To "BJ"
Bobbie Jean—

Your Aunt loves
you and hopes you'll enjoy this
book; She says you're "energy plus",
so here's to you, one doer to another.

Love,
Deb, "Danny" Glenn
IDITAROD, 2006

TO DIE FOR JUSTICE

A novel

By

Danny Glenn

This book is a work of fiction. Places, events, and situations in this story are purely fictional. Any resemblance to actual persons, living or dead, is coincidental.

ISBN: 1-4107-1455-1 (e)
ISBN: 1-4107-1456-X (sc)
ISBN: 1-4107-1457-8 (dj)

Printed in the United States of America
Bloomington, Indiana

This book is printed on acid-free paper.

1stBooks - rev. 11/16/04

“Wisdom combined with goodness is called justice.”

Moses Mendelssohn

“Some of life’s greatest disappointments come to break a path for life’s greatest joys."

Danny Glenn

TO DIE FOR JUSTICE

Dedication

Thank you Lord for the difficult turns, for without them I might be a straight line. Bless the souls of those I've encountered who continue to thrive in adversity, that they too may someday experience your love.

Thank you to my grandparents, who set the stage for me. Just being around you made me feel happy and I steered forward from childhood feeling loving acceptance. To my parents, who never stopped encouraging me to be all that I could be, and who set an example of perseverance that has never failed me. To my two "little" brothers, Steven and Jeffrey, who I adore and who even now in adulthood can do no wrong – may their new families be blessed.

Thank you to my husband for standing by me as I "came to be" and for your support in all that I do. It is with you I have felt free enough to climb a mountain with the security to know you would be there to help me down if I couldn't make it. I love you. To my beloved children, Emily, Garrett, and Drew, who, along with my husband and me, suffered together our losses and challenges but grew stronger and ever closer in ways that could not otherwise have been achieved. I love you all around the world and back, and more than you'll ever know.

Acknowledgements

Thank you Norm for sharing office space with me so I could write this book. Thank you Beth and Mary, the first people to read my very rough draft and who gave me encouragement to go on. Thank you Holly and Connie who read and edited and "shared" my story with me. Thank you to my general editor, Emilie, for knowing where the commas go, and to my professional editors, Jessica and Mitch—you are irreplaceable. I appreciate you so much. Thank you to Peggy for the way you single-handedly validate people, particularly me. And to Lee, who read one of the final drafts, edited, and said, "Well, here it is," thank you.

Finally, to my "special" children: Jeremiah, his wife Nancy, their daughter Billie and son Wyatt. To Charlie, Joyce, Sarah and Madison. I am so blessed to have you in my life.

For my family
XXXOOO

Preface

History is written by its survivors. By watching, listening and reading, I have learned that each of us endures many levels of anguish in life, and that telling the story of one's own hardship can be just as important as recording large-scale historical events and national tragedies. No one person is exempt from pain. First we seek understanding and the strength to endure; after that, we search for justice in its many forms hoping somehow that wisdom will combine with goodness. Perseverance allows us to work toward these goals yet when the truth is revealed, it often finds us still seeking as we strive to serve a greater purpose outside of ourselves. Within that purpose lies the standard by which we define ourselves.

Music has been my lifelong friend. Even while writing, it takes me to places where I have never been, places of long ago, and never-forgotten places forever pressed on my heart. These feelings are illuminated by Thoreau in his 1857 *Journal*: "When I hear music, I fear no danger. I am invulnerable. I see no foe. I am related to the earliest times, and to the latest."

Charlie Parker said, "Music is your own experience, your thoughts, your wisdom. If you don't live it, it won't come out of your horn." George Gershwin said, "Music sets up a certain vibration which unquestionably results in a physical reaction. Eventually the proper vibration for every person will be found and utilized." And, in *The Sound of Music,* Maria von Trapp said, "Music acts like a magic key, to which the most tightly closed heart opens."

To those of you who read my book, may you too hear music and may it command your soul to a pleasant place.

Chapter One

She always heard music. Thoughts would enter her mind and melodically travel through different chambers in concert with the world around her. Spring wasn't just spring for Becky. April breezes flowed like Debussy, and she was so in tune with herself and nature that the music and her soul protected her from pain or fear, taking her to far off places, bringing beauty and tenderness to her world.

This spring wasn't like any other spring, though. As Becky sat on the park swing not far from her apartment, there was a chill in the air, a peculiar feeling that something different was echoing in her daughter's laughter. Something present that would change her life forever. Becky held on to Beth, and with her right hand around Beth's waist, she put her right foot under the swing and gave one big push. Beth giggled with delight as she and her mother shared a moment of the morning. Their long blonde hair danced in the wind and the rhythm of the swing blended now with the music in her mind as she pondered the world around her. Becky's left hand held tightly to the chain until her fingertips were shaded purple to white. Her strange feelings clashed like cymbals, and she put her foot down so the swing would stop. There was a slight jar to the right and then back again as the chain twisted from the abrupt change in movement. Then they both just sat there for a moment, motionless.

This spring was a time of rebirth for Becky. The divorce had gone easily for her, and she was becoming accustomed to being a single mother. She savored the feeling of being free and appreciated being able to make decisions for herself without being badgered or judged.

She sat poised staring forward and enjoyed the breeze on her face, with sweet Beth cuddling against her. They were both kept warm by their matching red wool plaid jackets. They were content being alone together, and hardly noticed what was happening on the other parts of the swing set. Three young girls had meandered up close and were climbing, hanging, and busying themselves. Becky was so caught up in her daydreams from the past and of the future that she did not notice their presence until one of the girls with short, dark brown hair grabbed the A-frame of the swing set and glided around to spin right in front of Becky's face.

"Hi, my name is Kim, and I'm nine. What is your name? Is this your daughter?"

Although she had never seen her before, Becky smiled with polite acceptance as the young girl inquisitively flung questions at her as if they had known each other for years. In fact, all three young playmates seemed intrigued by this woman and her two-year-old daughter and, before long, Becky was drawn into conversation with them.

"So, are you married?" asked Kim.

"Yeah," said another. "Are you?"

"Oh my goodness," Becky said. "That's quite a big question coming from such young ladies." The timing of the question was almost as if they had been part of her daydreams. Becky paused to think about how she would answer and decided to keep it simple. "No," she said. As soon as Becky answered, Kim asked, "Well, what kind of guy are you interested in?"

Becky looked at them in puzzlement and shook her head. "Boy, you're really getting into this, aren't you?" The inquisition was personal, but the girls were so cute she could not deny their innocence.

"Well, you see those two guys over there playing tennis?" the girls asked. Becky had noticed them quite a while before, but was content to watch them volley the ball back and forth as she thought about fun, freedom, laughter, and simplicity. "The blond one is cute," Becky said.

Before Becky could think, the three girls were off and running toward the courts in trilogy of mischief.

Becky could see them as they ran right up to the blond-haired man and giggled, "Are you married?" Without much notice or pause in his game, the man shook his head and said something to the girls. Becky couldn't hear because she was too far away, which made her glad because it also meant he wouldn't see her red face, had he cared to look in her direction. She didn't want him to think she was party to the interruption of his game, but wondered to herself why she would even care what he thought.

Up until now Becky had not paid serious attention to what she was really saying to the three girls, but she could no longer ignore their actions and found humor in their antics. The game was a bit amusing to her, and made her smile. This hadn't happened in a long time.

"No! He said no!" Kim shouted as she ran back to report her findings to Becky. She stopped short and stood before Becky with her arms outstretched in exclamation. "He said he's not married. I'm going to tell him you guys have a date!" And without pausing long enough to catch her breath, she spun around and was off running back toward the courts.

Caught by surprise and the quickness of the girls' spirited nature, and before Becky could even fathom what had transpired, the girls were at it again, chattering little nothings to the tennis-playing stranger. For a second, Becky thought she should hide under the slide or at least duck behind her daughter's back lest he catch a glimpse of her embarrassment. Or maybe she should get up and leave the park. Instead, she chose to enjoy the moment, and she smiled and drifted back into the sway of the swing.

She began to think about the few dates she had been on in the last several months and how disappointing they had turned out to be. Although they were few in number because she turned down more advances than she accepted, each date was pretty much the same—cute guy, nice, professional, bright, witty, well dressed, and considerate—the perfect combination for a nice evening. However, she came to expect disappointment. Her daughter most often was not included in the invitation and, to Becky, that was the first problem because she didn't want to leave Beth with a babysitter. Then the date ended on a dissident note of predictability—the guy asking to come in for a nightcap, but never expecting coffee. Becky did not want a relationship to begin in her bedroom. She seldom went out and instead chose to spend time with Beth. She enjoyed doing this much more than dating.

Becky had been working in a hospital for the last two years, and there were plenty of available single men there: maintenance guys, cooks, doctors, and pharmacy technicians. Even though the hospital was large, many people knew who she was and would wave good morning when she first arrived and when she walked the halls to her office where she coordinated and staffed the Pharmacy and Therapeutics Committee. Becky felt drawn to the medical profession; her early childhood fantasy was to become a physician. She enjoyed the medical field, though fate seemed to have different ideas, and Becky now appreciated any way she could to be around that environment. During her lunch break she ate the usual apple, crackers, and cheese from the brown sack she'd thrown together, and as she sat on the green space to the left of the children's hospital she would watch the medical students coming and going, still longing to be one of them.

Her most recent date had been with a doctor. She considered doctors to be bright and caring individuals—two of the strongest characteristics she most admired in people and a common thread she could relate to. He picked her up in his Mercedes, and on his way to a party wooed her with his romanticism, stopping on the side of the road to retrieve a bottle of vintage wine and Waterford crystal out of the trunk. He even had a great sense of humor, was an engaging conversationalist, and blended well at the party they attended. This gave her hope that indeed he might be one she would consider dating again, but the result was the same, and it wasn't what Becky had in mind at all. Becky loved being a mother and included her daughter in most everything she did. Babysitters and bedroom scenes with men who weren't her husband wouldn't cut it. Family life was absolutely what she was looking for—baking cookies for the school bazaar, going to church on Sunday mornings, and picnics. A special husband and father would be needed to complete this picture.

She had been a wife since she was eighteen years old, and during the ten years of marriage she had come to know what she wanted and expected from a man who would be her life mate. She found the discomfort she felt playing the dating game was conclusive evidence that taking up company with different men in search of the elusive Mr. Right was not for her.

Before long, the girls were running back with what they felt was good news. "We set you up for a date in March!" The girls were so young they didn't realize that March was ten months away, and Becky chuckled as she watched the children delight in the idea that they had arranged a date for their new single friend.

The unnamed mystery man ended his tennis game, and he and his partner walked slowly toward the swing set where Becky, Beth, and the three girls were still standing.

"Oh, look! Here he comes!" Kim said, putting her hand up to her mouth like she could hardly believe he was walking their way. Becky rolled her eyes, took a deep breath, and looked away for a second as she realized she would soon have to fess up to being an accessory to the charades. At the same time, however, she was curious about what he would look like up close, what he thought about the girls interrupting his game, and what it was about the morning that had her feeling different.

Becky felt the mild breeze at her face once again, and this time it brought with it the fragrance of sweet lilacs from a nearby bush. The scented memory brought her back to her grandmother's backyard, forget-me-nots, a picket fence and Grandma nearby in a pretty cotton dress.

Becky looked up to see the medium-sized, blue-eyed blond getting closer to her, and she could see that his hair was sun bleached and straight, falling just below his ears, and he was just tan enough that Becky felt sure he spent a lot of time outdoors. He walked with self-confidence, and he had his racquet thrown back and resting on one shoulder. The girls had gotten off the swing and were scurrying here and there and even got in his way, almost making him trip. He stopped just short of Becky's right foot, which protruded off the park lawn and into the sidewalk leading away from the tennis courts. His friend kept on walking to his car, but in an inquisitive way, he stayed, and for a moment opened up to conversation.

"Well, I guess we have a date in a few months," Becky said shyly as she smiled at the tennis player. He was now in plain sight and looked like a hybrid of Clint Eastwood and John Denver—woodsy, weathered lines drawn into his face, and smirking grin of "good ole' boy" contentment with a down-home, flannel shirt kind of simplicity.

"Yeah, so I hear," he said and then extended his hand toward Becky, smiling. "Hi, my name is Will." His voice was strong and deliberate. His handshake felt easy and self-assured.

Becky smiled back. "Hi, I'm Becky, and this is my daughter, Elizabeth—Beth for short." She paused. "So, I guess we're supposed to meet back here in about ten months." She smirked and shook her head as if to say, can you believe this?

Will chuckled back. "So I understand." He bent down to re-tie his tennis shoe and, as he stood up, he looked around and asked, "Do you live around here?"

Becky was looking at the sweat that was dripping off his forehead. She was trying to figure out as much as she could about him with one sweeping glance. She liked a man with a rugged, outgoing nature who was refined enough to engage in a gentleman's sport. It mirrored both sides of her, too, and the commonality stirred her curiosity.

"Yes, I do," Becky said. "You see the whiskey barrel up on the second floor deck over there—the one with pansies in it?" She pointed to the first set of three buildings that sat adjacent to the lake in the front of the small complex. "That's my apartment." Becky surprised herself that she told him where she lived, and even more when she boldly asked back, "Do you live around here too?"

"Yes," he said, "but not in this apartment complex. I've got an old farm a little west of here."

Becky watched Will's mouth as he spoke, and she wandered again in thought, reminiscing about the beautiful things that had attracted her to her ex-husband, the father of her beautiful child. He too was blond with blue eyes, and intellectual, which was important to Becky. Ben had been her high school sweetheart, and together they had made great plans for the future. He was going to become a doctor, and they would have five children, and they would live in a large log cabin in the rural outskirts of a small town.

Becky was young and naïve when they married, and it was easy for Ben to sweep her off her feet. She was like a horse with blinders on. She ignored the disrespectful comments he would throw out every now and then while they were dating because she wanted so much to marry him after they graduated from high school. Ben and Becky forever, the perfect fairytale.

She could have used her academic scholarships to attend college, but instead chose marriage as the most practical choice for her at the time because she could not fathom how she could work full-time to be able to afford college, even with a scholarship. The townsfolk who knew her were disappointed in their local girl. They had gotten to know her because she did so much in the community: volunteering at the nursing home, helping organize exhibits at the county fair, and they had read about her at one time or another in their four-page daily newspaper because of local accomplishments like ballet performances, singing, scholastic achievements and when she was crowned Posture Queen for her Brownie Troop. When word got out that she was planning her wedding for one week after graduation, she became gossip at the beauty parlor and the local tavern where community events were discussed and friends' problems were solved.

During her senior year, her mother was asked more than once how Becky was able to attend high school during the day and take night classes at the community college, where she took a court reporting classes to help ensure she would be able to get a good job to support her husband-to-be through college once they were married. When she did not go to school, she worked weekdays and weekends, too. She somehow found time to be Maria in her senior class play, *The Sound of Music*. The three major things in her life then were school, work, and her wedding.

Ben went into the service for a three-year military commitment after the wedding, and it was during this time that her husband's narcissistic tendencies were exposed as he abused Becky to satisfy his need to control others. She suffered, but felt in her heart that if she gave her marriage enough time she could figure out how to make it work—reasoning that intellect, hard work, and determination could solve anything. Her decade of sacrifice only served to prove her wrong. When she mastered the courage and strength to leave Ben, Beth was not yet two. Becky no longer needed to suppress the person she had come to know and like inside of herself, and she looked instead toward happiness and peace that she convinced herself she deserved.

"Just me and my son," Will continued, as he gestured toward the little boy with brown shaggy hair and blue jeans scurrying toward him. Will told Becky that Will Junior was the only child of his divorced parents, and he had custody. Together they lived on the farm that Will bought from his grandparents' estate after they died. Will's own parents were also divorced, and it was because he had chosen to stay on the farm to help his grandparents when his folks moved to Florida with his three sisters that Will became attached to country living.

"Hey Dad, are you ready to go?" Will Junior pestered, eager to hop into his Dad's Jeep and go four-wheeling on their property. That was a pastime they both enjoyed, and they didn't hesitate to say so. Will Junior was used to getting his own way.

"Well, I guess I'm heading out," Will said, as he put his arm around his son and gestured toward the parking lot. "It was nice meeting you. Those girls are sure cute." Becky and Will both turned to catch a glimpse of the girls who were now chasing the ducks and laughing as they ran.

"Yes, they are," Becky said, as she picked her daughter up and kissed her cheek. "But my Beth is the cutest!" and she kissed Beth's cheek again and wrapped her arms around her in loving adoration. Becky and Will smiled in mutual admiration of their children.

"Maybe we'll see you here again," Will said.

"Maybe so," Becky replied. "Maybe so."

Chapter Two

It was Friday night, and Becky felt tired. As usual she had gotten up at 5:30 and had put in a busy week at the hospital. She looked forward to spending some quality time with Beth, and they planned on meeting another single mom and her daughter at a local pizza parlor so the girls could play in the indoor amusement area that had become a favorite local spot for families with children. The fact that families would be there and that her family was not complete with a mother, a father, and other siblings bothered Becky.

So even though the evening seemed easy and fun on the outside, the emotional pain on the inside was not easy on Becky. She looked forward to listening to Beth giggling with laughter and joy, but she longed to be part of a healthy, loving and nurturing family unit. This was the way normal families ought to be, Becky thought with conviction, and she wondered how long she would have to wait before she found someone who would be special enough to be both a good father for Beth and a loving husband to her.

She was washing her face in the bathroom when the doorbell rang. As she ran to answer it, she swooped up Beth and gave her a hug. With Beth in her arms, she peeked through the peephole in the door to see if she knew who it was, and much to her surprise it was the guy she had met at the tennis courts the week before. She opened the door.

"Hi!" Becky said, holding Beth on her hip with one hand and opening the door with the other.

"Hi!" Will said, not appearing at all awkward, but rather matter-of-fact about his presence as if he belonged where he was. "I was just sittin' around my place and thought, well, I thought that maybe you might be interested in sharing a little wine."

Will was dressed in khaki shorts, hiking boots, and a casual shirt. His hand supported the brown paper sack that was covering the wine that rested on his shoulder, accentuating again Will's casual demeanor. He looked handsome and wholesome with a wind-roughed face and strong jaw, and was cheerful, and content—a welcome respite for Becky who was moving past the days of Ben and was eager to accept lighthearted conversation.

"I'd love to share some wine with you, but I can't tonight," said Becky with slight chagrin. "I have other plans."

"Well, that's okay. I just thought if you didn't have anything else going on tonight you'd like some company."

Becky reached down to the table beside the sofa, picked up a pen and paper from the top drawer and handed it to Will. "Maybe some other time," she said. "How about if I give you my phone number, and then if you want to get together sometime, you can give me a call?"

"Okay, I'll look forward to that," said Will.

Becky knew she was in control this way and could back out if she wanted to. This made her feel comfortable. Becky and Will exchanged phone numbers, and Will left, taking the wine with him. Out of curiosity Becky peeked around her patio window blinds to watch him leave. Then she looked down toward Beth who was standing by her mother's leg, holding it and searching too to determine what her mother was looking at. *Well*, she thought, *he can't be all that bad—he drives a Jeep!* Becky did think he was inconsiderate and cheap for not leaving the wine. *At least he was polite*. Down the hall Beth played with her stuffed animals while her mother went into the bathroom to continue getting ready to go out.

Becky looked at herself and thought how grateful she was that she was still young. She thought how blessed she was that she and Beth were healthy. It had not been easy starting over as a single mother with no child support and no one to share the parenting. Ben refused to pay and was an absent father, which on most days suited Becky just fine, but she felt sorry for Beth that her dad did not show much interest in spending time with his precious little girl. Becky never could figure him out and, over time, quit trying. She did not try to enforce child support because she thought having to hire a lawyer and go to court was something she did not want to do. Thus, she was poor, and she had the stress and responsibility of raising a child alone. There were difficult times, but they survived well, and Becky did not take her blessings for granted.

Since her divorce, Becky got up most mornings to face the same routine. She would hurry to get Beth's breakfast and then get ready for work. Her heart would be torn at having to leave her at a daycare when what she really wanted was to stay home and raise her herself. Then she'd put in a full day at the office, come home during winter after the sun had already set, and spend what was left of the evening trying to create a family for her and Beth. Both of them went to bed early so they'd be ready for the next day. Most nights Beth shared her mother's bed. They had each other, and they were very close. Becky thought that nothing would ever come between them. Their routine was set—day after day, week after week, and month after month.

As a single parent, Becky worked and created play. Being a single mom was the most challenging thing she could think of. Once in the middle of the night when Beth was awake and crying from an ear infection, Becky walked her up and down the hallway in her apartment until her arms were about to fall off. She bounced her up and down trying to bring her comfort. There was no father to give a reprieve. Becky's arms ached and tingled with numbing pain, but her duty never wavered, and she wondered when the endless night carrying her crying baby would end, or if it ever would. She paced back and forth praying that her daughter would feel better, and she pictured the day when a real father would be there to love them both.

This Will fellow was simply not considerate enough, she decided, as she leaned over the sink and finished putting on her mascara. She was afraid of finding Mr. Wrong again.

Becky was glad that she really had plans for the evening and that she had seen a side of him that she observed was just not good enough. She lifted Beth up and gave her a quick hug. "It's time to meet Debbie and Kristin." Debbie was a friend Becky had made working at the hospital. Both she and Becky, being single mothers with little daughters to raise, shared much in common and enjoyed spending time together. They would analyze why their marriages failed while their daughters played together, and they shared conversation of the joys of motherhood, the sorrows of looking for a mate, and going over the gossip from work.

When they pulled up to Pizza Land, the parking lot was crammed almost to capacity. Becky looked around for a parking space and noticed the many minivans that were used to transport families to dinner this evening. She looked around and saw other moms and dads entering with their kids. She leaned over and kissed Beth on the cheek and said, "Well, honey, if wishes were horses, then beggars would ride, right?"

Beth looked at her mother. "Horses Mama, where?"

"Oh, not real horses," Becky replied, "Just horses in a thought I had."

Becky pulled in to a space, put the car into park, turned off the engine, and unbuckled Beth from her car seat. Once inside they met their friends, and while the girls enjoyed the play equipment, Becky told Debbie about Will—how he had showed up with a bottle of wine, and how he took it with him when he left. They laughed together and shook their heads in agreement that it would probably be a long time before either of them would find someone they might enjoy dating.

About a week later Becky got a phone call. She put the dishtowel down beside the dishes she had just finished washing and ran to pick up the phone before the last ring.

"Hello?"

The voice on the other end had a familiar down-home country accent. "Hey, this is Will. Remember me? How are you?"

"Oh, Will. Yes, I remember. I'm fine, thank you. How are you?"

"I'm doing great. I was just calling a bunch of my friends to invite them to a get-together at my place. We'll sit around the fire and strum a little guitar. I wondered if you would like to come too. You know, bring Beth—she can run around with the other kids. What d'ya say? Come about five o'clock Sunday. We'll throw some chicken on the grill and cook a few dogs over the fire."

Becky sat quiet for a short pause, gazing around her apartment, and thought about his invitation. It might feel good to spend time outdoors in the country that she so loved. She hadn't had a real break in months. Between work and the apartment, she rarely found enough time to do much of anything else except maybe take Beth out to eat once a week or for a short walk after work. On weekends she needed to catch up on laundry, clean, and to grocery shop. It seemed she never had time to just relax outdoors.

Why not go to Will's party? It would be a nice change. She could expose Beth to the wonders of nature, peace, and serenity offered by the great outdoors, not just for a short walk by the lake or in the park. After all, if Becky had her choice, this is how Beth would be raised—surrounded by trees and gardens where she could cultivate her imagination and laugh with the birds rather than be surrounded by the concrete of an apartment's parking lot. Becky accepted Will's invitation and she asked if it would be all right if she also brought Honey, the beautiful golden retriever that Becky had raised from a puppy.

Becky had shared custody of her dog with Ben. Before and after their divorce, when he took out the married and unmarried nurses with whom he worked, Honey would be left alone indoors for too many hours. Becky hated that Honey was alone so much, so she was excited to think she would take her along. She was glad she had decided to accept Will's offer and began looking forward to the weekend. It would be good for all three of them.

Becky had a difficult week at work, and the weekend could not have arrived too soon. She had recently taken a new job as the manager of an ophthalmology clinic, where she had hoped to earn a better wage. She had seen almost fifty patients every day that week and, as Becky tidied up her desk and prepared to leave, she shared her weekend plans with the last doctor who was still around. She also discussed the last patient she had seen.

"Mrs. Hemphill's glaucoma is no better, is it, Dr. Heich?" she asked as she hung up her lab jacket and retrieved her purse from the drawer of her desk. Becky had learned a great deal about ophthalmology from the home study classes she had to pass in order to be hired for the position.

"Yes, I know," said Dr. Heich. "I don't know what I can do for her now outside of surgery. And at her age, I don't know if that's the best thing for her. Her son is not around much either you know, and I think the recovery phase would be extra hard on her."

"I'd like to take her home with me," said Becky.

"I know you would, Becky. You'd take in every stray if you could. It'll probably work out. I think her heart will get her before blindness does," said Dr. Heich. He was usually too direct.

"Maybe, but I sure hope she can continue to make those great chocolate cream pies for as long as she still needs to come to the clinic," Becky said as she walked over to the pie Mrs. Hemphill had brought for the staff. "Did you have a piece?"

Becky looked around to see if Dr. Heich had heard her. He was gone. No doubt ran out through the back door like he usually did. Becky put the tin foil back over the pie, put it in a bag under her arm, and turned the lights out behind her. She walked down the long hall toward the elevator to the main level where she routinely passed by the statue of St. Francis, never missing to ponder his message: "Lord, make me an instrument of thy peace." She passed the hospital cafeteria where she said goodbye to Flo, the supervisor, who had been there for years and who wore bright pink lipstick every day to go with her bleached bouffant hair. Becky was kind to most everyone she met and, as she walked through the emergency room and out toward her car, she wore the same smile as she waved to the staff, addressing each one by name as she left the building.

Becky picked up Honey on her way to get Beth from daycare. Ben wasn't home of course, but Becky had a key. Honey was so excited to see her, but she didn't jump up. She just wagged her happy tail and looked up at Becky and smiled. Becky bent down on one knee and wrapped her arms affectionately around Honey's neck.

That evening the three of them headed out of the city and onto the two-lane road that cut through the country fields on the way to Will's farmhouse. Becky rolled down the windows of her 12-year-old Oldsmobile and felt immediate relaxation. By the time they were only fifteen minutes down the road, they were half way to their destination as the sun began to set. Becky heard peaceful, light and airy music then, and the May breeze pampered her face, and she felt free. She sang out loud thanking God for her blessings.

Becky turned onto Blaine Lane. It was named after Will's family, as was the little valley town. The gravel threw up dust behind her car as she approached the grassy area where others had already arrived and parked. She scanned the other vehicles: several old trucks, Will's Jeep, and a couple of new cars. Becky wasn't embarrassed to be in ole' Betsy, as she called her car. It fit right in.

Will sauntered toward her as soon as he saw the dust in the lane. Becky got out of the car in her tight blue jeans, followed by Honey, who stayed close by as she went to retrieve Beth from her car seat. Will walked straight to Beth's door and opened it for Becky—a polite gesture that somehow made Becky think maybe the judgment she passed on the wine incident had been a bit premature and harsh.

"Hey Becky!" he hollered over the hood of the car as Becky worked to get the leash attached to Honey's collar.

"Hi Will. Boy, this is a great place you've got here." Becky said as she scanned the farm lots and the old, asbestos-shingled farmhouse. "I like the porch. Did you add that on yourself?"

"Yup, I've pret'near re-done everything around here at least once in the last twenty years. New roof, windows, and porch. The new siding is almost finished."

Becky walked to the other side of the car where Will was standing and reached over to pick up Beth. Together then they walked down along the fence row and toward the tall, high-pitched, unpainted, gray barn to a small gathering of Will's friends around a bonfire. Becky sat on the ground and leaned up against a hay bale. Beth was introduced to some of the other people's kids, and she didn't waste any time running off to the yard and around the cornfields where new stalks were just sprouting. The children played tag for a while before Beth returned to sit on her mother's lap. Honey lay beside them. The warmth of the fire wrapped them like a fuzzy blanket. As dusk turned into darkness, Beth cuddled closer into Becky's arms; Becky ran her fingers through her daughter's hair.

Will's friends Stan and Ed played their ole'-time instruments. The fiddle kept time with the spoons, and the mouth harp bent the notes in such a way that almost everyone's toes were tapping. Crickets were humming in harmony in the distance, and the moon shed a warm glow in the sky. The fire was bright. It was black to their backs. There were no streetlights—only stars. Becky wished the night would never end.

When Becky left that evening, she had an unusual sense of contentment about her, even more than she had felt driving there. What was it about "Wild Will" that had her captivated? He was earthy, yet at times maybe too earthy. He hadn't paid much attention to her that night. Most often he was off on his own talking with his friends, laughing, singing, and strumming. Becky had to search for him to tell him she was leaving. Thinking about him on the drive home, she thought she deserved more attention than he gave her. But he did have some redeeming qualities, like the way he interacted with his son. Will Junior appeared close to Will. They were very much at ease with each other. Even though Junior was only seven, he and his father were great pals like Becky and Beth were. Watching their lackadaisical mannerisms, Becky surmised they just went about their life with no specific thoughts about how to live—they just lived. Simple and sweet. That was what Becky wanted.

Another week passed, and Will invited Becky and Beth to join him and Will Junior for "a bite to eat." Becky accepted, and again they had a great time. Before long they were spending more and more time together. They camped together. They rode bikes together. The two families were becoming one, and together they shared many blessings. Will Junior now had a mother figure around to add the special touch that mothers sometimes do, and Beth appreciated the male companionship only a father could provide.

Becky enjoyed what they had together, although she wondered if Will was versatile enough to possess the well-rounded personality she would need to sustain her in a long-term relationship. She took time to find out, for she had the time. Her only restriction was the biological clock that ticked away inside of her, for she knew she wanted more children. If she wasn't going to stay with Will, she needed to move on. As she explored her needs, she recognized in herself that the "country boy" did intrigue her, and she saw many sides of him as they spent time together on various outings. There was much more to be savored outside the barnyard door, and very possibly it could include Will.

So Becky and Will continued to explore each other, and Becky appreciated Will's repertoire of attractive qualities that kept her very much interested in their relationship. Over the course of the next several months, she was able to admit to herself that she might be falling in love. The two of them often spent long evenings together after the children went to sleep. They would listen to jazz while having cheese and crackers to accompany their wine. They went dancing, and they spent quiet time reading. They also spent time together riding double with their children on horseback, shooting archery, water-skiing, and canoeing. They dressed up, and they dressed down. They were always together—indoors and outdoors, daytime and nighttime.

Will was indeed diverse both in interests and talents, and Becky felt vibrant with him. They both thrived on the old-fashioned values they each knew they respected and cherished, but there was also a wild side to Will that drew Becky out of her sometimes all-too-serious shell, and she enjoyed that, too.

Autumn was bursting all over, just like their friendship. The sugar maples painted the lane from the main road to Will's farmhouse and escorted the new blended family home after all of their outings. The farm was the perfect picture of life in rural America, and Becky cherished all that it was and meant. She felt as invigorated as the dried leaves appeared to be as they whirled around in late September's air, and the children felt that way too.

It seemed that Becky and Beth never wanted to go back to their apartment at night, and they looked for things to do with Will and Junior that would bring them back to the farm. Even though Beth was only two and a half, she and Junior played together well and enjoyed their pseudo-sibling status. With their parents' help they built a tree fort. Beth enjoyed the rope swing that dangled from the tallest branch, and Junior found it was perfect for climbing up into the fort. Together the four of them enjoyed the scent of autumn as they raked and piled up the maple leaves that had fallen from the big old tree in the front yard, and their imagination and togetherness helped them bond with laughter from dawn until twilight. When crickets warned of nightfall, Beth and Junior had to be pried from their playful projects to come inside.

The foursome went almost everywhere together, and they shared the simple things that Becky had missed out on during her 10-year marriage to Ben. She was now the happiest she had ever been. Even the slightest occurrences that most people would take for granted stood out to her. Waiting in line to go through a spook house on Halloween almost brought Becky to tears as she looked around at what she had and how her life was almost perfect. Becky had Beth on her shoulders. Will stood beside her with his arms around Junior, and the night air was typical for October. Becky felt blessed to be out in it. The wind blew her hair across her face as she turned to smile at Will. He winked at her and smiled back with the coy grin that made only one side of his lips turn up. They had become family, and it felt secure to share their life together. The evening was cool, but their hearts were warm.

One day led to the next as weeks turned into months with almost all of their time spent together. One day after Will had been sitting next to the sofa and staring into her "baby blues," as he called them, and he whispered as he pulled her head down into his lap, and moved her hair out of her eyes, "You know, you're almost as cute as a speckled pup." Then he slowed down his words and said, "What am I going to do with you?"

Becky remained quiet and gazed into Will's eyes as if searching for answers that she too wanted. He broke through the awkward preoccupation and asked Becky if she and Beth would like to move in with him and Will Junior. It was the only proposal he could make.

After talking the idea through, a process that revealed how timid they each were to make the move, they got over their reservations and decided to do it. They no longer would have to go back and forth between residences picking up stuff they had forgotten when they wanted to do something. Sleeping bags, tennis shoes and, as winter approached, ice skates and skis, would now all be under one roof. Their new arrangement was practical. They would test the waters of the kind of togetherness that had burned them both in the past, but with the shared understanding they would not marry, at least not just yet. Becky's moral conscience broke through her decision and haunted her with agony as she struggled inside and searched for an acceptable excuse for living together without marriage, for not waiting until they had decided if they loved one another enough to make a formal commitment before God.

Winter brought with it many cozy nights warmed by the fire, but the old farmhouse brought more than draftiness. It brought mice, broken water pipes, and many nights when the furnace would quit working. Will would get out of bed, clang something with a wrench, and the furnace would start up again. All of this was much more than Becky had bargained for, yet the many challenges of maintaining a 120-year-old home helped strengthen their family even further as they worked together to bring in firewood, to keep the mice to a minimum, and to scrape the frost from inside the windows in the morning. Becky read the children bedtime stories every night. They had family dinners together, and Becky felt spoiled because not only was Will a great cook, but he was happy to do so often.

It was a sweet reprieve for her to have someone to share the responsibilities of raising Beth. Family was what she wanted and, in her mind, that meant a mother, a father, and children. And even though Will and Becky each had a testy side, they respected each other, which made working things out when there were differences much easier. Will was thoughtful, and his thoughtful caring was a pleasant surprise to anything she had ever experienced. He even started her car in the morning to warm it up before she left for work. He was hard-working too—he worked harder than Becky could ever have hoped or imagined he would, and she provided a motherly touch that Will said he hadn't experienced since he had lived in the old farmhouse with his grandmother after his parents had divorced. He shoveled snow. She made pies because they were his favorite dessert. The aroma of them baking floated from room to room, making the house a home, and Becky could see that Will seemed content.

They continued to enjoy the outdoors too, skiing together, sledding, and building snowmen together one evening after a heavy snow. The four of them put lights on the fencerow during the holidays that spelled "Merry Christmas to All," and to them it was a merry time.

Chapter Three

Spring came early their first year together. About the time they began planning the summer garden together, Becky thought they should also perhaps plan a wedding. After all, their lifestyle brought everything they both enjoyed. True enough, Will and his farm weren't what she thought she would marry into the second time around, and Will too had doubts about giving up his bachelorhood to the formal "foreverness" of marriage. But as long as they both kept planning, spending, and enjoying time together, they agreed they might as well get married and raise their family as husband and wife. Perhaps a marriage based on a secure friendship could find love. That was what Becky thought, anyway. She couldn't admit to herself that what she had with Will was the deep passionate love she had sought after and, although she didn't care to admit it, she did not feel Will ever wanted more than a close friendship with superficial love—light and easy. There would be less of a risk of failure. Seemed backwards, but Becky thought if she waited for the man who had everything—one who was gentle yet strong, kind, supportive, intelligent, down-to-earth, a Christian who liked to help others, hard-working yet willing to be a family man, and especially someone who would make Becky feel like she was somebody's something special, she'd be too old to have more children, and Beth would have missed out on having a good father around. Becky didn't like the live-in arrangement though, and both she and Will knew they should either marry or move on. They recognized that their first marriages had been so disappointing that they didn't want to risk losing the peace and contentment they had worked so hard to achieve, so they were slow to initiate marriage. But once they had decided to go forward, they expected the second marriage was going to be one that had to last forever.

The garden soon began to grow like their commitment to each other, and they began to plan their wedding. The date was set for early August. Through the summer, Beth and Becky picked beans, snapped them for dinner, and sat under the old oak tree that offered shade to the weary gardeners after an afternoon under the sun. Both she and Beth wore bandanas on their heads, and Becky loved to watch Beth kneeling in a garden path picking vegetables with her little hands and placing each one into the brown wicker basket that lay next to her. Becky used and reused old strawberry crates she had found in the shed, ones Will's grandmother had left there. Will and Junior mended fences and tractors after work and on weekends. They worked together and separately. It was a forever-family waiting to happen, and Becky was glad to know that by the time Beth started pre-school, she would have a married mother and father.

Neighbors and family from far and wide drove up the long lane to the farmhouse to take part in witnessing their outdoor wedding. Many had waited a long time to see who Will would marry, as it had been almost seven years since his divorce. He had lived on the same farmland for almost thirty years, and the old neighbors who went as far back as knowing Will's grandparents, kept a watchful eye on him from the time he was born. They watched him being "raised up," and paid attention to who he would take as his bride. From everything Will had heard at the local supermarket and gas station, feed store, and restaurant, most folks approved of Becky.

The wedding was a perfect example of "the farmer takes a wife." No wedding cake—Will's sister from Idaho and Becky's mother made pies instead. First thing after sunrise, Will took Junior and Beth out in the field to pick wildflowers for their mother's bouquet, and they brought enough flowers out of the field to cover the arch they had rented to outline an altar. Arnold the pig, the one that Becky had given to Will when it was still just a piglet, had grown up and stuck his nose through the fence. The young girls who had introduced Will and Becky by the tennis courts some fifteen months before were also in attendance. They had really matured in that short time, and they were tickled to death to stand up for Will and Becky's wedding.

Becky looked over to savor a lingering glance from her ninety-five-year-old grandmother, who had made the twelve-hour trip from Michigan with Becky's mother. She looked natural in Will's grandmother's old, whitewashed, wooden lawn chair. A gentle matron who, without saying so, gave approval of the union by simply looking on as the distinguished centurion Becky adored so much. Grandmother wore a peach pantsuit that made her caring, soft complexion and wrinkled face stand out. Her sweet blue eyes looked like forget-me-nots in the morning sun. She sat peacefully eyeing Becky, and Becky thought her grandmother was probably reminiscing the heartfelt significance of her own wedding day because Becky's grandmother on her mother's side was like that. She smiled a gentle smile at Becky and, at that moment, Becky felt like she possessed everything that mattered in the world. She stared back at the tender grandmother she had loved for so many years.

Arnold stuck his head out through the brittle, split-rail fence and made pig sounds every now and then, acting as if he too approved of the union. Many of Will's friends, being farmers anyway, didn't even notice. Becky did. *A pig at my wedding, if that doesn't beat all!*

The mighty barn that had served five generations towered steadfastly in the background, and the marigolds that lined the fencerow put the finishing touches on the outdoor chapel, whose alter bouquets were Will's great-grandmother's peony bushes. Will had placed the rented heart-shaped arch in the middle of them. He also had borrowed chairs from the church and set them up two sides of six rows with an aisle down the middle where Becky and he would enter with their children.

When the procession started, Beth walked ahead to lay down rose petals and handed a rose to her grandmother and great-grandmother. Junior was the best man who would hand his dad the ring. Some well-wishers had carried their own lawn chairs, and they opened them up where they wanted to—under a shade tree or by a farmer friend they wanted to sit next to. Will's long-time buddy played a delicate melody on his guitar as the wedding party walked slowly down the winding sidewalk from the old farmhouse that met with the grassy aisle between the garden chairs. The picturesque morning was aglow, as were all those in attendance, including Will's mother and stepfather and sister Carol's family all the way from Florida, and his other sister Diana, with her son from Idaho. The Blaine family preacher from way back gave a strapping country Baptist rendition of vows and then closed with a solemn prayer.

Becky and Will were now husband and wife—Mr. and Mrs. William Blaine!

Becky got pregnant the first month of their marriage, and it was not soon after that the Cinderella-like tale began to fizzle. Will's temper sometimes surfaced, bringing intermittent chaos and much too often unnecessary tension. People outside the home never saw Will's anger, but Becky sure did.

Will left earlier and earlier for work, and he snapped at Becky over little things like not staggering the flower rows next to the house, or for accidentally letting the horses out when she went to help him change feed lots, or for cooking the fresh beans too long, or for spending too much time at the grocery store. He became impatient around little Beth and lied to Becky about his work schedule so he and Junior could be alone for a while after he picked him up from school and before he came home at night.

One afternoon, in a fit of anger, after Becky had questioned him about where he was going, he punched a hole through the bathroom door. Becky did not understand where his anger and aggression came from, and their arguing occurred more frequently, even though Becky tried to suppress her responses so Beth could be spared the anguish. Tearful and alone, Becky struggled to figure out what the source of Will's frustration was and the driving force behind his unstable state of despair.

Becky continued to attend church with Beth in hopes that her faith would bring her the answers she prayed for, but knowing she needed prayer came as only a bleak reminder to her that perhaps another marriage had gone sour. How could she have made a second mistake? What was wrong with her that she could not spot trouble in the backfield? Was she to blame for the transposition of good energy into bad? These were questions that haunted her days and kept her awake at night.

"I'm going over to Sutton's place to help him get some strays back in," Will told Becky early on a Saturday morning before breakfast. "They walked over the back fence last night after the rain made the river swell and forced a bend." He headed toward the door.

"I thought we were going on a picnic at Leger's Pond?" Becky said.

"That's the problem, Becky. *You* thought we were going. I never said I was going, and Junior isn't going either. He is going to help me. I'll be back when I get back," Will said as he turned his back on Becky to leave.

"I don't think sounding so angry is fair, Will," Becky said. She realized she needed to confront his bizarre bursts of anger and short-sided, off-the-cuff, impatient behavior.

"What did you say to me?" Will said rather gruffly.

"I want to know why you changed our plans," Becky said. "That's all." She was begging to have answers to why the very man she wanted to have plans with was the very one she was disgusted with.

"Don't challenge me. I do what I want when I want," Will said. His voice became more loud and intolerant.

"No, you can't! You can't be this way to me. I've done nothing to deserve you being so angry," said Becky, and she began to cry.

"I can be any way I need to be," said Will. Out of total frustration he grabbed a potted plant nearby and broke it over Becky's head. "There. Now you have something to cry about!"

Will stormed out the door. And there Becky stood—alone, afraid, and a hugely expectant mother with dirt in her hair and down her face. The pot had been made out of thrown clay, not glazed ceramic, so it appeared worse then it was, but Becky cried just the same. She hurt both mentally and physically, though grateful the twin babies she was carrying were not in harm's way and that Beth would not be able to notice the small knot on her mother's head.

In the months that followed, Becky worked harder at protecting Beth from realizing that her mother felt she had made yet another error in judgment, fooled by another man. Becky wondered how she could have been so blind and what method she could have relied on as a means of predicting a different outcome.

The twin boys, Eli and Erin, were born that May. It was a beautiful and uncomplicated birth at a hospital about half an hour from home. They were the cutest babies their parents, brother and sister could have imagined, with blond hair, blue eyes, and giggles. They were not identical twins, but it was hard to tell them apart at first. Eli's fingers and feet were quite a bit longer than his brother's, though, so when it was feeding time Becky would look at their feet to see who she was picking up first. Becky continued nurturing the facade she had created around the perfect family unit she had so desperately sought after and yearned for as long as she could remember. And she worked harder yet to preserve the possibility that with the foundation of friendship and giving love and time, all things were possible. She admitted now that she did love Will, but just didn't *like* him very much sometimes.

Chapter Four

Will and Becky continued with their day-to-day duties. Becky took a much-needed respite from work, although the newborn twins, Beth and the farm kept her busy. Will worked overtime in his contracting business to pay the doctor bills. Becky enjoyed motherhood, cuddling with the children, cleaning, making homemade meals and doing crafts. She was also fond of hanging clothes outdoors because the smell of fresh linens from the line was a real source of pleasure. She could see joy in Will's face whenever he spent time with the children, and she loved that. Will did not appear as aggressive and edgy as he had been before the twins were born, and Becky figured her prayers had been answered. Maybe it was her pregnancy that had not been easy for Will. Some men go through resentment and fear, Becky rationalized, though she knew that was no excuse for the way he had behaved. She continued to work at forgiveness and at moving on for her sake as well as for the children.

Christmastime neared, and Becky decorated the old farmhouse like a Currier and Ives painting. She only wished the sentiments were as pretty. When it came time to open presents, there wasn't one under the tree for her. She didn't understand why, and it hurt her. If the reason Will hadn't wrapped a gift for her was that he didn't have money to spend, she figured a small token of affection or a hand-written Christmas card would have been wonderful. Becky ached inside often from the imperfections of her marriage that she couldn't seem to fix, but focused most on the cherished simplicity of country living and her beloved children. With those three gifts she was happier than words alone could describe. As much as she tried to include Junior in the family picture, his real mother, who was jealous of Becky, worked to keep him out, interrupting family dinners with selfish motives, refusing to let him be with Becky on outings and, in Becky's mind, manipulating Will, who even years after the divorce harbored unresolved issues.

The twins were almost eight months old when Ole' Man Winter began to pound on the shingles of the old farmhouse, making much additional work for Will and Becky. They spent long evenings on the remodeling project they had started to keep the drafts at bay and enlarge their living space to accommodate their new family of six. The double-paned windows they installed helped a great deal, and the added insulation around the pipes seemed to keep the mice out.

Since Becky was still on maternity leave and was home during the day to be with Beth and the boys, she got a lot accomplished outside of routine motherhood chores. She spackled and sanded one hole Will had punched in the wall before they were married. She filled the hole that Will had punched in the bathroom door, too. She also rubbed linseed oil into the new plank floor Will had laid and wallpapered the kitchen.

When the boys napped, she and Beth often played learning games to prepare Beth for kindergarten that fall and, right after lunch they all would go for walks to the end of the lane where Becky picked up the mail. She couldn't carry both twins, but she could pull them on the sleigh that Will had rigged like a wagon. She watched as Beth walked to her friend's house across the narrow road. There Beth played with her friend Julia until Junior came home on the school bus at about three o'clock and walked her home. Some days Becky had Julia come back with them to play. Julia and Beth got along well, and Becky enjoyed watching them play house with their dolls or make snowmen outdoors, and all the little games and creative pastimes two young girls could come up with. During the quiet time, which was a rare occasion, Becky worked on the remodeling plans—choosing wallpaper for the bedrooms, coordinating paint colors, deciding where to add walls or to knock them out, where to put a door, how long the dining room table should be, and other details to adapt their 5,000-square-foot, 120-year-old farmhouse to fit their lifestyle. She enjoyed the planning and even the labor because it helped her get her shape back and to lose the twenty pounds of the pregnancy weight she'd gained.

She and Will worked well together on the remodeling project almost as soon as he came home from work, though Becky felt sorry for him that he had spent all day remodeling other people's homes. He spent time in the barn doin' things with Junior, too, until supper, and they would all eat together which was a busy, happy time. Will played with the twins too, and he always had time for Beth. He just couldn't resist her soft-spoken pleas for attention.

Becky admired Will for the way he knew how to work with wood and nails, just like her grandfather had done as a carpenter. When Becky smelled sawdust on Will, it made her think of her grandfather and her childhood, and it made her feel cozy. Will had never had any formal training in carpentry, but he knew how to rewire, re-plumb, insulate, grout, or lay a floor. Like Becky, he was a hard worker and, because of their instinctive dedication to hard work and family, within two months after the start of the major remodeling, they were just about done. They felt mutual pride in their accomplishment.

It was almost suppertime when the phone rang. It was Will's cousin and his wife inviting them out to dinner. Will would have declined, but they offered to have their babysitter watch all of the kids, and since the smell of the linseed oil he and Becky had used on the wooden floor was so strong, they decided to go and get the kids out of the house for a while to give it a chance to air out.

Becky was thrilled with the idea of getting out of the house for a while, and the cold weather didn't dissuade her as she enjoyed bundling up and feeling the wind nip her face. She knew the children would be fine. In fact, they probably would be too warm because Becky was overprotective, and would layer them in blankets and scarves even though it was a short road trip. She felt tickled as she put on her black sweater and slacks she hadn't worn in ages. There was no particular reason why she hadn't worn the outfit other than she didn't go out any more and had no opportunity to wear it. She watched as Will put on a mock turtleneck shirt and a sweater instead of his usual plaid flannel. He still wore his jeans though, and he put on his favorite boots that fit like a glove, and they made him even in height with Becky. That night as Becky watched Will adjust his jeans over his boots and run his fingers through the sides of his hair and away from his face, she was conscious of how very much she cared for him.

It was understandable why Becky and Will rarely went out because there was always so much to do. Caring for the twins took a lot of time what with two diapers to change instead of one, two feedings—double everything. The remodeling also took a lot of time, and Becky was glad it was almost complete, because she was eager to sign up for college night classes. She and Will worked together, played together—though rarely—and took care of their children together, which brought them joy. Becky hadn't seen Will's temper flare up in a long while, so the prospect of going back to school seemed all right. She didn't get much in the way of affection from Will, but she was much too busy to really miss it. Their blended family worked well most of the time. Indeed, it was a rare occasion when they took the time to enjoy doing something away from home, like eating out. Becky thought back with effort to remember the last thing they had done alone together and remembered a time when they had sat on the back porch listening to the crickets and gazing off at the moon. It had been almost four months.

It had been a pleasant evening as they realized then they still shared some common dreams. They had closed on the mortgage papers on the old farmhouse earlier that day and, instead of renting it from his grandparent's estate, they now owned it. Will had paid off his two uncles, buying them out, and now the house, barn, two outbuildings, and ten acres were theirs. In celebratory fashion then, they came in from the porch, turned on Will's grandparents' antique phonograph and, to the sound of the century old tunes, they danced. The windows were open, and Becky could still hear the crickets, which comforted her. They didn't talk to each other much, but moved slowly, arm in arm, but not too close. Right before the record finished, Becky laid her head on Will's shoulder. It seemed they had adapted to their situation as husband and wife for the good times and the bad.

As Becky put the finishing touches on her make-up, she thought back to another night they had really enjoyed together, right before the twins were born. She and Will had invited some of their long-time barn party friends to come over, relax, and "sit a spell"—like they used to do when their attraction was new, probably why they enjoyed that kind of time together so much. It reminded them of when they were first together—free, when they got along well together in spirited, youthful unrestraint—when their time together felt fresh and alive. Will had made a large bonfire that night and shared a couple beers with Stan and Ed, his old "valley boys" friends as they jawed about nothing and whittled sticks for the hotdogs. They leaned back with ease, cross-legged by the fire, cooked, and reminisced. More friends showed up when they darn well felt like it, for there was no room for formality at Will's place, and laughter and good times echoed through the cornfields.

Many friends who came that night brought an instrument of some sort, a guitar, banjo, or mouth harp, and Becky was intrigued and attracted to a lifestyle she was experiencing firsthand that she had only seen on country western shows on TV before. The pickin' and singin' was accompanied by someone "packin'" the spoons, and Becky felt free and easy. Most of the people there had grown up with Will and, because of their friendliness, Becky felt almost as if they had been long-time friends of hers too. They were sincere and honest folk, good-ole' boys, down-to-earth, hard-working, and fun-lovin'. The atmosphere kept her situated on the border of reality, though, because it felt so good that at times she questioned whether she was part of a fantasy. The stories they told captivated her attention endlessly and, as the night air drifted in and brought the fog that settled down around them because they were in the valley—Blaine's Valley, she listened on. People around her were either sitting on the ground or on bales of hay that had been placed around the campfire, and the coolness at their backs went unnoticed. Many stayed the night, drifting off to sleep when they felt like it, leaving it up to the misty morning to wake them up.

Tonight should be fun too, Becky thought, *but different.* They had actually gotten dressed up to go out this time. Becky was now ready to go and started to bundle up the kids because she knew Will would not like the hassle. She knew Will enough to know that if too much "futzing" was involved, too much chaos, he would cancel going. The more she thought about it, she was amazed that he had even accepted the dinner invitation in the first place with all the little details that needed to be done to make it happen. Diaper bags, bottles, and scraping the windows on the minivan because it had begun to snow so hard. The weatherman had warned that when the snow stopped, the temperatures were going to plummet, which meant that before they could leave, Will would have to haul in extra wood and stoke the fire in the fireplace they used to help the furnace keep their large home warm. Becky and Will had planned on installing a new furnace, but they just hadn't gotten to it yet.

Dinner was enjoyable. The company was entertaining, and Will seemed to be having a good time talking with his cousin, Mark. Much to Becky's surprise, she found out in conversation with Mark's wife that Will was the one who had suggested they go out. The food was good too, and Becky was again surprised that although Will was a meat and potatoes man, he ate tacos with no complaints.

They stayed long enough to have coffee with Irish Crème and fried ice cream for dessert. Will got up from the table to phone the sitter to check on the kids and, by the time he got back to the table, the women had decided they wanted to call it a night. It was late and was the coldest night of the year. They were chilled, and they wanted to go home, put on some flannels, and crawl into bed.

So after the restaurant bill was paid, the women made sure to tighten their scarves, and the four of them put on their gloves, heavy coats, and hats, and then left the restaurant to brave the elements. When they got to Will's cousin's place, Will left the van running while he and Becky ran in to get the twins. Beth was spending the night with Ben and his new wife, so she wasn't with them. Neither was Junior. Although Will had custody, Junior often stayed with his mother.

"This has to be the coldest I've ever felt," Becky muttered as she ran toward the house. "My nose is sticking together every time I take a breath."

"I know," Will replied. "There's no way I'm shutting off that engine. It probably wouldn't start up again."

Before they left Mark's house, they covered the twins' heads with an extra blanket. They buckled them into their car seats, and then left for home. Becky could hardly wait until everyone was in his or her own bed, cozy and warm.

"Tonight was fun, wasn't it, Will?" Becky asked as she rubbed her hands together and folded her arms for warmth. She turned around to make sure the extra blanket she brought was still covering the boys. She gave them a pat as they fell back asleep.

"Yes, it was," Will replied, and said no more.

The ride home wasn't a long one and, after they went over the big hill on Bluff Road, they knew they were almost there. When they rounded the corner that came at the bottom, Becky sniffed the air and said, "Boy, it seems like a lot of people must have their fireplaces stoked tonight. I can smell them in the air."

"Probably so," Will said. "It's so cold. I put extra logs in ours before we left. I wanted to make sure the lines wouldn't freeze."

They were just about to cross the last main road when they realized there was a fire truck in front of them. "Gosh, Will, where could they be going?" They were only about a quarter of a mile from their lane, and the truck was headed in the same direction they were. Becky and Will knew there weren't many houses out their way and, as each nanosecond went by without the truck turning, Becky began to panic.

Three thoughts raced through Becky's mind: either one of the elderly people at the end of the road was having a medical emergency; the guy who lived by the levy and liked to drink and argue with his two sons and throw his wife around was involved in some kind of altercation; or someone had a fire.

The fire truck and the Blaines' minivan both crossed the highway. Then Becky and Will saw their black lab, Ozark, out of his usual territory and out in the road beyond the end of the lane. Ozark never went past the end of the lane. Something was wrong.

Will skidded the van to a stop, and Becky opened her door, pulled Ozark into the van and onto her lap, and Will then jerked it into drive and they flew down the lane. In half a second they could see that the fire truck they had been following was headed right toward their house. Actually it was the third one to arrive on the scene. Their farmhouse was being eaten alive by flames that shot some forty feet into the air.

Will slammed on the brakes, and the minivan slid sideways somewhere on their front lawn. He left it running, opened his door, and tore toward the flaming structure that represented his entire life and heritage. Becky watched as the flaming lion's head leaped out of the front window above the sink of her house where she usually looked out at the wintered hydrangea bushes while she did the dishes. She wept as the wreath she and Beth had made from willow branches they picked on one of their many walks disappeared from the window frame where it had hung.

Becky struggled to stay in the van because she wanted to run out and try to help Will. But there was nothing she could do to help. The twins were sleeping in their car seats, and she couldn't leave them. She just sat there mesmerized and feeling helpless. Seconds later, she opened her door as her anguish compelled her to do something other than just sit there. She would get out, she decided, at least to stand outside right next to the van. She got out and leaned against it. A news reporter who had been sent to the scene after hearing about it on the police scanner ran up to Becky and stuck a microphone in front of her face. He asked for comments toward the cameraman.

"Get away, please," Becky said. "Don't you know this is *my house* on fire?"

"Where were you when the fire broke out?" he asked.

"Just leave us alone!" she cried in desperation.

"Is there anyone in the house?" he asked.

"No, please, I don't want to talk right now. Can't you respect our privacy? Turn the cameras away!"

Becky put her hand out toward the camera to shield herself and turned her head away. With fear in her voice, she yelled, "Will, can you hear me?" Inside, she prayed, "Will, are you okay? God, please help us."

A woman from down the road came up with several other neighbors to watch the fire burn. She was empathetic toward Becky and put her arm around her as her heart went out to her. Becky was shivering, more from anxiety and fear than the cold, and the woman took off her scarf and wrapped it around Becky's head. Becky didn't seem bothered by the howling winds that set the wind chill records that night. She was too consumed with the fact that the life she was just getting settled into was once again going to be a pile of miserable rubble. What would her husband do without the farm? How would he react to her without the security of the farmhouse to ground him? What would they do?

Before long, the fire chief had figured out that Becky was one of the owners, and he too came over and began to ask a series of questions. Becky felt obligated to answer. They were similar in nature to the ones that the reporter had asked, and Becky answered as best she could. She kept looking away trying to catch a glimpse of Will. Where was he? Becky knew he was the kind of guy who took chances and, for all she knew, he was up on the third floor attic trying to do something heroic, like trying to save some of Grandma's china that was packed away there. Or for that matter, maybe the floor had given out and he was lying in the back room breathing smoke and half dead. Becky knew that because Will was so familiar with the layout and all of the nooks and crannies, he would be able to elude the firefighters who would try to stop him from entering.

The neighbor, Mrs. McGruder, came over and put her hand on Becky's arm. "Come on, honey. We've got the boys inside now. You come in too. There's nothing you can do for Will now by just standing out here cryin' and freezin'."

"You don't understand," Becky sobbed.

"Sure, I do, but Will is with the firemen, and you need to stay out of their way."

Becky dropped her head and, with sunken soul and heavy feet, she headed for her neighbor's house. She walked inside and took off her wraps. The twins were indeed safely inside, and she looked down at them in their infant seats, side by side on the floor. Erin and Eli were awake from all the commotion, and were restless. Becky took out two bottles from the diaper bag. Her infant sons sucked just a little and drifted back asleep. She wanted so much to pick them up and hold them against her, never letting go. She needed the comfort and felt so blessed and grateful no one was trapped inside and that they weren't home at the time the fire broke out. However, she wondered if the fire would have gotten so out of control had they been home. How had it started? The old furnace, the new wiring, the wood stove? With the boys sleeping, there was no reason to continue holding the bottles, so she put them away and sat down on the floor next to them. She put one hand on Erin's hand and one on Eli's hand, and she just sat there staring straight forward.

Becky thought about calling her parents, but they were six hundred miles away. What could they do for her? They would just worry. The neighbor agreed with her and suggested that she call after she was more informed about the condition of the house. She would wait until her emotions had settled down a bit to where she might be able to tell her story in a way that would be the least upsetting to them. She would wait now for Will. Becky thought about Will Junior and Beth and missed them. She was sickened more when she thought about how they would react when they found out the world, as they knew it, was gone.

The neighbor handed Becky a cup of hot chocolate and tried to make comforting conversation. It was a sweet gesture, but Becky couldn't make out what she was saying. She was in shock and could only see the woman's mouth move, her voice inaudible, rambling with no discernible words. Becky's mind was a million miles away now, and she could hear music. Her body numb, she got up off the floor and sat in an overstuffed chair staring at the front door.

Becky's father had been right when he warned her years before that whenever things seemed to be running smoothly, look out—that's when you get blind-sided.

After what seemed an eternity to Becky, the front door opened. A cold draft swept across the floor. Will stood in the doorway brushing a mixture of snow and soot off of his shoulders. His face was tarnished with ashes. Blood dripped off his brow. Becky eyed him, motionless.

"Is the fire out?" Becky asked.

"It's gone, Becky," Will said.

Becky felt her heart well up as she took a deep breath and looked at Will with a blank stare. A tear fell down her left cheek. "What will we do?" she whispered. "Where will we go?"

In less than three hours, the fire had devoured the structure that stood to represent over a hundred years of the Blaine family history. Their heirlooms and keepsakes went up in smoke. One minute Becky and Will had a beautiful old farmhouse that they had almost finished renovating themselves. The next moment it was gone. Nothing was left but the ghostly gray curls that lifted off the smoldering embers, and the three-story chimney that stood alone in the cold, bitter winter—the only reminder of where a house once stood. A matter-of-fact event had occurred, and now they had to deal with survival.

During the two weeks that followed, Will and Becky worked with the cleaning crew the insurance company had hired, and the debris was cleaned up. By the third week, they had purchased a trailer and had it placed on the property not far from where the old farmhouse stood so that their children would be able to live with a similar routine—similar except for the new toys they could play with and a different bed they now had to sleep in. Going from a farmhouse to a trailer was a dramatic change, even though the trauma had been for the most part substituted by acceptance. Whenever one of the babies woke up in the night, everybody was awakened because they were so close together. Whenever Will's son wanted to have friends over to play trucks, there were no longer the long wooden hallways for the kids to use as roads. And Beth soon learned that security didn't lie in her special bedroom, but in her mother's arms.

The ladies from the church had been helpful by providing them with the staples they lost to the fire—an iron and ironing board, used pots and pans, and blankets. The women from the Blaine Valley Methodist Church made several trips to the trailer delivering clothes that the congregation had donated. The priceless antiques that had been in Will's family for over a century could never be replaced, nor the ones Becky had handpicked at the market to finish decorating their home. But they had their memories, and that was something no one could take from them.

Because of the age of the farmhouse and the fact that there were no fire hydrants close to their home, there wasn't much insurance available to the Blaines. So, after the second mortgage that they had taken for remodeling expenses was paid off, there was barely enough money left except to put a minimal down payment on the trailer. Will and Becky spent endless hours trying to figure out how they would recap their losses so they would be able to build another home and afford to buy the furniture to fill it. Will offered to discuss the matter with a friend of his who was an engineer for a highly respected firm in town to see what he could come up with. They still had the ten acres, and that surely would be worth something. Becky agreed and started to envision how their acreage might be divided up for a profit. Selling off part of their land would be the only way to start over.

Chapter Five

It was lunch time on a Thursday at the old diner where Will used to have breakfast with his grandfather when Will and Becky met with Will's long-time friend, Lonny. Some of the old farmers still came into the diner around 5:00 in the morning, after the cock crowed, just like they used to. Some came to eat, but most came to see their friends first thing to talk about the farm report and to jaw over a cup of coffee. At least the ones who were still around came. Most of the old farmers that Will knew when he was a kid had long since died. As they entered, Will said "Hey" to two guys in bib overalls, one wearing a baseball cap and the other a railroading hat. Will and Becky found a table. As they sat down, Will told Lonny, "You can always tell who is a farmer—look at those 5-buckle rubber boots pulled over his shoes." He pointed to the guy one table over. "Five buckles always left open and always tellin' stories." Will was endeared to the farmer friends he'd grown up with.

Lonny was a surveyor employed by Coston Engineering, a firm that was best known for designing large strip mall developments and high-end suburban housing projects. At first Will didn't recognize Lonny because he had grown a beard, and he didn't expect him to be wearing blue jeans. Lonny later explained that that was his usual attire, except for mandatory board meetings. Like Will, he had grown up a Valley Boy, and they wore jeans as often as they could get away with it.

They sat across from one another, Becky next to Will, at a small table with a red and white checked tablecloth and next to a small window. Will could see his farm through it. No sooner had they sat down when two groups of locals came in. Recognizing Will, they greeted him with a friendly nod and tip of the hat. Will and Becky smiled and Will waved back, then ordered coffee from the tall, bleached blonde waitress with the white apron on. She was chewing gum and had a pencil behind one ear. The apron had a large front pocket where she kept her order tablet and, from the bulge and sound of change that made noise as she approached the table, it also held her tips. She pulled the tablet out, took the pencil from behind her ear, and waited to see if they'd order more than coffee. Lonny and Will exchanged small talk before they got down to business, and Becky just listened.

"Boy, I'll tell ya," Lonny began, as he looked around the restaurant. "Some things never change, do they?"

"Nope, they really don't," Will said. "I've been comin' here for years, and I think those are the same cobwebs in the corner that my grandfather used to talk about."

"I used to come in here some times as a kid too," Lonny said in a way that sounded like it was a fond memory that he missed. "My dad used to say this place had the best sunny-side-up eggs around!"

"How long has your dad been gone, Lonny?" Will asked.

"Almost seven years now," Lonny said.

Will shook his head. "Man, time doesn't wait for nothin'."

The two of them paused, and Lonny took a deep breath. "So, what can I do for you two?" Then he looked at Will and said, "I was surprised when you called and told me you needed my services. My first thought was what does an independent contractor who builds a couple of houses a year need from me? You thinkin' bout a big project?"

"Well, not exactly," said Will. "I need to pick your brain. I need someone with your expertise to see what platting ideas you could come up with for the farm."

"The farm?" Lonny said. "You planning to tear down your house, the barn, and all those great outbuildings and do a subdivision?"

"Well," said Will, making a painful sigh. "I don't have a choice, Lonny. I've got to do something. Our house burned down, and we can't afford to rebuild. We've got to think of a way to utilize what little we have left so we can try to get our family back in a house again."

"Fire." Lonny shook his head in disbelief. "When did that happen? I'm so sorry. Is everyone okay? I mean, was anyone hurt?"

"Everyone is okay—well physically anyway," Will said, nodding matter-of-factly. "I'm surprised you hadn't heard about it yet—largest fire the Valley Fire Department had ever worked on. There were reporters there and everything. It was somethin'."

"Oh my God," Lonny said and paused briefly. "Were you home when it happened?"

"No, we had all gone out," Will said.

"Lucky for that, or maybe not so lucky," Lonny said. "Think it could have been stopped if you had been home? I mean, do they know how it started?"

"No, not really," Will said. "They figured maybe it was the old wiring in the kitchen."

"That's a shame," Lonny said, and he paused again looking down into his coffee cup with a blank stare. He picked up his spoon and began to slowly stir his coffee as he pondered the news. "So how can I help you now, Will? What exactly are you thinking?"

"Well, we need to sell off some of the property," Will said. He hated to think about this because he and Becky wanted to keep their horses and maintain the isolated feeling that they enjoyed being positioned in the middle of ten acres before the fire took their home. They didn't want close neighbors. They wanted seclusion and all the property they could have so the horses could run freely. Also, the property had the last remaining section of the Old Central Canal that lay on the eastern border, now a linear demarcation of where the house once stood. They didn't want to disturb the historic canal bed that was still of interest to the Indiana Historical Society members, to the Canal Society, which continued to bring tours of visitors by even after the fire, and to the Blaines, who honored preservation. The remnants of the canal were also significant because the founders of Blaine's Valley, Will's descendants, had owned the abandoned waterway all the way to the toll way. The Indiana canal system was abandoned when the railroads came, but this section would have been abandoned anyway because it had a large aquifer under it, the ground being so porous it would never have held water. Selling part of their land was an uncomfortable compromise to Will and Becky, and it seemed to make the devastation of the fire even that much worse.

"You're right that I have quite a lot of experience designing development," Lonny assured him, and he took another sip of coffee. "But I don't think a development is what you were thinking of, was it Will? You just wanted to figure out how you could partition off some of your land to sell and maybe which part would be the most economical to get rid of, right?"

"I don't know, Lonny," Will said. "I never thought about it before. I never thought I'd ever see myself getting rid of more of my land. What would you do?" There was a pause, and Will looked away, then said, "Does a small subdivision seem feasible?"

"Oh boy, Will," Lonny said. "How about giving me a couple of weeks to think about this? I'll try to come up with something."

Will took Becky's hand and they thanked his friend for his time, and Lonny went back to work while Becky and Will went home and walked their land and considered other ideas like moving and selling out completely. Many times over the week or so that followed before Lonny would get back to them they would talk together on the back steps of the trailer, at the small kitchen table, or while leaning against Will's truck before he left for work, and even in the middle of the night when they were both awake and tending to the twins, or when they just couldn't sleep. Eventually they decided they would divide the land with three splits—two one-acre parcels by the main road, keeping a third parcel for themselves in the back by the barn and still keep the horses. To them this seemed like a reasonable conclusion that would bring in enough cash so they could qualify for a new home-construction loan and it would be the least complicated solution so they could hurry and start digging to lay a new foundation yet that spring.

Lonny kept his promise and got back to Will. But the results of his thinking were not what Becky and Will had in mind because his idea would be time-consuming and costly to get started. Their friend also reminded them that the City of Indianapolis had jurisdiction over the small rural suburbs that bordered their property, and would probably refuse to allow them to partition off buildable land unless they installed a city sewer system—an option that the Blaines couldn't afford. Will lifted up his hands in a gesture of confusion as to what to do, and scuffed his feet in the dusty gravel of the old lane that now led up to their trailer instead of the old farm house.

"What should we do now?" Will asked. "It will cost, I bet, a quarter of a million dollars to put in a city sewer."

"That's right," said Lonny, "but you could look at the bright side. If you sell off smaller parcels and more of them, your costs would be offset, and you'd still come out ahead."

"Come out ahead of who?" Will answered as if cornered. "We won't be able to keep the barn or the horses, and our property that we'd build our house on would become a city lot. I'll have to think about it, Lonny." He patted him on the shoulder. "Thanks for looking into it for me. Becky and I will let you know what we decide." Will turned as Lenny was getting into his truck. "Say 'Hi' to Patty and the kids from us, will ya?" There would be no more barn parties, thought Will. He knew those days were over.

Becky and Will spent a few more days going back and forth looking for the best possible answer, but they knew they were limited to Lonny's idea if they ever wanted a house of their own again, keeping at least a small piece of Blaine land and their children in the same school district. They could have waited a few years to rebuild after they'd had time to save while living in the trailer, but it seemed to them most logical to follow Lonny's plan to partition off enough parcels so they could offset the cost of the city-mandated sewer system. That would leave them with enough money to build a house after all was said and done, and their mortgage debt would be one they could afford. Will hated to give up any of the family land, but he and Becky didn't want to live in a trailer for the next five years, either.

In between bottles, diapers, cooking, helping with homework, and the special times she spent playing children's board games and baking with Beth, Becky worked at the kitchen table drawing lines on the plat map that Lonny had given them to use, trying to come up with a suitable land division. She used pencil to draw and redraw where she thought the layout of lots should be according to the layout of the land. In her mind she walked the property as she had come to know it, struggling as she drew to preserve the integrity of the land, its natural swells, the big old trees, large lilac bushes, and the old canal bed. She chose house plan options for each lot as she was able to imagine where the house would be staked out, where the garages would be built, and how large the side lots would be so that the subdivision would be aesthetically appealing while maintaining as much of the natural layout of the land as possible. If a house had to be set back further to protect the old oak tree, then it would be. If a house had to be designed with a walkout basement so that part of the canal wouldn't be disturbed, she drew it that way. Becky saw to the smallest details.

The final subdivision plat allowed them a one-acre lot for themselves. And, if Will decided to build the twelve houses on the plat himself, it would give him solid work for the next two years or so and ensure him a reputation as a large home builder that would keep a good business growing into the future. Ten of the twelve houses would be built on lots along the east side of the property line; one would be built at the end; and one more would be built so that the lane would wrap around to the north curving back to form a cul-de-sac. Becky pictured the large house at the end of the cul-de-sac to be theirs, but eventually she and Will settled on the first house started at the entrance of the subdivision—the one they began first as a strategy for visibility of their project and moved in as the most financially efficacious. Eventually they hoped to be in a house on the acre lot by the barn.

After Becky and Will got accustomed to the idea that they would no longer live on a farm, they focused on other aspects of their new plan—aspects that would bring them enjoyment and satisfaction. Working together on a common goal was good for their relationship because they worked best as a team when their time together was defined by the focal points of their projects, whether it was the goal of being the best parents they could be, the most involved couple at church, or the best subdivision planners.

It was a Saturday morning, the snow was almost gone, and the daffodils and crocuses had just begun to show their heads to springtime. In anticipation of an early spring and twin toddlers to keep happy, Will was building a fence around a small section of grass outside the back of the trailer so Becky could more easily keep track of their little boys who were now at the perfect age to toddle out into the cornfields that would soon be over their heads. She never had pictured herself being the mother of four children, living in a small trailer, being married to a southern hick-type fella, wearing an apron, and baking several pies a week, but she felt happy. The children seemed happy, and so did Will. He was a dutiful man and was content when duties called.

"You know how the valley is named after your family, Will?" Becky said as she brought him a glass of lemonade.

"Sure," Will replied as he swung a nail deep into the fence picket.

"Well, I was thinking…"

Will interrupted with a teasing smile that pleased Becky. "You were thinking—that's trouble."

"Yes, I was thinking." Becky smiled in return. "Since your forefathers were the founders of this settlement, the farm, the school, the church, etcetera, why don't we have it dedicated as an historic landmark? An epitaph of sorts to the founding family. We could make the subdivision authentic—you know, make it look like the community must have looked like back then. We could install gas lamppost lighting for street lights, cobblestone walkways instead of traditional sidewalks, and Victorian architecture."

"Hmm," said Will. "You mean the real ornate kind with fretwork and turrets?"

"Yes, and then we could enhance the area by emphasizing the fact that we have the last remaining, untouched section of the old Central Canal. When I think back on how the valley was settled, I mean the end point of the canal system that ran the entire state, even connecting to other states, I think, and the toll booth, it's so unique. We should preserve, well, preserve it as a significant part of history." Becky went on rambling, and Will went on pounding—but slow enough so he could still hear what she was saying. He looked up occasionally to acknowledge to her that he was listening. The twins were bouncing up and down on their small rocking horses. Beth was busy picking flowers and green weeds to make her mother a bouquet, and Junior was off running the field somewhere, probably with the McGruder boy, who was the same age.

"The timing would be perfect to advertise its significance, Will, because the downtown elders are renovating the canal system there in preparation for the Summer Olympic Games that will be held in Indianapolis this year. You know as well as I do, buildable land especially with unique amenities is scarce in this area." Becky could feel her excitement building. "The Bible talks about making beauty out of ashes. I don't think that's what the author meant, but the basic premise sounds appropriate here, doesn't it? We could do research and make it as authentic as we can." Becky continued to see Will on her idea. "Imagine that each home would have its own character . . . the American flag flying, white picket fences, and flowers. Oh, Will, wouldn't this be fun?"

Becky was happy when she noticed she was feeling how they could be focused on a project that would not only serve to solve their housing problem, but that would give them something really fun and exciting. Having a positive sense of purpose would be good for each of them and for their marriage. It would help lift them out of the doldrums that had began to turn into a mild form of depression for each of them. They were having difficulty sleeping even though it was hard to tell if the real reason they couldn't sleep through the night was because the twins were still waking up often. Eli had chronic ear and tonsil problems that often woke him. Then it was like a chain reaction—Erin would wake up, then Will, or Becky, or both of them.

Becky still planned on finishing the semester of night school because the organic chemistry class she was taking was the last requirement she needed to apply to medical school. She would not plan summer coursework, but would do research for the subdivision project to help design the first spec home. A spec home was usually built as a showcase—a sample house where realtors would meet prospective clients. But in this case, Will and Becky would occupy their spec so they could sell the trailer and use the house as a model when they needed to. Becky would return to school in the fall after the subdivision was well underway. Realtors would sell the houses built by Will's company, and, although different from the farmhouse days, life would go on.

Will had a good rapport with the Valley Bank's employees, from the tellers to the president. He had gone to high school with several of them, and knew them all on a first-name basis, so it seemed they wouldn't have any problem getting a loan, especially once the plat was listed with a realtor, and when lots began to sell. The project would not be viewed as too speculative then. Will figured they might not even need a loan if four lots sold right away—pre-selling them and creating a waiting list with down-payment money that would earn interest while in a holding account was how most developers in that area got started. Becky and Will were eager to see evidence that their idea was viable. The sooner they made decisions and got things going, the sooner they would be able to move out of the trailer.

Becky had grown since the days of Ben. Adversity had been her best teacher, and she felt strong and more personable. Once again she had shown herself that she could overcome struggles that had always been part of her life. She was happy now with the way things were going for her and her family.

Will had been a carpenter ever since he had gotten married right out of high school, and he needed to work so he took up the trade that seemed most natural for him. He had renovated over fifty older homes in Indianapolis since he went into business for himself as an independent contractor. He was looking forward to building new homes now, from the foundation up. No more partial remodeling jobs, like a kitchen here, a bathroom there. He would build whole houses from start to finish—he would be a builder instead of a contractor.

The subdivision was born and, over the next several months, the Blaines, Lonny's firm, and infrastructure contractors Will and Becky hired kept very busy turning their vision into reality. Will was at ease in an environment that he was accustomed to, and Becky was having a good time. She did not feel overwhelmed with trailer living because it was new and small enough in size that there wasn't much to clean, and Will helped with the children. He was never a stranger to a dishcloth, which Becky appreciated, too, and she would come home from night school to find the dishes done. The twins were attending nursery school five half days a week, and she had adequate time during the day to spend planning and organizing the subdivision project. Their older children had settled into an uncomplicated routine that had begun to show signs of acceptance and contentment with their new lifestyle, especially when the weather warmed up and they could play down by the barn.

Their living space was enlarged to include the extension to the outdoors that Will had fenced in. The land around the barn remained unchanged, so they still had the fields, the pond, the dirt lane, and many outdoor activities that hadn't been changed by the fire, for which they were grateful. The trees and fields adjacent to their property were where they had always been and offered them stability. The barn still housed their horses, bicycles, and other things that provided them with many hours of pleasure and leisure activities, including the rope that was tied to the center rafter. They used the hayloft and farm implements to play hide and seek after school and on weekends.

The final plat was technically prepared and drawn up by Coston Engineering and formally submitted to the downtown Planning Commission. It was approved by the City of Indianapolis late that April. The timing was flawless, as it provided the opportunity for Will's new company, Valley Builders, to survey the land and pound the first stakes as soon as the ground thawed. The corner stakes were set in place for their new home—the spec house that was to be placed on Lot One, the first house that sat on the right as the soon-to-be Blaine Lane wound down to the cul-de-sac which circled around in front of the barn, then up another two lots on the other side of the lane not far from McGruder's place. Becky enjoyed watching Will direct the workers as they began construction on the two-story home. She was proud of him with his working knowledge of building and, until now, she had not realized how talented he was. She took pictures for the keepsake album she had started.

Memorial Day was the first holiday the Blaine family celebrated in their new trailer home. Becky began the week by putting out the American flag in the holder attached to the small front porch post. Will Junior taunted her for being so namby-pamby, but Becky was adamant about displaying things that added memories and significance to the time-honored traditions she valued and wanted her family to value. The Stars and Stripes waving at their front door was only the beginning of the flurry of activities that would steep the children in the richness of their predestined birthright as citizens of the United States. Becky laid out her homemade, patriotic and country-style crafts and engaged the children in projects that included such activities as painting dowel rods for mini flagpoles, and adding glitter on projects in the form of stars. She adored that kind of time with and for her children.

They had a barbecue that weekend too, and they all went to the hometown parade. Becky and Will took turns pulling the twins in the red wagon Will had taken out of the barn loft—the one he and his two sisters had been pulled in as kids. The older two children caught candy the firemen threw from their trucks, and when the uniformed servicemen passed by in their ranks, Becky instructed them to place their hands on their hearts. Becky felt grateful appreciation for the great men and women that had worked and fought for their freedom, and it brought tears to her eyes. The marching bands were next, and their feet tapped in unison with the bands' cadence. After the parade was over, they followed the last float up the hill to the antebellum cemetery where the guns saluted, "Taps" was played, and a wreath was thrown into the river to commemorate those who had died for their country.

Becky and her family wore the poppies they had purchased from the volunteer Women's Auxiliary that promoted their cause. They sat under the shade of a Jack Pine tree that bordered the cemetery, for that was tradition too. The white grave crosses were the backdrop to the speeches given each year by an elderly war hero, the mayor, a Boy Scout, and a pastor. The hometown band that had been a constant for eighty years, or so locals had told them, played "The Star Spangled Banner" and "God Bless America" and those sentimental songs resounded once again the tunes for Old Glory, independence, God, and country. The slide trombone player in the front saluted Becky, as he had grown accustomed to seeing her every year sitting in the same spot and no doubt realizing through his smile that he was aware of how her family of two had grown to include

Will and Will Junior, and now Erin and Eli. They never spoke out loud, but the shared smiles acknowledged a pleasant familiarity.

The following Monday, Becky got right back to work even though most businesses were closed. She began planning the Open House she would have together with the realty company she and Will had hired to sell lots. She designed invitations and decorated the old smokehouse they had turned into an office. She painted "Canal Estates" on the outside of the building and designed a logo not only for the subdivision, but also for Valley Builders, painting over the old Blaine Construction Company sign. Being a valley boy and the only direct descendent that still lived in that area made it seem right that he'd call his new company Valley Builders. And he hired many of the guys he had grown up with, Valley Boys perfectly suited for the project.

Becky was exposed to talents she had only recently seen in Will since the inception of the project, and she admired them. Her creativity was exposed when she went to the newspaper to get an ad designed. She found it was much easier and more fun to design the advertising herself than to let the ad designers do it. With a little persuasion, they let her sit at a design desk to explore ideas and create the layout. She was in her creative glory as the subdivision logos, office space, invitations, and advertising were designed with minimal effort and a lot of joy. Becky was not bored with her intermission from taking classes now that her semester was over, and she and her family were enjoying the sunny days of an Indiana summer.

The project had only been listed with a broker and advertised in the newspaper for slightly more than a week when they sold their first lot, Lot Three. It was exactly one week before the Open House, which was perfect because they would have two "sold" signs up when visitors came. As with any new project, though, there were issues to work through that were necessary and mundane like opening up a company checking account, trying to find title insurance, making sure there were fresh flowers in the office, and that there was always someone in the office while Becky was with the children and while Will was pounding nails. For the most part, all was well.

Becky and Will started looking for investors that would loan money for the improvements for the development—water mains, sewers, sidewalks—infrastructure money that would be paid back as lots were sold. An old friend who Becky had met in bimolecular chemistry lab, Henry Roth, showed up on their doorstep one day, and having served on the Board of The Canal Society and having brought a group to tour their land, he was surprised to find that Becky was one of the owners of the property that he had been leading walking tours on for years. Becky told him she was not a legal owner of the property because Will would not let her name be on the mortgage. Technically, not even part owner, but that it was *their* project just the same. Becky noticed after she had verbalized the technicality, that it irritated her like the whistle of a teakettle that needed to be shut off. Henry would become an investor.

Becky had met Henry in class while he was working on his Ph.D. after retiring as an executive at RCA. He had never been satisfied with only a master's degree, but he had shared with Becky that starting a family back then and needing to support it had interrupted his plans to further his education, like the Canal Estates subdivision had been doing to Becky. Henry was now retired and was almost seventy years old. Becky admired him for not letting go of a dream, and for taking on the challenge rather than succumbing to numbers. Henry and Becky enjoyed a mutual admiration for each other. They were quick to resurrect their past friendship.

So that afternoon while Henry and Becky walked the historic property they chatted, reminisced, and brought back to life again fond memories they had enjoyed through three semesters as chemistry and physics partners. As the tour group took its time absorbing all they could about the layout of the land, Henry and Becky paused by a fallen tree and sat together on its trunk. They continued to get caught up on what each had been doing in the year since they had last seen each other. Henry shared how he had been involved with the preservation of history and had been since he first became involved with The Canal Society, which he joined to learn more about the part of the canal that was close to his property north of downtown Indianapolis. He had been an avid member of the Historical Society for years. He shared with Becky that he was occasionally hired by artifact museums from around the world who hired him to authenticate past presidents signatures. Becky shared all about the twins' birth, the fire, and the plans to develop the Victorian subdivision, assuring him they would maintain the integrity of the historic Central Canal.

Henry suggested ways that Canal Estates could be used to echo what the Downtown Historic District was doing to enhance its own section of the old canal, designing commercial walkways and pedestrian-friendly paths around new landscaping, drawing the past in with the present, and for the future. Henry walked with Becky to meet his friends from the Board who had come with him that day to see if perhaps some of his colleagues, particularly the University history professor who was a personal friend of his, and another retired statesman and friend, might be interested in becoming silent financial and general supporters of the subdivision project. The day ended in a spectacular way, good news for Will, who was eager to accept administrative experience and financial help.

Once Henry was made privy to the investment needs of his friend's project, he stepped in to assert his ability to provide capital. The fact that he had retired from a successful company gave him almost unlimited capability to obtain investment money because he had a secure background with an established and respected reputation. Henry and the Blaines met to exchange legal documents for loans that would be used for the needed improvements using part of the land as collateral. The two biochemistry pals worked together on several occasions to plan a ceremony to dedicate the Blaine land with its last remaining section of the old Central Canal as an historic landmark. They invited a state representative and the principal of Blaine Valley Elementary School to the ceremony.

Becky continued to work toward the upcoming dedication event. She dug through old Blaine family scrapbooks that she had retrieved from Will's grandfather's trunk—the one that Will's sister had given them after the fire. She read through old documents and faded papers. She was intrigued and appreciative to realize that they had possession of a certificate from the early 1800s that officially made Will's great grandfather a Justice of the Peace, and it had been signed by the then Governor of the State of Indiana, Thomas A. Hendricks, who later became Vice-President of the United States. Henry authenticated the signature.

Becky published the ceremony schedule in the newspaper and wrote an article to accompany the announcement:

> "Around 1836, America became enthralled with the idea that it was in need of developing alternative forms of transportation used for trade. Canals, their tolls, and their taxes would enhance the transportation of goods, while at the same time give revenue to the state. Indiana went all out with an Internal Improvements Bill in an effort to realize its dream to completion. However, the porous geography in the southern part of Indianapolis proved unable to hold water. At the same time, the railroads came into existence as a further revelation to internal trade, and, as a result, before 1840 rolled around, the state had undergone bankruptcy, and the Canal System was abandoned. Renovation and preservation have found their way through city planners and historians alike. In 1971, the Indianapolis Water Works Association designated the Indianapolis Water Company Canal a National Water Landmark. Its plaque is located at the Indianapolis Museum of Art. This Thursday at 10:00 a.m., the last remaining section of the Central Canal will be designated a National Historic Landmark realizing the importance. The property has been in the Blaine family for over one hundred and fifty years since Blaine's Valley was founded. The current owner, Mr. William D. Blaine, the fourth generation and direct descendent of Archibald, currently owns this property, and he, along with his wife, Rebecca Blaine, have worked with state and local agencies in an effort to preserve yet another piece of Indiana history. It is with this enthusiasm that the June 1st unveiling of the historical marker will find its way into the permanent archives of Indiana Canal History."

Henry continued to hold a captivated interest in the project, and he was present at the ceremony in trinity of mind, body, and spirit, despite the windy, rainy day that kept many folks away. The ceremony was well attended with about sixty or so who made their way despite the weather. Henry arrived early and helped Becky prepare coffee and other refreshments for the reception they held afterwards. Becky was happy not only to have found an investor, but to have a companion who agreed to be a sounding board she could count on and a friend she could enjoy as they both related to their new professional relationship—one where they both stood to make a profit. When the ceremony was over, Henry made his way to a corner of the canal and stood with his notable friends and colleagues, and they talked about the significance of the landmark, the planned subdivision, and the impact it would have on the city. On the television news later that evening only umbrellas and raincoats were visible.

As time went on, it became more important for Becky to hold on to the idea that what she and Will were doing wasn't simply building houses—they were preserving part of history and honoring the Blaine heritage for their children. Becky was serious about her responsibility. Long after the ceremony was over and the historic sign was placed in the ground, she continued her research in the Indiana State Library studying turn-of-the-century architecture, paint color combinations, fretwork, turret styles, cupolas, wraparound porches, and gazebos. Although she kept it to herself, she hoped the quaint subdivision, like others found in authentically preserved antiquated neighborhoods, would perhaps one day be seen and appreciated for its successful replication of the Victorian era that marked the beginning of Blaine's Valley and that would become the epitaph of sorts to the Blaines who had founded it. She planned to make the new homes they would build to be indiscernible from well-preserved structures from the past, and she hoped that her husband would win notoriety as a designer and builder. Will and Becky often took long drives out into the country looking for Victorian houses, taking photographs, and making notes. The children went with them, enabling work to be quality family time.

Becky felt an affinity for the past, feeling connected to the Victorian era where leisure, luxury, and common sense frivolity were paramount. She also found the dedicated work ethic that stood out along with strong family values that became apparent through the books she read to be a symbol of what she too felt important. Reading about the Victorian era showed Becky that she shared similarities of thought, for women of the that era took time to appreciate the simple things in life like poetry, watercolor painting, arranging fresh-cut flowers and crocheting doilies. They enjoyed the things that enlightened their existence—music, children's laughter, culture found in art and literature, and the peace found in idleness that could not be confused with laziness. Quiet easiness found in the serenity of sipping lemonade while rocking in a front porch swing. Becky was sentimental too, and she tried to add similar elements to her family's lifestyle because she wanted these types of experiences for them.

Will, on the other hand, had his own set of priorities when it came to the subdivision, and Becky appreciated that they were both intrigued and captivated by Victorian architecture. She was proud too that the carpenter she met and married was able to build the ornate buildings and had transformed into the business man he needed to become to handle the responsibility of home building and the development of the subdivision. He took the necessary initiative, and together he and Becky designed a portfolio of plans from the photographs they took, cataloguing ideas from the many homesteads they passed. The Victorian lifestyle became inspirational to them.

Once again, although for different reasons, Becky and Will shared a common interest, and a mutual goal besides that of raising their children. They appeared content and tied to their joint venture, and their children seemed happy and content in their daily life too. Although activities were based on routine so their parents could get a lot done, Beth still attended dance lessons and swimming classes at the Y, and the twins continued to spend five half days a week at a nearby nursery school, where they eagerly looked forward to socializing with children their own age. Junior rode his little dirt bike around and up and down the mounds of soil that were created when the construction crew began work on the road cuts, and

Will spent from sunup to sundown working on their brick home that would be prominent and sturdy like the mountains he loved. Will was captivated by mountains and dreamed of climbing one someday.

Becky read journals and nonfiction books steeped in the traditions of the bygone era that she studied. She began to know herself in ways she never thought possible. She was strong and capable after all, despite the fact that her ex-husband had worked so hard to convince her otherwise. To the contrary, she was not stupid. She made all of the financial arrangements for the subdivision loans—the lots, the mortgages, and for property improvements. Becky worked with brokers and bankers on a day-to-day basis. She met with realtors to solidify house plans and to find the best way to entice a well-suited clientele, consummate caregivers to a neighborhood of its character, and who would be able to afford to live there.

Becky too transformed from housewife and student to ardent businesswoman, her wardrobe changing like the many new hats she was wearing. But she never lost sight of the not-too-distant past when she owned nothing more than three pairs of jeans, a few tops, and three white uniforms that she alternated wearing to the hospital where she worked. She felt blessed not only for the opportunity for change, but to be aware to be thankful for it. In those days, she did laundry every third day so she would always have something clean to wear. Now she took nothing for granted.

One day after a successful business meeting, Becky felt particularly refreshed. As she was getting out of the car, she noticed her reflection in the window. She fluffed her hair, and, feeling flirtatious, decided to find Will and try to get his attention in hopes of spending time together inside the trailer before the kids returned from their friend's house. As she looked for Will, she had a spring in her step because she felt so happy. She saw Will standing up on a ladder. When she got closer to him, she sucked in her stomach, forced her shoulders back, and yelled up to him, "Hey, Will, what ya doin' up there?"

Will didn't reply, but motioned for Becky to move away from the ladder as he climbed down. As soon as his right foot touched the ground, Becky moved close to him and kissed his neck.

"Hi honey," she said. She drew away from her kiss and attempted to follow it up with a hug.

Will seemed annoyed. He dropped his hammer and said, "Damn it, Becky, can't you see that I'm busy?"

Becky's feelings were hurt, and she went from feeling good about herself and the day into the all-too-familiar feeling of being rejected by Will. She tried to tuck her feelings away in the protective place she put the other hurtful things made her feel bad in the past, but she couldn't get the words there fast enough. A tear fell down her face, and she turned to walk away.

"Don't walk away from me! You don't just come and bother me and then walk away. What do you want?" Will retorted. Becky continued to walk back to her car that was parked in the lane. Will began walking after her, and Becky felt the sick feeling she had experienced before in her life. Even though she wanted the moment to end, Will would not let it. He grabbed her arm in a way that would leave a bruise, got in her face, and said, "Don't ever turn your back on me, understand?"

Becky moved her hair that had fallen into her eyes and onto her face from the jarring of Will's grip and whispered, "Sure Will—no problem."

"That's better," he said as he raised his arm up before he headed back to the ladder, and it made Becky flinch. "I've got work to do."

Even though the project unified them, Becky could not figure out why Will often seemed edgy, even when it seemed things were going well. His short temper was unbecoming. It stressed Becky out, and she worried he might sometime show his temper in front of a prospective client. She would have tried to dilute the potential for his sudden bursts of discontent, but she could not figure out their cause, and she could not get Will to talk about what might be bothering him. His unpredictable mood swings annoyed Becky too—maybe, she figured, the project was too much for him—maybe it was too much responsibility—too much pressure.

Maybe he was afraid he would fail. Whatever it was, Becky felt like she either needed to rationalize his behavior, or that she needed to try to cover it up when the kids were around. She tried to protect them from chronic exposure to negative feelings. She tried to keep potential clients from seeing that side of Will by setting up meetings in the office when she knew he wouldn't be there.

As time went on, it seemed Will was becoming resentful of Becky's contentment. At least it seemed that way to her. What else could it be from? Yet Becky knew she wasn't good at figuring out the cause and effects of people's miseries. She had never been able to make sense out of dysfunction that came into her life from people she loved and, at times, she wondered if perhaps she was the cause. Meaningless supposition did her no favors, so she figured she would just look for more effective ways of dealing with Will's unpredictability. She distanced herself further and further from him. They still planned family outings and did a lot together. To outsiders like their neighbors, business affiliates, and church family, everything appeared to be great. But in reality, she gave up on the possibility of a renewed sense of togetherness that could be born of common goals and dreams.

Chapter Six

It was a sultry Indiana summer day, humidity so heavy Becky's lungs had to work overtime to push the moisture out so breathing could be sustained. She had the windows closed in the trailer and had the air-conditioning on even though it didn't help that much because the trailer wasn't insulated very well, and the kids kept going in and out of the back door. Erin and Eli played in the little plastic wading pool and Beth played with her dolls in her playhouse. Sometimes the children went out the front door to the barn, where they played in the shade. But the twins could only be down there when someone was with them, and Beth didn't like being around the earth-moving equipment that was being used to level the land so the asphalt company could complete the cul-de-sac. Sub-layers of sand had to be hand shoveled into the forms, and there was too much going on for Becky to let the kids run free like they did in the days before the fire. The platted subdivision that for a short time had only been lines on a piece of paper had come to life.

The culverts were already in the ground with open spaces left where the laterals would be sunk for each new home, and even though the road and cul-de-sac would soon to be ready for the asphalt, it would not be poured until the dirt dumps and tree spades were finished tromping through the area. Will and Becky saved all of the deciduous trees by either planning around them or moving them. The tree spade pleased Becky because they were able to save the many evergreens, pine, and spruce trees that she had looked at from her bed while falling asleep in the old farmhouse. Now the children watched as they were transplanted where Becky would see them from her new house. Becky walked the property and marked each tree that had a trunk diameter of twelve inches or less because that meant the seven-foot spade would be large enough to encapsulate the root ball, and those would be chosen for moving. There were three houses that had been started and each were in different stages of construction by the first week of July. Becky felt confident they could be in their new house by the time the children started school.

Becky was just about to go out to the small garden she had planted right outside the trailer, which was about one-twentieth the size she had cultivated the year before, when she paused to put a bandana on her head. She spent long hours working in the old garden that was between the farmhouse and the barn because she enjoyed working the land and watching the vegetables and herbs grow out of seeds. The garden was the same one Will's grandmother had worked for years, and his great-grandmother before that. However, Becky didn't have time for field farming now with everything else going on. She tied her red bandana behind her sweat-dampened hair and picked up her garden gloves and spade as she reached to steady herself between the door and the stairs so she could help the twins down to the vegetable patch she would weed until suppertime. The patch was very close to the trailer, so it wouldn't be at risk to be trampled on by the trucks and equipment that moved around just about every inch of their land daily for whatever reason—pipes, trees, road, utilities. But before she could leave, there was a knock at the door. Becky opened it and found herself face to face with a sheriff—a Marion County sheriff dressed in a khaki-colored uniform with a bright badge and a side arm.

"Oh, hello," Becky said with a question in her voice. "What can I do for you officer—is something wrong?" Right away she went through the many possible scenarios as to why he had come. She was disturbed that he might be there to deliver bad news, but he dispelled that thought.

"I'm Sheriff Watson and I'm here to talk to your husband about a case we're working on—is he here?"

"No, he is not. But what's the case about—can *I* help you?"

"It's a nonviolent crime, ma'am," the officer said in a not-to-worry tone. "A third-degree offense that I would prefer to talk to him about. Do you know when you might expect him to return?"

"Is it something Will did?" Becky asked with vague skepticism.

"I'd rather talk to your husband, so you can tell him I'll be back." The officer turned to leave without giving Becky even a hint for the reason for his visit, and she felt anxious to learn what had brought the officer to their small trailer on an uneventful summer's day.

"Well, he's due home for supper," Becky said, as if it would buy her time to convince him to tell her the nature of his calling. "I'll tell him you were here." She pulled at the knot in her bandana in nervous gesture. "Should I tell him you'll be back tonight?"

"Yes, ma'am. Tell him I'll be back sometime after supper," he said.

Because the sheriff said it was a nonviolent crime and it didn't seem like talking to Will was urgent, Becky found comfort thinking the situation had nothing to do with Will.

The sheriff thanked her for her time and left. Becky wiped the sweat off her forehead with her apron, then closed the door behind her. She watched through the top window of the door as the sheriff's car disappeared in a cloud of road dust as he headed down the lane.

Becky took a deep breath, then peered out the back window as if watching the sheriff pull onto the main road would somehow give her more information. Her mind was racing with random possibilities that her unexpected caller knew but wouldn't share. She wondered if Old Man Stan from down the road at the levy had gotten into trouble like he had been in before. She convinced herself that this was the most likely reason for the sheriff's visit since just the week before Stan had a run-in with the law over where he was living. He had been married to the same woman for thirty-some years when she left him for the trucker next door—a guy who had been their neighbor since they bought the only house they'd ever lived in. So Stan moved himself into an old school bus that he kept on the back forty of a friend's farm field up next to the river and adjacent to the levy itself, down the main road not far from the Blaines. He had lived in the bus and had been minding his own business for over two years when one afternoon some law enforcement officials who were walking the levy to check water levels found him cooking his supper over a large kettle he had gotten from Will. They saw smoke rising from the little wood stove he had rigged up inside of the bus where he slept, which gave them reason to assume he lived there. The officers looked at him as a vagrant and they ordered him to leave.

Stan didn't take kindly to orders, especially when he knew he had permission from the owner to be where he was, and he wasn't hurting anyone. He just wanted to be left alone in the field by the water and the woods that bordered his little home site. When Stan refused to leave, the officers returned with a search warrant and pulled their weapons out. Stan pulled out his shotgun and, for a while, there seemed to be a standoff, at least according to the *Valley Voice*. The officers left to regroup and gather back-up and, while they were gone, old Stan started up his bus and moved it down river about fifty feet where he would legally be in a different county. The officers couldn't touch him, and Marion County couldn't have cared less that he was there. Stan was a Valley Boy like Will, and their friendship went way back to the days when Will was just a kid. Stan would have done anything for Mac's grandkid. Valley Boys *always* stuck together.

Will had always been there for Stan too, kind of kept an eye on him, leaving a six-pack of beer every now and then on the steps of the bus, even though Will knew Stan was inside but wanting to be alone. Will wouldn't have stayed long to jawl anyway because the "skeeters are so bad down by that levy," but for a guy who smelled like wood smoke and beer, the mosquitoes didn't bother; they much preferred blood to Milwaukee's Best. Stan was like a street person most of the time—just existing from day to day.

Becky hoped Will wasn't in any kind of trouble. She set out to put her mind at ease by weeding her garden as she had planned. She heard music while she labored—old gospel tunes that turned her heart to silent prayer. The soil between her fingers felt good. The sower worked the land and breathed the good earth in all its black richness. Becky felt the sun through her bandana, and it bathed her with soothing warmth. She felt peaceful and content. But the mesmerizing state of mind did not last long, as not too much time had passed when Becky heard Will's truck coming up the lane. She stayed outside to wait for him so the children wouldn't be able to hear their conversation. Will pulled up to the trailer, stopped his truck, got out, closed the door of his small-size extended cab, and slowly passed by the garden where Becky was standing and waiting. Will was exhausted from the long day he had spent out in the sun building and, as he neared Becky, he panted a quiet "Hey, Becky," and raised his left hand just above his waist in a vague gesture of a hello.

"Hey, Will," she said as soon as he got a little closer to her. Then she walked up the first step and stayed in front of him so she could keep him outside while she said, "I had a visitor today."

"Oh yeah, who?"

"A sheriff."

"A sheriff—what'd he want?" Will asked as he stepped backwards.

"Says he wants to talk to you, Will. Do you have any clue as to what he's inquiring about? He wouldn't tell me a thing." Becky eagerly awaited Will's reply.

"No, I don't."

"He said he'd be back to talk with you after supper. Are you sure you don't have any idea what this could be about? He said something like it was a nonviolent, third-degree thing, but he used the word crime."

"Well, it doesn't concern you anyway, so don't worry about it," Will snapped unexpectedly.

"Don't worry about it, what?" And Becky stepped closer to get in front of Will's face. "You *do* know what he was here to talk about then. Why can't I know about it? There you go again, Will. I want to feel close to you but something always gets in the way. What is it with you?" And she pressed his shoulder to move him sideways so she could get by him and go inside.

"Nothing is wrong, Becky," Will said.

"Yeah, that's right Will—denial—you're the king of it. Pretend there's nothing wrong and then there isn't, right? You and your ex-wife never fought either, right, Will? And you and I get along okay too, right? Deny we have problems, Will. Deny everything—what the hell!" And Becky turned and stomped up the metal stairs and slammed the trailer door behind her.

A couple hours later, as the sun was beginning to set on the horizon adding an effervescent glow to the fields of tilled crops that framed in the west side of their property, Will and Becky noticed the sheriff's car driving up the lane. He had returned as he promised he would. Will walked out the door to meet him, and Becky stayed inside minding her own business. She watched out the window from behind the drapes to observe Will's body language as he met the officer and shook his hand. Together the two men walked over to the old smokehouse building, the one that had since been converted to the business office of Canal Estates and Valley Builders, and there they conversed. Neither one of them showed much expression, so it was difficult for Becky to get any clues about what might be going on. She wished she could read lips. Just when Becky thought about withdrawing from the window, Will's hand went up in the air. He was demonstrative when he shook his head no, and he looked down at his feet. The officer showed no outward signs of emotion. Will shifted his weight to the opposite leg as if agitated. Then, as the sun began to throw their silhouettes against the tool shed, Will shoved his hands into his pockets and the two quit talking. As they walked back toward the lane, Will took one hand out to shake the sheriff's hand and then the sheriff left. Becky retreated from the window and quickly sat down to play blocks with the boys so Will wouldn't realize that she had been watching. He came indoors and said nothing.

Becky didn't look up to attempt to engage in conversation with him either. She let him be alone with his own thoughts, and she stayed with hers—a necessary division. Her sense of aloneness that came from an empty marriage became more prevalent just then as she ached for him to draw her near and share with her whatever was going on in his life, no matter what it was. She looked around where she sat and appreciated the terrific and satisfying role she had as a mother. The children were unaware of the distance she felt from their father, and Becky continued to work hard to conceal her pain and to cover up Will's distress.

For many days following the sheriff's visit, Becky was bothered. Of course she wanted answers, but if Will wasn't going to offer them, she wasn't going to pry—that would only precipitate an argument. She didn't want that; neither did she want that for her children. Whatever it was, it would be something Will would have to either take care of, or it would go away. At least she tried to convince herself of that.

Chapter Seven

The move from the trailer at the end of the lane to the new, three-thousand-square-foot gray house that Will built was completed on schedule about a week before the two older kids started back to school. It had been a great summer for the children, with many sunny days. Junior had spent a lot of time riding his dirt bike, his favorite pastime, going up and down the swells created by the waterless canal banks and the mounds made by the earthmovers that altered the landscape for Canal Estates. Many times Beth rode behind Junior, her long, blonde hair trailing like the mane of a winged Pegasus. But the highlight of the summer came early one morning just after dawn, when she went with Will on horseback to help round up cattle that had gotten loose from the old farmer's pasture down the road. Beth and Will had a special bond that surfaced every now and then, despite the fact that he was her stepfather—but she was still Becky's pride and joy.

Becky was home most of the time now because she was finished with school until she could enter medical school—if she ever got the chance. The work she did for the subdivision was done right there on the property, either in the smokehouse office or in their home. The smokehouse was comfortable even as the weather got cooler because Will had added recycled barn wood siding to keep out the drafts and he installed an old potbellied stove he found up in the barn loft. It was still easier to meet clients at home. New clients preferred to see Will's work firsthand anyway. The spec was built with that in mind, although it meant Becky had to keep it looking picked up. She cooked large evening meals that the family ate together, and they continued to do casual, simple things together after work and school that an unrestricted, rural environment allows, running through fields, picking wild berries, and riding bikes. The family especially enjoyed their bike rides together. Will would take one twin behind him in a bike seat, and Becky would have the other one behind her. The older kids weaved in and out. But the family couldn't ride together as often as they liked because Will worked long hours often until after dark. Junior, who was now twelve, enjoyed chasing squirrels, fishing, and catching frogs in the creek at the back of their property that ran deep into the woods. It was the same creek that Will used to fish in when he was a kid. The twins were usually not too far behind. Beth kept track of her two brothers, who found joy ducking in and out of the corn stalks of Charlie's field that was to the east of the Blaine property, still further east of the canal, until harvest time took away their hiding places. Catching fireflies after dusk was often a favorite activity for the whole family too, and Becky always got grief from the children when she had to call them indoors for the night.

The move into the new house hadn't been easy because Becky felt pressured, as she wanted the house to be in order before the kids got up to get ready for the first day of school. Even though much planning had been done, none of them could anticipate how much stuff they had accumulated in the trailer in such a short time and how many trips it would take to move it. It was almost as if their belongings multiplied when they hit the air. Yet everyone had waited such a long time to move back into a house that their excitement gave them the energy they needed to complete the task. And with eager anticipation and appreciation, the children boxed up their toys, clothes, and books. Becky packed the dishes, more clothing, and extras. Although they were only moving a quarter of a mile down the lane, they still packed breakables well because of the bumpy dirt road. Whenever they left the trailer for whatever errands they had to run, they made sure the back of their car and trunk were full of packed boxes to be left at the new house, which they had to drive right by on their way out, anyway.

The kitchen tile had not yet been installed, nor was the wallpaper hung when they moved in, but they knew they could do those kinds of things as they had time. Will continued to stain and put up trim, install a few light fixtures, and complete other aesthetic features that were last on the list. The important thing by far was that they were finally feeling settled again. There were many rewards from a job well done.

Trailer living hadn't been too rough on their family even though there were six of them in such cramped quarters partly because of the façade of a much larger living space created by Will's fenced-in extension. But Becky was ready to get back into a house.

She had gotten used to mice from living in the farmhouse, but the trailer had become overrun with them getting in around the cheap trailer plumbing, and gnawing through the thin walls. Becky heard them every night, and she saw them every day during the cooler months. Too close quarters inside the trailer and the air-conditioner that barely kept up with the summer heat made Becky feel like she had spent the summer in a sardine can by the time they moved.

Will was proud of the house he had built, and every now and then he would stand out in the lane that was now a hard-surfaced asphalt road to take a look at what he had accomplished. He was also proud that he was able to provide for his family financially with his other building projects, though he didn't give himself enough credit. Becky praised him often for his many talents and abilities because she recognized and appreciated his hard work. Will had done the framing, all the wiring, insulation, drywall, painting, and the entire structure from the foundation to the shingles all by himself. Becky was amazed at what he had achieved in such a short period of time.

The drywall had been the most difficult for him because there were over a hundred sheets that he had to hang, and they were awkward and heavy for one person—a job Will should never have considered doing alone. Becky felt sorry for him because unlike those who did drywall work for a living, he didn't have a hoist to help hold each one while he nailed it in place, and she worried how it might affect his bad back. Becky marveled at how he instinctively knew how to tape and mud, and she watched him sand and re-sand. He never complained about how hard he worked. He just got up every day and dutifully toiled till sundown. The worst memory she had of the new house building was the day he was shingling on the steep pitch of the roof without a harness on, and he slipped carrying up a large bundle of shingles. He began sliding down and came close to falling off the roof, but he caught himself on the guttering that, thank goodness, had been installed before the chimney shingles were completed. Will dangled in place for a few seconds before swinging himself into an open window space that was within arm's reach—the window that hadn't been installed yet. As he pulled himself inside the house through the window opening, he hit his eye, slicing open its corner. To make matters worse, almost a pitiful comedy whenever they recollected the event, was that when Will landed, his foot was pierced clear through by a 16-penny nail sticking out of a two-by-four that had been left out of place, which often happens at construction sites. It hadn't been Will's day that day, but it made for a good story that was repeated to the Valley Boys, to Charlie and Ruby next door, and to friends from church. Becky always chimed in, "And he never went for a tetanus shot, either!"

Becky's two brothers, Steven and Jeffrey, came down from Michigan a couple of times during their summer vacation from college to help lay the foundation and to help put up the first walls of the framing. Even though they were in college studying computer science, they appreciated the summer income and how much they learned from Will. Jeffrey, the comedian of the family, enjoyed telling stories about experiences and near misses while helping Will with the house that summer. There were several stories that all three of the guys told over a cold beer at the end of a long workday—a telltale sign of a construction worker. The one they enjoyed the most was what happened one day when Will and Jeffrey had just finished framing up a wall. Openings had been pre-measured for the front door and windows, and they were ready to stand the wall up and brace it down. Will counted to three as Becky videotaped the first wall going up. The wall was almost erect when the two men realized they weren't going to be able to hold it up long enough or in the right place to get the braces attached. The wall started to bow and sway. Becky was just about to put down the camcorder to lend a little muscle when Jeffrey saw Will bend his head into the wall for added support from his neck muscles, and immediately followed suit. He couldn't straighten his neck for days. He made fun of himself for doing everything Will did and, best of all, Becky had captured the escapade on tape. But to hear her brother retell it and embellish it with demonstrative antics was even better.

The children had helped with the house too, picking up loose nails, sweeping up sawdust, and doing go-fer chores that Will called grunt work. The family worked well together and diligently to recover from what the fire had done to them.

Becky marveled at the way Will knew how to build a house with no formal training. "Not too many people could have accomplished what you did," she would tell him. He was quick to jump to a cause where he was needed—he had been like that his entire life. Will expressed fortitude and even enthusiasm when he had reason to labor. Becky was happy that she and Will could both feel a certain amount of contentment now that they were in the new house. Becky was happy for Will that he was finally able to move away from building *parts* of houses when he was remodeling and renovating older homes to historic perfection, to building one from start to finish with fine historic replication.

Becky was also relieved to see that Will appeared more focused. She questioned him now and then about what could be bothering him deep down because he had trouble holding on to the "good ole' country boy-love the fresh air and good earth" attitude that was so engrained in his soul. It seemed to Becky that there was always a chip on his shoulder waiting to avalanche into a boulder, given the right jolt. Maybe his demeanor seemed at unrest because of the responsibility that resulted from the birth of their twins, or perhaps the losses from the fire, or both. But Becky never let loose of the possibility that the sheriff's visit may have had something to do with Will's mood changes, or perhaps it was as simple as the chronic pain from his bad back. On the whole, though, she felt that working on the new house project as a family helped them bond. Becky knew he had to be overwhelmed with the thought of the subdivision project and having a wife and four children to support. He was tired most of the time, but she hadn't experienced one of his anger outbursts in a long time.

As the cool autumn evenings brought a reprieve from the sweltering Indiana heat, Will finished constructing the porch and the banister to the stairs that led to the front sidewalk from the side of the house and sloped downward into the bed of the canal. The creative architecture was beautiful and highlighted the already magnificent street appeal.

Will and Becky worked into the night in those days, driven by a common source of motivational high energy. They worked well as a team. Some nights they hooked monitors up to the twins' rooms after they had fallen asleep. Then they went down to the barn to cut wood or work on staining the boards they had cut and stacked the night before. If Erin or Eli cried, they'd hear them through the monitor receiver, and it only took seconds for Becky or Will to run back up to the house to tend to them. This setup was perfect because the barn allowed them to keep working even when it was raining or windy. It was the perfect place to keep the wood dry, and to keep the mess of woodworking and the spray of staining out of the house. In a matter of weeks, Will had finished making all of the antique-looking trim pieces by hand, and Becky had sanded and stained them.

As time went on, the house became even more beautiful as Becky and Will got more creative with ways to finish their new home—ingenious ways they never could have imagined they'd think of or accomplish, and they enjoyed doing these things together acknowledging at times it was even more fun than a date. They hand-painted the little two-inch balls between the frets on the porch. Will framed the glass mosaic into transoms. Becky designed and Will constructed the window boxes that she later painted. They laid the brick fireplace together—Becky mixed mortar and handed bricks to Will.

Becky sat on the steps of the wraparound porch painting one afternoon while the twins ran around the yard and rode their little trikes on the long porch that made for the perfect "road." She felt blessed as she watched her precious children at play. Will worked long hours trying to pay off the medical bills from the twins' delivery too, and together, he and Becky did what most people would never fathom trying. Maybe now that the babies were older, the fire well behind them, the house almost done with the children in rooms of their own and enough space for all of them to spread out, the entire family could rest, relax, and be more content and happy.

The new house was one to cuddle all who entered because of the old-fashioned amenities that made it like a visit to grandma's house. The outside was inviting, and the plants in the bay window, the hand-crocheted doilies, and the family pictures placed here and there made for a congenial abode for friends and neighbors to visit. Becky and Will enjoyed sharing the results of their hard work. The kitchen was done in Wedgwood Blue and had hand-painted flower tiles to match the wallpaper trim. Will had designed many special trim pieces for the corners, windows, and door frames that added to the vintage look. Becky purchased a refinished ice cream parlor table for the middle of the tip-out area, and the chairs fit as if it had been designed around them. The African violets on the windowsill were just like Becky's grandmother had always displayed and cared for, and the sunlight in front of the three-paneled window was perfect to keep their variegated blooms of white, pink, and purple.

There was also a family room in the house with a fireplace, and Will had made a mantel for it in deep, rich mahogany. There was a parlor where Becky put her piano, and on it she placed framed family photos from the collection her parents had made for them after the fire to replace those she had lost. Pictures of her grandparents' wedding taken some fifty years earlier, and pictures of her brothers when they were much younger. Also displayed were photos of Will's sisters, his parents, and of course their own children. So when Becky played her piano, she had her family right in front of her. They inspired her playing, and it made her feel good all over just to look at them.

The wallpaper in the parlor was accented with an old-fashioned print of pink roses—large peony-type roses with blended shades of mauve and burgundy. And there were two statues of painted ladies, a crystal vase, and crystal candlesticks donning Becky's favorite claw foot table. The accessories were placed on two separate and different turn-of-the-century tables displaying memories, which made the room a place of solace for Becky to retreat to. She could gaze through one of the four parlor windows and enjoy a view of the porch painted two shades of gray with rose-colored accents, so it blended well with the room and extended the warmth to the outside. A gazebo on the end of the long porch faced the sunset. The front door was embellished with leaded glass, and the angled pieces often brought prisms of light onto the walls of the parlor.

Becky seemed to have a natural ability for decorating, and the eclectic rooms were designed to highlight the diversity of both Will and Becky. The family room where the mahogany fireplace mantel was became the focal point of the rustic Western aesthetic that Will enjoyed. They hung a skull of a steer they had found on a trip out west when they first started dating and just before they got engaged, and they mounted it on the wall opposite the entryway to the family room. A colorful Indian blanket was hung above the couch, and a bear rug was laid in front of the fireplace. There was a Remington statue next to the firewood cache, and, in the corner, an 1820s take down rifle in a leather and suede-fringed case that Becky had hand-tooled as a gift to her "Wild Will."

The children enjoyed what they called their own space and arranged their belongings the way they wanted to. Becky continued to unpack and display keepsakes she believed would illuminate the timeless traditions that she felt kept families feeling secure and loved. Since most of her personal treasures had been destroyed in the fire, she relied on family members to replace them with something of their own. As she had been the keeper of sentiments, so to speak, the things she received as gifts paled in comparison to what she had had in the old farmhouse, but still she appreciated them.

Since Becky had always had an affinity for the elderly and the way they kept their houses, the sturdy well-made furniture she and Will owned was, if she had her way, usually handmade by a relative with some unique story attached to it like, "Uncle Archie made it before he went off to war," or "Your great-grandfather carved this wood himself and gave it to his son, your grandfather, for a wedding present." Becky savored the way elderly folks more often than not gave their love unconditionally, and the way they seemed so happy just to have Becky visit. What was it, she wondered, that they had learned in eighty some years, to be pleasant no matter how difficult their lives had been, and to give absolute love? Becky determined that she would try to be more like them. The keepsakes made Becky feel cozy and they reminded her of her grandparents, whom she loved, and their parents before them, who she had only met through stories. Although she hadn't known them, she respected how they had lived, and felt lucky to even be aware of and care about their traditions.

The house had come together, but there was one important thing left to do that would make it truly become home—hosting a dinner for friends—a dinner that would include the pastor of their church and his wife, and the Blaines' favorite neighbors from down the road, Charlie and Ruby. The meal would be home-cooked, of course. So Becky called Charlie and Ruby, who had been friends of Will's grandparents and lived next to the Blaine family for sixty years. They had become Becky's most cherished friends. They said yes, as did the pastor and his wife. Becky admired Ruby as a woman after her own heart. Ruby loved to take walks with her hands in her pockets. Becky liked Ruby also because she kept an orderly home and cared about gardens, home-cooking, church, the welfare of others; and she was dedicated to Charlie, who lived the idealism from the 40s—hard work, discipline, and patriotism. He had great wit and even greater wisdom, which both Becky and Will enjoyed. He still hunted on his property, and he could get away with it because it was just outside the City limits. Charlie paid attention to what was going on around him, how the crops were looking, and what the Valley Boys were up to. Like Ruby, he was a pillar of the church and the community. Ruby met Will or Becky almost daily by the split-rail fence that separated their two settlements and that was hidden for the most part by the sweet pea vines overgrowing it so that there was no obvious delineation between the properties. There they shared a story or two, discussed the weather, their gardens, or the church service from the Sunday before, or any subject that caught their fancy.

Becky and Ruby could chat about little nothings all day long—whether there had been enough rain to give a good harvest of strawberries or when Ruby's daughter might finally get the geraniums planted in the window boxes around her front porch. Ruby's daughter helped around her folks' place and Ruby, in return, babysat her great-granddaughter so her mother could work. Sometimes Ruby and Becky would end up walking along the fencerow talking about flowers or birds. Becky would have her apron on, and her long hair would be pulled back in a ponytail with wispy ends flowing in her face. Ruby would be wearing shorts, anklets, a good pair of walking shoes, short hair, and a man's cap that helped Becky recognize her at a distance. Also, Ruby was taller than Charlie, so when they were together out in the field, or talking down the road with a neighbor, it was obvious who they were.

Ruby was a very practical woman, and she knew her way around the outdoors, the names of most odd and rare ferns, wildflowers, trees, and bushes. She knew not only how to tap maple trees when it was running time, but all about canning and how to keep a clean house, and how to keep a good man happy with a delicious meal at supper time. She knew just about every homemade remedy, and often shared her advice if one of the kids got stung by a bee or into poison ivy. Once Beth got too near a bees' nest while exploring and got three stings around her ankle. She did not run home, but instead ran straight to Ruby, who stuck tobacco into her mouth, moistened it with her spit, and then packed it over the welts to draw out the poison. Becky admired Ruby, and she used her as a role model as she exemplified the kind of woman she felt akin to—strong, confident, and self-assured. Charlie, on the other hand, just put up with women's chatter, or at least he gave that impression. However, he really adored his wife, daughter, and both of his grandchildren, his only great-granddaughter, and Becky too. Becky teased him about the toothpick he often had between his teeth, saying that it probably hadn't left his mouth since he first picked up the habit as an army infantryman during World War II.

The neighbors would do anything for each other because their mutual adoration went farther back than their bloodlines would show, having been Valley folks for as long as anyone in those parts could remember. Ruby and Becky would chuckle as they listened to Wild Will and the worldly, brilliant, and cantankerous Charlie solve the problems of both the Valley and the world. The four of them straightened up when they were in church though, and were polite to members of the Blaine's Valley United Methodist Church, where both families had attended as far back as 1823 when the Blaines had first settled the Valley. The Methodists who attended this church did not show much emotion past a hand-shake between men or a hug between the women, but Will and Becky knew how much their family was loved by Charlie and Ruby and their family, and the feelings were mutual.

Becky planned the dinner for the first opportunity their calendars would permit, scheduled between Junior's hockey practices and games, Beth's dance practices and recitals, and both their parents' building and research obligations.

When the chosen day arrived, Becky started to clean the house as soon as her feet hit her slippers that morning. Then, shortly after noon, she started to make her specialty—baked chicken. To go with the chicken she planned to serve mashed potatoes, cottage cheese, Will's favorite white corn, her favorite cucumbers—sliced thin with onions, vinegar, oil, salt and pepper—the way her dad liked them (and his father before him), homemade biscuits, cranberry salad, and stuffed celery with a dash of paprika for color like Becky's mother always prepared when guests were coming to dinner. She felt so good to be in her own kitchen again. The trailer hadn't given her the right blend of space and coziness to think about cooking large, family-type meals. She felt fragmented there. But the new house smelled like home as the rosemary and bay leaves simmered their way into the meat and their scent drifted out of the oven. When she walked by the window ledge on her way to dust off the pictures in the music room, she could smell the mixture of yeast from the dough that would be ready to punch down around two.

She made an apple pie from scratch the way Charlie liked it—with the apples not too hard but not so soft that they became mushy, and she made only one pie because she knew the children wouldn't eat any. Becky watched the oven with timed precision to ensure that the pie would be cooked to perfection. Before their guests arrived, Will changed from his suspendered work clothes into one of the three pairs of clean-up jeans he owned, and helped Becky finish mopping the kitchen floor. He was comfortable in the kitchen and with household chores, and Becky appreciated that.

The oval dining table seated eight. Becky planned to be at one end, Will at the proverbial head of the table, the Pastor and his wife seated to the right of Will so they would be facing the picture of the shepherd and his flock that was mounted on the main wall, and Charlie would be seated next to Will so the guys would all be together. Ruby would be seated next to her husband in front of the two long windows so she could watch the sunset, and the kids were placed wherever they would fit in—the twins in their high chairs and Beth and Junior sitting picnic style in the kitchen—their choice so they could finish eating and play sooner without being forced to sit still and endure adult conversation.

Before dinner began, and after all had been seated, Becky motioned for each of them to extend their hands together in a prayer of appreciation, and the moment was solemn because they all knew what the Blaines had been through with the twins' birth, the fire, and rebuilding even while Will worked a full-time job in construction.

The conversation at dinner was divided between talk of the stockyards as the Pastor recalled how Charlie and Will's grandfather used to haul pigs there four times a year, and the ice-cream social that the Women's Auxiliary was sponsoring a week from the following Sunday. It was a special time, the group acknowledged, that they could gather together for dinner in the home that Will, Becky, and their children had worked so laboriously to finish.

After supper was over and all the guests had left, Becky was sitting alone in the darkened kitchen, the only light being that from the moon, and Will walked in to join her. The children were asleep, and Becky was sipping the last cup of coffee with her legs propped up on the chair next to her. She put her legs down so Will could sit next to her, and she looked forward to quiet conversation with him before they went to bed.

"Why did you squeeze my hand when we started to pray before dinner?" Will began.

Becky sat up straighter in her chair. "Oh, well I was afraid you might say something about not wanting to, and I didn't want to be embarrassed in front of the Pastor."

"Well, don't you think that should be my decision, Becky? I'm a big boy—you're not my mother!" Will said.

Becky was surprised by Will's need to challenge her about something she didn't even think twice about and replied, "Actually Will, it would have been special to me if *you* had initiated grace." Becky was strengthened through prayer, and she wanted to thank God for their blessings in front of the children. She wanted Will to set an example that he and Becky relied on prayer not only for themselves, but for others less fortunate, in the same manner Becky's grandfather had always done which had made her feel good inside—safe and taken care of. But Will wanted no part of it.

Will said, "So don't do that again."

"You know, Will, don't tell me what to do, okay?" Becky said.

"Don't tell *me* what to do or how to be," Will said, and his voice was anything but patient or kind.

Becky sat in stillness, but her mind was filled with noisy chaos that brought her back to other unpleasant and unexpected incidents she had experienced with Will. Once again she questioned herself as she wondered if *she* was the cause of his disdain. She convinced herself that even if she had expected too much he still could have been nicer to her. She thought he had come to sit down next to her to exchange pleasantries. *What a foolish waste of loving moments!* Becky lamented to herself as she hardened herself to the misguided ways that Will found necessary to deal with the pressures and circumstances of life, and she felt pushed further away from him.

Will got up and retreated upstairs without saying good night. Becky was left to sit there alone in the dark with her thoughts.

Chapter Eight

Applications for medical school were due no later than January 15th for the following year, so Becky began filling hers out that fall, preparing her personal statement, and arranging for letters of recommendation because she knew it would take time to get it all together and to get her transcripts sent. Simultaneously, she studied for the Medical College Aptitude Test, known to the undergraduate pre-professionals as the dreaded MCAT. She took classes on how to take the test from a local test preparation center. It seemed to her, however, that her years of hard work and sacrifice were about to pay off. She knew getting the subdivision to a point where it sustained itself was important to the success of the project and to her future medical career. The timing for medical school was not as she had envisioned, knowing she'd be one of the older students, but it coincided nicely with the ages of her children and where she was in life. Diligence, hard work, and persistent attitude enabled her to break the downward spiral of lost opportunity she had sometimes felt about her past, and now she orchestrated her life to be in concert with the world around her.

Becky had worked her way through college, satisfying most of her course work as a single parent though she never compromised her time with Beth. She had been very conscientious and caring, studying only while Beth slept, while she played at a park, or while Becky was somewhere where she could enjoy time with her daughter and do a math problem here and there. Sometimes she even read to Beth from course material in physics or microbiology. Becky was amused at the retention skills of her daughter who, as she got older, referenced back to what her mother had read to her and asked her the oddest but connected questions. After Becky met Will, she had more time to study because he would cook dinner or drive Becky to class so she wouldn't have to spend what sometimes would have been a half an hour looking for a parking space.

When Becky went to study for the MCATs, Will was home with the kids. She would drive to a secluded area to study without distraction, usually parking behind the hockey arena where Junior played because there was a grove of evergreens she enjoyed nestling her car into. She would park as close as she could get to the trees away from the noise of people, and then she'd get a lot of good studying done. She usually brought water or coffee with her and, when the weather was right, rolled down the car windows. The conversation from a good book blended with a steeped cup of coffee, fresh air, trees, a soft breeze, soft music from the radio she kept on low gave her serenity. Becky felt then that all was well with her soul. To most people the day-to-day schedule would probably seem too difficult and not worth the trouble, but to Becky it was perfect. She felt very content and blessed. She, Will, and the children were healthy; they had food on the table; they had access to good books; they could be together and worship as free citizens and now, with the subdivision well underway and her family complete, she could focus on becoming the doctor she had always wanted to be.

She told Will that by the time he was forty, he could probably retire because she would be happy to supply the family's income from her practice as a rural family physician. He wouldn't need to work. Will was reluctant to accept her proposal because he was a hard worker, and he couldn't fathom *ever* retiring. The whole idea of Becky going to school for another four years didn't sit well with him either. "I told you when we first got married that I expected you to work, and my position on that hasn't changed. If you want more say-so in this relationship, you'd better start bringing in some money," were words Becky heard from Will all too often. He didn't consider the work she did to help the subdivision a job because it didn't add to their income. Maybe he was just more practical than Becky was. Becky's philosophy was vastly different from Will's when it came to investing in formal education.

One morning, as Will was getting ready to leave for work, Becky approached him to give him a hug goodbye. "Will," she said, "if I don't go to medical school, what could I do for work? You're so good at what you do, and you didn't need college to learn it."

Will opened the door as if impatient to leave and said, "It's not fair for you to get to go to school and not have to work all the time."

"But school is work, Will," Becky said, "and it will train me for something useful."

"No, we need your income from a job now." Having made his point, he walked away.

Becky tried not to let his attitude get her down, and she continued to fantasize about the days when she could get up early to do rounds in a nursing home somewhere in a small town. For twenty some years already, since she was almost nine years old and made her first visits to play checkers with residents at a local nursing home that she passed on her way home from school, she had been committed to work with the elderly. She loved them, and their wisdom and wit delighted her. She respected where they came from, the reasons they gave for their longevity, and she was amused by the stories they told that she could sit for hours and listen to.

Becky continued her nursing home visits even while she was in high school, and she made friends with several of the residents there, sometimes bringing them little handmade gifts, but usually just stopping to chat or to hold hands while visiting. Fran was a ninety-year-old woman who Becky befriended there. Fran had permed hair, and she relied on Becky to come by every Thursday to style it. Fran had no family, and all of her neighbor friends were gone. She had dentures that moved when she talked and dimples that still formed beneath her wrinkles every time she smiled—no doubt the same dimples her parents had thought were so cute when she was a baby. Lucy was Fran's only friend at the home, and they played cards to pass the time. They would report to Becky who had won the most hands that week. Lucy wore a lot of jewelry she had purchased in her younger days from the five and dime store and, although her fingers were bent with time and arthritis, almost every finger still displayed a tarnished gemstone ring. In their minds the nursing home residents could still chase rainbows; it was just that their bodies couldn't keep up. But Becky saw them as youthful playmates.

Then there was the man who always wore the blaze-orange hunting cap with a bite of chew stuck down into the side of his cheek. He walked daily arm-in-arm with the unknown lady who lived in a room not too far from him. That lady, who chose not to talk to anyone but her "hunting friend," had a faux tapestry purse with vinyl straps frayed from use. Becky never saw her without it and figured she must have thought she was going somewhere. The purse pocket was usually open exposing dollar bills that had been jammed into it along with the grocery coupons she still cut out of the daily newspaper, more out of habit than necessity. These were the people Becky cherished, and it mattered to her if they felt lonely or if they didn't get the kind of medical care they deserved. She advocated for them if they needed it, whether they needed a clean bib, were out of diapers, or wanted to use the phone. Becky sought time with them, for they gave her much richness. Beyond that, she sought after the mental challenge and intrigue that the field of medicine offered, and she was determined to become a doctor.

Becky had come a long way since her divorce. She acknowledged to herself now that she had grown and recovered enough to deal effectively with the rigors of medical school. Yet every now and then she wondered what ignorance had compelled her and what unnatural force had kept her in such a sick relationship for so long. Maybe she wasn't so smart, she questioned during times of stress or weakness, but quickly dispelled her doubt. She did not ask for much out of her first marriage, nor her second. All she ever wanted was to feel loved—to be somebody's something special. With Will she had independence and room to grow, but she yearned for more—more emotional gratification. With Will she was her own something special, but she *was* learning to love herself.

Becky and Will were enjoying watching the second house being constructed in Canal Estates two doors down from their home. The Robins family, a young professional couple with no children, selected Lot Number Three. Since they bought the first lot in the historic subdivision, they could choose from one of the eleven that remained available. Becky knew they would make the perfect neighbors because one of the first things Mrs. Robins and Becky realized was that they each had carried in their purses the same house plan from a magazine published four years earlier. They laughed about it and experienced an immediate bonding. The Robinses were impressed with the uniqueness of Canal Estates, and they looked forward to becoming part of a turn-of-the-century landmark, as they too held an affinity for the type of architecture prevalent in that era. Mrs. Robins had already selected wicker furniture for their front porch even though the house was still in the framing stage.

Becky met with many prospective buyers over the course of two months, and each meeting gave her a sense of satisfaction. Most clients were drawn in from their advertising because of the historical significance of the project and the character of the subdivision. Becky agreed that the subdivision had much to offer in the cozy neighborhood, cobblestone walkways, lamppost lighting, and charm. The terrain was hilly, and the Blaines were careful to create Victorian house plans using those they had seen or that customers themselves brought in, and each one seemed to be designed with authenticity. Clients met Becky by appointment mostly in the old smokehouse office now that the children were back in school. The corners had been singed from the heat of the fire, though, and whenever Becky entered the little building she was reminded of their tragedy. As the autumn evenings were often chilly, Becky burned wood in the pot-bellied stove whenever she had an appointment, and the smoky aroma from the fire mixed with the potpourri she had simmering on top, blended with the soft hues thrown by the yellow bulbs she had put in the lamps. Becky hoped this ambiance would help to sell lots. It wasn't long until all the lots were spoken for either by closed contract sales or sales pending financing.

Becky worked hard to maintain the professionalism she felt necessary to attract the type of people that would not only be able to afford to build in their subdivision, but clientele who would appreciate the unique opportunity to live there. She worked all phases of the business and, when Eli broke a window by accident one day, and Will was too busy to fix it, she fixed it by herself. She shopped around at various antique dealers, met with personal bankers, realtors, contractors, and engineers, and she felt right at home with all of them. She felt spoiled by the challenges and with all that was good.

It was after the Robinses' home had been framed and the wiring was being installed that problems began to surface like crude oil in an ocean disaster. The McGruder neighbors to the west of the subdivision filed a petition with the City of Indianapolis remonstrating the development of Canal Estates.

While Becky and Will were standing outside of the smokehouse discussing plans, the McGruder neighbors came out of their backdoor, walked across the lane and began conversing before he was close enough to shake Will's hand.

"So why didn't you ask us what *we* thought about this subdivision?" Mr. McGruder said, ignoring Will's outstretched hand.

Becky, trying to protect Will from their neighbors' harsh approach, said, "We were so caught up in trying to recover from .."

"It's my land," Will interrupted. "I need to do this, and I haven't had time to get approval for something I need to do."

Becky looked at Mrs. McGruder who was standing by her husband and said, "I was hoping we could get together over coffee, but I've been so busy. You're right, we should have met sooner."

"Damn right," Mr. McGruder said, not letting his wife answer. "You never offered to sell to us. If you needed the money, why didn't you just sell?"

"We didn't want to move," Will said. "I know you've always wanted my place so you had more land to put your equipment, but it's my land, Joe, not yours. You're just angry because I wouldn't sell last year when you asked."

Mr. McGruder took his wife's hand, turned around, and walked away from the Blaines, leaving them to watch them walk home.

Becky said to Will, "I didn't expect them to be so angry. It wasn't that long ago that she brought me stawberries from her patch. I feel so bad, Will."

"Bad, nothin'. He just wants what he wants. Well, guess what, I want what I want. It's my land and I get to choose."

"They're right, though," Becky said. "We've always been good neighbors to each other. We should have asked them over once we had the preliminary plat. After all, these houses and the people who live in them will change things around here. We should have talked to them."

Until the summons and complaint arrived, the Blaines hadn't thought anything about whether or not the McGruders would be against their building the subdivision. For several years the McGruders, Will, and Becky had exchanged pleasantries back and forth over the small fence that divided their land to the west, opposite Charlie and Ruby's place. It was odd that their attitude toward Will and Becky was so quick to turn against them. Still, Will had heard rumors through the Valley-vine that McGruder probably started the fire so the land Will had refused to sell him would become available.

"Becky, we don't owe them anything," Will said. "You're beginning to think like them. We don't owe them our land, and we don't owe them an explanation for what we do with it. Do you think they thought about asking us before they had their cousin who works in planning and development downtown file a petition against us? No!"

Just then Mr. McGruder yelled back from his house to Will, "I'm gonna cost you so much time and money, you're gonna lose everything!"

The McGruders hired a lawyer and initiated litigation over a contrived three-inch, property-line dispute. The situation cost the Robins family a large number of delays in the completion of their home. For as long as there was a dispute regarding the surveyed property line, a "meets and bounds description" outlining the setback requirements could not be determined. The McGruders' complaint cited the original plat that had been approved by the City of Indianapolis as inaccurate. McGruders' cousin solicited from his colleagues that a Stop Work Order be written on the house until the conflicts were resolved. Becky and Will were forced to hire legal counsel in hopes that they could resolve the ridiculous situation as soon as possible and get back to the business of finishing the Robinses' house and pouring the foundations for the other two that were already staked off.

Becky walked in the front doors of the impressive downtown Indianapolis City-County Building and, rather than being upset, found herself intrigued by the experience. The rooms were large and showy with grandiose marble pillars and solid cherry wooden shelves filled with leather-bound books. A well-dressed receptionist greeted her, and she was led to a room off the main lobby. Her lawyer walked through a set of side doors with an air of distinction. He came across like so many of them often do, delivering opening remarks with double entendre, almost Shakespearean in nature. Although Becky was amused by his comical antics, she would have enjoyed the entertainment more if she knew she wasn't paying a pretty penny for his show.

The secretary offered Becky coffee during their meeting, and she was impressed with herself to be in a position where a secretary was offering *her* coffee. She recalled her younger days when she was employed as a secretary, and she was the one who got coffee for visitors. Becky enjoyed the role reversal, even so she did not relish the fact that she and Will were having to fork out a lot of money to solve a foolish, mean-spirited discrepancy regarding a property-line issue contrived by neighbors who were now more like enemies than the friends they once were. After paying for a few hours of legal advice, Will and Becky decided to give the McGruders the land they were fighting over, just to get the matter over with so they could get on with the subdivision project. Of course this meant they had to have the plat redone, which cost them a few thousand dollars and even more time, but at least for the time being, they were free to move on with their project. Grandstanding with a lawyer did no more than lend credulity to the absurdity, and although the solution was expensive, it had turned out to be simple. With the alteration to the property line and the plat plan revised, the Blaines got the Stop Work Order removed, and Will's crew continued work on the Robinses' home.

The McGruders continued their fight with fervor, however, using despicable and immoral tactics to accomplish their goals of trying to destroy the historic subdivision. Their "city connection" advised them next to file a complaint that alleged that the Robinses' home was in violation of the easement requirements—too close to the road. By the time this complaint was filed, a feud had been created in the Valley, and the gas station, pool hall, and diner had become congregating places from each camp—those who wanted the subdivision and those who didn't. By and large, most folk were on the Blaines' side, but it didn't matter because what had become clear was that the McGruders intended to keep at it, causing the Blaines as many problems as they could for as long as it would take to stop it.

But Will and Becky knew they too could play the game, had they wanted to. Will was well aware that when the McGruders built their home, they did not get a building permit for the swimming pool they had installed. The McGruders hid and slid through the system—no doubt with their cousin's help. When Becky went downtown to look into the neighborhood records before she met with her lawyers the first time, she found that the McGruders' records were not available. Their microfiche had disappeared from the file. Becky and Will believed that the McGruders either removed their records or they had their cousin remove them. Either way, no one would have been able to prove their wrongdoing had they gone to court. But Becky and Will knew they too could file a case with the County Board against McGruder, knowing he had violated City mandates and codes, and maybe even cause them to have to dig up their pool. But Becky convinced Will that being vindictive was not the answer. Will was frustrated that she wouldn't support him in his effort to make others as miserable as he was.

One afternoon, Becky saw Mrs. McGruder nosing around next to the property line. She watched Mrs. McGruder as she stuck her face over the grudge fence her husband had erected. Becky couldn't help herself. She scared Mrs. McGruder half to death yelling out from a place where she couldn't be seen, "Hey McGruder, let thee that are without sin cast the first stone." Becky felt hot inside from her pent up hostility. She would have rather at that moment given Mrs. McGruder a blow to her head with her fist, but she held back and simply yelled—feeling bad later for having done that. Will enjoyed Becky's story that afternoon, but she told him she should have known better than to act that way. Will encouraged her to really let loose if there was ever another opportunity, and Becky felt bothered that she knew she had it in her if she really wanted to.

The Blaines' kind-heartedness earned them no favors. The City came late one afternoon after Will had put in many hours pounding nails, told him that the house he was working on was seven inches into the right-of-way of the road, and they would have to file for a variance if they wanted to be able to keep the house where it was. To Will and his crew this meant that the Robinses's timeline to get into their new home by Christmas would be out of the question. After much deliberation, Will decided he had no choice but to contract with a house-moving company to come and lift the house up off its foundation and move it back a few inches—the only immediate solution that would solve the latest of the McGruders' diabolical plans. Becky helped Will out with the phone calls so the problem could be worked out with the least amount of stress on Will. The idea of moving the house seemed outrageous, but what was just as unsettling was the effect the whole charade had on the other ten customers who were in line to have their homes built. Valley Building Company had more than its fair share of problems before having barely gotten off the ground.

No matter what Becky and Will did, however, their problems with the McGruders not only remained but got worse. As soon as one problem was solved, another would take its place. The Robinses no longer wanted to live in Canal Estates. They had grown to harbor animosity toward the people who would have been their closest neighbors, and they just didn't want to be part of the hassle any more. Will and Becky couldn't blame them. They were frustrated, too, that the Robinses' dream home carried an imposition that was more than unreasonable. The Blaines would finish the Robinses' house and sell it.

Becky never imagined that there would be anything that would keep her from applying to medical school that year, but here it was. Becky prayed about their problems and how they might go about ridding themselves of the obstacles that finally had been done as the McGruders had threatened. It caused Will and Becky so much time and money, that unless there was some miraculous plan to earn large amounts of money in short order, there would be no point in continuing to try to develop the Canal Estates. However, the Blaines could not afford to just quit, either; they were in too deep, and they already had taken loans out at the local bank in great excess of what they alone could afford. In addition, they had spent money held in escrow for infrastructure that would have all been for nothing, and they owed money to Henry. They would have to secure more loans on Will's good name, the name of his family, and the fact that their property was now part of an historic landmark—a soon-to-be subdivision. The project had to continue. To acknowledge their predicament was to suggest that perhaps it was now the beginning of the end.

Chapter Nine

The Robinses were very lucky that Becky and Will were so generous. Becky and Will could have held them to their contract, but chose instead to buy them out. As a result, the Blaines endured more financial and emotional pain from losses they incurred as a direct result of the McGruders' actions. It was difficult to lose the contract on the first house in Canal Estates because it diminished the momentum they had going, and it put a damper on the Blaines' enthusiasm. Becky and Will would not allow themselves to be defeated, though. They were familiar with how to make the best out of a bad situation. So, a meeting was held, a quit-claim-deed exchanged hands, and a check to the Robinses made the buyout official.

As Becky and Will left the notary public's desk, Becky put her arm wound Will's waist and said, "Will, we'll just have to pull ourselves up by our bootstraps—we'll be all right."

They reclaimed ownership of Lot Number Three, House Number Two, and began to strategize the schedule of progress for the takeover. Before they returned to construction on the Robinses' house, they called their insurance company to change coverage so the framed-in structure would be in their name, as well as the entire process of building to completion. They were surprised to learn they were denied coverage because no one could officially work on the house. The City had not lifted the Stop Work Order, even though the moving company had moved the house back as the City had requested and even though the house had passed inspection. The paperwork had not caught up with the action taken. While Will and Becky waited for the City to work through its bureaucracy, which they knew could take weeks, even months, their ability to withstand adversity was once again tested. It made them work harder.

Bedtime became a welcomed part of the day—a time when they both tried to give in to the nothingness that eventide can sometimes bring. This night, the strong winds of the storm passing through pelted rain on their windows, tap-tapping proof that the last of the autumn leaves would bare the trees and ready them for winter. They hadn't been asleep long when they were awakened by a peculiar sound, a loud, heavy disruptive noise that was long enough and loud enough to get their attention. They both sat straight up in bed and looked at each other. "What was that?" Becky asked.

"I have no idea," said Will.

Within seconds both of them were peering out the window through the trees. They could see nothing but the silhouette of the owl that often hooted peacefully when the night was still. He didn't make a sound this night. "Oh well, I don't see anything, Becky—let's go back to sleep," said Will. Becky, whose apprehension and awareness made her hypersensitive, went to each of the six windows in their bedroom searching out the cause of the noise before she gave in to the darkness and returned to bed.

The next morning, as Will began to get ready for the day and drove his truck to the barn to load lumber, he noticed the top of the Robinses' house could no longer be seen above the old walnut tree. He slammed on his brakes and said, "What the hell!" He stepped out of his truck and ran through the brush and there stopped dead in his tracks.

Becky had looked out the living room window to see if Will had left yet, and when she saw what Will was looking at, she ran out the door toward him. "Oh my God!" she yelled as she ran. "Oh my God, Will!" She began to cry and rushed up to Will and hugged him. "The wind . . . It's gone, Will."

He said nothing, but put his arm around Becky as they both stared forward in disbelief as their eyes scanned the location where the house once stood. Will took off his hat and scratched his head, then let go of Becky and sat down on his haunches, his head down with exhaustive pain. The strong winds that had passed through the night had blown down the house. That was the noise he and Becky had heard in the night.

"There's no home to finish now," he mumbled to Becky who put her hand on his shoulder and just stood there.

Over the course of the next few weeks, they looked for an equitable solution, but there were no easy answers. They had already spent several thousand dollars trying to take care of the McGruder complaint, many more thousands on the engineer to redo the plat, thousands on advertisements to sell Canal Estate lots, seven thousand moving the house back because of the set-back complaint, and then over sixty thousand buying the framed timber back from the Robinses. Now they were left with a pile of boards that lay on Lot 3. Becky and Will sat at their small, round table in front of the window seat where Becky kept her African violets. They looked out past the cornfields and on to Charlie and Ruby's and were able to distance themselves. Becky paused to stare at her violets and focused mentally on their kind-hearted neighbors. She picked up her cup of coffee and smiled at Will.

"What do you want to do, Will? Did you get the other contract you put the bid in for last week?" Becky asked.

Will replied, "No."

"You didn't?" Becky asked.

"Nope. Our bank won't back us any more Becky. You know how the locals talk. The Valley Boys tell me that McGruder's cousin—you know the one who works for the City—has filed another complaint. I guess they feel that the pile of fallen lumber is a danger to the neighborhood, and they'll file a Stop Work Order again until the mess is cleaned up. The guys were at the diner this morning and they told me it was reported that we *abandoned* the building on our property and that it is not only dangerous over there, but that it is an eyesore. Oh, and they said we'll be getting a citation." He paused and made a dejected sigh. "They'll notify us to clean up the mess right away or we'll be fined I think about a hundred dollars a day for every day it's not cleaned up." His voice softened. Becky did not reply, but moved her gaze from out the window to the coffee in her cup, swirling it with her finger, watching the circles form, and she bit her lip and took in everything Will had said.

Will looked out the window and saw his buddy pulling into the driveway—Stan, the good ole' Valley Boy from down the road in his rusty, red pick-up truck. Will moved his chair back, stood up and, without saying another word, opened the back door and stood in the driveway as Stan stepped down out of the truck cab, took his sweat-stained hat off with one hand, and reached with his other extending a friendly "Howdy do" to Will. Becky too got up from her chair, put her hands into the back pockets of her jeans, and listened to Will and Stan's conversation through the open window.

"Hey Stan," Will said, with a wiped-out, unenthusiastic drawl. "What brings you around?"

"Well, I was just havin' some eggs down there at Frankie's, and folks—well, they's tellin' that things ain't goin' so good for ya'll." Stan paused to spit some juice from his chew. "Will, now you know we goes way back. What ya say you let me take care of them McGruders—no one will ever know. I'll just crawl through the fields some night." He sort of crunched down and moved his hand from the center of his abdomen and out level with it as if to scan the area where he'd hide.

Will interrupted shaking his head. "Stan, you know I appreciate that man, but you can't do nothin'—you know that."

"Damn straight I could; ain't right what's goin' on." The two of them kept talking.

They would have to take the broken house apart, load the wood into a truck, and sell it for scrap lumber. To make matters worse for Will and Becky, money was really becoming an issue. They were running out. The infrastructure costs of road cuts, sewer, architect bills, attorney bills, and payments to the lumber company for a house that didn't exist anymore and that they couldn't finish and couldn't sell were eating up their funds. Will had no choice but to spend as much time as he could tearing down the fallen house, so he didn't have much time at all to work outside of Canal Estates to bring in much needed income. It wouldn't have mattered even if he had the time to work outside of their own project, because their bank wouldn't lend him any more money for contracts.

Will put in what seemed hundreds of hours tearing the lumber apart—floor joists, roof rafters, wall and door jams—everything that had gone up had to come down. Every nail he had pounded in two months earlier had to be extracted. It was backbreaking and heartbreaking. Nothing seemed to go right, even the simple things. Eli, being only three, wanted to be like Dad. He put on his little tool belt one afternoon, and went to the wreckage to help Will. He wasn't there long when he got a nail stuck in his foot. Poor kid. He needed a tetanus shot. Eli wanted to help his father because he had heard him tell Becky many times that it didn't seem like he made any progress; the pile never seemed to get smaller, and he wasn't able to get the area cleared fast enough. Will worked well past midnight many evenings trying to clear the area where the house had blown down. None of this should have happened. The conflict between the Blaines and the McGruders was past serious, and the stress it caused Will's family was taking its toll on him. He often looked out their bedroom window after dark and talked about how he would love to take a shotgun and shoot all of the windows out of the McGruders' house. Becky wondered if he was serious for she never underestimated the part of Will that was unpredictable and malevolent.

Meanwhile, both Becky and Will's health was deteriorating. Neither one of them felt well most of the time—stress began to show its effects. Will developed intermittent but consistent chest pains, and one afternoon after a hard day pulling nails out of two-by-fours from the fallen house lumber pile, Becky found him slouched in the living room chair clutching his left arm. She took him to the hospital, thinking he was having a heart attack. They gave him nitroglycerin under his tongue, and his symptoms went away, and he was released. He was supposed to have a follow-up doctor visit but never did because they didn't have health insurance anymore. It had run out when they couldn't make the payments. If only the McGruders had not schemed to cause trouble, the house on Lot 3 would be finished by now, and the Blaines would have their money, and the other homes would be well on their way to being finished. They wouldn't have the mess or several thousand feet of lumber to clean up, and they wouldn't feel that the world was closing in on them.

Becky thought often about Job from the Bible when she couldn't fathom things getting any worse, but they did. What she felt was real to her, and though she felt connected with the story from the Bible, she found little comfort in reading the verses. She tried to gather strength from the words and faith to help her have strength to persevere and find understanding, but she was tired and scared and the words made no comfort. There was continual worry. In Will's family, most men didn't live past sixty-five because they died of heart attacks—a genetic predisposition that left Will and Becky both knowing Will was at high risk, especially if their lives didn't settle down.

The McGruders were relentless in their pursuit against the Blaines. Becky told Will one day, "I bet you money they're the ones."

"They're the ones what, Becky?"

"They started the fire just to get our land, I know it."

"Over my dead body they'll ever get it, Becky."

The Valley was becoming more and more split as a result of the turmoil, and neighbors met at their clotheslines or fencerows to talk about it. Some felt Will and Becky were taking on too much with the house and kids—others agreed that they had no choice. In a small town, words traveled fast, and neighbors quickly formed alliances with others who held their viewpoint. Long-time friends occasionally took issue with each other, and even Will's relatives who lived down the road took sides against their own cousins, saying Will had bitten off more than he could chew and probably should have stuck to pig farming like his grandfather. Others didn't like it that the farmland had been torn up by big city machinery, and they were glad. The McGruders were fighting against the subdivision. And even though it wasn't Will's fault, human nature would take on many different forms before the struggle was over. Becky couldn't stand all of the ugliness, and she was feeling like nothing was worthwhile.

"Mama, you don't go out in the field with me and the boys anymore. Can't we go and pick wildflowers?" Beth would all too often ask her mother.

"No, Beth. Mama's got a lot of paperwork to do right now. The wildflowers will have to wait until tomorrow. Sorry."

"You said that yesterday," Beth said.

"I know Beth, but I can't help it. There are things I need to tend to for the business," Becky said.

"Well, I don't like the business, Mama." Beth stormed out of the kitchen where she had been waiting by the door to go outside.

Junior was bothered too because ever since the fire, his mother had tried to bribe him into living with her, making him feel guilty because he had always lived with his dad and didn't want to leave. But there was so much stress around the house that he started to spend more time at her house and away from home. Will was on edge not knowing how to handle any of the pressures, and Becky just kept thinking how much she'd like to just move and start over. There was a price tag on peace and contentment, and for them it was clearly becoming too expensive.

Becky realized that she needed to get her mind on other more positive things or she would go crazy. As a distraction, Becky decided to do something she had always wanted to do—learn to ride a horse. Not just any horse, though—she wanted to ride seriously and to take lessons. The discipline required would help her focus. She knew there were riding stables relatively close to their home, so she decided to drive around that area one afternoon to see what she could find out. Her friend, Henry Roth, who had lent them money for the sewer pipes for the subdivision, had volunteered another small loan should she realize that indeed the distraction would be good for her. She took Beth and the boys along so they could enjoy being with their mom away from work and enjoying the countryside and being around farm animals.

When Becky drove down the lazy road that wound around to the stables, she could see that the stables she had heard about on this horse ranch were not run-of-the-mill. There was more to it than a few horses penned up with a fence ring. Right away she could see several riding arenas, at least four large outbuildings, and two heated barns that Becky soon found out were filled with almost thirty winning horses, some worth more than she could fathom. She parked in a gravel spot and, as the dust settled behind her car, she put her sunglasses away, looked in the mirror to check her hair, and took a deep breath. She prayed that God would be with her in all that she did. She felt blessed for the opportunity just to be there for the experience.

Becky and her children entered one of the barns through a side door and looked around, hoping to find someone they could talk to. The floor of the barn was concrete, and there were many stalls on each side of two long rows. Each stall contained what Becky and the children considered to be a beautiful horse. Erin loved to reach up to feel the velvety noses that poked over the stall doors. The barn smelled good and, even though it was still early in the morning, Becky could see that the farmhands had already been very busy. There were green hoses that lay in little puddles of water near the sides of the walkways; no doubt the horses had already been watered. The horses were chewing loudly so Becky showed the children that they had already been fed. Becky looked around and saw at least three men clad in black rubber boots. Two of them held pitchforks. Then she saw a stocky man wearing tight jeans, a western shirt, large belt buckle, cowboy boots, and a five-gallon hat. He looked more groomed than the others so Becky approached him thinking he may be the owner.

"Are you an employee here?" she asked.

"Not exactly," the man replied with a southern twang. "I'm one of the owners."

Becky began to explain why she was there. By the time she was finished, the man's wife had joined them and both were enthralled by Becky's eager character and enthusiasm toward riding. They explained to her how long they had been in the business and how very successful they had been in the world circuit. Becky listened in amazement, as she could hardly believe she had run across what seemed a spectacular opportunity. She hadn't known that they were world-class trainers. The owners went on to say that they had a horse in their stables right then that had taken second place in the World Championships the year before. Of course Becky wanted to see him. She was mesmerized as she walked through the corridors by all of the beautiful horses that smelled so good. She reached into many stalls over the top half of the door and tried to pat the nose and manes of some, and she talked to others as she went. All three of her children had found barn kittens and were satisfied to stay with them as she meandered contentedly.

The large barn doors were open wide as she passed another entrance of the barn that was open so that a tractor could get back inside after the hay bales had been moved. There was a morning breeze that brought in sweet odors of freshly cut clover. Starlings dodged in and out chasing off the other smaller birds and, even though it was early, there was much commotion about. The owners and Becky took one last left-hand turn, and there he was—tan coat, handsome face, and very large stature. This wonderful horse named Billie Jack Straw took a couple of steps closer and stood before her with big brown eyes and a welcoming look. Becky readied to pat him. She could barely reach his withers he was so tall, but her fingers found a soft place to stroke at the ridge between his shoulder bones.

"He is so tall," she told the owners, "and overbearing." She felt a lump in her throat as she struggled with the fear that was slowly taking over her as she envisioned riding him. She continued to reach up to pet the eighteen hands of beauty and masculinity.

"Here, Becky, go inside and take a look at him," the owners told her.

"Oh, I don't know if I should do that," she replied.

"It's all right really—check him out," they said. Pat reached past his wife, Jan, and lifted the latch. Then he took Becky loosely by the arm and guided her in. Becky was reluctant. She didn't know what to do—she just stood there feeling afraid and stupid.

Billie Jack Straw bent his head down, stretched forward until his nose reached Becky's neck, and nuzzled her like a lamb to his mother. At that moment Becky fell in love with this horse. She loved horses, and Billie apparently loved her. Her mind raced through several things at once. Would the current owners be willing to sell him? *Wait a minute*, she thought, *what would I do with a world-class horse? Why ride him, of course*, she thought to herself. *Ride him where*? Becky turned around in the stall to ask the owners her questions out loud and, as fast as her mind would let her, she began chattering away with a myriad of questions to the owners who were not used to novice questions.

"Slow down," they told her. "There are many things to consider before investing in something like this. Have you ever ridden in a show? How comfortable are you around horses? How capable are you of learning? Our business is a serious one, not just your everyday spend-an-hour-riding-a-week class, but lengthy classes with other serious riders—we take horses and riders to Nationals and the World Show, Becky. That's our business, and it's an expensive one."

"How much does it cost?" Becky asked.

"Well, first things first." They suggested Becky try a few riding tests to see if she was even trainable. Then they would talk about which horse might be most compatible for her, though they could tell she wanted Billie.

"Well, I'm interested, so when can I do this? Ride, to try things out, I mean," Becky said.

Pat looked at her husband and gestured for him to answer. He said, "Well, you wanna get in a saddle now? See what you can do?"

Becky paused, then smiled. "Sure."

The owners motioned to their barn hands and requested that they get Billie ready to ride. "No saddle," Pat told them. "Just brush him out, pick his feet, lunge him on a line, and then put the bridle in his mouth." The trainers seemed eager to get Becky involved, because no one had come forward to buy Billie yet, and training for Nationals was less two months away. They didn't know Becky had no money or time.

Training fees would be expensive for both the horse and Becky, but she was in love with Billie Jack Straw, and the inspiration he seemed to give her pretty much closed the deal before they began. She began to contemplate how she could convince Henry to loan her the money. Becky was enthusiastic about the challenge, the distraction, the passion and the opportunity. She knew once she signed the contract, she would be determined enough to take the horse all the way to the top in competition. The owners agreed that Becky could consider purchasing Billie if all went well during testing because she had already appeared to trust him. To Becky, Billie's nuzzles indicated that she would be quick to develop a relationship with him. However, she needed to feel safe, not only because he was so tall, but also because her lack of equestrian skills made her especially fearful in the unfamiliar environment.

The horse was taken out of his stall, and a halter was put on him with a long lead rope. The horse and trainer assistant entered the ring and began to warm up. The trainer stood in the middle and clucked and "kissed" orders to Billie, prompted by a whip—not for hitting, but for the sound. The horse seemed unusually obedient from Becky's point of view as she observed him from behind the fence. He stopped when he was told to without a second of pause, and he changed gaits when he was told to. He seemed perfect to

Becky mostly because he was so beautiful, and he seemed to obey commands. She wasn't used to being around World Class horses, only the ones from the Fair Grounds in her hometown when she was a kid. When he was warmed up to the trainer's standards, the trainer opened the gate, walked over toward Billie, took hold of the halter, and motioned for Becky to join him.

"Where's the saddle?" Becky said. "You forgot to put the saddle on!"

"You don't need a saddle, Becky—just get on," the trainer said, as he motioned to his hired hand to retrieve the bridle from the nearby rack.

"How am I supposed to get up there?" Becky asked, as she pointed way up to the very top of Billie's tall back. She was very green, and it showed, which was probably a good thing. The trainer was accommodating. After a few full-hearted attempts to no avail, the trainer cupped his hand as a stirrup and helped hoist Becky up—almost too much, as she nearly went over Billie's back to the other side. The trainer then asked her to do many unusual movements that were foreign to her. She trusted him and went along with his requests, though seemingly preposterous at the time for a novice like Becky. She loped, not holding on. She stood up on his back and balanced herself. She told the trainers they were crazy, but she did as she was told. She put her fears aside and trusted the trainers not to put her in harm's way. As Becky rode around the ring, they taught her and then judged her to see if she could make the horse change gait while loping with the correct lead leg forward to the wall. Stop to a walk, then trot. Becky began to relax and feel comfortable. Then she heard music, a cadence that helped her focus, a proud tune that helped her decide right then and there that she had to find a way to purchase Billie Jack Straw and make it to the World Championships.

Within a week, Becky had purchased the world-class horse with a loan from her friend Henry and began training. She couldn't find much time to ride, but she seemed to have a natural ability for it. It was plausible that she stood a chance and, despite Will not understanding the risk of wasting money, the respite from their troubles helped Becky's mental state with the satisfying distraction.

She loved riding and she loved her horse, a combination that helped her improve at a rapid pace.

Qualifications were in Virginia, a little more than a day's drive away. Becky was reluctant to spend the time and money because her training sessions had been so few, and she had never ridden in an actual show, but she had committed when she bought the horse, so she'd have to figure something out. Becky and Will couldn't afford to fly to Virginia, which meant Becky would have to drive. She would be very tired by the time she arrived to perform in the competition. Becky told Will she didn't care what it took—she had to get there and give it her best. If she lost she had tried. If she won first, second, third, or fourth, she'd qualify for the World Championships. She had not been able to attend any other pre-qualifying events, which would have at least shown her protocol and an opportunity to watch others and observe her opponents. Now it was just up to her and her friend Billie. Perhaps it was better that she was naïve to the demands of her competition, anyway.

She loaded up their four-wheel drive vehicle that already had some hundred thousand miles on it, said a prayer, and headed for the hills. Her long trek to the east would take her about 18 hours. As she drove, she was drawn into the countryside, to all of the scenic landmarks, and away from the ugly corruption that haunted her dreams back in Indianapolis. As Becky wound around the curves of the old two-lane highway that hugged the hillside sloping upward and that had long since become an outline of the past, she enjoyed becoming absorbed in a time and place that was no more. She stared into the old empty tobacco barns as if she could smell the fresh leaves that once dried on their slats. She thought of the people who worked long, hot hours in the fields and wondered if they were a more content lot than the people she knew who worked nine to five in air-conditioned buildings in the city.

Becky thought of many things while she drove, but she tried to stay away from thinking about the problems of the subdivision. She worked at staying focused on what was to come in the arena less than a day away. She would meet Billie there. The horse was being transported to Virginia in a horse trailer with five other world-class contenders who would compete in events outside of Becky's class—Hunter Under Saddle. As a kid at the country fair, she never paid attention to what the 4-H members did to get ready for their shows, and was only a casual spectator at the equestrian events. She enjoyed watching the horses, and loved smelling them and patting their heads as she walked through the horse barn. So much of the process was foreign to her. She was on an adventure.

Shortly after arriving at her destination in the hills of Virginia, she looked for a place to park her SUV. She would sleep in the back of her vehicle for the two nights she would spend there. The cramped quarters of the back end would be her kitchen where she kept a packed cooler, and her bedroom was a sleeping bag crammed along side of it. She was entering a world-class competition on a wing and a prayer. She was not only a novice who had never attended a horse show as a competitor, but the long drive and sleeping arrangements probably wouldn't help. All the other competitors were either wealthy themselves or had sponsors. They had the best of accommodations available to them—fluffy beds and hot tubs after a long workout in the arena. Becky had nothing but herself, her horse, and the cold, damp SUV. The first night the temperature dropped to just above freezing, and the rain pounded unrelentingly on the roof, keeping her awake half the night. The rain finally stopped after 3:00 a.m., and Becky was finally able to fall asleep until about six o'clock when she woke up for good. She grappled around to pull a fresh change of clothes from the bag that had become jammed between her back and the front seat. She opened the door for her first whiff of a Virginia morning. With arms stretched upward, she moaned slightly as she worked out the stiffness in her body, then grabbed a towel and headed toward the barns.

There were no competitors at the barns when Becky first walked in and looked around. It was too early for them. She scuffed through the straw and made her way to the pavilion where she figured the horses were probably readied for show. She found a shower there, and in her shirt and shorts she let the cold water clean her hair and flush the dirt from her skin that she had accumulated on the drive. She was showering in the same stall where the horses showered. The cool water felt good even though warmer water would have felt better. The only audience she had were the mice that scurried back and forth stealing grain from the bags meant for the horses only. They too were taking advantage of the time when no humans were around. She ate a pre-packaged fruit pastry, and dried off. The Mexican stall-hands were just coming around from their night watch. They slept in an empty stall, waking up from the cots in their makeshift bedrooms; they were there to make sure no one tampered with the horses. Six slept in one stall, but Becky could see that they looked comfortable and content, and figured that they had probably enjoyed much frivolity during the night telling stories to one another. Becky could see playing cards lying near the cots next to a battery-powered lantern that was sitting on a hay bale propped up on its side. *Who had the better life?* Becky pondered.

Back in town, the motels were serving large, hot smorgasbord breakfasts to the other competitors. She later found out when her trainers described the delicious spread they had enjoyed. They knew Becky had slept in her vehicle, but didn't ask her why. Yet, as the sun rose, Becky realized her spirits did not need to be lifted as she was already very happy and content with what she had already experienced, and she was in no need of anything.

Becky's instructors, now that they were together, got her going in the direction she needed to go. The first thing was to get her horse ready, and she was to take him into the ring to be lunged and worked out. His ride to Virginia had also been long. Billie Jack Straw was still sleeping when Becky entered his stall. He whinnied a hello. Together they would embrace the day. With stiff looking legs, he stood up and nuzzled her neck, as he always did. Becky loved that, and she wrapped her arms around his neck and petted behind his ears. She brushed him down, took a pick to his hooves, and put on his halter. Becky led Billie Jack Straw out of his stall and the barn and through the side lot to the ring, which had been designated for warm-up. She used the whip only as a directional tool and marveled at the beauty of her magnificent friend as he loped around the arena. They had the whole place to themselves. To Becky this was heaven—with the birds chirping and the smell of her horse against the freshness of last night's rain.

It took a while before Becky noticed the well-dressed audience that had begun to congregate as owners, competitors and trainers got word of the new rider they had not seen at any of the other shows. Her competition was now eager to see if they felt she was any challenge to them. Becky had no idea what was going to happen during the day as the events of such an affair started to unfold, but the one thing she could tell from the whispers and size of the crowd that had gathered around while she practiced, was that this was no county fair. She saw that there were many classes of people there—those that would ride, those that would clean, those that were officials, and those whose only job was to watch. The spectators really stood out in their tailored, old-money outfits. It was their job to observe the horses and their riders and report back to the trainers. There was a buzz on the fence line as many ascot-like ladies began to wonder who the blonde-haired woman in the center ring was and where she had come from. They recognized Billie from the year before when he had taken second in the World Championships, but rumor had spread that his dapples had gotten too large for the popular look that year, and that no one had invested in his purchase.

Because of Becky's schedule, Billie Jack Straw and Becky had not been seen together at any of the other qualifying events throughout the year, and the observers took for granted that all the horses and riders they had counted on when calculating the winning line-up were solid. Becky was the one who would upset the apple cart with her prized buddy and confident posture. After warm-up, when Billie had been put back in his stall to eat, Becky heard a rumor from one of her trainer's friends that the owners of a large chain of department stores who owned several of the horses to be shown that next day would be her most stiff competition. They probably were relatives of the ones who had watched, whispered and pointed on the sidelines that morning. Becky's trainers were stopped by many who had grown to know them over the years in the circuit, and asked them for details. The Wolgberg Ranch sent word to have their best horse, Blazerunner, arrive later that afternoon. He was resting in preparation for the World Championships, which he had qualified for by taking firsts at other shows that year. In fear that

Billie would earn more points from a win at Nationals, they did not want to risk that their prize horse would not remain in first standing as he entered the world competition. Becky, on the other hand, although competitive, was not there to take first. She just wanted to qualify for the World and enjoy the reprieve she had away from her problems by delving into a fantasy world that she found she loved. She really didn't care much what anyone thought.

The next morning, the day of her event, began by meeting her coaches at Billie's stall. Becky was dressed in her competition attire—black stirrup pants, black English riding boots, white blouse, black riding cap, a gray tweed blazer that was not the style for the year like the beige and rust outfits she had already seen and that probably would have matched Billie's coloring better. But she liked the outfit she had chosen, and her trainers told her it would certainly make her stand out before the judges. Becky was given her number that she would pin to her back and final instructions. Her coaches told her they would watch by the south fence and use the finger motions they had practiced to give her advice and positive vibes. Becky held her breath while she mounted her horse and entered the ring. She and Billie were one as they were in Becky's mind every time she rode him. For the moment she was in her own environment—secure and confident. Though Becky took in her surroundings, she barely heard the noise from the onlookers as she entered in line with the other horses to begin walking before the judge. She glanced at the others for signs of unfamiliar formality. She was surprised to see the judges were dressed in Western gear with large hats and pointed boots, because her class was an English-style competition. The shiny, expensive belt buckle on Judge Number Two told Becky that he had been around, and that it had been given to him as a prize for "Best of Show" in other years when the judge himself had been a competitor.

Blazerunner and rider were one horse-length away from Billie and Becky in the line-up. Becky glanced over Blazerunner's stance without moving herself. Neck positioned down for the perfect line. Confident. Poised. The class started. Becky clucked her order and made sure her posting matched the trot. "Walk your horses, walk your horses," the judge announced. Becky made sure

Billie's neck was down. "Now, lope your horses, lope your horses," the judge continued. The command to go from a walk to a lope made Becky tense up because she knew she had to make sure Billie didn't get even one trot step in during the transition, an error he had made before in practice. She had to maintain control. He went directly from a walk to a lope with nothing in between, his lead leg forward at the fence, matching the direction they were going in the ring at the time. Perfect. So far so good. Becky continued to pay strict attention not only to the judges' commands, but to her immediate response to them, relayed instantaneously to Billie.

They performed together well in the first third of the event. They had worked past the start-of-the-competition jitters, but just ahead the large gate at the far end of the arena where they had first entered became unlatched and was moving slightly. Becky knew from practicing that Billie was shy of it even when closed, so she tightened her reigns slightly to let Billie know she was in control and that everything would be okay. Her hand movements were subtle and undetectable to the judge. Billie's head started to turn slightly to the right. Becky moved her little finger about five-tenths of a centimeter in the opposite direction, and he followed her order. He behaved like a finely tuned race engine—shined and polished. He responded to Becky's softest and most gentle commands. Becky put a slight pressure on her inside thigh, and he righted himself after he got too close to the outside wall as soon as he turned the corner past the gate. Everything was smooth again, and Becky looked grand in her black riding pants, tall leather boots, and English hat. Their presentation was almost flawless. They won first place, and they had qualified for the World Championships!

Her trainers said they didn't think she breathed through the entire competition. Becky was not conscious of whether she breathed or not. All she knew was that she was on her way to the World Championships in Dallas, Texas. She was so excited, and she wanted to share her excitement with someone. The only person she could think of to tell was her mother; Becky thought that no one else would really care. But even her mother could not have fathomed what Becky had accomplished because her parents lived over twelve hours away and had never seen her ride, even though phone calls Becky made to her parents kept them somewhat abreast of her eclectic and busy lifestyle. Henry didn't answer his phone and Becky figured Will probably didn't care to know because he had never even taken the time to go to the stables in Indianapolis to watch her practice. *Oh well, it doesn't matter anyway*, she told herself. Becky was her own best friend, and she was happy and proud of herself.

The World Championships came and went. Becky took fourth place, and she hated to face that she'd now have to sell Billie. She couldn't afford him or the lessons any longer, never could. She loved him and cried the day he was hauled away. She often remembered the day he first nuzzled her neck. She remembered the hills of Virginia, too—the one exceptional night when the air was thick with a mixture of the fog rolling in and the powder smoke from a Civil War re-enactment that Becky had decided not to watch for fear that Billie would spook from the rifle shots. She felt particularly close to him that night. She rode him bare-backed away from the barns and up to the top of a small hill that overlooked the countryside. She bent down and put her head on his neck. She put her arms down toward the front of his withers and hugged him for a long time. Billie was her beautiful and loving friend. Becky wished with all her heart that she could keep him forever. Reality demanded the sale. Billie was gone.

Autumn winds were now chilled by winter weather eager to rot the pumpkins in the field and to give the farmers last notice to condition the tractors and get them put away for winter. Will began to layer his clothes when he headed out to work on the fallen house where the ruins still laid waiting to be completely removed. He didn't have much time left to clean up the lot of debris before the City of Indianapolis would stop giving him extensions and fine him. He had ripped thousands of nails out of lumber that he now had to stack in a place he had yet to find. They planned to sell for scrap. He looked pitifully worn. His hair was unkempt and shaggy, and his face unshaven. The depression he was made to endure tearing down his house was exacerbated by the pain in his head, back, and sometimes his heart. But he stuck to his task and, board by board, nail by nail, continued to take the house apart. Becky watched Will from the window. One evening as the sun began to set, she could still see his woolen cap-covered head bobbing up and down as he stacked lumber. He wore gloves without fingertips so he could control the hammer and, when he came in and readied for bed, Becky gave him lotion for his cracked and weathered hands. This was the only help she could give him, aside from trying to think up ways to pay the bills and take care of the children. She woke up that following morning about 4:00 a.m. with an idea of what she could do to make a difference financially and in short order.

Becky didn't know where her idea came from, but it was so clear and directed that she gave credit to divine providence. She had a vision to start a conservatory named "Music Masters and the Arts." By 6:30 a.m. she had much of it planned. There would be about fourteen classes. Even before intergenerational issues around the nation were truly addressed, Becky planned that she would work with senior centers and retirement communities so seniors could work with children. Together they could do art and music projects. *Elderly folks could have "grandchildren" so-to-speak, and children who didn't have grandparents around could enjoy the love and laughter of a stand-in.* A nine room conservatory seemed a challenging concept, but she thought, *if this is what I'm supposed to do, then so be it.*

By the end of the first day, Becky had designed in sketch what would become the multifaceted learning center. She went out that day to explore a vacant space she had seen for rent across from the children's dance studio where Beth took jazz and ballet classes. It was still for rent, and it was the right size—with a little imagination. The second day she met with the owner of the building and signed a lease. She designed the construction plans and went over them with Will, who at the time thought she was crazy to even be thinking of such a thing in the middle of all that they were doing. But Becky was determined that the start-up costs would be minimal and, if she found the right secretary once it was set up, it would require minimal time on Becky's part to maintain. The financial business plan, if classes would fill, would make the Blaines a handsome profit. And the time she would spend there, the twins could be with her, and Beth would be in school. She convinced Will that it wouldn't cost them much more than the scrap lumber, some spackle, and a little paint. She would talk a local music store into loaning equipment in exchange for advertising. She would coordinate sign-up for classes to coincide with the dance academy and make their little district an artsy alley. She had faith that the project would go well.

On the third day she contacted the university's music school and found two young doctoral students who were willing to teach the classical and jazz components of the piano and violin classes on a contractual per-student basis, so Will and Becky would have no payroll, at least not at the onset. Becky made arrangements with a local theater director to teach the drama classes for free until the class size was large enough to support a paycheck. She signed a contract with a music therapist to work with the emotionally disturbed children; the teacher, anxious to subsidize the meager income she made working part-time at a community clinic, was willing to work unpaid until her client base was built up. Becky planned how she would meet with each retirement community in the area to arrange transportation to and from her facility.

Becky worked with the sheriff's department, the court system, and juvenile centers, making arrangements for children with problems so they could attend classes and come to a supervised environment where they could work out their aggressions in a positive and constructive way. She had a class called "Exploring the Inner Rainbow," where a teacher with a Ph.D. in psychology integrated different emotional energy levels associated with certain colors, like red for anger and black for stress, designed to help people of all ages reflect quietly and transform their emotions to a more positive state of mind. Beanbag chairs were provided so students could be comfortable and relaxed. There was a class combining audio-visual stimulation that incorporated tactile movement orchestrated to go along with sound. In this room, students were exposed to many cultural activities. They folded origami while listening to Japanese lute music. They wove baskets while they listened to the twang of a country fiddle, and they brushed impressionistic watercolors to the bend of a blues harp. *What a wonderful opportunity,* Becky thought, *for people to become all that they could be!*

Within a short time they were ready for their grand opening. Will had worked diligently alongside Becky, and together they completed all the carpentry work on schedule. Becky praised Will for his many special talents as she watched him quickly assemble the eight walls that divided up the solo piano practice rooms. The music store delivered seven pianos. Will also helped Becky unload the chairs she bought with a charge card from a local department store to be used by the 1930s Players and Singers Group, a fun gathering of singing seniors who would reminisce through practice. Will watched the twins while Becky interviewed for a secretary. Becky admitted if it hadn't been for Will, she never would have been able to move to completion with such expediency. They made a good team, and although Will could not believe Becky had made such an unexpected turn in her life, he came to realize that if Becky set her mind to do something, it would be done.

Classes were almost filled within thirty days as their facility was completed in time for registration. Becky had coordinated with the dance academy owner, who had a great reputation and a strong client base, to do a joint registration. The conservatory looked beautiful. A grand piano greeted visitors when they first walked into the building. Becky's office was to the left, and above her chair was a framed poster of Einstein. The saying on the bottom of it echoed Becky's sentiments: "Great spirits usually receive violent opposition from mediocre minds." Could this have been a harbinger of things to come, or was it a phrase that had captured Becky's life to date all in one sentence?

Music Master's success was going as planned as the Christmas holiday approached, and they had a stipend left over by the end of October. That meant that Becky would soon be earning a salary. The problem was that all of October's surplus money went to pay the lawyers who had been hired to get Canal Estates back on the right track again. Becky would have to work harder.

Becky couldn't stand what was happening at home. She and Will were struggling just to keep their home mortgage payments up to date and food on the table. Becky opened her Bible often and read scriptures to Will in an effort to give both of them strength. They waited for the architect to redraw the plat so they could restart construction the next spring. With all of the issues that still needed to be cleared up, they lost potential buyers, and Will had to look for other work to support them during the winter. They so desperately wanted to save the subdivision.

While they waited for the engineers and lawyers to finish their work, Becky came up with yet another idea. She would produce and direct a Broadway musical through "Music Masters and the Arts." She would use her conservatory as a way to get into the largest performance hall in the state. She called Lowes Hall and asked what the seating capacity was. She extrapolated numbers in her head, weighing the costs of costumes, director, orchestra, choreographer, conductor, rehearsal hall, advertising, props, royalties, and stagehands against the number of tickets she thought she could sell. Becky decided she would do it.

Lowes Hall had a reputation for selling out to Broadway hits and world-renowned orchestras. She figured she could make about forty thousand dollars with a two-day show. Although Lowes only put nationally recognized performers on their marquee, Becky knew she would still try to convince them that MMA and staff could produce a successful, heart-warming Christmas show for the community. Becky was driving Will crazy.

"Will, I've calculated everything. We should make over twenty-thousand each night," Becky told Will just before they finished doing the dishes and headed upstairs to bed one night. She described her ideas as if they were easy and no big deal, like telling him she was going to fix him some hot chocolate. Easy preparation, won't take long—no problem.

"Becky, you've never done anything like that before. What makes you think you can do that?" Will said.

"I just know I can—you wait and see," said Becky.

Becky was extremely excited to put her ideas in motion, but Will couldn't sleep that night. The next day Becky made an appointment with Lowes' manager, put on her best suit, jewelry, and business attitude, and drove to the meeting. She spoke with professional ease and, in less than one hour, she had sold her way into a market where most everyday, inexperienced people like Becky entered only as part of the audience. Within a week Becky had hired dancers from Broadway and choreographed what she wanted to see on stage as the opening number. They would be paid after the show, their contract the binding assurance. Her drive surpassed her enthusiasm.

She rented a lighted sign for the front of her conservatory to advertise auditions for the musical. She decided she would produce "Babes in Toyland"—a perfect choice for Becky because she adored Christmas, and the timing was just right. A Christmas musical would give her even more happiness and unending energy. There was light at the end of the tunnel, for the prospect of financial success was real—happy, delightful success.

She researched and found out how to get the rights to the musical, and she made arrangements to have the orchestration and scripts sent to her. She read about royalties and made an appointment with a conductor she had been referred to from the symphony orchestra director in the city that she had called. The magnitude of the fact that Lowes would even consider her musical was inspiring and brought credibility to those she worked with to accomplish her goal. She had the magic. Ticket Master would be promoting her show.

Becky needed a place for her actors, actresses, and dancers to rehearse. She checked with high schools, but found they charged too much for even an hour or so in an already empty auditorium. Becky needed to be thrifty in finding space. After all, this was the reason she started the project in the first place—to earn money *for* the subdivision, not to *spend* it. Eventually, she found a rural town hall that had enough room to accommodate her large crew. She located a dance company and recruited dancers who had previously performed on Broadway. Arsenio Hall's trumpet player, Henry Mancini's percussionist, and other great musicians made up her twenty-one piece orchestra.

Becky decided to have about eighty children on stage all dressed up in toy costumes for a live rendition of Santa's Toy

Shop for the finale. This would let all the children who didn't have a speaking part participate in the program. She didn't want any one of them to feel let down. Becky had fun going to the costume store, and she either chose or designed all of the wonderfully bright and colorful costumes. She called around to find out which high school had won first place in its band competition and hired it for a meager price in exchange for the recognition it would receive from performing "The March of the Toys" scene. The band would be in red uniforms and march down the four aisles with trumpets blaring—the dramatic finale.

Becky went to several churches to listen to the small group choirs. She surmised that a church choir might sing for nothing, and Becky would be pleased to have church folk involved in her musical. She spent evenings listening to small choral groups practice from several churches until she finally found one with the right blend of voices—cheery and with a well balanced sound. This choir of eight were willing to perform with less than six weeks of rehearsal time, and they had just the right mix of harmony and sweet, fun-loving personalities that would comprise the Victorian singers who would open up the show. Becky planned that after the overture, the choir, which would be dressed in costumes to make them look like they had just stepped out of a Dickens's Village, would then have lights dimmed on them to create a silhouetted still-life in the shadows. The curtain would then open to the first act. Becky envisioned an old Victorian street scene with snow falling and dim lamppost lighting. The dancers who would enter during the first song would be dressed in blue velvet, the women wearing white fur pillbox hats and carrying muffs. Their short skirts would have a white fur trim on the bottom. They would act as if they were skating onto the stage with their male counterparts, four couples gliding to the opening number.

Becky held auditions at the conservatory and played the piano for potential lead actors and actresses as they tried to impress her with their talents so they would be chosen. The ad she had put out in the newspaper solicited almost sixty, and she was thrilled with the tremendous response from the art community as word spread. Enrollment at Music Masters increased. Experienced actors, actresses, and singers helped Becky find make-up artists and background set-design people. Word-of-mouth by starving artists served Becky well as many things were still left to do in a short time. Becky attended all dancing and acting rehearsals as she attempted to choreograph her visions. For a while Becky acted as both producer and director until she was able to locate a director suitable for the job, one with a good reputation who would accept a pay check that fell within Becky's restricted budget.

Becky sold advertising to local shop owners to help defray the cost of printing the program that she had designed. She also designed the professional-sized stage sets, and Will skillfully built them. Again their teamwork paid off and while they worked together, they were happy. Late one evening, after the children were asleep and one day before opening night, Becky and Will spent the night together finishing up one of the larger props they were making outdoors. By the light of the moon they walked hand-in-hand down the old canal to the ruins of what used to be the Robinses' home. They took apart one of the last standing walls so they could use the lumber for a prop. The moon provided the light, and the only conversation was between whatever creatures were watching them that night—wide-eyed night creatures who hid nearby as Becky and Will shared love, happiness, togetherness, and contentment. It would be one of Becky and Will's fondest memories.

It was the morning of the first performance, and Becky was tired and dirty from being up all night with Will, when the eighteen-wheeler finally showed up about 6:00 a.m. to transport the last of the props to the performance hall. The driver told Becky he was hired to bring the rig and to drop it off *only*. A car pulled in behind the rig to take the driver back to the garage. There was no one to drive the semi to Lowes Hall. Becky tried to persuade the driver to do it, but he continued to refuse. He had another contract and had to leave. How would she get the truck to the hall without a driver? Will had to leave for work as soon as the children left for school. The huge truck just sat where the driver had stopped. Becky said, "Well, I guess I'm just going to have to drive it there myself." And she did. She opened up the door and hoisted herself up into the driver's seat. "Jeez," she said as Will watched in disbelief. "How do I do this?" As the sun was beginning to rise over the treetops, Becky shifted the truck and navigated toward the sunrise. She arrived at Lowes Hall without a hitch, but her stomach was near her throat the whole way—a half hour that seemed to her like eternity.

When she arrived at Lowes Hall she remembered how the dock entrance in the back of the building was where trucks unloaded. She wheeled the truck around. It was a tight squeeze, and there was no way she could tackle maneuvering the huge rig into place because of the extreme finesse it would take. She stopped, put on the hazard lights, hopped down and ran into the building where the union loaders were waiting. She looked around for their boss.

The stagehands glared at her. "What ya doin' here so early?" one asked. "We ain't startin' yet. Haven't had coffee." They didn't know who she was—she had no make-up on, and she still had not changed out of the dirty cargo suit and the old wool cap she had worn all night. They knew no better than to assume she was the truck driver. She looked different from the day she was all dressed up and sold her way into the place. She stood on the stage waiting for a boss to come over to her, and while she waited she looked out over the two thousand empty seats that she hoped would be filled for that night's performance. Half the tickets were already sold in a presale.

When the boss finally approached her to see what she wanted, it took him about a minute and a half before he realized who she was. "Mrs. Blaine, is that you?" he asked.

"Sure it's me. Can you have one of your helpers please move the truck for me? It's out in the street, and I can't move it in next to the dock," Becky said.

"Oh, well sure, Mrs. Blaine—anything you want," he said.

Becky chuckled to herself, and as soon as she knew things were under control with the props, she called her friend Deb for a ride home. After a shower and a change of clothes she made dinner. While it cooked, Becky picked up her relatives and her high school music teacher, Mrs. B, at the airport. Becky included Mrs. B as a guest because she had been such an inspiration when Becky herself was on stage playing Maria in *The Sound of Music* and when she had sung in other high school musicals and competitions. She was excited to have Mrs. B in her new home that Will had built with a little help from his family. For the holiday season, Becky had decorated the house with over twenty poinsettias. Burgundy, lace, and old-fashioned ornaments hung on the tree in the parlor. The family tree in the living room was trimmed in the keepsake ornaments they had only recently begun to accumulate as their old ornaments had perished in the fire. The frame of the house was outlined in white lights and evergreen boughs. But the best part of the evening for Becky was knowing who would be in the audience. Becky had contacted the Methodist Home, the Children's Hospital, and hospice centers and gave away a thousand tickets for their patients to be able to come and enjoy a Christmas memory. Becky could hardly wait to see Beth on stage as Red Riding Hood, and knowing the twins, her parents and brothers, Mrs. B and Will would be present escalated the anticipation of opening night. Junior wouldn't be there. He didn't want to go, and Will did not encourage him to do so. Becky knew she would enjoy her fantasy despite the shades of gray, but Becky's heart was a Junior-sized bit empty, and there was nothing she could do about it.

Becky made the front page of the entertainment section in the *Indianapolis Star* that night—the show was a hit. She was a household name overnight as regular ticket holders paid attention to the venue, and the show sold out for the second night. When the tabulations were complete, Becky was able to deposit over twenty thousand dollars in the bank to help their family and the subdivision. They could now focus on finishing the subdivision. Becky felt her prayers had been answered.

Chapter Ten

Becky and Will got the lot of the fallen house finally cleaned up. Time had put distance between the subdivision and the McGruders, the City had lifted the Stop Work Order, the sewer was in the ground, and the road cuts were almost complete. "We've got to get these lots sold Will," Becky said one morning at breakfast before the children woke up.

"No kidding, Becky. Are you trying to tell me something I don't know?" said Will sarcastically. Becky had changed since the fire. She'd grown to appreciate happiness and life more, and she felt more open. Will was still the same, though, like he was in a miserable rut. Becky really didn't know what would bring him out of it. For as long as she had remembered, even when things were the best she'd ever known between them, he had a mysterious side—a side that punched when provoked and raged when given a chance.

"Maybe we should sell the land to the McGruders after all, Will. They've always wanted it, and we'll just move and start over."

"No, Becky—for the same reason I wouldn't sell the farmhouse. The farm is part of me. Either I have it or no one does." That was the end of their conversation.

Becky and Will closed another land deal, but they'd have to wait until spring before they could start building. Only one-third of the lots had been sold now; the other buyers had left as the problems came. The Blaines were hopeful that the historic subdivision would be a success. They met the most recent buyers at the mortgage company and were all set to sign when the secretary came in and handed the closer a note.

The closer read the note and said, "Guess we have a problem, Becky, Will. You cannot sell this lot because the current mortgage holder has encumbered all the property, each and every lot."

"What?" Becky said. "How could that be? We've had a title search done before every closing, and there has never been a problem before."

"Probably because you used the same title company, and they made a mistake on the first one," said the closer. "The same paperwork must have been used for the others. No, we can't close because the original mortgage company that gave you the loan on your house has mistakenly included all the land on the mortgage." Becky was bothered for the inconvenience of everyone, but knew the problem could be easily rectified, so they would just reschedule a meeting after the problem was fixed. All the mortgage company had to do was take a closer look at the legal description, and it could ascertain that it only held title to Lot One, Will and Becky's first spec house. The rest of the lots should have been free and clear to sell. But Becky felt compelled to try and get answers before they adjourned.

"Let's look at the title policy. There are no encumbrances," Becky said. "May I use a phone? I'm going to call Mr. Allen, the manager of our mortgage company, and bring this to his attention and see what he has to say about it. Surely they had everything in the proper order before we closed. Maybe you have part of an old file before the new deeds were recorded."

Becky got up from the table and paced a little as she dialed. "Hello, Mr. Allen—this is Rebecca Blaine," she said after dialing the mortgage company.

"Oh, yes, Rebecca. What can I do for you?" he said.

"Mr. Allen, we have a problem and could use your help."

"How can I help you?"

"Well, I'm at a closing right now, but we can't seem to close. It seems that the paper work we received from your office used the wrong legal description when our mortgage loan papers. The old legal description was used, the one from before the subdivided plat was approved. The 'meets and bounds description' that was given to your office by our engineering firm was not used. Can you revise that section, I mean even now, fax something over with the correct legal on it so we can close this loan? We're all here to sign now, and that would be so great."

"I'll have to pull your file out, Becky. This is the first I've heard about it. How about if I get it out this afternoon and call you back when I see what's up?" said Mr. Allen.

"What's wrong with right now—I mean, we could wait a few minutes and you could call us back."

"I have a four o'clock appointment, Becky, then I'm out for the rest of the day. You're just going to have to tell your people they have to wait."

"But we'll all have to reschedule," said Becky.

"I'll get back to you when I have what you need."

Becky had no choice—he had control. "Sure, I'll look forward to your call," Becky said, with hesitation in her voice. She wanted to be more persistent, but chose to keep her composure in front of the buyers, even though she was frustrated inside. Everyone was inconvenienced, and they left the meeting with the understanding they'd all check their calendars and get back with one another after the situation had been corrected.

Becky waited around at home all afternoon but no one from the mortgage company called. She kept walking into the kitchen by the phone feeling pressured that they might lose another sale. There was no time for ineptitude. That night she tried to stay busy to keep her mind occupied, and the next morning she still felt impatient. At nine o'clock, she called Mr. Allen. He was not in so she left a message. No return call that day. On the third day she called him yet again, and this time, she wasn't going to take "I'm sorry, Mr. Allen is tied up at the moment," for an answer. She had his secretary on the phone. "You know, this may not be a priority issue for Mr. Allen, but I really need to get this resolved," Becky explained to her.

"Mr. Allen has told me that he is having difficulty getting some answers about your file," said the secretary.

"What answers?" Becky said. "We don't need any answers on anything. We have a small problem, and it needs to be fixed, that's all!"

"I guess it's not that simple, Mrs. Blaine. Look, I'm sure that Mr. Allen has your best interest in mind, and he will be getting back to you soon. At this point, that's about all I can tell you."

Becky felt manipulated and was bothered that she could not control a rapid resolve. She thought about driving to the mortgage company, but thought if Mr. Allen wasn't in, the trip would serve no purpose. It appeared there was nothing she could do but wait. Becky tried to think of ways in which she could expedite matters, but she came to a dead end every time she realized she couldn't even get Mr. Allen to return her calls. Corporate America—just like Monopoly. Throw the dice, and wait your turn.

Over a week passed. Becky, Will, and the buyers, being more than frustrated at this point, decided to contact the loan officer who had originated the loan. Maybe he could give them some answers.

"Hi Cliff, remember me? It's Becky Blaine."

"Oh, hi Becky—long time no hear," said Cliff.

"Yeah, I know. I've been really busy with the subdivision, MMA, and the kids," replied Becky.

"Yes, I see that you have. I drive by your conservatory every day on my way to work. It looks real nice, and I read the great review of your recent musical. Congratulations! So how's the new house and everything?"

"Well, Cliff, that's why I'm calling. We have a problem. Will and I went to close on another lot sale the other day, and the closing staff told us we couldn't, that there was already an encumbrance on the property. It seems that your people inadvertently used the wrong legal description and now all of the lots in our subdivision are tied up in our mortgage. I've already called Mr. Allen—heck, it was last week already, and he hasn't returned any of my calls. Do you know anything about this?"

"To tell you the truth Becky, I have heard something about this, but I've been instructed not to talk about it yet," responded Cliff.

"What do you mean you've been instructed not to talk about it? What's *it*? I mean, what's the big deal? You knew we were building a subdivision and what our intentions were for the loan. What's the problem? What's the big hush-hush about?" asked Becky.

"Look Becky, I'm really not in a position to discuss this. I'm sorry. I'm sure Mr. Allen is taking care of things and that he will get back to you soon."

The rhetoric sounded all too familiar to Becky. She wasn't getting anywhere with Mr. Allen or with Cliff. She expected more from Cliff, who she had befriended way back in the beginning when they first initiated the construction loan. Cliff had been out to their place with Mr. Allen on several occasions, walking the subdivision; unlike Mr. Allen, who had taken an interest in the historical aspect, Cliff seemed to take an interest in Becky. She was surprised that he would shun her concerns with a simple "don't-worry" attitude! He didn't flirt with her that day—he seemed more concerned about not making waves than he was about fixing Will and Becky's problem.

As she and Will readied for bed one evening, Becky said, "I can't get through to them, Will." She pulled her pajamas down over her head.

"Through to who?" Will asked as he sat on the stool next to his closet and took off his socks.

"That damn corporation. They got what they wanted out of us, schmoozing us all the way, then, that's it. I can't get through to them. I can't get the documents changed."

"I know, Becky, and we have to soon because if we don't close on another lot before snowfall we're gonna be hurtin' through the winter."

"The loan document has to be changed or there will be no more building," Becky said matter-of-factly.

About two weeks had gone by when Will announced, "I know how we can get their attention, Becky. We'll quit making mortgage payments until they fix their mistake. We've got too much on the line. You're right, we're going to lose more than one sale if things don't get cleared up soon. Here we go again."

"That's not the answer, Will. We need to make the payments to keep up our good credit."

"Becky, it won't work that way. As soon as we quit making payments, we'll get their attention."

"Fine, whatever, Will. We'll try it your way." Becky had no other solution to offer.

Becky was the one who paid the bills, so when their mortgage payment came due, she ignored it just like she and Will had agreed to do. Feeling guilty, she scribbled a quick letter about why they weren't paying and enclosed it in the same envelope with the billing statement, then sent it to the home office of the mortgage company.

The home office gave no reply so when the next month's bill came she did the same thing. This time though, she wrote a lengthy and more formal letter outlining all the details with dates and times, and she enclosed copies of their mortgage, legal descriptions, title work binders, and a request for reply.

Two weeks later she got a letter from an attorney. The letter informed the Blaines that they were two months behind in their mortgage payments and threatened that if payments weren't caught up, the mortgage company was entitled to begin foreclosure action if it wanted to. "What?" Becky screamed out loud when she read the letter. Becky was crazed with outrage, and she stormed upstairs in search of Will, then down the stairs and outside until she found him.

She waved the white envelope as she went, and when she found Will shoveling on the side lot, she walked up to him hitting her hand with the white envelope. "We haven't done anything wrong, the mortgage company has! We can't even get them to call us back about their mistake. Now I have to call their stupid lawyer."

Will stared at her, then said in a downtrodden voice, "Now what?" Becky went on to tell him about the letter, what she thought, and she didn't even stop to listen for a reply from Will. She turned and headed back to the house where she was going to phone the lawyer right away. She paced back and forth in front of the file cabinet where the phone was, then decided to pause, take a deep breath and cool down before making the call lest she might say something she'd regret later. About thirty seconds later and with trembling hands, she placed the call.

"Dan Shortino?" Becky asked when a man answered.

"Yes, it is."

"This is Rebecca Blaine. I received your letter today. You know, the one that threatens foreclosure? What's going on here? I mean it has been less than sixty days and, we have made you aware, well, we informed the mortgage manager about a problem with our loan papers that needs to be fixed. He never returned the calls. We quit making payments to get someone's attention. The incorrect legal description needs to be fixed."

"That's right," said a smug sounding Mr. Shortino, who didn't offer any more language to the conversation than necessary. "I sent you a foreclosure letter."

"That's right, what?" asked Becky. "What gives you the right to send a letter like this?"

"This is how we handle bad creditors."

"Bad creditors? We've never had bad credit in our lives. The only reason we quit making our mortgage payments was to get someone from the mortgage company to take notice that we had a problem that nobody was fixing! You guys are the ones at fault here, not us." Becky paused to calm down so the intonation of her voice would not be misconstrued and so she'd sound level-headed and sincere. "Why don't we both get to the bottom of this right now, and we'll all be able to go on about our business—okay?"

Mr. Shortino didn't say anything. Becky knew that he didn't have to. He was hired to collect mortgage money, not to pass judgment on communication techniques from the company that hired his services. "Say something, Mr. Shortino. What am I supposed to do here?" asked Becky.

"Pay your mortgage," he said.

"But what about the problem we have with the legal description? We can't sell lots in our subdivision until the mortgage company releases the encumbrances on the lots they mistakenly tied up on our mortgage."

"Nothing's going to change. Either bring your mortgage payments up-to-date, or we begin foreclosure proceedings against you," Mr. Shortino said. He had been trained well as a collection lawyer, like a dead fish—cold and with no brain activity.

Will and Becky weren't just people who weren't paying their mortgage. They weren't bad risk people. They were people who had a real problem, and no one in the corporation would listen to them. Mr. Shortino finally offered, "You'll have to get a lawyer."

The situation for the Blaines went from bad to worse. The title company had missed First Trust Mortgage's mistake. They ran a new title search just to make sure. Someone had taken shortcuts, using old information already on file downtown at the Recorder's

Office. Corporations making big money were once again taking the path of least resistance at the expense of their client.

One morning Becky was still in her pajamas and slippers at eleven o'clock because she was too depressed to get up any earlier to go to the conservatory. All the money she made was being spent on the lawyers she had hired to try to fix their problem. As she sipped her coffee and scuffed through the kitchen and around to the cutting board, she told Will, "The path of least resistance might work for energy, but it's not working for me."

"Maybe I should just go kill 'em all," Will said.

"Don't talk that way—it scares me," Becky said, giving him a puzzled look. She couldn't tell if he was kidding or not.

"Well, like that guy that just went to prison for tying a shotgun to this corporate guy's head, he got his attention, didn't he?"

"Yeah," Becky said, "but now he's in a crazy house over it."

"So what, what's worse—this crazy house or that one?" Will asked, and he left the kitchen.

Becky yelled after him, "We used lots as collateral to Henry, remember. How will we pay him back?" But Will had headed down the canal where he used to run as a kid. Becky followed after him, saying nothing until he reached the barn and they both stopped, Becky several steps behind him.

"I just wish I could be a kid again, Becky," Will said, but didn't turn around to look at her. Becky continued her silence. "I wish I could talk to my grandpa and ask him what he would do."

Becky called their lawyer, the same one who had handled the McGruder problem. Their lawyer helped them understand the procedures, but told them nothing they didn't already know. Without lots to sell, Will and Becky could not make payments to the engineers for the platting, for the infrastructure, or to their friend Henry, who had been so good to them. Henry ended up suing the Blaines. He had to. Indirectly, he was a party to the whole mess, and he had to file paperwork to protect his interests.

Will and Becky didn't know what to do or whose advice to take. They couldn't sell lots so they couldn't pay their creditors.

The mortgage company needed to correct its error, but it wouldn't. Their lawyers wanted to foreclose. If the lawyers succeeded, Will and Becky would lose the family property, the historic subdivision worth several million dollars, and their home. They should about suing, but didn't know who, or for what, breach of contract, fraud? It seemed that First Trust Mortgage would be first on their list because it wouldn't fix its error, and it was threatening to foreclose. But the Blaines couldn't afford counsel for as long as that litigation would take, and the lawyers weren't willing to work on a contingency. They could sue the title company for making a mistake on its title search. After all, if the title company had picked up on the fact that there already was a first mortgage on all of the lots and if it had advised the investor and the Blaines of such, the investor wouldn't have lent the money, and the Blaines wouldn't now owe the investor money. But who was on first, and who was on second was a moot point. Only money could purchase justice, and the Blaines didn't have any. They couldn't sell lots to pay for the bills, and they couldn't build houses. They were stuck!

The Blaines thought long and hard and decided to take loans out on the two one-year-old cars they owned outright with the off-chance that a short-term lawyer could turn things around. They bravely hoped it wouldn't end up costing them their automobiles. Becky told Will, "We need to be prepared if we go out on principle, because principle might be all we will have left when this is over with."

The lawyer they hired thought the case would easy, and he was eager to begin. He assured the Blaines that he was more than familiar with the other firm and that he could probably work out a solution over coffee. He gathered information and vowed to get back with Will and Becky soon. In the meantime, he would file some sort of paperwork with the courts, nothing really complicated—just something to outline the problem and to propose a resolution in writing and hope for a meeting in person. He planned to speak of the situation as a mutual mistake. First Trust Mortgage had made an error using the incorrect legal description on the mortgage documents, and the Blaines had made a mistake signing it. The

Blaines trusted in a hired expert to get the problem solved. Quick, simple, amicable.

But it was not simple. The reply that their lawyer got from First Trust Mortgage was one that neither Will nor Becky expected. The mortgage company was denying that it had made a mistake and insisted it had used the proper legal description. It refused to alter anything already recorded. Furthermore, it was asking for legal fees for wasting its time on something that had no merit.

Time waits for no one. Every week that passed was another week they got behind on bills. Pretty soon creditors were calling—a first-time experience for the Blaines. "Bill collectors are ruthless people," Becky told Will. "They don't care what your situation is; they're only bent on harassing people who are already down on their luck." She knew the collectors were only doing the job they were hired for, but did they have to do it in such a condescending manner? Becky and Will weren't bad people who just didn't like to pay their bills. They desperately wanted to, but they just couldn't right now for reasons beyond their immediate control.

Tensions in the Blaine household were mounting big-time. Will's weakest character traits had now become who he was, and he acted them out daily. He existed on anger and resentment. He began to look old; his hair was unkempt; and his beard was stubbly. Their credit was going down the tubes with their livelihood. Becky, who most always seemed to be in control, couldn't make anything right. She was edgy with the kids. She sold Music Masters and the Arts. Why spend all of that energy into a profitable business only to give the earnings away to lawyers who weren't doing any good anyway? Finally, the lawyers recognized defeat and advised Will and Becky that unless they were prepared to spend years and hundreds of thousands of dollars in legal fees they should file bankruptcy and get on with their lives. This was against Becky and Will's grain. They had worked hard their entire lives for what they had. They always paid their bills and they had no intention of filing an ugly bankruptcy that would stick with them for the rest of their lives.

Becky's parents came to visit. She dodged the phone calls from creditors, but her mother knew something was wrong. Every aspect of their lives was affected. One night, about three in the morning, Junior happened to be spending the night, and he woke everyone up screaming, "Dad, someone is stealing our car!" He was frantic for his Dad to apprehend the perpetrator. The automobile wasn't really being stolen—it was being repossessed. They lost both of their vehicles the same way that week. Becky didn't know how she was going to get the kids to school—no cars, no money for cars, and no credit for one either. Will knew a friend who had an old beater. His friend was remodeling his garage and needed a door and some lumber, so Will bartered with him to trade a door and some lumber from the fallen house for the friend's old car. His friend agreed.

Beth cried when she was dropped off at school for the first time in the rusty old blue clunker that barely ran. She told her mother that her friends had made fun of her. "Why didn't you keep our new car?" Beth asked her parents.

There was no easy answer for the children, but Becky offered, "Material things don't make a person."

Painfully, Becky and Will continually struggled with what to do. Will still couldn't get work. They added the loss of MMA and the building's lease agreement to the bankruptcy that now seemed inevitable. Becky made several calls to Mr. Shortino again with a new approach, suggesting that *together* they work on closing the lots that already had down payments on them. This way, the Blaine's first mortgage could be paid off in its entirety, leaving the remainder of the subdivision free and clear of encumbrances. Shortino wouldn't budge. He didn't have to. What was his motivation? Did he have a secret desire for the Blaines to initiate litigation so he could ensure himself continued employment with the mortgage company? *Why were they so stupid?* Becky told Will she wasn't surprised that Mr. Shortino wouldn't settle. There was no incentive for him to settle. The longer he was in litigation, the more his client had to pay him.

Becky continued to try to make sense out of the bizarre situation and how they had gotten to this point. Surely, she thought, there were better ways to make a living. Couldn't Shortino settle their case and free himself up to go after someone else? A person with scruples and morals would have found a sensible solution or at least settled and gone after someone who intentionally wasn't paying their bills. Becky doubted whether the corporate home office even realized the magnitude of the situation. Maybe they just knew the Blaines simply as a name on a list of debtors. Maybe what their tributary counsel told them from this distant town was all they knew. So Becky wrote to the home office. Nothing changed. She didn't even get a reply.

Will and Becky were both depressed and lethargic. Becky kept trying to hold things together. As a diversionary tactic for Will's dangerously fragile well-being, Becky tried to think of ways that she could boost his spirits. In the back of her mind she was hoping and praying that God would somehow think of something better for them to do with their lives, something that would promote His will and not theirs. She read the Bible for hope and found in James, "Life is full of difficulties, but be happy, for when the way is rough your patience will grow, and you will be ready for anything, strong in character, full and complete." And from Peter, "Don't repay evil for evil, instead pray for God's help for them." Becky called Will upstairs to where she had the Bible open on their bed, and she read to him. She asked him to kneel and pray with her. She asked to hold his hand and feel close, for they had each other, and their children were healthy.

Becky researched amateur climbing expeditions for Will because he had always wanted to climb Mt. McKinley. Maybe she could at least give him a taste of his dream—a fantasy that would divert him from ugly reality for a while, like she had done with Billie Jack Straw. Diversion and escaping could be a short-term solution with long-term benefits. Maybe he'd come back with new ideas or better able to focus. It would be a diversion for Becky too. The more she thought about the fun surprise and the research it would take to coordinate something she knew nothing about, it challenged her, and it made her happy. She called many places for information, and one phone call led to another. Eventually, she was given the phone number for the author of the *Seven Summits*.

During another phone connection, she ended up talking to a retired Navy Seal. Becky chuckled to herself. Imagine, in the secrecy of Beth's room, she was planning Will's special surprise. He was only two doors away in their bedroom. He had no idea what she was plotting, but he would have been amazed to realize she was talking to a Navy Seal. One of Will's greatest fantasies from childhood was to become a Navy Seal. Becky's simple wispy thought was taking shape, and after calculating a plane ticket, rental equipment, and guide costs, she decided to throw caution to the wind and spend the last money they had gotten from selling the antique pot-bellied stove from the Canal Estates office on Will.

Becky decided to give him his surprise gift on Valentine's Day, so every morning the week before then, she left a small riddle on Will's pillow as a clue. She wanted to build up the excitement and anticipation—give him something to look forward to each day. They had fun together playing the game, and Will really looked forward to trying to solve a clue from the riddle. When Valentine's Day finally arrived, she made his favorite chicken dinner and had the children wrap their gifts to Dad so that they would be opened one by one before she would unveil her gift. One gift was a puzzle of Mt. Rainier, and another was a gift certificate to a climbing store. Another was a scrapbook with a mountain picture on the cover. The gifts contained more clues. Will was completely taken by surprise when, by the end of the evening, he opened up the card that housed his airline tickets. He balked at spending the money—the first thing out of his mouth, but did give in and accepted. The children were happy because they hadn't seen their Dad so happy in a long time.

"So, Will, are you going to start working out to get in shape? You're going to be a part of a climbing adventure and you'll need upper body strength and stamina." Knowing he didn't have any work, there was no excuse for not getting in shape, which Becky thought might help with the depression she thought he had. Becky watched Will throw a rope up over the large oak tree in the back yard and climb it several times a day, hand over fist to the top, shimmying up with the aid of his legs wrapped around it. After about two weeks she noticed he no longer needed to use his legs—his arms carried all the weight as he dangled below the waist. Becky could tell Will was getting excited. He slept better at night.

Three weeks later he left for the mountains with his old orange backpack carefully filled with food, flashlight, knife, carabineers, white paste to keep his nose and lips from freezing, maps, a compass, survival gear he had accumulated in the garage from years of camping, waterproof matches, windproof matches, a small roll of toilet paper, and band aids. He borrowed a friend's Gortex pants, and he took his and Becky's down sleeping bags and stuffed them together for a better protection rating.

The trip turned out to be one of the high points of Will's life. He made friends, and he told Becky they slept in candlelit tents at night, and that he loved to hear the wind howl. He also said that the crew of eight practiced lowering into ice crevasses and spent two days in an ice cave they built. They tried to summit but couldn't because of bad weather.

But Will did not stay on his high—he left that on the mountain. When the elevation lowered so did his spirits, for although his time away was a welcomed respite, he couldn't run from the fact that he was losing everything he had worked for. He was beside himself with anguish. Responsibility and hard work were all he had ever come to rely on to get him through hard times, and now he didn't even have that. Becky was in pain. Her whole family was in pain. *You don't live your life today for what may come tomorrow,* Becky thought. *You live it today as if it may be your last.*

Becky anticipated when Will was going to come home for the day early, because he was only pulling scab labor. He was pounding nails for the same guys that only four months previously had actually been his workers and employees. Funny the way fate twists things. Here he was working for ten dollars an hour for the same people that had been on his payroll for years at seventeen dollars an hour. That was the best that he could do, and he felt indebted to them that they would even add him to their crew. Becky filled the Jacuzzi, the one that Will had installed in their bedroom the year before. She lit candles, poured a glass of wine, and sat on the edge to wait for Will. She read a book until he got home, then invited him to take a nice refreshing and relaxing soak in the hot tub. She told him that she had some things she wanted to talk to him about.

"What's going on, Becky?" Will asked.

"Don't worry about it, Will. Not too much really. I just have some things that I want to talk to you about."

"Wine? Where did this come from?" asked Will. It had been almost a year since they had shared pleasant conversation over a glass of wine.

"This is a rather important day for me, Will. I've made some decisions for myself—decisions that will impact the whole family. Here, just get in the tub," Becky said.

"Get into the tub? It's the middle of the day for me, Becky. I've got things to do. I can't be lazing around in a tub," Will said.

"Please, Will, for me? Just for me this once—won't you relax? Please, just get in."

Will gave Becky a sideways sneer and reluctantly gave in.

Becky pulled out the atlas she had laid on the sink near the tub. She handed it to Will. Will was careful not to get soap bubbles on it. "What am I supposed to do with this?" he asked.

"Just open it—anywhere you want to," said Becky.

"Anywhere I want to—what for? You don't think we're going on a vacation, do you? You know we can't afford that. What are you thinking?" said Will.

"You are the man of the family," Becky began, and Will's eyes gave a disbelieving roll. Becky tried not to be insulted. "You are the man of the family, Will, and I will go wherever you want to go." She paused, then looked him directly in the eye. "I want to move. I want us to sell everything and move far away from here. Our dreams are gone here—there's nothing left. There's no other way out."

"What do you mean, move?" asked Will. "I've lived in this property for almost forty years. This land, well, I can't let it go."

"I know, Will," Becky said. "When your grandparents died, you still had the land. When your parents split, you still had the land. When your wife left, you still had the land. And now, after the fire . . ."

"I can't give it up. And what about my friends?" Will asked.

Becky said, "Will, you haven't done anything socially with friends since, well, the night of the fire, I think. You'll make new friends if you want to, and your old ones will always be there."

"What'll I do for work?" asked Will.

"What you do for work now. I care about us, Will, our family. But I have to leave here." *With you or without you*, she added in her head.

Will would not discuss or make a commitment about whether or not he would consider a relocation. Eventually he agreed to move. He was angry at Becky—like the whole thing was her fault. He left it up to her to decide where they would move to and what job she would get to support the family. Now more than ever everything seemed to bug him, and he acted trapped because that was the way he felt.

Will started a fight with Becky one night. Beth stuck up for her mother. The twins cried as they watched their father rage from the hallway by their room. Beth tried to protect her brothers from witnessing the argument and her stepfather's behavior. She called for her brothers to join her in her room. They quickly ran in and slammed the door. Will was out of control. He pounded on her door and demanded that she release her brothers. She would not, claiming that she just wanted all of them to be left alone and for him to please stop yelling. Will broke the door down and almost broke Beth's wrist. She lay crying on the floor. Becky ran to pick up the twins. Will grabbed them out of Becky's hands and screamed, "I'm leaving and taking the boys, and you're never going to see them again!" Becky struggled for the phone and called the police. Will tried to grab it out of her hands, but Becky had already successfully made contact. Will ran out the front door without the children. He just left them on the front steps crying.

The officers arrived within minutes to find the leftovers of a defeated man. Becky was shaking and crying, hugging Beth, tending to her aching wrist, and summoning the twins indoors. She comforted them through her tears that everything would be all right and that Daddy would be home when he felt better. The policeman turned out to be someone Becky knew. She was embarrassed, and he felt sorry for her. He put his arm around her to comfort her, and it felt good to her—his gentle touch. "Leave him Becky—this is no way to live," he said. She felt he was right. "Don't settle," the officer said. "You're very special and loving—don't ever forget that."

Some three hours later, when things calmed down for Will, he returned. Becky told him that she was leaving within the week and that maybe he should just stay in Indiana. Will told her that he would never allow her to leave the state with their children. Becky decided that she would let Will think that they were working on their marriage while they made the transition to relocate, and then she would divorce him. At least then she could move like she wanted to and not be stuck in Indiana the rest of her life.

Becky began to pack and, for the remainder of that week, she and Will were copasetic toward each other. They were too busy to argue, and once they had both agreed to the move, it seemed some of the pressure of what to do had subsided. Becky decided they would move to Madison, Wisconsin, because that was half way between where both Will and she were raised. Also, Becky had found out in a popular magazine that Madison had been voted the number one place in America to raise a family, and that it had a good medical school. Over the course of one week, Becky made two trips to Madison—one to find a job, but she was not lucky, and another to find a place to live. They had no money for a down payment to buy a house, so the choices of where to live was a problem. When she returned to Indiana, she and Will continued to empty the house, selling more family heirlooms and anything they could think of to get what Will called a bankroll. They sold Beth's Victorian playhouse—the one that Will had made for her. They sold Grandma's two rings. They sold dishes, pots, and pans—some for a quarter each at the flea market.

It was five o'clock one Saturday morning when Will loaded tons of stuff to sell in the old beat-up, pick-up truck. He looked like a true junkyard dog with two days growth on his beard, dark rings under his eyes, and defeated posture. His jeans were stained with dirt and grease, and one leg had a hole both at the knee and at the crotch. The old truck sputtered as it tried to start. Becky rolled change she collected from the toolbox where Will emptied his pockets each day after work for two years, since they had lived in the gray house. They stopped to put three dollars worth of gas in the truck to make it to the market. Eventually, Will and Becky tore out their kitchen cabinets and sold them too.

Becky worked emotionally each day at letting go of her church family, who had been a large part of her life ever since she met Will. Once again she relied on her inner strength, God, and the courage and wisdom that had carried her through many days of anguish in the past. Now here it was, the last Sunday to attend their church, and they would be gone.

Becky got the children up extra early that morning. She wanted them all to have a bath before they dressed. She coordinated their outfits from the few remaining clothes that hadn't been packed yet. After breakfast, the children got in the car, and their seatbelts were fastened. Will wasn't with them. She drove as if she were part of a funeral possession, idling down the all-familiar country road she had been on so many thousands of times. This time she was careful to take in her surroundings so as to never forget the happy feelings she had going down that road on Sunday mornings. Becky noticed the purple and white tops of the clover in the fields. She glanced at Charlie and Ruby's place as she passed, but could barely stand to look too long, but she did notice Ruby's pansy bed that encircled the tree in her front yard. She passed the house where a guy she knew fed dog food to the fish in his pond. She would see him at church. As she turned into the parking lot of their church, which was only a couple of miles away, she passed the sign which read "Blaine's Valley United Methodist Church," and she paused to cherish all the Blaines who had attended the little white church with the stained glass windows.

After the children went to Sunday School, Becky walked down the center aisle toward the third row from the front on the right where she always sat. She walked as if she were a bride on her wedding day—taking proud, slow steps, eyes gazing frontward while noticing folks on either side. She took even slower steps so the Sunday morning ritual would never end but be captured in her memory forever. Just before she sat down she reached forward to touch the shoulder of the woman and her husband who had sat in front of her since the first time she attended this church five years ago. Then she turned around and looked back at Charlie and Ruby, who always sat third row from the back on the left. As the organist began an anthem, a steady stream of tears flowed down Becky's cheeks into the handkerchief she held tightly in her hand.

Chapter Eleven

It was the last night that Becky would ever spend in the gray house that she had come to love and appreciate so much. She would miss the creak in the second stair step. She would miss the many sunsets sitting on the front porch, and she would miss seeing her little blonde-headed boys running through the cornfield down to the pond to catch frogs. Becky looked out the back window and up at the moon like she had done many nights before. Tonight was different because it was her last. The darkness was blue—that special blue that separates the sky and the sea. The moon was full and golden, dark sepia outlining another world—the colors beautiful, mysterious, and hauntingly peaceful. To her it exemplified the awesome nature of God's splendor. The moon was bright and firm in its convictions about its placement among the stars, lending light and constancy. The greatness bore through her as her mind fell heavy and she strolled through the many special moments that she and her family had shared in their home. She looked around the kitchen behind her and visualized herself cooking, and she looked at the floral tiles behind the sink, the tiles she stared at when she did the dishes. She looked the floor over and out into each corner and thought how she would never wash it again. The future was uncertain, and joy was now something that had to be created. Nothing felt natural anymore.

Becky noticed a light was on in the new neighbor's front yard. Two women had recently purchased the old Burgess home. Becky had been there the morning that Ed Burgess died, and she had prayed with his wife, Ruth, as they sat waiting for the minister, ambulance, and church friends to arrive. The house had been empty for months. Becky felt empathy for what was left of Ruth's life—empty of the life that once filled her home, changed forever in an instant. Right then Becky felt blessed that her family was healthy. Will spoke often of Ed. "It's funny how little things from your childhood stick with you forever," he'd say. When Will was a young boy, Ed was feisty and strong, and Will enjoyed spending time watching how he took care of his tractor and put away his tools. Will said that Ed always had a greasy rag hanging out of his back pocket. And when Ed would meet Charlie and Will's Grandpa in the road to talk farmin', Valley news, or about the weather, Ed would take that old rag and wipe his sweaty brow with it, and it didn't bother him about the grease.

Becky kept watching out the window. One of the new owners was raking fresh mulch by the light of the moon where Ruth had once grown a climbing country rose. She was changing the landscape, the proof that Ruth and Ed had once lived there. Becky yearned to meet her, as if exchanging words with someone who would someday become neighbors with whoever moved into the Blaines' home would bring satisfaction and closure. Becky didn't really want to talk, but she wanted to go outside and be with her—to rake in silence with the woman who would now become part of the valley that Becky and Will had to leave behind. Becky wanted to share a moment with her as if to give her permission, her approval, wishing she could say, *"Hello, I'm Becky. I want to stay and be your new neighbor, but I can't."* The story of why she had to leave would be too long and complicated to tell, and it didn't matter. As soon as the valley found out they were gone, the news would be fodder and speculation, and the new neighbor would have to decide what to believe and pass on.

Becky opened the front door and gently closed it behind her. She slowly walked across the darkened street until she entered the light. She stood there momentarily until she was noticed. Ann recognized Becky right away and raised her hand to signal a cordial hello. With a nod of her head she acknowledged Becky and Becky wished their friendship would have lasted longer than the evening.

Becky asked, "Could you use some help?"

Ann said, "Sure," and pointed to a rake that was propped up against the house. Becky picked up the rake, and without another word they both went to work. Becky heard music as her arms made the rake oscillate like a cradle in a tree. It was an interlude of peace. For over two hours the women shared the midnight air, touched by the smell of dry leaves, moonlight, and togetherness. It would become one of Becky's fondest memories. When she left they hugged, and Becky went home and climbed into bed for what would be the last time in the gray house.

Morning came too early. Eli was the first one up of course, and ran outside as soon as the morning doves cooed. He was ready to start his day. He was usually the first one awake, always refreshed and rejuvenated. This day he was eager to pack the car and go, and the brightness of the clear morning seemed to cheer him on. He knew it was a big day, but his reasons were not the same as his parents' reasons. He picked a flower and gave it to his mother, and she fought to hold back her tears. She took the precious flower and kissed her son on his forehead. Becky walked over to her purse and retrieved the little diary that she always kept with her in a side pocket. She put the flower in the middle of the diary to press it and then recorded an entry that read, "Flower picked for Mama by Eli the last day in the gray house." She dated it and closed the book.

Beth woke up soon after that, followed by Erin. Will had been up a long time doing chores down at the barn, and she pictured him reminiscing the many days and nights he had spent there helping his grandfather take care of the hogs—even staying up all night in a snowstorm to make sure the heat lamp didn't go out. Now the barn was empty, but Will found excuses to be down there anyway. Becky knew he would continue to do daily chores, whatever they were, just to keep the sameness of the past going for as long as he was able. The plan was that Becky would take the children and drive to Madison staying only for a day or two to look for a place to live. Then they would drive on to northern Michigan to visit her parents. Will would pack what was left in the house after all of the flea market sales, load up the rented truck, and drive it on to Madison. Becky and the children would heal faster if they didn't see everything leaving the house. Becky also knew that Will would probably appreciate a few days to be alone before he vacated the family homestead forever—the land that had been his security blanket for almost forty years.

By ten o'clock Becky had started the car and turned on the air-conditioning, then loaded the children in the car. Even though it was the middle of August it was still hot and humid in Indiana. Wisconsin would feel like fall in comparison, especially at night when the nip in the air would require sweaters. Becky went back in the house to say goodbye to Will. She walked into the empty kitchen and saw Will through the dining room window standing on the porch facing west and leaning on a post. This was the spot where the two of them had often shared their dreams as they watched the sunset after a hard day's work. Now the sun would set far away from the porch of the big gray house without their admiration. Becky felt no animosity toward Will right now. The Lord had blessed her with a sense of closeness to him—a tenderness that drew her toward him. They both peered forward and Becky gently took Will's arm and put it around her. She looked into his eyes and said, "I love you. Everything will be all right, you know." Will did not reply. Together they stood for what seemed an eternity. They both wanted the moment to last long enough for the whole nightmare to just go away.

The kids started to honk the horn to let their mother know that it was time to leave. To them this was a vacation. After all, there were many similarities. Their clothes were packed like they always were when they were going on a vacation: books to read, mazes to figure out, their favorite pillows, stuffed animals and snacks.

Becky knew they didn't realize that this would be the last time they would live in the home that had sheltered them from many storms and that had protected them tenderly from the rain while their mama baked pies from the berries they picked from the bushes in the canal and brought to her in an old tin pail. This had been the cozy place where scraped knees had been tended to and where laughter was enjoyed. The marks on the door jamb were the children's heights recorded as they grew, and Becky's heart was so heavy just then she thought it would burst. As she turned to walk away from Will she kissed him on the cheek. Becky went through the house alone one last time. She walked into each of the children's rooms and looked around. The beds were bare. Becky tried to soak in as much as she could so she wouldn't forget. She blew a kiss to each room and whispered to herself—*I've loved you, house*.

She walked down the stairs and out the back door, looking over at Charlie and Ruby's house, her all time favorite neighbors, who had watched Will grow up, attended their wedding, and watched their children grow. She knew Charlie and Ruby would miss the children. As she stared at their house and beyond the cornfield that separated their two side yards, Becky thought how she loved them too, and how she would miss them. Becky chuckled to herself as she remembered how Ruby always brought a side dish even when Becky asked her not to worry about bringing a thing. Then Becky reminisced about how after dinner Charlie always got up from the table and went into the living room, expecting Will to follow so they could talk men things and watch a football or basketball game on television. He would yell at the referees about a certain play in between their sentences, and Will would yell, too.

Becky knew that Charlie was raised in the days when the woman stayed in the kitchen after a meal to clean up. Becky thought this ritual was precious and went along with it, cherishing every moment. But when Charlie wasn't there, Will always helped in the kitchen. Ruby thought nothing about it. When Becky knew she and Will had decided to move, she waited months to tell Ruby for she could hardly bear the thought of telling her. She didn't even like to hear herself say the words. Becky walked over to Ruby's pansies one afternoon and picked a few with the cutest faces, and then she pressed them in her homemade press. When the flowers were nice and preserved, Becky put them on paper and inscribed a sweet verse of remembrance to her dear, sweet neighbors, and in honor of Ruby.

Becky didn't stop by Charlie and Ruby's when she finally left, but she looked in the rearview mirror and whispered to herself, *Goodbye*.

The road was as long as her thoughts, and many miles passed before Becky truly left the gray house. She stopped when she needed gas and when the children needed a restroom break. From then on, the trip became just that—a trip, and she tried to block out her heartaches. After almost six hours and a few more stops, they were almost to Madison. Becky pulled into a wayside to look at a map, and she planned which exit she needed to take to get to the Holiday Inn. It turned out to be the same Holiday Inn that the family used to stay in whenever they took a vacation up north to Michigan to visit Becky's family. It sure didn't feel the same to Becky when she got there, though. She had a different agenda this trip, and she felt awkward to acknowledge that Madison would no longer be a vacation stop, but their home. But the children had fun. There was a big swimming pool with large glass windows that exposed the outside while people swam, and the children changed right away into their swimsuits. Becky called Will from the phone by the pool to let him know they had arrived safely. The children went to bed early that first night in the motel and slept soundly. Becky collapsed on her bed and took out her journal and wrote:

Oh in the midnight reach I find
the touches of those times
that canter through the windswept age
where youthfulness passed by.

In splendid verdant meadows ran
the girl with golden hair
to gasp at moon drawn shadows there, the
delight of all within.

So catch me now, my reminisce
and keep me there just now.
Don't let me leave, just tenderly
hold still my all in all.

To drift away past yesterday
and never leave behind,
caresses of the days been spent
yea, they're to live again.

Becky spent the next two days looking for a place to live. She didn't have any luck. Disappointed, she and the children left and drove to Michigan—about four and a half hours away to spend the next week with her parents. It was easier to spend time in her hometown than in Madison because she was accustomed to going home, and she could pretend she was just visiting like she had done so many times before, not making it obvious to friends and relatives that she was going through a traumatic transition.

Becky was glad to be home, and she paid attention to all the little nuances she could treasure. As she stood in her mother's kitchen, she looked out the window, and there she saw her father in his garden with Beth. The two of them were nose-to-nose picking onions, and Becky savored the moment. Grandma, of course, ran right away to get her camera. *Grandma and her ever lovin' pictures!* Chili cooked all day on the stove. The dartboard on the kitchen wall right next to the spoon rack that displayed spoons from the many places relatives had been, entertained her parents each night for an hour after supper and before watching Jeopardy.

"You've got to call Grandma, Becky. You know, let her know you're in," said her mother. Becky could hardly have one foot in the door when Becky's mom was after her to call the grandparents. *Once a mom, always a mom,* Becky thought.

"I know, Mom, I planned to," said Becky. She enjoyed visiting her grandparents. She loved her childhood memories of time spent with them. "I was actually hoping we could go over and visit them this afternoon."

"Okay, well just let me know when you want to go," Becky's mother said. She put her dishrag down and went upstairs to freshen up. *Hmm*, thought Becky, *mothers and their dishrags*—a symbol of motherhood, she guessed.

When they got to Grandma Tezak's house, the first thing Becky saw as they pulled up were the clothes hanging on the line. Grandma always had clothes on the line. Even in the dead of winter there were pants rocking back and forth as stiff as paddleboards. There was nothing like the smell of fresh linen from the line, her grandmother would say. Becky's mother had always hung clothes out to dry too, and Becky wished so much that she had her own home and clothesline back. They knocked on the back door, not like they had to because they never waited for someone to answer—it was just ritual to knock, then walk right in.

"Hello, Grandma. It's me," Becky hollered through the doorway.

"Oh, Becky," cried her grandma, as she briskly walked toward her, straightening her apron and her hair. Grandma's hair was the same gray as the other women in town—familiar purplish tint because they all went to the same hairdresser. There was only one in town. Her hair was a bit over processed from a perm too, which she insisted she needed. Grandma never missed an appointment, not only because how she looked was important to her, but also because she didn't want to miss out on any gossip. Becky looked her Grandma over to enjoy her, and she could see the same two rings on her right hand that had always been there for as long as she could remember, pressed into swollen fingers, bent over time by arthritis and hard work.

"I'm so glad to see you!" exclaimed her grandma. Her youthful dimples still showed through the wrinkles, which proved to Becky what her mother had always told her: "Inside every grandparent is a young person trying to get out."

"I didn't know you were coming for a visit. No one ever tells me anything," said Grandma. Becky's parents had worked hard at keeping Becky's problems a secret, so they hadn't thought to tell Grandma she was coming. Becky's family did not talk about things that went wrong in the family. It was understood that you always painted the happy side of your life and denied the rest. As far as Becky's family was concerned, anything that could be denied didn't really exist, similar to the way Will dealt with problems. So for all Grandma knew, Becky was indeed just visiting.

"Yup, just thought the kids and I would come for a little visit," said Becky.

"Where's Will?" asked Grandma.

"He needed to stay home and work," Becky said.

"Yes, there's a lot to be done with that subdivision," Grandma said. "I'm so proud of you two, Becky. You guys just seem to know how to do everything."

Becky didn't respond. She was thinking about how far from the truth Grandma's last comment was and how she and Will actually knew nothing about anything, at least that's how she felt right then. Otherwise, why would they be in such a predicament? She didn't labor too long on these thoughts, however, because after many agonizing hours of analyzing, she knew that there was nothing she nor Will could have done to prevent what had happened to them.

It didn't change the cloud of worthless despair that followed them, either, and Becky sure wished she had some happy stories to tell.

Becky and her grandmother pulled chairs up to the kitchen table and sat down. This was habit too—same table, same chairs, thirty-five years, and Grandma always had a bunch of leftovers cooking in the oven, usually heated up together and it was difficult to figure out exactly what it was. There was always warm food to eat. Grandma got out some homemade goodies, and they sat and drank coffee and talked about everything that was going on in the small-town world of Becky's Grandma. Nothing that was said had any major impact on Becky's life, but it all mattered. She loved to hear how Grandma had won at bingo and how she got ten percent off at the newly remodeled five-and-dime store the first night it reopened—the one that now lit up at night. This was a major change in town where most buildings, except the bars, were dark after five. As Becky sat listening, she could predict almost everything that would be said because nothing ever changed. For as long as Becky could remember, her grandparents remained ageless. When Becky was with them, her life and theirs was timeless.

Grandpa always made high scores at the bowling alley, and as the stories were told, none of his buddies could believe what an impressive bowler he was. Grandpa was also a fine hunter. He shot five birds the day before Becky arrived, commenting that there were more birds in the woods this year than there had ever been. Grandpa was a tough bird himself—of solid Czechoslovakian build, large hands, strong character, and straight from the old country. Lots of guys were not only tough in Becky's hometown, being loggers or miners, but they usually were rough around the edges too. Many were World War II vets with a smoker's cough and a beer belly from a life of cigarettes and good booze—the male counterpart of families who then, in turn, gave their sons and daughters to war. And they liked to gather at the local taverns and tell stories. Most of the guys wore orange hats from the beginning of hunting season until spring. Grandpa would have a patch of chew in the side of his cheek telling about the time he beat the one-armed bandit at the reservation down the road, then hitchhiked home after 2:00 in the morning. "And why not? Nothin' but old black bears out there!" Then there was the story about the time when he spotted a deer from the blind in Pelton's Swamp that he missed because he was busy eating the peanut butter and jelly sandwich his wife had made him for lunch. "Damn near shot myself in the foot. I missed da other one 'cause I was writing my name in da snow," he would say with a Yuper accent, and then his audience would all laugh.

Friday nights the family met at the American Legion Hall for a fish fry. As Becky walked down the old marble stairs to the basement of the Memorial Building, she could smell the familiar blend of stale beer, cigarettes, and fresh fried fish. The American flag was to her right, and she revisited viewing the patriotic symbols. There were pictures of past mayors, reproduction snapshots of past presidents, bayonets and regalia, framed lists of those servicemen and women who bravely fought for the huddled masses to breathe free. Had any one of the wall decorations ever been removed, their outline would be forever marked from over fifty years of smoke and grease. The old piano that Sam plunked was still there, and both were out of tune, but it didn't matter. Everyone was in tune in a different way—in tune with the camaraderie left by the spirits of those who had returned home, and of those whose names were on the wall. Becky felt lucky to come from the sort of stock who laughed hard and worked hard, yet whose sentimentality molded honor and respect. She could see the toughness in the faces of old family photos Grandma had saved from way back. But they routinely went to church. They were never so tough that they'd try to go this world alone.

Grandma hated to see Becky leave, but they had to if they were going to see the other grandmother before she went to bed. Both grandmas were well into their eighties, and their bedtime was shortly after dusk. The sun was setting, so they would have to hurry.

The ride from Grandma Tezak's to Grandmother Courtney's was a long one for a small town, but a short one for Becky—it was only about three miles. She knew when they were getting close when they passed the hospital on the left and wound around the big curve to the hidden dirt road that turned in front of Grandmother's house, and that Becky and her mom missed more than once, so they slowed down.

Becky got out of the car and stepped onto the part of the sidewalk where her grandfather years before had used a stick to engrave the date in the sidewalk he had laid back in the 40s. Grandpa was very handy that way—he had even built their home, just like Will, who was in many ways like him, both being strong-handed carpenters with a carpenter's bump on their hammer hand wrist, were usually soft-spoken and patient, and wore a scent of sawdust. Becky remembered stories of when her grandfather went off to Greenland to do construction during World War I because there was no work in their small town. He was not afraid to leave his family to do what he had to do. At least he gave that impression when he told the story, and he didn't change the intonation in his voice when he told how long it took to recover from smallpox, and the fact that his one small son never did. It was different back then—people didn't complain as much.

Becky supposed it was stories like this that made her realize at an early age the sacrifices that Americans had made during wartime and the price they paid for freedom. Becky's Mom had lost another brother—her older one died in the Battle of Luzon in the Philippines. She remembered Grandma telling of the day a letter arrived from her son, two months after he died. It was charred from the mail plane that had been shot down carrying her son's words home. Life went on in their home after the news, and the family didn't talk about it much. But Uncle Archie's picture, the one where he was dressed up in his army uniform, had a special place on the wall. Becky looked at it every time she went there because she was proud of him, and she wanted to acknowledge him in the room with her, and she only wished she could meet him and talk to him. He looked gentle and caring—so young to have died at seventeen. When Becky went through the stamp collection he left behind, she ran her fingers across the stamps as if touching them where she knew he had placed them would somehow bring the two of them closer. Bonnie, a friend of the family, had lost her husband in the war too. She had worked hard for the war effort. Every Saturday night and Sunday afternoon she worked putting together care packages they'd send out to the field. No doubt it was her way of giving her husband a hug and a kiss. She never wavered from her labors. Her husband never came back to her, but freedom came in his place.

"Oh, Becky, for goodness sakes!" greeted her Grandmother, who was sitting in a kitchen chair not far from the front door. She waited for Becky to walk over and give her a hug.

"Grandmother, I love you so much!" said Becky.

"Here, let me take a look at you, and oh, look at the children! I hardly recognize them. Boys, you've grown up so much you'll be as tall as Grandmother soon! And Beth, you're such a young lady. I've missed you," said Grandmother.

After the comforting hug, Becky went over to the leaded-glass transom window and looked out at the last place she had seen her grandfather alive, putting a new coat of white paint on the old picket fence he had made by hand. Then she looked over to the two living room chairs in front of the television, one where Grandmother sat and the other where Grandfather had. Becky swallowed hard because she missed him so.

Becky was her grandfather's favorite grandchild, and they had a special fondness for each other. Their birthdays were one day apart, so for as long as Becky could remember they'd go out and have a banana split together—just the two of them. He always had a spare hug for Becky, and she missed that and the popcorn filling the house with its aroma whenever she spent the night. Another favorite memory of her grandfather was the way he made his special sundaes—vanilla ice cream, fresh strawberries, peanuts, and bananas. They were wonderful! As an adult, Becky still ordered her sundaes the same way. Mornings at her grandparents' home smelled of instant coffee and toast, and the basement always smelled musty. Becky wondered what it was about these familiar smells that made her feel good all over.

Becky noticed that although she had practically been all around the world and back with experiences since she had left home, life in the small town as she had remembered, had pretty much stayed the same. Her memories meant so much to her.

Grandma's dentures still moved when she talked, but she wouldn't think of seeing a new dentist because the one who made her dentures, the one who had been retired for years was the only one she trusted, besides, she liked to entertain the grandchildren by easily slipping them in and out of her mouth. Becky felt blessed to *feel* life the way she did. She appreciated little things like seeing her grandmother's dentures or the cardinal on the crimson-forest green bough outside her window. She appreciated her grandparents for their tender ways, and she was grateful for the memories of when they would kneel down by the sofa together every morning and hold hands while they prayed. She tried not to think about the day when the other chair would be empty.

Becky and the children didn't stay long at Grandmother's either. It had been a long day. Becky said her goodbyes and walked out to the car. The kids gave hugs and followed behind her. As they were pulling out of the driveway, Becky looked up to see the familiar picture she had in her mind from days now gone, Grandmother and Grandfather were standing in the window waving goodbye. Grandfather had one arm around Grandmother and the other high in the air waving. Grandmother had one hand in her apron pocket and one arm wrapped around Grandfather's belly. Grandmother stood alone and smiled and waved as the car pulled out of the driveway.

It wasn't long before the week Becky had planned to spend at home had passed, and it was now time for Becky to make her way back to Madison to meet Will and all of their belongings. She felt empty and afraid because neither she nor Will had found a job yet or a place to live. They were financially broke, and so was her spirit. She suspected Will's was too. Becky relied on her faith to hold her and to keep her, but could only speculate for Will because she hadn't spoken to him since she had first arrived in Madison because their telephone in the gray house had been disconnected, and they were only going to communicate with a call to her parents' house if there were an emergency.

The trip back *to* Madison was longer than it was *from* Madison, no doubt because Becky didn't want to leave her parents and the comfortable security of her grandparents' love. Becky would try to make a perfect life for her three children—find them a cozy home in a nice neighborhood, find a job that paid good wages, and make homemade soups and pies. She would have to find new friends, a new church, and new places to create traditions—where to share in an Easter egg hunt, where to find the closest library to take the children to. Many questions ran through Becky's mind—would Madison's library have a children's book club? A Saturday morning children's hour like the one they enjoyed in Indy? Her mind drifted as she tried to visualize her life, but there was nothing to see because no memory was there yet. She would have to make them. The responsibility was great, and she could feel the stress mounting as they got closer to the Holiday Inn that would be their temporary home. Becky tried to focus on the new world that had opened up to her, and the past she'd have to deal with as soon as Will arrived. She and the children were glad when they got to the hotel, and the children wasted no time hurrying their mother to get a key to the room so they could change and splash into the pool right away.

Becky helped the children feel eager that their dad was going to be there soon, but she herself felt empty. The short time she had been away seemed like months, and the distance she had put between herself made Indiana seem like half way around the world. The irony that she was feeling as empty as her gray house was, seemed eerie. There were tables and chairs in a cluster by the pool, and Becky sat at one of them as she watched her children laugh and play while she looked up more than occasionally to see if she would see Will arrive. She was tired and looked forward to having him around to help with the children. She was afraid to see him though, for she knew that packing the trailer and leaving Indiana would have been physically and emotionally grueling for him, and she didn't know what to expect. Nothing could have prepared her for what she saw when he arrived.

Staring out of the large glass windows she saw the old, rusted blue truck that Will had traded for a garage door, a toilet, and a sink from the fallen house. Then she saw a U-haul truck and knew without a doubt that it was Will and Junior. She wanted to go outside to greet them, but she had to stay at the pool to watch the children. She saw in her periphery someone walking in. It was Will, followed closely by Junior and his friend John. She hardly recognized her husband, who looked like he'd aged ten years. His beard was thick and shaggy. His eyes were dark and sullen. Becky walked over to him and put her arms around him as if to help hold him up. "How was the trip, Will? I see you made it okay." She paused and meekly said, "I missed you."

"Yeah, we made it all right. That damn cat meowed the whole way, though! I was afraid the truck Junior drove wasn't gonna make it for a while. And the moving van trailer slipped gears every once in a while. The three of us stopped and got oil about five times. I ended up having to rent a U-haul—too much stuff. John volunteered to ride with Junior so he wouldn't be alone for the trip back home." Junior was only sixteen and hadn't had his license very long. Becky was glad John would be with him—not just the driving part, but she couldn't imagine Will, Beth, Eli, and Erin saying goodbye to him and watch him pull out of the parking lot alone in the old truck to head back to Indiana where he would live with his mother to finish high school. Becky's heart ached when she thought of the separation—for Will, for Junior, and the obvious changes their family was going through. It would seem strange starting school that fall without smelling Junior's aftershave in the morning as he left, and not having him at the dinner table. They had gotten used to Junior not being around all of the time because after the fire happened he stayed at his mom's more, but to know they would no longer be in the same town was painfully difficult to accept.

"Are you hungry?" Becky asked Will. "We haven't been here too long—just long enough for the kids to work off some energy in the pool, so we haven't eaten. Boy, have the kids been rowdy."

"Yeah, we're hungry. I haven't eaten in two days—really. Just didn't feel like it," said Will. "I suppose I'd better eat something." He motioned to Junior and John who were playing video games in the game room by the pool.

Three days passed, and neither Will nor Becky had found a job or a place to live. They were down to their last hundred dollars. After that was gone, they didn't know what they would do. Becky's parents drove down to be a part of Beth's birthday and met them at the hotel where they observed what appeared to be a dismal future for their daughter and Will. They brought with them the only presents that Beth would open this birthday. Becky had wrapped up a necklace of hers with pretty pink paper, and she blew up five matching pink balloons she had purchased for fifty cents. Beth would love the gifts that her mother gave her. Becky was glad that her parents had come. While the kids swam, Becky's mom questioned her about what they were going to do. They sat and chatted at the same table and chairs where Becky had sat to wait for Will. Becky's mother commented that she and Will seemed to be holding up okay. "We've got faith Mom—something positive will happen," said Becky. Will walked over and sat down by the two of them. He hadn't said much since he arrived, but this morning his appearance was different. He had shaved, and he looked well rested. He had on a nice button down collared shirt instead of a wrinkled tee shirt. "Hey Becky," he said. "There's an ad for a job in today's paper that I'd like to go check out. Can you and your Mom watch the kids for a while?" He appeared unusually and unexpectedly cheerful.

Becky got a peculiar feeling inside about that time. God hadn't let them down. It was after ten in the morning. Becky looked at her mother and said, "I think I'll call the University of Wisconsin. I had been in contact with the employment supervisor of the Family Medical Clinic Department several months ago trying to get hired. I sent her my C.V. and interviewed, but they had no openings then—maybe they do now." She went to her purse to get the phone number but couldn't find it. *Oh no,* she thought, *what did I do with it?* She thought she had saved the direct number to the lady's office, and Becky continued to search for it because she couldn't remember what her name was either. They had already spoken enough times for her to know Becky's situation, and the woman already had a file made up with her application, references, and noting the type of job she was interested in. Becky finally found the piece of paper, and she waved her arm up in the air flapping it with the name and number on it to her mother. She used the pay phone by the video game room next to the pool and dialed the number. The phone was answered after the first ring, and Becky introduced herself.

"Mrs. Blaine, I'm so glad you called," said the secretary. "We've been trying to get a hold of you for almost a week now. Your phone number has been disconnected."

"I'm sorry. I know. We made the final move. We're right here in Madison now," said Becky.

"Perfect timing. We were just about to offer the position to someone else."

"What position?"

"We have an opening in the West Side Department of Family Practice—the Director is leaving permanently to be with her young child, and she's expecting again."

"You're kidding. That would be wonderful."

"Great, I'll set up another interview. Then I have another question—have you found a place to live yet?" she asked Becky.

"Actually, no. We're here at the Holiday Inn trying to scout things out."

"Well, we have someone on staff here who locates housing for university staff. Is there a number where I could reach you?" the secretary asked. "I'll call her and have her phone you back with details."

Becky gave her a number and arranged for a joint meeting with the secretary and with the director, whose job she would be filling. She went and told her mother, who was elated for Becky. The kids finally got out of the pool, and they went back to their room to change. Less than an hour later, a call came to Becky. It was the university locator who told Becky she felt she had the perfect house for her family of five in a great neighborhood and in the price range she thought they could afford. "But," she said, "You'll have to go look at it right now and decide because the children of the homeowners—a retired physician who had recently died and his wife who was now in a nursing home—are just about to leave to fly back to their home in California."

How sad, Becky thought, *that they had to leave their home*. But without wasting a breath she replied, "I'll hurry." Becky could hardly believe her ears—a job and a house all in one day. It was too good to be true.

"Mom, you're not going to believe this. Not only do I think I've got a job, but the University found us a house! But we have to go look at it right now. I know you and Dad were about ready to head for home, but could you just stay with the kids a little while longer so I can run over to this house and take a look at it? You and the kids can order pizza. Will that be all right? I'll hurry."

"Sure, Becky, go ahead," said her mother.

Right before Becky was ready to leave, Will walked in. With much excitement in her voice, Becky told him to hop in the car with her, and she'd tell him all about her job and the house they were going to look at. They were driving to the location according to the directions Becky had written down. Will pulled out the city map he had used to check on the job in the newspaper, and it was then when he told Becky he too had found a job—one he thought he would like and with good pay. With a surge of enthusiasm that neither had expected or experienced in a long time, they smiled and hugged.

When Becky and Will pulled up to a large, white, modern farmhouse with a white picket fence, they thought for sure that Becky had misunderstood the rental price. Surely she misheard by a thousand dollars—at least. The house was in an upper middle class neighborhood. It looked like it had at least four bedrooms, and it had a manicured lawn, a wildflower garden, and a tire swing hanging in an old maple tree that had already begun to turn yellow at the top. The place was beautiful.

The owner's fifty-year-old children were already in their car pulling out of the driveway to head for the airport when Becky and Will got there, just in time. It had taken longer than anticipated to find the house. The owner's children assumed that maybe Becky and Will had changed their minds. The two couples exchanged pleasantries and the four of them entered through the front door and into the vestibule. Becky could see that not all of the furnishings had been removed yet, and in fact much had not been moved in over thirty years. The two adults accompanying them, a brother and sister, had been raised there. Becky absorbed what she felt their household was like.

There was a grand piano in the living room. Its presence made her feel good, and she heard waltzes in her head. One of the rooms they walked into had been the dad's library, and on the wall were shelves with books about history and medicine. These subjects were Becky's other two favorite interests. Becky thought, *I love this house and its feelings of music, history, and medicine!* As she walked from room to room, she felt cuddled by the presence she could feel like her life was entwined with theirs only a generation before, now one family closing a chapter and another opening theirs. Becky paused to give reverence to the owners' parents, but couldn't spend much time on the first floor—they still had the upstairs and the basement to look at, and they still had to discuss prices and lease options. Their mother had been on the board of the Civic Center, and playbills were stacked in the basement closet off of the laundry room. Becky noticed them and felt so at home—*what a blessing,* she thought. *This house would certainly ease the transition for everyone, large and affordable and surrounded by the woods and the arboretum.*

The two families quickly negotiated a price, and a lease was signed. The owner's children were eager to get on their way and had decided that Will and Becky were just the sort of tenants they were looking for. It had come as a shock to them when their father got ill so quickly, and then their mother not soon afterwards, and they too felt lucky to have fallen into the right situation at the right time. Becky's emotions moved right in as she shared the passions of the owners' past. It was perfect that the Blaines would occupy this home and exude the sameness of the place in a continuum that would serve both of them well.

In less than three hours, Will and Becky's world had turned completely around. Their prayers had been answered. Just when they didn't think they could go on for another moment, and they knew their money would run out by the next day, they had been provided for. Becky's mother and father were happy for them. Becky's faith helped her mother with hers too, because peace had befallen them all, and hope was restored.

After they had settled in, Becky never ceased to be moved by all the things in the home that kept her feeling connected and in appreciation of the family that had once lived there. When Becky went to put their clothes away in the closet, she noticed wooden hangers that had been engraved with the father's initials on them. She thought of the suits that were probably hung on them and put back on the hanger again perhaps after a speech he had given to the medical faculty. Or maybe an awards event he had attended because he had been a prominent physician who had made a name for himself at the University where he taught, and in his community where the Blaines now resided. Becky put her toiletries away only to find a tube of the mother's lipstick and some powder still in a bathroom drawer. Becky pictured her getting ready to attend a play or a board meeting, but most probably an opera because she was an opera singer herself—before her Alzheimers had progressed. She would entertain the neighbors as she enjoyed walks and sang as she went. The neighbors told Becky that they missed her. Becky went to unpack more boxes and to put away her kitchen dishes, and there were Christmas cookie decorations and baking soda still in the cupboard. Sometimes their past life in that house was overwhelming to Becky, and it made her feel again how important it is to have a positive influence on the people you meet every day and to make your life matter in a good way. Becky brought back to life an old Christmas cactus that had been left by the owners' children in the rubbish pile. Becky knew that when they too moved from this rented home to perhaps a permanent one they owned, that they would take the cactus with them so that year after year as Christmastime approached, she could watch it bloom and Becky would think of the mother she had grown to admire and respect, but whom she'd never met. It was Becky's way of keeping that mother's spirit alive, and maybe the spirit inside herself, too.

Chapter Twelve

The year that followed brought many positive changes for the Blaine family, and Becky played into the 'fresh start' theory right from the beginning. She made friends with the neighbors and began to integrate the children into local sports and activities doing anything she could to help them feel part of their new community. A neighbor had given her a directory of the area—a book that listed the family names, how many children they had, and their ages. So, before the children started school, Becky took them on a long bike ride through their new neighborhood, and she pointed out where all the children lived that were their age. Some of the kids were outside playing, so Becky stopped and took the opportunity to introduce her children to them. A couple of boys were playing soccer, so Becky made them aware that her children too were soccer players. She did everything she could to promote relationships for the kids.

"Mom, you're so eccentric," Beth would say, but Becky knew that Beth was glad that her Mom was helping her break the ice to gain new friendships. Beth was apprehensive about starting a new school where she didn't know anyone; the shift to middle school alone would be tough no matter where she was, and not having friends would make it that much more difficult. Beth would have nothing to worry about though because her Mom's efforts paid off and, before the day was over, Beth had made a great new friend that she met on their bike ride. They both had pink bikes, which for these young preteens was a sign they must become friends. The girls made plans to walk to school together on the first day, which was now just a week away.

Becky found a local ice cream parlor to celebrate their happy day and thus began a tradition that brought familiarity to their surroundings. The ice cream parlor became a favorite celebration stop. Soon a great playground was added to their list of places to go, a park next to Lake Wingra, which was three blocks from their home. Several bike paths meandered through the woods nearby. It didn't take long before the children had all sorts of extracurricular activities planned. "A busy body is a healthy body," Becky always said. She searched out a community choir that Beth could audition for and helped her prepare a song for auditions. She also helped a new friend's son prepare himself for an audition. Becky enjoyed playing the piano and felt blessed that she could do this for the children. Both Beth and Becky's friend's son ended up being chosen as members of the Wisconsin Children's Choir.

Beth was excited to start rehearsals. A choir like this was one of Beth's and her mother's fantasies, for they both adored music. What made it even more perfect was that rehearsals were held at the First United Methodist Church, where Becky had been taking the family for over a month since their move, so now the church was a familiar place for two reasons, thus adding comfort to the children's life and to Becky's.

It was a shame that Will didn't feel better—he still held on to bitterness, relished his resentment, and nurtured his discontented feelings by dwelling in the past and refusing to move on. He told Becky that he yearned to hear the owl at night and the morning doves at dawn, and despised hearing Joe up the street yellin' at his dog and the mother next door yellin' at her kid. Becky, on the other hand, cherished her new surroundings and sought out the beauty and serenity that Madison had to offer.

By winter, things had settled down quite a bit for the family. Will was getting used to his surroundings and found small places of acceptance. The pain in his heart and spine from the strain of the move to Madison were subsiding, and the headaches that had surfaced during the major time of transition seemed to be under control, and they were less frequent.

There was a lot of snow that winter, and Becky played outdoors with the kids often, enjoying the winter wonderland with them. She urged the children often to put on their mittens, to get dressed up all nice and warm, and to go outdoors during snowfalls—even during blizzards. The kids loved it. They built tunnels and forts, had snowball fights, and their imaginations gave them freedom and enjoyment. They stayed out so long at times that Becky had to remind them of the possibility of frostbitten hands and toes. They hadn't experienced that much snow in Indiana, ever.

One evening when the snowflakes were as big as half dollars, Becky announced to the children that she and Daddy were going to take them for rides on their sleds. With great enthusiasm the children were outside before Will and Becky could get the sleds down from the garage rafters. Becky had waited until nightfall before suggesting the rides because she knew it would be cozier to be riding by the light of the moon. Becky had Beth trailing on a sled behind her, the rope looped around her belly. Will had a larger sled with Erin and Eli together. Eli's legs were wrapped around Erin's legs to hold him in place. Huge snowflakes fell on their caps and eyelashes as they walked. The pace was gentle and easy. The flakes danced and swayed as they fell. Peace was all around.

Becky's mind started to drift, and she heard music as she thought about how she yearned to feel romantic with her husband, for romance would have completed the perfect picture just then. Instead, she simply felt dutiful. Sure, here they were, one big happy family to most outsiders, but inside she was empty and unfulfilled beyond the love she felt for her children and that which her children spontaneously gave her in return. She yearned to feel adult affection, to feel close to her mate—the man in her life. She sighed inside at the thought of having a man by her side that would be happy and playful—one who could convince her that she was somebody's something special—someone who seemed genuinely content. *Couldn't he laugh just once and maybe put his arm around me, or kiss me?* she thought. She had lost spontaneity with Will. The carefree loving gestures just weren't there any more. She didn't feel close to him or comfortable with him. She felt lonely.

"Mom, can you please keep up with Dad?" Eli asked. "Erin and I are playing a game. We're trying to hold hands while you pull us." Eli had rolled off the sled, and he was walking hand-in-hand with his Mom, and Dad was pulling ahead with Erin. Beth had decided to lie on her back and let her arms drag in the snow. She gazed up into the sky, then gently closed her eyes and let the new falling snow blanket her face that was already blushed pink from the chill in the air. Becky turned around to watch the expression on her beloved children's faces. They were happy and content. Knowing this brought her satisfaction.

"Will, you don't have much to say tonight," whispered Becky.

"Oh, I'm just thinkin,'" he said.

Becky could tell that Will had a lot on his mind, but as usual, she didn't know what it was about because he never opened up. He kept his feelings in until he got mad about something—then all heck would break loose. One could say outside of doing things with the kids, they didn't share much. Although Becky had her children around her and a wonderful home, she still felt alone and unsettled. Her future with Will was uncertain. Becky knew she couldn't continue to try to make everything okay for Will. She worked at making things okay for herself and her children. She thought Will was a big boy and needed to begin to help himself heal. In fact, the more Becky pampered him, the worse he got. Becky felt there came a time in life when people who had trouble should stop making excuses for their misery, quit blaming their past, pull up their bootstraps, and get on with life. *Enough is enough,* she thought.

"Mama, when we get home will you make some of Grandma's hot chocolate?" asked Eli followed by a second from Beth.

"Certainly," Becky answered. Becky loved that they would even ask because she enjoyed creating cozy memories with her children, and what could be more memorable than a sled ride by moonlight on a snowy night with their mom and dad, followed by hot chocolate! Becky built a fire when they got home and, while she was in the kitchen making hot chocolate, the children sat Indian style around the warmth, and she could hear their laughter. Will had disappeared in the garage. He was probably hanging up wet jackets, snow pants, and the sleds. Becky wished he were in the kitchen with her, maybe showing outward signs of affection—a kiss on the neck or an arm around her waist with a hug. She heard music that soothed her loneliness, and before long Becky was humming out loud to fill the void. It was a church song "Keep the Candle Burning." She kept humming the same verse over and over as if keeping vigil on her tender emotions.

Sweet misery, why couldn't Will have built the fire? thought Becky. Maybe he would have if she had asked him to, but why didn't he take the initiative to do it himself? *Maybe a fire didn't matter to him any more,* Becky thought. *But he sure enjoyed fires before we were married—campfires and fireplace fires. Maybe he is too depressed.* Will didn't *feel* life anymore—he just existed in it. Becky was sick of analyzing why Will didn't engage enthusiastically in what he was doing.

That night when Becky got into bed after kissing the children goodnight, the loneliness she felt inside put an ache in her whole body, like lyrics from a song she knew, "Lying Next to You is the Greatest Emptiness I've Ever Known." She laid flat on the bed looking straight up at the ceiling, and the yellow light that came through the blinds from the street lamp showed two parallel rays on her face and neck—an omnipotent flow which reminded her she was not alone, for God was with her, and that comforted her. Even though she relied on her faith at times like this, she still yearned to share her feelings for she too had lost much and had been forced to adapt to change. She desperately yearned for the male companionship she felt she was missing. It seemed like Will was there in body, but not in spirit. As she lay there alone, she wondered where Will was now—he probably was downstairs watching television. Becky picked up the pen and paper that she kept in the nightstand beside their bed and found solace as she began to write:

The night comes.
The quiet tomb withholds pleasure,
And the temptress beckons the solitude of sleep.
Away, long away, lies the key to what should have been.
Oh merciful gloom, why must it be so?
Shadows of the want, lying close.
Passion between four lips and all about.
The need, the want to be fulfilled.
Loving, cooing the one sweet touch.
Tears of joy, to be loved; it should be so.
Empty I wait.
Forever I will wait.
Sadly I hold the perfection of a dream.
When the time is right and luck should have it.
I know it is there somewhere.

Half-truths I have seen.
Half-truths I have known.
I have felt it at least, to know it exists.
And the dream goes on, and the dreamers do dream.

Frustrated from the want, but comforted just to know.
For some do not even know—poor souls.
Even poorer than I.

The night moved on to another day, and Becky continued to take her destiny in stride. There was still one more day to the weekend. She was bound and determined to have fun and live life to the fullest regardless of how Will needed to live his. She called around looking for an ice rink and found one not too far away that rented skates, and she took the children skating. At Becky's prompting, Will joined them. Sometimes he seemed to be enjoying himself. Will had skated a lot when Junior was on a hockey team. It had been quite a while since Becky had been on skates, but it came back to her, albeit awkwardly. She wished so much that Will would rush up enthusiastically behind her and reach for her hand, but of course he didn't.

When they got home, they all were tired. "Whew, I haven't worn myself out like that in a long time," Becky said. Will noticed the smell of the dinner Becky had started in the oven before they left. The chicken simmering in a sauce spiced with bay leaves and marjoram was almost done. Becky was making a lot of home-cooked meals lately, and this was a sign that their new life was normalizing. She baked, cooked, and involved herself in various activities intentionally to make everything *seem* like all was well, even when it wasn't because she felt that even an appearance of contentment gave stability to the family.

The children were doing well in school having adjusted with unwavering resilience. Their life too was becoming their own again. Will and Becky attended the kids' programs; Becky introduced herself to the choir director at the children's school and was invited to become their accompanist. Again, most anyone who noticed the new family on the block would assume they had no problems. No matter how well Will and Becky got to know people, they did not discuss their past. No one knew what the Blaines had been through, and they guessed that it didn't matter.

Becky worked at keeping her mind away from the part of their Indiana life they had left. Will still had a hard time, though, and Becky knew he was struggling with the past. She hadn't given up totally trying to do whatever she could come up with to help make him feel better, and she continued to work on their marriage as well, even though she too was tired. Again and again she noticed that outside of doing things with the children, she and Will did little to nothing together. On a whim one afternoon, Becky decided to spontaneously drop by where Will was working and surprise him. He was still in the construction business, working for a local builder. Becky had an approximate idea of where the company was putting up a house. She drove around in the vicinity for quite a while looking for Will, his truck, or for any signs on the lawn advertising of the company he worked for. She knew that if she showed up it would make him feel better, and maybe it might even turn out to be enjoyable for both of them. She crossed her fingers that she might see him smile.

Becky passed several beautiful homes that had been built on lots next to the lake, and she couldn't help but think of her beautiful gray house back in Indiana. *Stop thinking about it,* she told herself. *It's over, done, and gone.* But she wondered if anything had happened with the mess they had left and, more importantly, if some other woman was raising her children in the home where the growth marks of her children were still on the kitchen wall. Becky continued to drive, looking down every side street for Will's truck. Luck was with her, and her perseverance paid off because she finally found the house, having seen Will's truck on the front lawn of the framed structure.

The picture she saw as she drove up the lane was chillingly reminiscent of Dr. Zhivago's ice palace. The sun shone through the piercing crystal spears that hung off the rafters, and the snow glistened 'round the treated beams and roughed-in wires from a house not yet complete. Becky got out of her car and walked around being careful of what she might step on as she looked for Will. There was no sign of him. She hollered and heard nothing back. She thought, *I hope he's not hurt!* Becky knew only too well that the possibility of getting hurt on a construction site was a real concern, especially when everything seemed to be covered with a thin sheet of ice and was slippery. Back in Indiana, Will lost one of his best workers in a freak accident in a crawl space. He was wiring an old house, and the grippers he was holding were only rubberized for insulation on the ends. He hadn't turned off the main power source, and when he went to pull the hot wire, he got shocked. The shock forced his head back where a part of his neck touched on an old tube of conduit—the perfect ground. He had current running through him for over four hours before Will found him.

Now all Becky could think about was that Will had been up on the third story, slipped, and had fallen his death. She wished she wouldn't think the worst, but she had been so used to misfortune that she looked for it even when she didn't need to. *He's not afraid of heights,* she thought. *No, he's a natural climber. He'll be safety conscious.* She tried to convince herself that Will was all right. *But in the past he took stupid risks. He even let the twins up on the second story of the gray house when they were only two, and the walls weren't up.* As she continued to walk around inside the house structure, she noticed there were no sidewalls up, and the wind off the lake brought snow inside and piled it in drifts. She saw no footprints. *Will must be cold—where is he?*

Becky heard a large icicle crack and saw it fall and hit the frozen, snow-covered dirt mound behind her. She looked up startled, and there above her was Will, suspended by ropes anchored to the roof some three stories up the framed structure. With the wind chill, the temperature was about twenty degrees below zero. The gloves on his hands exposed bare fingertips because they were torn out so that he could hold the nails while he pounded, and he had icicles hanging from his nose. Becky's heart went out to him. "Will, you're such a hard worker," Becky told him. She cupped her hand by her mouth and shouted, "Isn't there a better way to make a living? Will, hey Will—can you hear me up there?" Will didn't respond right away, but looked down and motioned to her to let her know he knew she was there. Becky climbed a nearby ladder to get closer to him. She was afraid of heights so was doing good to position herself on the top rung and yelled again, "Will, do you hear me?"

"Hi, Becky, what are you doing here? How did you find this place?" Will asked.

"Oh, you know me. Can you come down from there please? We're leaving," she said.

"What do you mean we're leaving? Becky, I've already had my lunch," said Will.

"It doesn't matter, you are coming home with me. This is no place for you—you can find something better."

"Maybe, but right now Becky, I have to keep this job. The family has to eat!" said Will, and instead of coming down to greet her he kept working.

Becky felt appreciative to have such a hard-working and dedicated man, but she only wished that he'd reconsider leaving with her. She also wished that Will were dedicated with the same intense commitment to his love for her. *Many women would be pleased just to have that.* Becky was reminded of Robert Frost's poem and thought, "I have miles to go before I sleep." To Becky, this was Will—he had miles and miles to go before he'd sleep. Even though she didn't feel completely loved, she appreciated what he had inside.

Becky persuaded Will to leave after all, but not without hesitation. She was happy to get Will to agree to try to find a different job. "Come on, Will, let's keep our faith—you'll find another job—an even better one! You'll see. This is no place for you," she told him. Becky's mothering ways were allowing her to be convincing. It was a vehicle that enabled her to protect him from the harsh outdoors and his own blind persistence.

"*Your* faith," Will reminded her. "I don't have any anymore."

She knew he could find better work if he only tried. But she also didn't want him to be a martyr. Poor Will. Maybe this was part of the problem. He needed to quit thinking about "Poor Will."

Will did get a new job, and it didn't take him as long as he had predicted. One week of looking in the paper, two interviews, and he was Vice-President of a large building company. The new job was indeed a godsend. Becky's sixth sense or whatever it was that day had proved to be right on target. She was excited for him, and she went to Shopko and bought him two new pair of pants for his new job. She also went to Goodwill and found him a couple of shirts—and a blouse for Beth too. Beth's choir concert was coming up and she needed a white blouse. Becky and Will were poor, but not too proud. Becky took the shirts and the blouse home and washed and ironed them right away. Although Beth never knew where her new blouse came from, she was happy to get it and thought it was pretty. Nobody would be the wiser that Becky had paid only a quarter each for the shirts and the blouse.

Will worked in his new job for almost two years. Becky worked on the staff of the University, attended graduate classes part-time, and was active in the children's school and extracurricular commitments. Beth entered a beauty contest to try to win a scholarship. She won the title of Wisconsin Junior Miss and a scholarship investment bond of $5,000 to be put toward her college of choice upon graduation from high school. Eli was working on his black belt in karate, and Erin spent time daily with the horse Becky and Will had given him that Christmas. They paid $50 a month for the horse to be kept at a stable not far from where they lived.

The elderly woman who owned the house that Will and Becky rented died that spring. The perennial bulbs that she had planted some thirty years before still bloomed. Her children put the house up for sale. Will and Becky would have liked to have stayed in the house, but the only way they could do that would be if they could buy it. There was no way any lending institution would give them a loan. Even though they were both responsible and always had been, had good jobs, and financial stability, no bank would give them money with a history of bankruptcy and litigation on their credit record. It was a very inopportune time that Becky would have to take time away from her studies and her job to look for a place for them to move to again. She knew if she left it up to her husband, he'd wait until the last minute and take whatever was available. It was predictable that when Will was faced with a complicated situation, he went into the "wish-it-away" mode that if he chose to do nothing at all, the dilemma would just go away. He especially could not work through complications that ruffled up memories of the past. So, Becky took care of finding them a place to live. She acknowledged that Will was a hard worker and a good father. He just couldn't handle emotional things. Over the last several years he had survived by putting his nose to the grindstone until it was practically worn off. If there were a need for any emotional energy, it would have to come from Becky.

Becky looked long and hard for the right place to call home, and found an apartment with less than a week left before they had to be out of their house. The move was hard on Will's back. The trip from Indianapolis to Madison had worn it down, and the move now to the apartment caused him so much pain he had to see a physician. The doctor revealed to Will that he had a degenerative disease that was eating away the disc material between his thoracic vertebrae, and it would require surgery to stabilize his back and to ease his pain. The doctor then told him he should go on disability. Will was too stubborn to give in to that idea, but the pain forced him to finally give in to have the fusion operation. Surgery was scheduled and once again, without Will working, the lack of money became an issue in their lives.

Becky and Will had learned how to be a strong family unit, yet faced with even more uncertainty, Becky was growing frail from a lack of emotional support from her companion. Even knowing Will would undergo a lengthy surgery didn't bring them together. It was business as usual for them. Becky wanted more for herself as she thought about the waste of all the love she wanted to share with her husband, who seemed not to care if he had her love or not. *Will could die on the surgery table. Why can't he get close to me? He's going to need me for strength to recover, for courage to sustain us through the difficult days that lay ahead, and for a lot of patience for a smooth recovery.* She backed off from expecting too much emotion, took a look at the whole picture—their life, as it was—not through the picture she painted, and she just dealt with it. Now both she and Will just existed. Sure, they went to church together, but only the family unit was in attendance. She still questioned whether this was all she was supposed to expect out of marriage. Maybe it was God's will that she should be the strong one and not desire anything more. Becky remembered trying to help Will feel a part of the church, a part of anything that involved her. At the Christmas program she was directing she asked him to help light the candles for the children. Her request didn't go very well—in fact it was terrible. Will threw the matches at her in front of the children and said, "Do it yourself." Becky should have known better. She was pushing him to be the way *she* wanted him to be, which was not the way *he* wanted to be. He resented it, and he just wanted to be left alone.

As she sat in a chair sipping coffee the morning of Will's operation, the children already off to school, she continued to think about many of the events that had taken place in the last several months—even years. She thought about how Will hadn't been there for her surgery or for the World Championship horse competition. He never even cared to see her ride. Will had already left for the hospital by himself, but Becky wanted to go with him and be there. She felt the wife *should* be there. She felt Will was cold-hearted and uncaring to leave without her. As she rocked back and forth in quiet desperation, she recalled a New Year's Eve when the family went out with another family to celebrate. They should have enjoyed a nice dinner. But Will's steak didn't come done the way he liked it, and he started to yell at the waitress right in front of the children and their company. Becky tried to gently calm him down, but he cursed at her and then got up from the table and walked home. Becky had to ride home with the children and their friends without Will. *The entire evening had been ruined. Why?* Becky's rocking had been getting faster and more forceful as her nervous tension and unwitting irritation grew stronger. She abruptly stopped and got up with purpose. She drove to the hospital despite Will's apathy. But she told herself that as soon as Will was better, she was going to insist on having some serious discussions with him.

About six weeks later when Will was out of pain and still receiving unemployment compensation, they spent an afternoon discussing separation. The children were at school. The bottom line for both of them, the one thing they could agree on, was that the family unit would survive much better with two parents living together. Although they both agreed to pull it off, knowing there would need to be changes, neither Becky nor Will felt much love for one another, and they wondered if the children could tell. They made a vow to try and show more respect for each other. Becky asked Will if he could make an effort to at least *appear* like he was enjoying life and to try to control behavior that seemed angry. Will didn't request any changes from Becky, though she wished he had come up with something so she would have deliberate things she could do to prove she was trying.

On a chilly day in February, Becky bundled up and left the house to attend a healing service at church. She was going to pray for people in need. She did not go to pray for her marriage, even though there was a need, and she tried to ignore the tug at her heart to give in. Becky argued in her mind with God saying to him through prayer that the way she was feeling was appropriate. She didn't want to pray for her marriage to get better when she already knew she didn't even want the marriage. But she gave in and prayed. That evening when she went home, Will's attitude was different and more pleasant. Becky tried to provoke him, to test God, for she would not believe that prayer had changed Will even though she was praying for other people that night with a belief and expectation that it would help them. Why should she expect less for herself? Nonetheless, even if Will had changed, she would have to change. God would have to heal her broken heart.

Becky kept busy and went on with life as usual by working part-time and, now that Will was back to work, soliciting her letters of recommendation for medical school. She could no longer put off what she had hoped to do since before high school. Will now seemed proud at the thought of being married to a doctor, and their marriage was showing signs of getting better. They went out to a social event that Becky recalled with particular fondness. They attended a celebration of all the new homes that were built in the Madison Parade of Homes. Will had built one of them, so they had a reason to get dressed up, go out, and be together. Will gave off a sense of pride and accomplishment. He had worked on being better with his emotions, and that night showed significant change. Will seemed happy, but Becky was still lonely. Sure she was with him, happy for him, and proud too of his title and position with the company. But for so long she had felt disconnected and empty with Will. She was tired. She was with him but didn't feel close. She accepted the fact that the way things were was the best they would ever get.

Becky made herself feel good by reading the recommendation letters for medical school she had received from friends, colleagues, and professors that were in support of her becoming a physician. She especially liked the one written by her former history professor, which read, "I have known Becky Blaine for fifteen years, both as a student and as a friend. She was an excellent history student of mine at Indiana University in Indianapolis, and we have kept in touch since. We still discuss books, history, literature, music, and poetry. I have been a guest at her and her husband's home. I feel qualified in recommending Becky for admission to medical school. Mrs. Blaine's ability to ingest knowledge with rapidity and to retain it with tenacity is remarkable. For example, some years ago, I recommended that she read Wynn Wade's *Titanic*, and then a few months ago I was telling her about the ship's first officer who perished, but whose friend mysteriously and briefly appeared at a Senate hearing in New York shortly after the disaster at sea. Although the scene was short, she remembered every detail. I am still impressed with her memory retention. This is not the only such incident. As for intellectual keenness and depth, I have no reservation in saying that we are considering an extraordinary intellect. She has an industrious personality, and I have seen her perform outside academic and domestic circumstances. I can assure you that her interactive skills are impressive. Once she accompanied me to a meeting of the English-Speaking Union. While addressing a Member of Parliament, she was easily communicative in a situation where rapport is requisite. She is naturally articulate. I have noticed that her children have been inculcated with the same ability.

"Regarding stability and knowing something of Mrs. Blaine's personal life, I can assure you that she is a survivor as she has had her unfair share of adversities and has endured where others crumble. At times the pressure has been almost unbearable, yet she has borne all. It is this kind of emotional tenacity, on top of the intellectual tenacity, that is obviously admirable. Her judgment is not only sure but also penetrating. Decisiveness immediately follows. In other words, conception is execution. That is due to a self-confidence which covers the area conceived or the plan to be attacked. She does not have to think long since the spring within is already coiled and prepared for activation. It is the essential quality we see in military commanders just before battle." Becky liked this statement because it came from a Ph.D. in history, whom she respected. This was probably the highest compliment he could have paid her.

"Independence is in Mrs. Blaine's personality. She is her own boss, yet not overbearingly or stridently obvious. She knows what she is about, so she doesn't have to parade her independence of mind. She is of responsible character. Beyond those qualities already mentioned, Mrs. Blaine has a desire—even a passion—to become a physician and that obsession has extraordinarily persisted despite agonizing delays and outrageous adversity. Lincoln said that '*Wanting* to be a lawyer was the most important element in becoming one,' and, if the same applied to wanting to be a physician, you have in Mrs. Blaine a superlative candidate who should some day make us all—and herself—proud.

"It is my pleasure to recommend, without reservation, the admission of Mrs. Rebecca Blaine to the University of Wisconsin Medical School."

Chapter Thirteen

Becky got into medical school that year, and it gave her exactly what she needed—a perfect relationship. It was something she could put effort into and, unlike in her marriage, she could get something satisfying in return.

Becky's favorite class was biochemistry because she needed to rely on a culmination of knowledge from all the years of undergraduate studies sort of rolled into one great class. It taxed her in every realm of past study, and she loved it. She applied the molecular configurations from organic chemistry to the practical applications of physiology, and she became invigorated every time she found a new revelation into the inner workings of the miracles of the human body, which biochemistry explained in microscopic detail. She learned the citric acid cycle and feedback inhibition. She learned about hormones and cellular activity and purpose. Becky was in her glory, and it bathed her with a sense of purpose and direction. She could sit in class all day long and never tire of what she was being taught. The more she read, the happier she felt. The days always ended too soon. She liked looking at the grades she got on tests—she was rewarded for all her efforts. Becky felt there was no other situation outside of her children that would guarantee satisfaction and results in reciprocal fashion than to do well in classes she liked.

Becky was thrilled to be where she was at thirty-eight years old. She was an older student, but she didn't mind because the things that the younger students did which made them stand out as young people were far away from where Becky was or wanted to be. Maturity and experience were calming features. It wouldn't have mattered anyway, for the things that enhanced the medical school tract to most other students were things that Becky never enjoyed anyway. She was never interested in where the next drinking party would be held, and she couldn't have cared less if everybody was going to the football game that night instead of studying for the next test. School was not a duty to Becky—it was a privilege.

The other class Becky really enjoyed was anatomy. At first she wondered how she would respond to working with a cadaver, but it turned out that her curiosity surpassed her apprehension and fear. She became fixed not only on what was expected of her, but what she expected of herself. Every morning as soon as she arrived at the lab, she put on her white lab jacket, took out her scalpel, and got to work. She was absorbed in what she was doing, dissecting through every layer of muscle, fat, and mesentery. It was easy for her to learn which nerves innervated each muscle, and what orifice they went through in the cranium. She learned about disease processes as she went along, the origin of certain tumors, and witnessed the dramatic effects of smoking on the lungs. She examined the staples left in the skull of one of the cadavers who had had a brain tumor removed before she died. All around was evidence that confirmed to Becky that she had made the right choice to finish school, and it simultaneously confirmed that life itself was a miracle.

The medical students were split up in groups of four—about thirty-two in all. In time, each group got to know their cadaver really well—all of his or her unique characteristics and medical phenomena. Becky found it interesting, noting no two people were alike, not just on the outside she thought, but on the inside too. Organs that might be expected to be the same in each human—a liver just a liver, a heart just a heart, were very different. Becky noticed that her cadaver had a heart whose main arteries that supply the heart muscle with blood were routed in an atypical way; the transverse arteries were not transverse and had not been since birth. Becky was astounded by the differences that make each person unique and how the miraculous human body can function well even if important organs were compromised. She had to study the science of probabilities and learned to accept that nothing is perfect.

Maybe there was one exception—the professor who came into class one Friday afternoon. He was absolutely perfect, and he made quite an impression on Becky.

It was about noon. The class was restless to leave the lab, and most of the students had already put their cadavers down and their dissecting tools in the light blue boxes that usually stuck out of their book bags—a sign to others who traversed the campus each day that they were medical students. The class stood ready in small groups by the door, waiting for Dr. Burns to dismiss them for the weekend. Most everybody had been talking all morning about their Friday night plans while they dissected the ear, the assignment for the first half of the day, and drank their coffee. The dialogue had exacerbated to an impatient mumble by the time Dr. Robert Raine finally entered to give last-minute instructions for the following Monday's lab. He walked in like a king with a sophisticated stride.

Becky kept her probe in place, deep in the auricular cartilage, and looked up over the protective glasses she wore in lab. She felt a surge of adrenaline as she convinced herself she had seen this professor before—there was a certain familiar sense—she guessed it was probably in her dreams.

He was distinguished, tall, and handsome, and she heard music, "The Nightingale in Love," a flute and harpsichord dancing a minuet together. He was balding just a bit, but to Becky it added to his debonair qualities. As she stared longer at the visiting professor who had joined their class for a few weeks in between his research project deadlines to help prepare the class for mid-terms, she noticed that his posture was strikingly erect. He was demure and commanding, in the sense that when he spoke the entire class seemed to become particularly quiet as if the reverberations from his voice demanded respect. His lips were full, and his hands looked soft and gentle, but deliberate. He spoke, and as she was quiet and breathed shallow breaths she listened to his monologue. Becky felt like a schoolgirl with a crush, and she struggled not to show her sheepish grin. Maybe she was just love starved, and the timing was right. But it didn't seem to matter what the reason was, her mind was drenched in the idea of how she wished he would walk over and kiss her. She fantasized about putting her arms around him, and just the thought of it made her body tremble. She sat down on the stool beside her and continued to stare with quiet yearning. Dr. Raine began to give the directions for Monday's lab, but Becky heard nothing.

As weeks passed, Becky got to know Dr. Raine a little better as she took interest in his innovative approach, which lent better connectivity between the lab and clinical application that he had developed in private practice before his research position with the university. One day, Dr. Raine stood near Becky while she was dissecting her cadaver.

"So, how do you do it, Becky?" he asked.

"How do I do what, Dr. Raine?" she asked, thinking he was flirting, or maybe just wishing it so.

"How do you get such good grades and still raise a family? How do you balance it all?"

Becky smiled. "You have a family, too, don't you?" she said. "Long days, but I enjoy it. Best of both worlds, you might say."

"Well, it doesn't seem like you'll need it, but if you ever fall behind or feel like you could use some help, let me know," Dr. Raine said.

"Thank you, I'll remember that, thanks a lot."

Becky waited one week before taking him up on his offer. After regular lab hours, she went home, prepared dinner as usual, and helped the children with their homework. They played for a while and, after they readied for bed she tucked them in, read to them and hummed a lullaby even though they acted like they were way too old for that. Beth, on the other hand, still enjoyed falling asleep to the rhymes her mother made up and put to music. As soon as the children were asleep, Becky left them with Will. He would watch television while she was at the lab for additional study. She was eager to return and ran down the apartment stairs, opened her car door, and flung her book bag on the seat beside her. She backed the car to the end of the cul-de-sac instead of taking the time to turn around first, and took off toward school. *Too many stoplights*, she thought. It seemed like she couldn't get there fast enough. She knew Dr. Raine would be waiting for her. The night air was brisk, but her excitement kept her warm, and she was full of determination to get to the lab to study for the next day before Dr. Raine might leave. She wanted to put the time in and do well in her class for two reasons—to help herself and to impress Dr. Raine. She couldn't park the car fast enough. Her eyes darted back and forth in search of an empty spot in a lot that usually was full. She drove around a couple of times while she waited for someone to leave. Becky was anxious and impatient. She turned on the radio, tapped her feet on the floor, kept her right hand on the steering wheel, and used the fingers of her left hand to comb through her long hair. She breathed deeply as her anxiety heightened.

She noticed a passerby reaching for his keys, and she watched as he opened the door to his vehicle, started his car, and began to back out of his parking spot. Becky pulled in quickly lest someone else would get the spot before her. She dug through her purse to find change for the parking meter. At last she was at the back door of the Medical Science Building. She entered the combination so the after-hours security system would let her into the cadaver lab. *Calm down*, she told herself, as she walked with a brisk pace down the long, cold, shaded hallway. The lights by the door were not on, so she figured Dr. Raine had not arrived yet. Becky prayed that he hadn't been there and gone.

Becky sighed, closed her eyes for a second, leaned back against the marble slab wall, and tried to relax. She thought to herself—*You're here now, and he isn't, so relax!* She then opened up her locker and retrieved her white jacket. She put her glasses on. Then she walked over to the stainless steel box that held her cadaver. She opened the lid and began cranking the body up and out of the preservative. With each turn, the stainless steel slab emerged from the fluid which then drained back down into the basin, forcing a sucking sound as the weight pressed it through the vacuum, causing it to cascade down over the corpse, where it fell in one large puddle of fluid, fat, and debris. She lifted the white gauze-like blanket that covered the corpse and kept moist what was left of the once intact body. Organs that had been resected out and studied already had not been put back where they originated. They were placed anywhere the students decided to put them so they could go back at a later time and study them over and over again.

In this instance, Becky had tucked the heart under the armpit so she could have access to it without reaching over the gut and under the rib cage. She would saw through the rib cage and open it up when the class got to that section in their studies. *Hmm, imagine*, Becky thought, as she held the heart in her hand. *This organ once had the capacity to feel—to feel something special for someone. How had it told the brain to feel? Did it matter to anyone now?* Her eyes tried to reach deep within as if to hear the story only a soul could tell—the story of when his heart had been glad, and she wanted to ask if his heart had ever been broken. The soul breathed life and meaning into rigid objects. Becky's own heart felt rigid. Her soul seemed all around her. She could feel it and understand it, but it had found no company with her heart.

Becky heard footsteps in the hallway. *Could it be him*? she questioned herself. She wondered what it was about him that made her excited to see him. Excited, nothing—she could barely breathe when he was around! She held her breath for a second to listen. Yes, it was Dr. Raine!

"Oh, Dr. Raine, it's you," she said with a subdued expression.

"Sorry I'm late, Becky. My eight-year-old needed help with his homework," explained Dr. Raine.

"You have an eight-year-old, too?" Becky asked, still working to contain her excitement. "I have twin sons that age. What school district are they in?"

"Really. It seems like we have more than medicine in common, don't we? My son attends Savannah School. It really wasn't homework but a special project I was working on with him. You know, the kind where the parents are expected to do most of the work? I hope I get an 'A'," Dr. Raine laughed, and Becky chuckled and acknowledged what he meant.

A few awkward moments passed while Dr. Raine got situated. His tall, statuesque figure stood out against the shadowed room where only a few of the lights had been turned on. He put on his white lab jacket that fell to his knees and not below—a look Becky had thought goofy on the other professors because as they walked their knees kicked up a flap at the bottom of the lab coat, annoying her with each step—up, down, up, down. His short, dark bangs wrapped around his forehead and into the receding hairline that framed his not-too-round, not-too-squared face in such a way as to expose the seduction in his eyes. He reached up on a shelf against the wall and retrieved his own copy of the students' anatomy book, then retrieved a small gray box that housed a probe, scalpel, and hemostat from his white jacket pocket with the University Hospital insignia on the right front side above his nametag that read "Robert Raine, M.D."

"Where should we begin tonight, Becky?" Dr. Raine asked.

"Well," Becky stammered and cleared her throat. "I thought we could start by going through all of the muscles. I think I know them, but if you could go through them with me . . ." She paused. "I will pick each one up, identify it, and tell you which nerve innervates it. That will help me the most right now. If I make a mistake—well, then I could use your help."

"That sounds fine—go ahead," said Dr. Raine.

Becky gloved up and proceeded to pick up the latissimus dorsi with her probe. She named it, identified the nerve, and then went on. By the time she got to the sartorius, her voice had become just an echo in her head because her mind was on other things. Her autonomic nervous system kept her going, with her fingers and mouth just carrying out simple tasks while her heart and brain were with Robert Raine. She could tell she impressed Dr. Raine with her anatomic accuracy, and for some reason that mattered. She wanted him to know that she knew what she was doing; his approval seemed to be important for reasons beyond a student-professor situation. Her cover-up had worked as to why she had asked him to join her in the lab. She really just wanted to be with him again, to see him, and to experience the unique chemistry that occurs outside of a science laboratory—the special attraction that usually only occurs once in a lifetime if one is lucky. She was aware of his body warmth. They passed a scalpel. She paid attention when he took a breath. They moved in synchrony to the next muscle and probed at a nerve. She wondered if he was happy in his marriage.

"You know the muscles well enough—nerves too. It doesn't appear you need my help—really," Dr. Raine said. They had worked well into the night. Becky could have stayed all night. However, they both were aware it was either time for a break or time to go home.

"Do you feel like some coffee?" asked Dr. Raine. Becky half closed her eyes in her disbelief that was only challenged by the reality that he had indeed suggested they extend their time together.

"Sure," said Becky, acknowledging a lengthy litany of emotions. She wanted time to get to know him better. She began to put her things away with a leisured motion to conceal her excitement. Becky wondered why he asked her out for coffee. Perhaps she was trying to levy too much from his invitation. Becky told herself that he must have reasons why he "allowed" himself so much time away from home, and she was curious about what they were. Even people who love their work like to go home and spend time with their spouse and children.

Dr. Raine helped Becky off with her lab jacket. *Oh, he touched me,* Becky thought, and her shoulders tingled, and her head went back just a little. She held her breath for a second before she took her jacket from his hands and hung it up. Becky looked up and smiled gently. She wanted to spend more time with him. They walked across the street to a quaint café that was out of the mainstream for passersby, a place where no one would probably see them together. Becky thought it shouldn't have mattered, but it did. The entrance was simple and inviting. The dining room was dimly lit and, despite the cozy Winstonesque music flowing out of the juke box, only one man was there sitting on a stool at the bar, and he didn't even look up when they walked in and sat at a small round table with two chairs not far behind him.

The middle-aged bartender ignored her three customers as she put last night's glasses back up on a shelf behind the counter. Robert spoke to the bartender quietly and ordered two coffees. Becky bit her lip and searched for a neutral place to begin a conversation. She was uncomfortable staying quiet.

Robert, on the other hand, seemed self-assured, as if the environment was a natural place for him to be. Becky fidgeted first with her purse, digging all around searching for something. She didn't know what for. Then she twisted her hair with her index finger but only for a second or two before she caught herself and put her hand down on her lap. She excused herself to go to the restroom. As she walked around two tables and toward the back of the room, she wondered if Robert was watching her. She closed the door behind her and stood looking into the mirror. She smiled to see what her smile would look like to him. She fussed with her hair.

She smiled again, and then said out loud, "Oh, forget it," and headed back to their table.

Once reseated, she said, "Well, I really think it is coincidental that our names are so similar, don't you?"

"Yes, I do," Dr. Raine said. As the initial conversation breakthrough had been accomplished, the rest of the evening that took them well past the midnight hour came easy. After a refill of coffee, they eased into wine. Dr. Raine mused at how relaxed they seemed with each other and how there were so many things they could talk about together. Becky and Robert didn't seem to tire. Regardless of what the clock showed, their eyes remained alert and on each other. They never did go back to the lab.

Robert poured Becky a second and third glass, and she was aware he was doing it, but she trusted herself. She had never been a drinker. She would not allow too much wine to put her judgment capability at risk. The situation between them seemed to be a matter of testing the waters of mutual respect. She was pleased that she could show Robert that not even a little too much wine would make her do something he knew she wanted to do. She was disciplined. They spoke of their children and discussed what marriage meant to them, careers, and destiny. Robert spoke openly that he was somewhat unfulfilled at home, and Becky acknowledged that her marriage had seen better days too. All the romantic bed and breakfasts in the world spent with their respective spouses wouldn't alter the truth they each knew—that they both felt empty! Together they decided it was the worst kind of loneliness to have so much love but no one to share it with.

Becky shared with him her interest in rural medicine and nursing homes. She could hardly believe it when he told her that internal medicine and gerontology were his line of work in private practice when he wasn't helping out at the medical school as a visiting professor. As they conversed, they each learned many intriguing things about each other—their strong sense of caring and commitment and the incurable need to share the love they felt inside with those in need. Her compassionate behavior met with his—somewhere between reality and fantasy. She figured he heard music, too.

Snow began to fall, and they both noticed it at the same time as they gazed through the large window near their table. They looked back at each other silently—another perfect moment. Becky looked back out to the white flakes making their way gently to the ground and smiled. They each wanted the night to go on, but they knew it was time to go. Becky stood up and told Robert that she had better get on the road before it got slippery. She didn't want to give in to the weather, but then again she reminded him that her test was the next morning. Robert politely stood up and reached for her jacket. "Here, let me help you." He pulled up the back of her hair so it wouldn't be pulled under the collar. Becky closed her eyes for a second and took a deep breath to absorb the moment of something pleasurable a little deeper and a little longer.

"You want me to drive you to your car?" Robert offered after he realized the sidewalks were snow covered.

"No, that's okay. My car is not too far from here anyway. Thanks again for tonight," said Becky.

They politely said goodnight to each other and departed in opposite directions after they left the building. They both turned back to look at each other. It only took her about 15 minutes to get home.

When she walked in her front door, Will greeted her. "Well, did you get as much accomplished tonight as you had hoped to, Becky?"

Becky was annoyed that Will was still awake. "More than that, Will," she said, with an indignant tone. "Much more."

It was just a couple of weeks before Christmas. Becky made plans to spend their vacation and her time off of school once her finals were out of the way taking the family to Michigan to visit her ex-husband's grandfather. Don lived alone, and Becky thought no one should have to be alone on Christmas—the family should gather together. Her ex would never consider going, and she felt blessed not only to be with his grandfather, but that her husband would not balk at the idea.

She and Will loved Don and looked forward to being together. He had spent Christmas alone ever since Grandma had died some eight years earlier, and their only daughter, Ben's mother, had died years before that. Becky could never understand why Ben and his sister never went to visit him, but then Ben didn't spend time with his only daughter Beth, either. It was just the way he was. Ben's sister hadn't visited her only brother in many years, and it appeared to Becky that they only cared about what was happening in their own lives. Becky and Grandfather chose to be together as often as they could, and they had spent many wonderful times together since Becky's divorce from Ben. Even though Becky lived nine hours away from Grandfather's by car, she saw to his every need. She made sure that his prescriptions were filled and appropriately dispensed into the pill packs every month, and she had daily conversations with him about his life. She knew when he had doctor appointments, arranged transportation for him if he didn't quite feel up to driving himself, and gave him the assurance that she cared. Because of their relationship, his life had a sense of purpose; he had someone to brag to about his golf game, to tell the details of where he went to lunch each day, and what the weather was like. She tended to his feelings, and he tended to hers as well, knowing all the details of the subdivision, her marriage to Will, and the trials, tribulations, and joys of raising her children. Grandfather loved Becky and Will's children, and he appreciated that they were all family and were willing to come and visit.

They often played out a ritual in which Becky would call and ask him what he had eaten for lunch, what he purchased at the store and if he had seen any of his neighbors that day. In turn, Grandfather would ask how her family was and what she had done all day. She wanted him to feel cared about, and the truth was—Becky really did care! Just knowing he was there and that she was part of his life made her happy whenever she thought about him.

Becky told him they would be coming to Michigan to spend Christmas with him and the dates of their arrival three months before they'd make the trip so that he would have something to look forward to for a long time. Becky herself had been planning the trip in her head and heart for longer than that, realizing that this Christmas would probably be one of the last opportunities she would have to create a Christmas at Grandfather's house—one that everyone would remember. He would be eighty-nine that March, and Beth would be going away to college before too long. The twins were involved in athletics that kept them tied to Madison for practices—soccer in the summer and hockey in the winter. The opportunity had worked out perfectly for this year to be the one.

Everything that Becky planned was intended to make a difference in the lives of those around her. She gathered cookie cutters and chose Christmas songbooks, wrapped presents, and packed the tree skirt and some old ornaments Grandfather had given Becky years before when he had decided to no longer put up a tree. She often wondered what it was about Grandfather's own grandchildren that made them ignore him so, and she ached for the way she knew it made him feel. There was nothing wrong with him. He had no offensive behaviors, and he wasn't selfish, boring, mean spirited, loud, or rude. He was a delight, reciting short stories to his great-grandchildren and thoughtfully buying their favorite snacks before they came for a visit. When Ben's mother died, Becky vowed to herself that she would do the best she could to keep the family together. She resolved this Christmas would be one they would never forget!

The day they were to leave, Becky directed the children to help take all of the decorations off of their tree at home so they could transport it to Grandfather's place. She was going to tie it on the back of their SUV. "Pick one ornament, children—one that has special meaning to you, and we'll take it with us and tell Grandfather why it is important to us," commanded Becky. Each child then picked out a special ornament to put on the tree at Grandfather's place. Then Becky dragged the tree down the stairs of their apartment and to the back of their vehicle. "What would Christmas be like without a real Christmas tree?" she told the children as she held the tree in place while Will put bungee cords around the trunk to secure it.

When everything was packed and well-organized, Will locked up the apartment, and they were off. The long trip didn't seem like it took twelve hours, but it did, and it was nice that there was no ice or snow on the roads to contend with. The children slept and read most of the way, so the trip was quiet and relaxing.

However, by the time they arrived, everyone in the car was ready to get out. They were anxious to unload all that they had brought and to decorate Grandfather's house. No matter how tired they were, their anxiousness kept them going. Grandfather watched in wonder as Becky and her well-trained team of experts prepared the house. Becky's months of planning and preparing precise details charted how they would occupy the next three days in Grandfather's apartment. She had the schedule down by minutes—the time they would have to leave Madison in order to arrive at his doorstep close to three o'clock in the afternoon, so they could unpack and have dinner on the table by four thirty, Grandfather's specific and unwavering dinner time. She had plans for what to get done before Grandfather went to bed. Becky had come to know his rituals, and she respected them and did not want to disrupt his routine. She knew how important routine was to him.

Will moved the coffee table out of the way and set up the tree. Becky hung the lights. Beth started to pop the popcorn that they would later string as a traditional, old-fashioned decoration for the tree. Erin and Eli made several trips to the car to bring in luggage, Christmas presents, and food. They took Claire, their cocker spaniel, for a walk. Family pets were part of Christmas too.

The children placed each present onto the red and green tree skirt that Becky had made sure not to forget. They set the cranberries on the countertop next to the popcorn so they would remember to string them. Becky asked Erin to set up the portable cassette player they had brought along, and she asked Eli to get out the Christmas tapes that she had hand-picked to bring. Music soon filled the air and mingled with the incense that Becky brought and lit to add an even stronger scent of evergreen than the tree alone provided. After the hustle and bustle of bringing Christmas indoors had subsided, the children strung the cranberries and popcorn in a way that would have made a true nineteenth century parent proud while Becky started to put together the ingredients for sugar cookies. Becky had remembered the needles and thread for the berries and popcorn and the cookie cutters too. She was bound and determined to make the Christmas fantasy come alive in Grandfather's heart.

While Becky stirred the dough, she looked over the counter and gazed at what was before her. The tree had a special glow. Eli appeared to be reflecting as he sat admiring the presents that had been tucked under the tree. He told his mom that he was trying to figure out what was in the packages that he had determined were his. Beth's eyes were half closed as she tried to keep herself awake. Claire was hugging Grandfather's chair as he reached down to pet her ears. Erin was listening to music with his headphones on, and Will was sort of walking around to see what Becky would ask him to do next. At this moment Becky appreciated Will very much. Becky was getting sleepy too and almost forgot the cookies in the oven. If it hadn't been for the neighbors who had smelled the aroma, they might have been ruined.

There was a rap at the door. Becky opened it to find Don's neighbors.

One woman, whom Becky knew was named Ruth, said, "We smelled something good in the hallway, Don. Is your family here?" She smiled at Becky. "He's been so looking forward to your visit."

Grandfather had shown them the pictures Becky had sent, so they knew the children right away and commented how grown up they were.

"Don, we saw your new wreath, too," another neighbor said. Becky had secured a wreath on Grandfather's front door to greet the holiday visitors she knew would come around because all of his neighbors were close with one another, sharing food, visitors, stories, pictures, and looking out for each other. In a sense they too were his family. If Becky knew Grandfather wasn't feeling well, she could easily call Ruth, who lived on the first floor of his building, who would graciously make her chicken soup (the best, according to Grandfather) and bring it up to him. They all came out ahead that way—Ruth loved to be needed, Becky appreciated that Ruth was there for Don, and Grandfather loved Ruth's soup!

Grandfather was very proud that he could show how much he was cared for and thought about at Christmas, so with great enthusiasm in his voice he announced, "Yes, my grandchildren came to bring Christmas to our house this year." Grandfather referred to his house as *our* house even though Grandma has been gone for many years. It would always be *their* home. Whenever Grandfather spoke of something that had to do with the life he had shared with his wife, he spoke in the plural form. Sometimes Becky would ask if Grandfather was in need of anything, and his reply was always "We are very comfortable."

Becky offered some of their cookies to the neighbors, who then sat down and commented on how beautiful Grandfather's place looked. The children were happy that all of their hard work was noticed, and Grandfather appreciated being able to share his joy.

Later that evening, Becky made hot chocolate and played Christmas carols on the portable keyboard she had brought along. The kids sang to their great-grandfather, and he sang to them. Memories were created that night.

The next morning Becky got to work right away cutting up celery and melting butter for the stuffing. She was still tired from all the preparations and the drive. She took out the roaster she had brought along. Grandfather didn't have one because he had given it to Becky years before. He had said at the time that he didn't have any use for it any more. *How sad*, Becky thought, *to have to resign yourself to giving up things that used to matter.* Over the years, Becky had watched all of the significant things in Grandfather's life become transformed to memory. *Who would have ever thought that the pan he gave me many years ago would make it back into his house to be used once again for our Christmas turkey?* Becky thought, as she put the bird into the oven by seven o'clock. The mouth-watering aroma woke the kids out of their sleeping bags. Becky had brought along pumpkin pies that she had baked right before they left Wisconsin, so those were done. Erin and Eli went sledding outdoors with Will. Beth took her time getting ready for the day, putting on the festive holiday dress she brought to match her mother's dress. They both wanted to look just right for Grandfather. He was attentive to the ladies and complimented them on how lovely they looked.

Grandfather sat in his favorite chair that morning and read the newspaper, then listened to the news on the television while Becky and Beth both worked in the kitchen. Every now and then Becky would look up to glance at Grandfather and, sometimes he was looking over his bifocals and above the top of the newspaper to look into the kitchen at both Beth and Becky. Once their eyes met, and they smiled at each other.

"Turkey sure smells good, Becky," Grandfather said. "Is it time to eat yet?"

"Grandfather, you sound like one of the kids!" Becky said.

"I know, but can you blame me? Nothing smells better than roasted turkey. How much longer?"

It was after noon, and the turkey was done. She took it out of the oven, and Will began to carve it as she made gravy. The family came to the table for their feast. Beth had set the table using the tablecloth that Grandma had crocheted herself—another gift from Grandfather. He had given it to Becky after Grandma died, and Becky had brought it as she felt it only proper it should be on the table that day. She reminded Grandfather that Grandma made the tablecloth. He didn't remark, but Becky knew that it touched him as she watched him run his fingers over the hand-woven stars Grandma had designed in her crocheting. The Christmas napkins resting on top were formed by Beth to look like doves. She had followed directions from a napkin-folding book she had her mom buy so she could help make the table look pretty. A poinsettia was the centerpiece. Everything was very beautiful. Becky especially took notice of the loving and joyful expressions on the faces of the blended family around the table. She didn't know what Will was thinking or if he even cared where they ate Christmas dinner.

Becky asked everyone to join hands in prayer. She knew the dinner prayer Grandfather recited daily. She had written it down during one of their telephone conversations earlier, and on their trip to Grandfather's, Becky had taught it to the children. As a tribute to him, she asked the children to recite his prayer. "Dear Lord, our Creator and constant companion," they began, and Becky's eyes welled up with tears. Grandfather sat proud in his chair at the head of the table with his family. This was a gift they had given each other! But as she prayed, Becky felt guilty because, as she looked over at Will, she was thinking about Robert.

Christmas came and went. Everyone was blessed. Becky returned to school when the semester break was over. She didn't run into Dr. Raine very often, though she thought of him frequently. The cold weather gave a reprieve, and spring once again proved to be a new beginning for Becky—a new life emerging from the stillness of winter.

Chapter Fourteen

The bike ride from Becky and Will's apartment to the medical school was not very far. Becky was taking summer classes and looked forward to her daily exercise of freedom in the fresh air. Seven miles was just enough to give her a good workout—about forty-five minutes of elevated heart rate. Approaching forty, she felt cursed by the genetics on her mother's side that would compete to replace muscle with cellulite. She looked for ways to enhance her appearance, and she felt the daily bike ride would help that. But more than that, she enjoyed waking up early, getting a jump start on the day, and feeling invigorated with the morning breeze all over her face.

Beth got up early too because she was working as a nanny for the two little boys down the street during the day while their parents worked. Will's job was getting easier on him. He did some of his work at home now that his role in the building company was more administrative. It enabled him to spend more time with Erin and Eli while Becky was in class. Most often when Becky got home, she would take walks with the boys to the park behind their apartment and meet Beth and the children she was watching, and together they would play while Becky studied. She loved hearing them laugh and would look up to them climbing a ladder or molding something in the sandbox. She felt blessed.

Will would go to the office while Becky fixed dinner. About the same time, Beth would get home for the day, and she and her mother would talk together in the kitchen, mostly about children. Beth, like Becky, loved to be with children.

As Becky rode through the neighborhoods to school, she couldn't help but be drawn into the coming and going of other families starting their days. She could tell by drawn curtains that some were still sleeping. She thought most families seemed very traditional compared to hers, and she wondered what it would be like to simply wake up, get the children off to school, and go to work like them, though she felt she would quickly be bored. Becky chuckled to herself as she saw one mother toting a briefcase that was overstuffed with brown lunch sacks, and carrying a baby bag, and schoolbooks with car keys hanging between her teeth and already stressed at 6:40 a.m. She remembered those early days herself and wondered which was more painful—leaving her children at a daycare when she would have loved to be a regular mom who could let her babies sleep late in the morning or struggling to complete her education while raising her family and earning a living too. It would have been so much easier and better for everyone if Becky had finished her education first and then started her family. *Children should be raised by their parents,* Becky thought. *However, you do the best you can with what you have at the time.*

Now she was years from the days when she suffered having to leave Beth at daycare so she could go to work just to feed and clothe her, and she was glad those days were short-lived by her marriage to Will. Being married to Will she no longer had to work so much and she appreciated how hard Will worked.

As she pedaled, she thought how she might see Robert in school and her feelings were in conflict. *How can I justify the feelings that I had that night with Robert? Why can't I forgive Will and put energy into adding quality to my marriage?* Becky didn't even like Will anymore. *God, how will you change my heart?* She heard the music that merry-go-rounds play, and pedaled harder.

Becky could tell she wasn't in very good mental or physical condition. The hills just about killed her and, by the time she rounded the last corner near school her face was red and her heart rate was soaring. She hyperventilated as she lifted her leg over the seat of her bicycle and took her helmet off. She stuck it on her backpack, strapped the buckle securely in place, put her sunglasses away, and locked her bike up to the rails in front of the medical school building. She looked at her watch and realized she only had about ten minutes before lecture started.

Once inside, she sat in her usual seat--front row next to the wall. She didn't want anyone sitting to the right of her where she might become annoyed at their nervous habits like tapping their pencil or bouncing their leg while she was trying to take notes. Her classmates' youthful anxious nuances bothered her. *Why didn't they just grow up and sit still?* Becky wondered. Sometimes the mother in her made her feel compelled to say something when her neighbor would fidget, and she took notice that little things were starting to bother her way too much. *How are those Nervous Nellies ever going to be able to sit still and act like a mature physician while taking a history on a patient?* she'd think, as she watched the girl next to her twist her hair and listened to her smack her gum. *Imagine going in to see a doctor and the doctor's leg is crossed and flipping up and down every thirty seconds while you try to describe how your digestion has slowed down and that you're suffering from constipation.*

Becky realized that the stress she was under was probably what was causing her to overreact to most normal situations, and she tried as hard as she could to concentrate on the lecture. Today, everything was making her tense—the sound of the heat registers; the guy next to her for no reason other than he had too much after shave on; she and Will weren't getting along; the apartment was too small; her family of five was on top of each other in the little place they called home, and she wanted the gray house back!

The pace of the lecture was too slow for her. She was bored, and her mind drifted toward all the things that distracted her. What was she going to fix for dinner? What extracurricular activities did she need to get the children to that evening? Why did she feel so old and tired? Would she ever be able to love Will again? When could she see Robert again? None of her feelings fit right, yet all of them had to function together, at least for now.

Becky felt impatient waiting for the lecture to end because she had decided she would try to find Robert. It had been four months since she had last spoken to him before her school break, and she couldn't get her mind off him and the night when they had shared glances and a glass of wine. She wondered if he thought about her any more, though she knew he had, even though he hadn't tried to get in touch with her, or at least not that she was aware of. She wondered if it was an escape she was in search of—an escape from the here and now of a bad marriage and the pressures of school, family, work and all she'd been through in the last two years. She was anxious to see what she would feel when she saw him again and even more eager to analyze what she felt he would be thinking and feeling.

She went over to the interschool telephone and dialed his extension. He was in. Her heart raced with excitement and feelings she didn't understand. He picked up the receiver and she asked him how his day was going and if he would like to meet and have a fifteen-minute cup of coffee. He accepted the offer, and said nothing more.

Eagerly she kept her eyes fixed on the stairs where she knew he would soon be descending. She waited, leaning up against the corner trim to appear nonchalant when he approached. She could hardly wait to see his body, his smile, and then—there he was! There were those soft, brown eyes that searched to find hers. They both seemed anxious and yet remained appropriately polite and more reserved.

"Hi, Robert," Becky almost whispered in a gentle way as to compensate for her racing emotions that had to stay undetected.

"Hi, Rebecca," Robert returned, with equal reservation. An awkward silence fell over them as they searched for neutral conversation that might seem appropriate. It was obvious to each of them that they longed for each other, and it felt right. The only problem was that they were both married to another person. Each knew that for their own reasons they had compromised themselves over the years for the sake of keeping the parental unit together. The children deserved that. Yet neither Becky nor Robert really believed they would ever be tempted by the reality that they could find the perfect mate.

Robert broke through the silence and asked Becky if she would like to leave the building and get away from the hallway noise where they could talk more peacefully. Even though Becky knew he meant privately, the word peace made her pause, for it was exactly what she was missing with Will. Becky was reluctant to leave for she knew it would probably be the beginning of something she wouldn't be able to control, but her feelings for Robert were so strong that she couldn't say no. They left the building without saying a word. They were caught up in their own daydreams—the joy and excitement of getting to be alone and together again.

"Your car or mine?" Robert asked.

"I don't have mine today. I rode my bike," Becky said.

"I usually don't have mine either," Robert said. "I usually get dropped off."

Probably by his wife, Becky thought, and suddenly felt uneasy. She knew that the feelings she had for Robert were wrong. She had strong Christian values and convictions that told her she was not where she should be. She did not want to allow herself to feel anything for someone else's husband—it was against her principles. She fought her feelings. It wasn't fair to the other person, she kept telling herself. She suspected that Robert felt this way too, and this understanding automatically took away from the beauty of what they felt for each other. How could they ignore that one of the very things they admired most about each other was the very thing they were going against so they could be together.

Robert unlocked the passenger side door and opened it for Becky, as a gentleman would. She reached over and unlocked Robert's side of the door from the inside. He got in and put his seatbelt on. Together they were where they shouldn't be. Traffic was congested, and she cautioned him to take his time leaving. Traffic wasn't the only reason she wanted him to idle forward. She wanted to allow her mind time to absorb the past ten minutes, to reflect for a moment, and to think about what she was about to do. She knew what would happen if she left with him. She hoped it would; yet she struggled with that fact. She thought about asking him to stop, to pull over so she could share her feelings and suggest that he return to work, and she would return to studying. She thought about kissing him and living out the fantasy of what she felt would be the perfect relationship. She thought about her children. She thought about her commitment to God. But selfish feelings overpowered her, and they continued to drive.

"Where should we go?" Robert asked.

"Turn left at the next corner—there's a little park near there." *What am I saying?* Again, Becky felt uneasy. If Robert had suggested a little café around the corner, it would have seemed less likely that something was going to really happen. But a park! The environment would enhance what they were both feeling.

Becky knew the park was next to a beautiful lake. There was a quiet breeze that flowed through the open windows, and the anticipation quickened the air. Never a minute rested without thought for one another since they were last together, though neither spoke of it, at least not then. Together—the water, the wind, and the geese were their only witnesses.

They were both aware that the short afternoon ride away from the "hallway noise" would manifest into a beautiful memory as each hoped it would. As Robert slowly pulled into the parking lot at the park, Becky's eyes scouted the perfect place to stop, anticipating the inevitable and wanting it to be the best it could be. She noticed a large sugar maple and decided since this was her favorite tree that was the spot where they should park, and she pointed toward it.

Robert put the car into park and turned the ignition to auxiliary so they could listen to music. Becky unrolled her window further so she could feel the breeze on her face. She turned and gazed into Robert's eyes and thought of Shakespeare's words: "The eyes say what the lips fear to speak." Becky thought briefly about speaking these words out loud but held back because she knew that once the words were spoken, they would illuminate the truth. Yet the truth was before them and could no longer be ignored.

She listened to her heart and, as she began to recite Hamlet's lines, Robert reached forward and took her hand. Becky's heart raced as she yearned to kiss his lips. He reached forward and touched her lips with his fingers and, bridling his passion, he put her hand up to his lips and kissed it in a manner befitting a princess. Becky leaned back and sighed at the perfection of the moment.

She put her hand over his and, as she held his hand, her mind was carried away. A seductive sonata swept like moonlight under her feet and in her mind she danced above the earth, drunk from the sweet perfume that escaped the musical composition to ensure that all of her senses were alert to the perfection of total bliss. She felt herself breathe a deeper sigh, and her eyes closed. Her head tipped back, and she became almost breathless as she drifted. Robert was everything, and Rebecca was everything, and they both knew it. He encompassed every crevasse of her soul. *Kiss me,* she whispered to herself. *Take me in your arms and never let me go.* Inside she wept, for she loved him so. *Dance with me until our feet lift off the floor.*

There was music within her, the private place she didn't share with anyone else—a place of calm and understanding. She would not have liked for anyone to know about her secret sanctuary of love and passion—the way she saw and felt life. She wanted to protect it. This was her private beauty. But she would share it with Robert because she knew he understood it, and he heard music too. Robert would understand, appreciate, and nurture all that was in her. He too had a special place, and they both knew it was with her. Only in her imagination was there ever a man like Robert, yet here he was, real. She drew close to him and could feel the warmth of his lips, though they did not touch.

Becky spoke within—*touch me!* She leaned over and kissed his cheek. Friendly, unobtrusive, yet steeped with emotion. She convinced herself she could get away with a small kiss without overstepping her bounds, although it didn't matter now—she had to do it. It felt natural and responded to what was in her heart. Whether or not she acted out her feelings further became no more than a matter of respect. Respect for what was left of the feelings she had for Will, Robert's wife, and what she felt for her children. What kind of mother would she be if she gave away to another man what should only belong to their father? How could Becky get what she yearned for and what she had been missing her whole life and still somehow rationalize what she was doing and how it contradicted her personal beliefs including her faith? She could throw caution to the wind and do what other people do if they begin an affair. Her desire scared her.

So she pulled back, closed her eyes again, and turned her head away from him. She imagined now being alone with no more than fantasy sitting next to her. But her attempts to ignore Robert were more than fate alone could overcome. She couldn't go away without coming back to the same place—eye to eye, the windows to her soul would not let her turn away from the reflection that mirrored their earthly existence. Her soul was staring at her.

Like two magnets, their energy captured in slow motion, Robert and Rebecca moved toward each other and their lips touched. They were like halves yearning to feel whole. Their togetherness was magical. They drew together again, and this time kissed longer.

Chapter Fifteen

Robert and Becky longed for each other daily, and they devised plans that made it possible to be together. Becky got herself a pager so she could be accessible almost anywhere without anyone knowing about it. She set the button to buzz, not ring, and she hid it under her clothes. They used coded sets of numbers as ways to communicate their love for each other and places they were to meet. A series of ones meant, "I'm thinking about you, and I love you"; a series of nines meant to cancel whatever was planned because something had come up. Like Pavlov's dog, Becky's heart raced with latent expectancy whenever the pager went off.

Today was like every other had been in the last several months. Robert and Becky were together again. Their hearts, like Faberge eggs, were rich in design, one of a kind, and delicately fragile.

Robert picked Becky up at the pre-planned location where no one would see them—one block down from the street lamp by the park off Monroe and Felia streets. She leaned against a tree as she waited. She would have waited all day if she had to, for when it came to Robert, time was infinite.

Robert pulled around the corner in his black Mercedes sports coupe, and Becky sighed with joy. *Yes, at last,* she thought, because he never arrived soon enough for her. He pulled up close to the curb and gave her the smile she had come to love and look forward to. He reached over to open the door, and Becky got in. They sat on the leather seats of Robert's car and played music as they drove. They could have driven forever. The road seemed as endless as their love. Robert pulled off to the side of the road just to look at her. They rarely spoke, for the unwritten words of their love were the most powerful. They took in the beauty of each other as deeply as they could, and together they made audible affirmation of the beauty they saw around themselves—no matter where they were.

Robert again pulled to the edge of the road, took his suit jacket off, and folded it behind the seat. He leaned forward and embraced her in a kiss. Their worlds came together in such a way that each knew that no matter how the story ended, they would remain inseparable souls into eternity. Life began and ended for them both right then, and nothing else seemed to matter—yet everything did. They could not dispel their feelings of responsibility to their children or their spouses—feelings they could not ignore. Even the love of a lifetime could not thwart the dedication they both felt toward an earlier commitment. This was their only obstacle. They discussed how they could be free, what would enable them to be together unrestricted, and decided the only way would be to outlive their spouses. Robert brought the idea into their conversation, but Becky thought the idea of discussing such a thing was inappropriate. Yet to Becky, she was too much of a realist to ignore that there were people in this world who killed their spouses or anyone in their way of having free access to someone they loved. *Certainly Robert wouldn't be capable of this, would he?* Becky asked herself because she was thinking about how wrong it was to be having a relationship with Robert. Wrong breeds wrong. Evil breeds evil. *Sure, some people make it through situations like this unscathed, but others do end up in a murderous ring of deception.* It was an ugly subject, far-fetched, yet a realistic possibility.

Her thoughts were random and drifting again, and she sat on the leather seat wondering what the purpose of anything in life was. *Hmm,* she thought, as she remembered something unusual about her grandmother—the one who wore cotton, floral dresses and whom she adored. *Perhaps Grandmother was a prime example of what Robert was talking about.* Grandmother had the perfect marriage—full of prayerful love and adoration for Grandfather. When Grandfather died, everyone knew that part of her died too. She and the family mourned not only his death, but also the end of their life on earth together. Yet, not soon after the funeral, Grandmother put a picture of another man out on her dresser. She was ninety years old. The family asked her who he was. For the most part, she ignored them. She behaved as if she didn't even hear them inquire. After a while though, she shared her secret with her daughter, Becky's mother. The man whose picture sat on Grandmother's dresser was indeed the true love of her life—the only man who her heart had been connected to for almost seventy years.

She was a young girl when he first proposed, and Grandmother thought herself too young to make the commitment. He was desperate for her and felt she would never be his. In an act of pure desperation, he killed himself. For all this time her heart was with his. She was able to live amiably with Grandfather all that time; at least she appeared to in Becky's eyes. To the rest of the family, too, she appeared to be a perfectly content wife and mother. But on sunny days, when she hung her babies' diapers on the line, she thought of Albert, and when she stirred her homemade bean soup, Grandfather's favorite, she thought of the poem Albert had read to her while she leaned on an old oak tree one autumn day when the air was thick with the smell of dried leaves and acorns, so many years before. She lived with his memory most of the time and all of the memories they missed making together. Now that Grandfather was dead, she brought her true love to life.

Robert and Becky both were aware, in their own separate ways, how they respected commitment and dedication and how they respected each other. They got out of the car and held hands as they walked over to a grassy knoll that had a deciduous tree line separating it from the farmer's field. The sun lit through the trees and made Becky's hair glow. She stared at Robert as he walked up the pile of rocks that lay stacked where some farmer had put them. The freshness of the morning outlined the freedom they felt when they were together. As they walked, the music she heard was like a holy place that awakened in her the spirit of prayer, forgiveness, understanding, acceptance, and love. She didn't know what to do with herself or what to think. She was so happy, but with Robert, not with Will. She no longer questioned how she should feel with the right man. Now she knew what it *should* feel like and *would* feel like, and it was wonderful. Oh, how they wanted to have each other as man and wife and all of their children to be theirs together as one family.

Robert stood on the top of the heaped stone fence like a king. He reached down to Becky and gestured for her to come near. Becky slipped off her shoes and stepped barefoot across the grass to meet him. She looked up at him and he cupped her face in his hands. The warmth from the sun bathed them, and her lips were full and ready. Robert moved Becky's hair to one side, leaned forward and kissed her neck. He pressed his lips against hers, and her body melted under his touch, like ice transformed to water by the heat of the sun. He would have her now, all of her. The way he wanted it. The way she wanted it. A moss-covered log became her pillow and the clouds her downy cover. The gentle breeze went over them, up and over, up and over. They didn't speak; they moaned. And when they were both still, the air too seemed to become motionless. They sat up then and looked out at their surroundings. Becky's breast was still uncovered and her blouse slightly open. She tilted her head to rest on Robert's chest and in his arms, and they smiled a small and unassuming smile that acknowledged the moment of contentment where all seemed at peace. The old fields of autumn where the soybeans and corn were just past harvest met with the green that lay like a patchwork carpet beneath the quiet golden poplar trees which moved only enough to make them shimmer. The wedding between two souls was consummated. The endless sky their cathedral and the wild birds their only witness. Then Robert's pager went off. It was his nurse. In awkward silence they removed themselves from perfect bliss into stark reality. Hand in hand, they walked toward his car.

They drove on, over hills and around meandering corners. They listened to music, that same music that had been playing when they first stopped and headed out into the field. Robert reached over and touched Becky's hand, his caressing a gentle assurance. Every so often, they would glance at each other and their eyes would speak. This, a once in a lifetime love.

Robert had patients to see. Becky had a monumental amount of work to do to study for her finals. They drove to where she had left her car. Throughout the day they paged each other back and forth using their secret code for "I love you," the honeymoon of two adulterous lovers.

Then, later that afternoon, they communicated through the pager and a few secret phone calls to arrange to be together again. This time they decided to meet on their bicycles. Becky pulled up to him at the corner meeting place. "Hi, Robert," she said.

"Hi, Becky," said Robert. They didn't stop long because they were still out in the open where anyone could recognize them. Instead, they gave each other the sign language for "I love you" and left in the same direction.

Robert already had in mind where he wanted to go, and he led the way. They rode through the cemetery by the lake on the bike path that was lined with overgrown spruce and oak, sugar maple, hydrangea, and spirea bushes. The ride was as beautiful as their love, and the music danced and allowed the child within Becky to play. When they got to the end of the asphalt path that passed over a small patch of grass connecting the old railroad tracks to the new path and down a small embankment, they decided to keep going.

"Robert, I'm going to fall!" laughed Becky.

"No, you're not, Becky—come on!" said Robert. Becky's legs were flying and flopping with every wooden four-by-four they went over. They dodged the tree limbs that stuck out in their way and took each bump in giddy stride. After almost an hour they neared the end. Robert kept on riding faster than ever.

Becky struggled to keep up. "Where are you going, Robert?" He didn't answer, and they both were quiet until they reached a small restaurant.

"So this is where you were headed," Becky said, out of breath.

"Well, I didn't have it in mind at first, but then it came to me as we rounded the last corner that this might be a nice way to end the day."

Robert and Becky parked their bikes and made their way to the front door of the out-of-the-way restaurant they had found. Neither one of them had been there before, and they wondered what it was going to be like. They entered to find that it was a quaint gourmet hideaway.

He ordered the best wine. Of course he was a connoisseur, or at least he pretended to be. His brother owned a winery on the Seine, and Robert had become very knowledgeable about fine wine. He told Becky that he could even discern which side of the river the grapes had come from. He also told her that the time of the day when the sun ripened the grapes mattered. They made a toast and sipped.

They brought their glasses to their lips, but their eyes never left each other. They displayed the closest signs of undying love that any two lovers could ever experience. The waitress remarked at what an apparently wonderful marriage they must have for they seemed to be so happy and so in love. Robert and Becky just looked at each other. Each knew they wished it were true.

Together they decided that they wanted to spend even more time together. The problem was how they were going to be able to do that. There weren't enough hours in the day with work, school, and spending time with their families. Robert suggested that they introduce their families to each other and hope for a cordial response. They would arrange to exchange handshakes at their sons' soccer game. Both Becky and Robert's sons were scheduled to play against each other in soccer the following week.

It turned out better than either of them could have possibly dreamed it would. Their spouses hit it off. Their children played together on the monkey bars after the game and, when it was time to leave, the boys begged to be able to continue playing together. "Maybe they could come and play at our house," Eli suggested. Becky let Robert's boys come over to her house, and they made arrangements for when they were to be picked up.

The two families became good friends and, after a few months, Robert decided to make plans for them to go on a joint vacation. Becky couldn't understand why he would want a lengthy vacation. She thought it might be uncomfortable to be in close quarters together for so long. Yet the idea of all the children playing together and them being able to watch them together seemed enticing. Becky and Robert had the best of both worlds.

Robert rented a large motor home and, after a brief planning session, their schedules coincided, and they left for a pleasant vacation. Each day that passed was even more wonderful than the last. By the third night when it was time to go to sleep, and all four adults were in one big tent, all Becky could think of was how she would rather be in her sleeping bag with Robert than with Will. Her empty heart told her arms to reach out and touch him as he slept—only a hand away—but she couldn't. Robert was braver and, sometime during the night, Becky could feel Robert's hand touching her fingers. They felt content and slept well. Their touching was innocuous and innocent—if their spouses happened to see it.

As Becky began to awaken that morning, she looked at Robert and Will lying there in the tent. She pondered many moments from the days she had spent with both of them on their trip. Many scenes rushed through her mind. She couldn't stand thinking about them anymore and left the tent for a morning run. Her jog invigorated her and allowed her to work off frustration. It wasn't easy being around Robert day in and day out, laughing and romping and just dying to hug and kiss. They could not show their emotions. She could smell the wet weeds as the warmth of the sun sent the aroma up in a mix of morning dew and sunlit mist. Becky felt Robert was watching her now from the opening in the tent where she had left the flap back.

The little boys had gotten very close and truly enjoyed each other. They too were up at the crack of dawn and went down to the lake together in search of minnows. Becky could see the four of them well after spotting them through the trees. They were lying on their bellies on the boat dock, barefooted, looking straight down into the water. The birds were singing all around that morning, and the scent of August in the woods with the thicket full of russet weeds and wildflower blooms made Becky feel like she was in heaven.

After she had returned to the tent and the four adults were awake, they began preparing breakfast. Becky thought about how she never really paid much attention to the way Robert's wife may have been feeling about the trip, nor had she given much thought to what Will's feelings might have been for that matter. Had either noticed their loving glances? Probably not. The four of them and their sons were just friends.

Becky gave a finger-puppet show for the children in their tent after dusk and before the adults retreated to their tent. All four boys laughed with excitement at the stories Becky told to go along with the creatures she created in the shadows.

Chapter Sixteen

It seemed to Becky that much time had passed since she and her family had left the gray house in Indiana, yet it seemed like only yesterday to her the trauma, the move and the happy times when free play in the canal among the wildflowers brightened their days. Despite the difficult transition, they had much to be thankful for. The apartment she settled on was really not too bad. The kitchen and dining room windows overlooked a park and faced west so they could stand out on the porch and watch the sunset or storm clouds rolling in before a rain. The park was large and had a playground, a basketball court Will and the boys enjoyed, a tennis court that Beth played on with her friends, much grassy space to fly kites, and the boys enjoyed climbing the trees. There had been a lot of snow that winter, which was good for shoveling out tunnels and building snow forts, and seeking victory in a snowball fight.

Claire, their cocker spaniel, could run forever in the field behind the apartment building and, most mornings about 6:00 a.m., Becky ran with Claire around the periphery of the field. They both got a little workout. She loved running with her dog in the snow, wind, or rain—it didn't matter what the weather was like. They braved the elements, and usually Claire led the way. Both of them appreciated being out in nature. Their path was obviously made clear from their routine because their feet flattened the grass down in summer, and Claire's feet and Becky's boots flattened the snow down in winter.

Every holiday, guests would find the apartment decorated for the occasion, with handmade projects Becky had made with the children. For Valentine's Day, the children worked on the dining room table creating elaborate lace cards of pink and white, and candy hearts were on the table in the same crystal bowl that Becky used every year. She wanted the sameness to create tradition and establish a sense of stability for the children. In the spring, the table was adorned with the same rabbits and eggs that had been put out in the gray house. Becky put the American Flag out about two weeks before the Fourth of July and would keep it there throughout the summer. The children looked forward to each special occasion with anticipation. Becky was a good mom.

But, deep down inside, Becky was aching. She ached to feel complete and loved, and hated that she had given in to an affair with Robert as the only way to have a fulfilling sense of adult affection. Every day brought more emotional emptiness because she knew it wasn't right. She continued to work on her dream of becoming a physician. Still, she knew that living two lives was not right, and the dichotomy haunted her.

Becky watched the children on the playground and kept watch over all that was good. Yet as grateful as Becky was, she wanted her marriage to be more fulfilling, and sometimes she yearned to have her gray house back. The trauma of what the First Trust Mortgage Company had done to their family was still with them and surfaced often as reminders that even though they walked away from their troubles and started anew, they were aware that they hadn't consciously made a move of a desirable nature, but one that had been forced upon them. They were all just trying to make good out of a bad thing.

Since the apartment was too small for her to open up the dining room table like she used to, Becky was unable to use Grandma's hand-crocheted tablecloth. Becky had wanted her children to have the memory of what that special tablecloth meant and how it looked. Maybe to most people something so ridiculously trivial wouldn't have mattered, but to Becky, the lace cloth was an important symbol of the past that she wanted preserved for the children. It was crocheted during a time in history when mothers spent hours making things for the family by hand. This was a lost art and one to be treasured. She also wanted her children to know how she valued their heritage, and the tablecloth was a lasting picture of their great-grandmother's table—a family connection and one not to be forgotten. The continuation of tradition was important to Becky. She loved her grandmother, and she wanted her children to feel the same love.

There were times when Becky felt like the four rooms were closing in on her, and to some extent they were. She often studied in the bathroom because that was the only place to go where she could close the door and have quiet, and it was the only place she could spread her books out and write. But the floor was hard and cold. *Many people have it worse,* Becky thought. *Besides, adversity breeds character.* Will still had difficulty adapting, and he was edgy with the daily routine of life.

Although Will no longer had outbursts like he used to have in Indianapolis, Becky still couldn't figure out what was eating at him. She felt guilty that she was able to find a comfortable refuge when she escaped with Robert. She tried to rationalize Will's behavior and prayed that someday he would overcome whatever was driving him crazy and perhaps, in the future, things would be okay between the two of them. She wanted to pray for Will, but she needed to pray for herself first. She could not.

Becky tried to believe that she should stay in school, even though she knew if she gave it up and got a job, any job to supplement their income, things would improve between her and Will. She felt guilty, despite the fact that Grandfather was paying for her school and subsidizing the family's income while Becky attended. She wasn't supposed to worry about working. Will didn't earn much money, and he didn't want handouts. Will thought Becky understood before they took their wedding vows: "My wife *will* work!" Becky considered leaving school several times a week, partly for financial reasons, partly for Will's concerns, and partly to get rid of Robert and her guilt. But she convinced herself that if Will wasn't complaining about her studying and not having a job, he'd find something else to complain about, and for now, she'd keep Robert, but wouldn't allow herself to get any closer with him in their relationship. No matter how she lived her life, she would never be able to bring happiness and contentment to Will. He would have to find it for himself.

Becky peered through the kitchen window as she often did while she finished the supper dishes. This was a place where her eyes could reach far to the hill off the west corner of the field at the back of the apartment lot, and her mind drifted as she scanned the cows making their evening walk up the thin path that led to a barn. This was the daily routine of the cows, and Becky came to rely on the peaceful countenance at the end of her day and theirs. As she watched, she was taken away from reality and brought into the safety of a distant world where things were simple and natural. She heard music, a Gregorian chant that was restful and inviting, whose rhythms echoed her breathing, and she sank deeply into a sense of relaxed spaciousness. The gait of the cows was slow, rhythmic, and relaxing in synchrony with her music. Becky felt tranquil at her window.

The sun was just starting to set, and by the time Becky finished at the sink, the silos were silenced to silhouettes against the evening sky. As the golden rays passed through the purple clouds that were streaked with pink, wispy feathering, dusk began to turn into night and Becky was carried into a heightened sense of awareness that brought her further into peaceful quiescence.

Another day of near perfect temperatures started Becky's third week of school that fall semester. It was hard for her to get back into the groove of studying after a long and terrific summer vacation. The summer had gone by quickly. The Blaines and the Raines had seen to that.

She had met Robert that morning. They sat on a bench next to the savannah behind the hospital, and spent a short time together before he went to make rounds. They were now seeing each other daily. Robert sat behind Becky, wrapping his arms around her shoulders. Becky had on a sweater to protect her from the early autumn breezes. Together, they watched the morning fog lift out of the valley and dissipate. The sun began to warm their faces and made Becky's blonde hair glisten. Silence was all around them. There wasn't much to say. The blind shroud that they hid behind was becoming a worn transparency, and they both knew that the status quo had to change.

Later that day she met Robert after his lecture, and they laid on the grass against the steep incline in front of the mezzanine between the music hall clock tower and church steeple adjacent to the law school. They gazed up through the russet and golden sugar maples to the partly sunny sky above, naming shapes of the clouds that moved often enough to give them a clean slate with a new shape soon to follow. Like young lovers they laid, Becky snug in her cable knit sweater, and Robert chewing on the end of a stem of clover. Students dotted the landscape, but neither the lovers nor the students paid much notice to the other.

By four o'clock, Becky was riding her bike home from the lab to get supper on the table for Will and the kids. Robert paged her. She turned around to meet him at his car in the vet school parking lot. They steamed up the windows with their breath, their kisses, and their desires. They didn't stay together long. They both left for home, alone and carrying empty longing of what could never be. What purpose does this serve? Becky asked herself. How long can it last? As they departed in separate directions, Becky turned back to watch Robert pull away in his car. He had his window rolled down, and his arm was outstretched giving her the sign language for 'I love you'. She turned to watch where she was going and, steering with her left hand, she held her right hand as far above her head as she could reach and held the same sign for him high up in the air.

She hurried home because she did not want to be late in arriving at her other life—as she now considered it. So she peddled hard. She turned into the cul-de-sac that led to their apartment, her hair flowing in the air behind her as she went, and stopped to get the mail before she pulled into the garage. She leaned her bike against the wall and threw her helmet haphazardly by the seat. Then she ran back down to the edge of the driveway to the mailbox that was full, as usual, with junk mail. *Such a waste of good trees.* Becky thought. *Hmm, Stubert's Fall Catalog. That can be pitched. Electricity bill. Veteran's donation. Wait, what is this?* She re-read the return address. *A letter from a lawyer?* The very word sent a chill up her spine. *Why the hell are we getting a letter from a lawyer?* She thought their Indiana problems were gone. Her heart raced, and her head began to pound with fret.

Becky felt light headed as she made her way through the front door and up the stairs to sit down on the couch to open the envelope. With great anxiety and frustration she tore it open. The thick fold of paper was difficult to extract. Becky pulled it out and began to read: "Adversary Proceeding, Plaintiff, First Trust Mortgage, the first mortgage holder on the property originally owned by William D. and Rebecca A. Blaine at 37 Wellbridge Road, Indianapolis, Indiana. That on March 8, 1990, William D. Blaine executed a mortgage to First Trust that was recorded on March 12, 1990, as Instrument Number 70003774. To secure said mortgage, the defendants, William D. and Rebecca A. Blaine, executed said mortgage, and it is attached and incorporated herein as Exhibit A. That in 1991, foreclosure action was brought against the property and Mr. and Mrs. Blaine, and prior to the filing of their petition for bankruptcy, the Blaines did willfully and maliciously remove and/or damage fixtures and other portions of the residence of said property. That because of the willful and malicious conduct of the defendants, plaintiff has been damaged in the sum of $83,314.37. That said sum should be excluded from the discharge of the debtors pursuant to section 523(6) of the bankruptcy code."

Becky could hardly believe what she was reading. No one she knew had damaged the gray house. It was fine when she left. She had no clue how to interpret the craziness of such an unfounded bunch of lies. "How can they say these things? What kind of damage? They are making stuff up out of the clear blue sky and expect us to just bow down and pay them almost a hundred thousand dollars? To even respond to such an allegation would be lending credulity to absurdity!" Becky said out loud, as she sat befuddled about what to think or what to do.

When Will got home she shared the letter with him, and he gave essentially the same response as Becky had. And of course he knew of no way to address the issue. He would leave those kinds of issues up to Becky. He more or less shrugged the whole thing off.

"Are you too overwhelmed to respond or what?" Becky asked. She felt the weight of the world on her shoulders again, and was miserable beyond reason. Her comprehension was vague, and she was outraged with despair. "Will, don't you realize that if we don't respond to this allegation, there will be a hearing set that we won't be present at, and they will be? First Trust will present evidence with no rebuttal from us, and they will win! We *have* to go to Indiana. This is a fact." She threw up her hands. "This kind of stuff doesn't just go away on its own, you know. You can't ignore it or wish it away either. When someone in a position of authority, like this lawyer who must be being fed by financial incentive, decides he has an opportunity to litigate something, it doesn't matter if the facts are lies and that the issues he sets forth to defend don't possess any moral character. Some lawyers are like that." Becky's voice got louder and more pronounced. "This First Trust group has been unethical from the outset. This is not a joke, Will. This is real, and somebody needs to respond to these allegations!" She paced back and forth in front of the living room window, thinking. Then she turned around to face Will.

"The only alternative as I see it," Becky said, "is to pack up the family and move to Canada. I mean, Will, there is no way I'll ever pay these lying bastards a dime. I can't believe that you're just sitting there and not saying anything."

"Well, what do you expect me to do?" Will said. "I don't know what to do. I mean, I guess I could just drive down there and tell them that what they are saying is a lie and they better knock it off or…"

"Or what?" said Becky. "What do you think that's going to prove? Threaten them? Yeah, right."

"Maybe in this case it's justified, Becky. Maybe I should just shoot 'em."

Becky shook her head as if to say neither Will nor First Trust made sense to her. "Will, this is serious. Now come on—what are we going to do?" Becky paused and then went on trying to elicit a remark that might help her. "First of all, we have to prove that First Trust Mortgage is lying and, secondly, we have to prove that what we have is the truth. God, I'm tired."

Becky sat down on the couch to think—not just about the allegation or what precipitated it, but what she was going to be able to do about it. They had no money to hire a lawyer; their car barely ran; a trip to Indianapolis could cost them their only mode of transportation if it broke down. Becky couldn't miss classes or labs, and Will was working full time and wouldn't even be able to go to court. Becky vacillated their options and possible solutions. She found no corner of peace, no empty chamber for study. She went to school and returned home. There was no time for Robert.

"What surprises me," Becky said to Will the next day, "is that even after First Trust took our land, destroyed our subdivision, kicked us out of our home and the entire State of Indiana, they still want more! They still won't let us rest. Who would believe they could be so cruel?" Becky went into their bedroom and paced from their bed to the window and back again. She picked up her stuffed animal off her pillow and held it up between her hands asking, "What are we going to do, Angel? Mommy doesn't know what to do."

The children came home from school. Becky dutifully cooked them dinner. She spoke to Will as she stirred a pot of homemade stew. "We can't get on with our lives for anything. I've had it, Will. I feel like I'm going crazy!"

"What are you saying, Becky? You don't think we can do anything? Are we stuck?"

"I don't know, but like 'ole Charlie always said, those son-of-a-bitches shouldn't get away with this!" she said. Once again a force outside of their invention or control was disrupting her family. The inability to move forward in their lives with any degree of freedom or certainty destroyed all sense of normalcy, again.

That evening and the morning of the fourth day Becky tried to ignore the feeling of pending doom. She got up like she always did, got right to business, and worked with Will to get the children off to school. She didn't speak with her usual enthusiasm, though, and when she took the butter out of the refrigerator to spread on the toast, her mind was struggling with how she would respond to their Adversary Proceeding. She was going through the motions, but her mind was somewhere else.

Maybe it is a moot point—maybe there is a statute of limitations to how long they can drag this out, Becky thought, as she gathered the children's lunchboxes and set them on the banister.

As she pulled the covers back to make the beds, she was trying to figure out what kind of damage might have been done to their abandoned house in Indiana and who may have done the damage.

Becky made sure that the kids ate breakfast and that they had all of their homework shoved into their backpacks. She kissed them goodbye and ran upstairs to finish getting herself ready to go. Will had already left for work.

The apartment was empty and quiet, but her mind was cluttered with noise. Becky shook her head in pity of herself and their situation—the disbelief, as she thought about the vast number of people she figured put on a veil of calm and peace every day and were able to carry on even though inside they were falling apart in a million directions.

Just think, I could turn on Mozart, lie on the floor, eat fresh raspberries by the thousands, and sink away into oblivion. I don't have any problems. Or better yet, I could bang away at the piano and let my mind carry me to a riverboat on the Thames. Hell, I could go dancing in Jamaica. I could drive to Indianapolis and shoot two ruthless liars in the head. No, I know. Take away everything they value, make up lies about them to the press, and make them suffer like us. Take away their law degrees and make it so they can never practice law again, make them have to let go of the career they worked so hard to achieve, and have nothing left in the bank to help. "God, please help me," Becky cried out loud and fell to her knees, hands clasped in prayer. "They're making me crazy." She started to cry. Where was the strength that Becky needed so desperately to rely on? *How can I be so weak? How can I let them affect me so much?*

She got up, put on her white lab jacket and left for school. She knew the importance of not being late for lectures. Any information that she missed could hamper her ability down the road as a physician to give the best treatment to her patients. She hopped on her bike and raced like the wind with her troubles to her back. *Keep focused*, she told herself, *keep focused, everything will work out.*

She rounded the last curve and glided up the sidewalk to the bike rail, got off the seat, put the stand down, locked her bike to the rail, and swung her backpack over her right shoulder in methodical routine. As she entered through the front doors of the old, red brick building she looked overhead and reread the words she had seen a hundred times before: "MEDICAL SCHOOL." The words meant much to her, deep down inside to reaches few could ever understand. Yet as she looked them over today, they were not words that were taken for granted as when she passed under them every other day. Today she looked at each letter.

As she entered the lab, the instructor was just beginning to lecture. "Today we're going to look at the spinal accessory and musculocutaneous nerves," said the sixty-some-year-old professor, who also had been the Assistant County Coroner for many years. "We will also need to look at the muscles that they innervate and the actions of the muscles, same format as before. For instance, on the pectoral girdle about each axis through the sternoclavicular joint, or each axis through the shoulder joint, please see 'Moores' reference, page 209 in your lab manual." The professor was speaking rapidly. "Make sure you can identify the brachial plexus and note the bifurcation." It was not out of the ordinary for the lecturer to speak quickly, but today, Becky couldn't keep up. Her notes were sloppy, and she had big circles drawn where she had missed what he had said completely. For all she knew, the actions of the muscles at the interphalangeal and metacarpophalangeal joints were to be decided by a judge. The opponuns pollicis were not thenar muscles—they were the opponents in the action about policies never written!

They are liars—all of them—liars!

Becky threw down her scalpel, slapped down her pen, and closed her book. She turned away from the professor and her cadaver and walked away from everything that represented her life goals, her success, and her personal satisfaction. *God, please help me. What am I doing*?

Becky began to cry as she started to leave the room, then began to sob uncontrollably as she walked past the clay models that were to be used for the next day's test. She walked past the desk where she usually sat every day for hours of lectures. She glanced up to the board and caught a glimpse of the all-familiar writing of Professor Laska, the notes for the afternoon's lecture that she would miss. She cried some more and put her head down, looking at the floor as she continued to walk. *Go back in—no one will question your tears—everyone has had his or her moment. Just walk quietly back into the room, pick up your scalpel, and get the notes you missed from someone later on. It's not too late. You're just having a hard day. No, you have to quit. You don't have a choice. You have to fight the allegations—justice will not stand alone.* Her options juggled in her head as she walked out the front door of the medical building. She didn't look back!

Becky couldn't discuss her decision that day. She was angry. She was bitter at Will for not having alternative answers for her. She couldn't face Robert. She felt cheated. She wanted to study medicine, not law! She questioned God for leading her down a path that she didn't understand. *Why would He take away my dream? Why would He want me to study in the law library, rather than the medical library?* Her questions didn't come with answers.

Becky remained sullen for days. The children had no idea what was wrong with their mother, who had not been attending class but instead cleaned the apartment a lot and cooked more. Becky did the best she could to give them the impression that everything was fine.

She wanted to talk with Robert about her decision, but she didn't want him to pass judgment on her. He would try to dissuade her from making what he would call a rash decision. After all, he was a doctor, and he had told Becky he was looking forward to spending time together studying and preparing for board exams. Her matriculation would be his dream, too.

Chapter Seventeen

Two more days passed before she was able to talk about what she had done. Becky woke up late with the sun in her eyes. As she lay in bed, Will entered the room. "Aren't you getting up today?" he asked. Becky just looked him over and didn't reply.

"Didn't you hear me? Aren't you getting up?" Will repeated. Becky took her arms out from under the sheet, putting one up and bending it over her eyes. As Will leaned over and tied his shoes, he said, "Well, I have a lot to do, and I'm sure you do, too. Not much will get done under them sheets."

Will had seemed unimpressed with the fact that Becky left medical school and made no mention of the culmination of the years of work she had put in to get there or the disappointment she must have been feeling. His insensitivity made Becky feel ill, and it propelled her further toward Robert. As she lay there listening to Will, she looked around and wondered where she was—where she had come in thirty some years. Her stone cold, emotional block helped her through the transition. She would survive this disappointment like she had other disappointment—work harder, do more, accept what you've got, and do the best with it.

The next day Becky forced herself out of bed by 6:00 a.m. and did motherly duties until the children left for school and the apartment was empty again. Then she grabbed all of her white lab jackets off the hangers in her closet, picked up her light blue case of dissecting tools from off her dresser, and shoved everything into the back corner on the floor of her closet. She did not want to see them or anything right then that reminded her of her pain and sacrifice.

I'll just have to do what I have to do, she thought, as she took out the phone book and looked up the number for the law library. She dialed the number. The receptionist answered and gave her the directions she requested. She hung up the phone, grabbed "the letter," a writing tablet, and two pens—an extra one in case one ran out of ink. She would not want to use a law school pen. She felt defiant, and was micromanaging the only things she could control—the pens she used had to be hers! No pens from the medical school, either.

The air was different today. Not because of the weather or an act of Mother Nature. It was different because Becky's mindset was different. She tried to breathe a breath of indifference, but it almost choked her.

Becky knew she needed to refocus, and she fought the idea of needing to focus on law. She needed to be serious and strong, because she was not going to simply respond to the Adversary Proceedings. She had finally had enough, and she was planning to file a petition for fraud against First Trust Mortgage. She wanted to be thinking and breathing medicine, but like a quick-change artist, she would be a lawyer now. *I don't want to do this today. I hate this. I'm not happy. I am driving to the law library. How awful! I don't want to do this but I have to.* Her hands gripped the steering wheel tightly, and she stared straight forward.

She drove the same route that she usually used when riding her bike to school, but today she drove her car, and she was reticent and sad. When she got to the corner of Ramsport and University, instead of heading left like she usually did to park her bike at the medical school grid, she veered off to the right. Reluctantly, she parked in the lot where the sign read, "Reserved for Law Students." *Yuck!* She slammed the car door behind herself and walked with purpose toward the front door.

As she entered through the dungeon-like doors, a smell like the musty, spider-web hollows of a haunted mansion slapped her in the face. *It sure didn't smell like this in medical school,* thought Becky, *no preservatives or cold drafts from air-conditioning*. Here, the smell was of old books—musty old books—permeating every nose hair. There were thousands of books, and Becky looked at her feet where the first shelf began and her eyes followed the books up as her head tilted back to the top shelf. *Every constitutional case ever tried over the last two hundred years and the musty old people who read them,* she thought to herself. Becky would soon come to realize that the multitude of foes she had identified that day would soon become her friends as they revealed to her a judicial system that worked—at least most of the time.

Becky looked up, down, and all around at the tens of thousands of books, stacks of shelves in many rooms and on many floors and thought, *Oh, where do I start?* She looked over the people reading books. Men who wore suspenders and big bow ties. *Get a grip! What showboat are you on?*

Becky walked up to the front desk. "Can anyone here tell me where I can look up the definition of fraud?" she asked one of the two women behind the desk. They ignored her. "Hey, I'm not asking where the key is to start the Titanic. I would like some help, please." One of the women looked hardly out of high school. The other one was a matronly looking woman who Becky mused needed a date and, from her condescending look, Becky couldn't have cared less how rude she was to her.

Becky felt cynical, yes, and she felt hateful and full of frustration. She couldn't help but think how these two women were acting just like Will. *If you ignore something, it will go away, right? It doesn't exist. Hey, you, straighten up and do your job,* she thought, and then she rephrased her question. "Can either of you two direct me to a reference book that would encompass the subject of fraud?" She was to soon learn that rephrasing questions would become second nature to her, as it would be prudent to her courtroom success.

This got their attention. They led her to the second floor of what appeared to be a separate building, passing through what seemed like a tunnel where some of the books were actually locked in cages. The darkened little alcove housed books that were categorized into different states and contained applicable state laws that were identified differently from federal laws. She was directed down two long, narrow corridors and through another maze of bookshelves. The matronly woman didn't talk, just walked and pointed.

The myriad of texts let Becky know from the outset that what she was trying to accomplish without training was going to be like using a cookbook to perform surgery. Again, she questioned what she was doing. She had no choice. First Trust Mortgage had given her no other alternative. She was broke and, in America, if you have a legal problem, the only way you can quest after justice is to either have lots of money and be willing to lose it all, accept defeat, or fight for justice yourself.

After considerable time had passed, Becky was able to find what she had been searching for, a definition for fraud. However, the first book presented only a vague and shortened description. One book led her to another and to another. She took notes as she went and continued to write all morning, citing text, pages, and paragraphs from which she had made notes. She stacked up several books that had paragraphs she wanted to photocopy. She looked for a copy machine room and, by the end of the day, she had copied about two hundred pages.

She befriended a library clerk who seemed to know what he was talking about whenever Becky had a question. The clerk shared ideas as to how she might look into other related topics, and he helped her search out more of the legal procedures for the State of Indiana. Becky continued to research the elements of fraud that she would have to prove, and she reviewed the format in which to submit them.

She wandered around trying to find a book or procedural manual that would explain how to go about filing a lawsuit, but couldn't find one, so she decided to call it quits for the day and went home to make a few phone calls. When Becky left the law library, she knew she would not have time to learn the system before she used it. There were time limits on how long she had to respond to each pleading, a fact she had picked up on that day. She didn't even have the time to figure out how much time she had. Everything was going to have to be done now, which meant she would have to learn as she went along. There was no quick-fix way to learn about laws and legal procedures. Everything took time to read, and everything she read would take time to process and comprehend. A trial with no law school would be brutal.

By the time she got home it was after 3:00 p.m. The children were almost done with school for the day. She made her calls before they arrived home. She did not want them upset by having to listen to her being upset as she was trying to figure out the legal system in a state nearly four hundred miles away. She was only too aware that the intonations of strained uncertainty would illuminate her fears and anxiety.

Becky's first call was made to Directory Assistance for the Indianapolis City-Country Building. *I guess this is where the courtroom would be,* she thought. The State courts were there, but the Federal courts were in another building. She needed to figure out was which court she would need to file in.

After a few operators telling her, "Just a moment, I'll connect you," or "Hold on please, I'll transfer you," she finally got her answers. She would later find out that even the decision of where she chose to file would be challenged. The clerk asked, "Will you be filing your case civil plenary or civil tort?" Up to now, Becky thought that tortes were only something to eat. Nothing was easy or straightforward.

Everything she did pointed to the notion that she was indeed on foreign soil, treading perhaps where she didn't belong. Yet she persevered methodically. It would have been easier and probably the most logical thing for Becky to just throw her hands up and say, "Well, I tried, but this is ridiculous. Will, this is your problem too—you handle it. Somebody handle it—anyone but me."

That evening Becky sat in her favorite chair with an amber colored light behind her and thought to herself how not much time had passed since she had walked out of the medical school lab, and again she questioned whether or not she had made the right decision. *If I went back to school, I'd be so behind in information.* Yet her decision to return seemed more desirable, almost reciprocal to every hour spent on the lawsuit, yet more improbable. Like a timeline that starts at zero—one point moving in the positive direction, and the other moving in the negative direction—and further apart with each move. *I've made my decision. Now even if it kills me, I'm sticking with it. Hmm,* Becky thought, *to die for justice.*

Robert was in a state of denial. After frantic pages and an arranged meeting, Becky finally had told him her decision. He did everything he could to side with her so that perhaps she would ultimately feel in control of her situation and return to class. He offered to go to the law library with her and hoped that surely she was just taking a short leave of absence. He watched her as she pulled book after book off the shelves and stacked some in his arms and the rest in her own arms. He followed her as she got change from the receptionist and exchanged the dollar bills for credit to use the copy machine. He helped her hold the books open while she made copies of pertinent case law. Robert's hand got in the way once and, without realizing it, she copied that, too. She didn't laugh nor was she flirtatiously amused. Hurriedly, she piled up the books on the return cart and told Robert she was finished and that she was going to leave now. The tone in her voice was indifferent. She was focused on her task, and there was no room for emotion. He tried to convince her that as soon as she took care of the "legal thing," as he called it, she should get right back to her studies. "Yeah, well right now I've got too much to do," Becky told him.

By the morning of the third day post "the letter," Becky had drafted her final copy. She had been up half the night. By noon, the original petition was done. Becky raced to the post office to have it sent by overnight mail to the Marion, Indiana, County Clerk. She enclosed a money order that she had purchased to cover the mandatory filing fees. The only thing she had left to do now was to drive to Indianapolis, look at the house that she believed First Trust Mortgage had damaged, get the police to make a report, and respond to the Adversary Proceeding. Becky was organized and had figured out that to work within the legal system and be good at what she was doing, she had to think two steps ahead of her opponent. She had *not* figured out, however, whether the Court would send a stamped copy of her petition to the defendants once a case number was assigned, or whether she needed to send the defendants a copy right away herself. It would be the small procedural details that consistently proved an annoyance to her. She went over what she'd taught herself and checked things off on her list as she stood in line to mail her petition return receipt requested. *Let's see, everyone listed in a complaint needs to be served with all the papers, but who serves the papers?* She called the Court but all of the people she spoke to on the phone told her the same thing—"We're not authorized to give legal advice; we cannot answer that question." Becky tried to convince them that her question did not require any legal interpretations, but nonetheless, they wouldn't comply.

Becky decided to send the defendants a copy without a case number and then again when one had been assigned—just to be sure. She was bound and determined to cross every "t" and dot every "i." In bold letters the transcript read: "Petition for Damages Induced by Fraud."

"Comes now William D. Blaine and Rebecca A. Blaine, Plaintiffs herein, *pro se* and for their petition for damages induced by fraud by the defendants, First Trust Mortgage. Plaintiffs were at all times mentioned in this complaint, residents of Marion County, State of Indiana. Defendant is, and at all times mentioned in this complaint, a resident of Marion Country, State of Indiana. On March 8, 1990, Plaintiffs and Defendant entered into a contract for the purpose of executing a mortgage on a house and one lot in the Canal Estates Subdivision. A copy of the contract is attached hereto and incorporated herein as Exhibit A. While Plaintiffs and Defendant were negotiating the contract described above, Defendant represented to Plaintiffs that the mortgage would be for a house on one lot as described in the legal description provided to First Trust Mortgage, by Coston Engineering. A copy of the legal description is attached to this complaint, marked Exhibit B, and incorporated by reference. The mortgage executed by William D. Blaine and Rebecca A. Blaine to First Trust Mortgage, was procured by fraud and or misrepresentation. The representations mentioned above were false when Defendant made them in that when the Plaintiffs were made aware that the mortgage had been placed on twelve lots and not just one, it was realized that the original legal description provided to First Trust Mortgage, attached and incorporated herein as Exhibit B, was not used to execute the mortgage loan, but in fact a legal description describing the entire subdivision had been used in its place. A copy of this legal description is shown on the front page of Exhibit A. During the time the Plaintiffs and Defendant were negotiating the mortgage of the house and one lot, the Plaintiffs made it clear to the Defendant, and the Defendant fully understood the purpose for which the Plaintiffs were entering into the mortgage. During the course of negotiations, the Plaintiffs and Defendant inspected the land and the Plaintiffs pointed out the boundaries of the lot to the Defendant. At the time the Defendant made the representations mentioned above, the Defendant knew they were false or the Defendant made the representations mentioned above with a reckless disregard for their truth or falsity. The Plaintiffs, relying on the representations above, and believing them to be true, did enter into a mortgage agreement with First Trust Mortgage. Immediately on Plaintiffs' discovery of fraud, the Plaintiffs notified the Defendant of the matters set out above and requested that the errors be corrected, but the Defendant refused to do so. As a direct and proximate result of the wrongful and fraudulent charges set out above, the Plaintiffs have been damaged in the sum of $1,200,000.00. Wherefore, Plaintiffs pray that the Court establish a debt against First Trust Mortgage, in the above sum, and for all the relief just and proper in the premises, and that the matter be set for hearing at the Court's earliest convenience. Respectfully submitted, William D. Blaine and Rebecca A. Blaine, Plaintiffs."

Becky sealed the 8-½" x 11" manila envelope, dropped it in the "out-of-town" slot, turned around, and left the building.

Becky soon found out that legal problems are like health problems: once you're involved, your life, as you know it, changes. Being involved in a lawsuit was like being afflicted with an illness. Her stomach ached. She threw up a lot. She had frequent headaches, and she seemed distant at times with the children, or at least she thought so. She'd be listening to them, but sort of looking through them, not at them. Quality of life, as she knew it, only two weeks post letter, no longer existed. Every decision she made for herself or her family became reliant on and fell victim to the defendants' motions and a courtroom's calendar. Vacation plans, how to spend Easter Sunday, doctor appointments, and even birthday parties, were entirely dictated by the timetables of when a brief was due, when a response to the defendants' motion was due, or when the judge had a trial date or a status conference set.

Chapter Eighteen

In the quiet of the morning Becky sat. Waiting. Waiting had become a way of life now. She waited for anything that might come in the mail and was sickened with the thought of what First Trust Mortgage would come up with. She actually feared the mailman. Just seeing his truck heading toward her mailbox gave her a cold sweat. She'd hyperventilate on her way to retrieve what he'd left. Her life seemed on hold during this time, yet it was moving. Her daily living evolved around the litigation, and her moods were dependent on it. She desperately tried to work past the effects, but she felt suspended, surreal, like she was a character in a screenplay. She loved being with her children. They were her unchanged, lifelong passion and commitment, but when she was with them, most of her smiles were intentionally drawn. She begged herself for spontaneity, but preoccupation colored it over, and joy had become a deliberate and solicited emotion. She could still see beauty and feel love, but the genuine freedom of the senses was tainted by oppression.

As the mist of the morning rose to the newness of the day, things around her seemed the same as the day before and the day before that. The panic and frustration stayed with her. Becky was rarely able to let her guard down. She would often look for distraction by immersing herself nature, like she used to in what seemed ages ago, taking time to cherish the bunny that came into their yard to eat clover, and the happy, little pansy faces blooming in the pot by the front door. Oh, how she yearned to feel content and peaceful like the beauty of the earth, but as much as she wanted to, she couldn't. She always fell back in. She had to. Like a chain saw cutting through a large piece of timber, the noise was there, and the chain would cut with determination until it went all the way through.

The afternoon mail came—the daily anticipation she couldn't ignore. *What would First Trust Mortgage try next,* she thought, flipping through the envelopes. Would the next letter raise the one issue she couldn't overcome? As she prayed for wisdom and strength, her esophagus became inflamed, and she had to work at keeping her coffee down. *Damn them for doing this to me, to us.* Her body, the human tomb that housed her soul, stood erect on the corner until each piece had been sorted. Her mind was numb. She barely knew where she was these days, rifted into survival at best.

The next day, again, Becky was aware and could feel her feet take every step as she approached the mailbox. She moved closer and closer, one foot in front of the other. *God, what will it be this time?* She slowly reached forward to open the box. *Lord, please be with me. Help me not to swear, help me be good, and help me to know I'm doing the right thing.* She retrieved the envelopes and opened the letter. There it was. *I knew there would be another one.* It had been eighteen days since she had filed her petition, and she knew they would come back at her with something. "They want to fine me now for trying a frivolous action," Becky yelled out loud, slapping her hand on her leg. "How can they say this is frivolous? First they take our land," Becky said to herself as she walked back to the apartment. "They rob us of our home, and now they are trying to throw us out on the street!" She gestured to emphasize her point. "They left us penniless! *Frivolous?* Those bastards!"

Once inside, she threw the mail down on the kitchen counter, and tried to calm herself. She knew she had to leave soon to pick up the children from school, and she needed to stay levelheaded. Read and research while the house was quiet. It was difficult to hold her emotions still. She would strangle the lawyers if she could. *Calm down,* she told herself over and over. But her sense of rage made her feel out of control. She paced back and forth in front of the couch and looked out the side windows as if looking into the distance would somehow take her there—anywhere but here. She felt panicky about what to do. Then it came to her.

I know, she thought, *I'll call the law library down in Indianapolis and ask them to read me the legal components of 'frivolous'. Then I can begin to dispel the elements.* Becky called, and even though the staff lectured the usual "No legal advice," they read to her what she wanted to know.

That night after the children went to bed, Becky sat down and, sentence by sentence, began to form the outline of her response. The war had been waged. She loaded her ammo and steadied her guns. *Type. Think. Type.*

It was almost midnight by the time she had finished her draft. Becky estimated that it would take another three hours to complete a final form. She had put in the equivalent of a day's work since she had helped the children with their homework and read the youngest two a bedtime story. *Time, always passing too quickly, and never enough of it.*

She got up from the computer that was on a table by Beth's bed, used the bathroom, and returned to the table. With grueling and painstaking intensity she typed, looking every now and then at Beth to make sure she wasn't interrupting her sleep. The printer was old and very loud. Becky despised having to use Beth's room, but the apartment was too small to put the computer and printer anywhere else. Becky was close to finishing her response to their allegations of frivolity—it was almost 3:00 a.m. *One thing at a time,* Becky told herself, *like in baseball. Try to hit each one as it comes. Stay focused on the one small thing coming at you.*

Beth stirred. "Mom, do you have to do that now?" she moaned. "I never get to sleep anymore. Do you realize that? You're always in here. How much longer do you have to do this?"

"I know, Beth. I'm sorry. I'm doing the best I can! I know it's hard for you to understand, but I have to do this. I don't have a choice. It will be over soon," Becky said. At least she hoped it would.

But the minutes were always hours. Becky dampened her voice in an effort to camouflage the anger she felt inside, her feelings wanting to spill all over as to how life had betrayed her. She continued to desperately work to protect the children from the effects of her own personal nightmare. It took discipline to master because her anger, frustration, and fear were always in the forefront.

She retrieved the twelve-page document up onto the screen one last time to run the spell check function. She glanced over to look at her precious daughter's face. Beth had drifted back to sleep. *So innocent.* Becky wanted to preserve the moment forever. As she stared at her, the picture of her sleeping child quickly disappeared into the face of the computer she'd come to know so well. She had a job to do.

"Damn, don't screw up now," Becky cursed out loud, as she slammed her fist onto the printer, which jammed as she tried to print her work. *Every time I'm in a hurry, this damn computer acts up.* Sometimes it would take hours of pushing, pulling, resetting, and readjusting to get it back on track. She rubbed her eyes. Her back ached. She put her left hand against her back and leaned on the desk, then leaned back against the wall and sighed.

The night was scripted. One thing first, followed by the next; each step was a challenge. Finally, the last correction was in place. "Cross your fingers," she whispered. *I hope I saved all the corrections,* Becky thought, eyelids half-closed. She could barely see the words on the screen.

Robert—no time to think about Robert now. But I need him. I can't have him. I want to see him. I want to hold him. She needed to be held in the protective arms of someone who would give her relief. But she was too busy that night or any other night since she had left school. Robert was like a cloud being blown away by a storm.

Becky fell asleep for about an hour, and then forced herself awake so she could head for Indianapolis. There were loose ends to tie up about the Adversary Proceeding, including how to dispel the issue of damages. The secondary claim that had followed in the mail accused Becky and Will of vandalizing the gray house, and there had been a status conference set that she had not attended. For some reason by the time she got notice, the meeting at already taken place.

Becky ran her fingers through the clothes in her closet, quickly selected a couple of outfits, and shoved them into an overnight bag. The she grabbed a suit and her toothbrush. As she went through the motions she was thinking of different scenarios as to what she'd be up against when she got to Indianapolis. She knew she'd see the gray house, and she was afraid of what it would look like.

She loved that house. She and Will had spent much blood, sweat, and tears in it. *Who would vandalize it and why? Maybe First Trust Mortgage did it so they could collect on insurance. Maybe McGruders did it so no one would want to spend the money to fix it up and then they could buy the property cheap at a sheriff's sale.*

McGruders always wanted our property. Maybe they had set the fire thinking Will would sell the land then.

Becky tiptoed into the boys' room and kissed them goodbye. Will was sleeping, and she scribbled a note and left it on his nightstand, reminding him that she would be staying with her friend Debbie and that Sarah, a neighbor, would pick the kids up after school. She grabbed her camera, papers, and bag, kissed Beth, and headed out the door. Quietly into the night she was on her way. The remainder of night's darkness was not long, but the trip was—daylight was only a couple of hours away. The road was lonely. Becky had taught herself to find comfort in her loneliness, though. How could she feel so empty, yet so full?

She had hours to think now with no distraction. As her eyes tired and the hum of the road made her even drowsier, she drifted back to her children. Their sleeping faces were so peaceful when she kissed them goodbye. Her body ached for normalcy, and she just wanted to go to bed so badly. *When will this nightmare end?* Could she ever wake up and find herself really living again? No, this was living. This was life. It was a dream that had turned into a nightmare! But it *was* life. *Move on. Get to it. Be diligent,* she told herself, and her foot pressed harder on the accelerator.

What will my next move be? How can I get First Trust Mortgage to produce the evidence that they're hiding? If only I had the original loan application and the appraisal, I could easily prove our intent with the mortgage and the fact that they were aware of our intent. She vacillated between three issues: their allegation of Willful and Malicious Damages through the Adversary Proceeding, her Petition for Fraud, and their Motion to Dismiss the case as frivolous. The headlights of passing trucks and semis made her tired head ache, and her eyes were becoming sensitive to them.

She knew in her heart that getting First Trust Mortgage to produce either document would reveal the truth. Then, the case would be easy, uncomplicated, and straightforward. She had phoned First Trust Mortgage and requested copies of the original loan application and the appraisal and even arranged a time to pick them up. But they didn't cooperate. They told her they had lost those papers.

Becky thought about Robert. *Dare I trust the music of the night?* She turned on the radio, and the night sky gave way to the sunrise that came just in time to help her stay awake. Her tiredness had taken away the boundaries of rational thought, and she drifted with boredom, becoming philosophical as she passed the time. Where had she been all her life? Where was she now? Where would she go? Why? Again, Becky reflected on the dream she had when she was younger. *Don't start this again,* she told herself, but her mind wouldn't stop. *It would be a perfect life.* Her husband would be a doctor; she would be a PTA mother. They would have five children. They would enjoy the fresh blossoms of spring and the gentle snowfalls of winter. They would have a perfect home.

I couldn't take the abuse. Leave it at that. Quit analyzing. Almost like her life was passing before her, she bounced around its entirety. *How had the fire started?* Becky had no reason to question Will about moving many of their things out of the farmhouse and into a safe place as he prepared the house for remodeling and before he tore out the walls. "After all, you don't want dust, drywall, paint, and sawdust all over everything," Will had told her.

But the question still haunted her. Where had Will gone for so long that night during dinner? The length of his absence had not been challenged. *He probably used the restroom after he called the sitter to check on the kids.* Becky, Mark, and Linda had continued talking while he was gone, she went over again in her mind. But now that she was thinking about it again, Will seemed different when he returned to the table. Becky had a perception about that. She had a sixth sense about many things. *No,* she told herself, *I'm just tired, and the long trip is starting to mess with my mind.*

Becky had been in shock for months after the fire. She had too many details to think about, and the Fire Chief had been satisfied with the origin of the fire. She had focused on keeping her family feeling secure and adjusted through the obscurity. She didn't need to think about anything else. *Until the sheriff showed up that one day. What was all that about*? Becky hadn't thought about that in over a year. And Will shrugged it off. Was her real challenge to prove criminal fraud against an international company, or should she be spending more time analyzing the other half of her marriage? *What if Will did set the fire?* She would have to leave him, of course, but then her perfect family she had worked so hard to create would be destroyed. No—she would have no more of that idea. *What am I thinking? Will didn't start the fire. McGruders probably did. They knew we were gone that night. Oh heck, no one started the fire. The Fire Chief was right—it was an accident.* Just leave it at that. *Quit thinking about it.* Her imagination was wearing her out.

Becky arrived at Debbie's house shortly after 10:00 with just enough time to shower, clean up, and head for the courthouse. It had been an arduous journey, but she had made good time. Now if she could just survive the rest of the day. Becky was ready though, fired up, and on a roll. After a cordial hello, Debbie told her, "I wish you'd slow down and be able to sit down long enough to have a cup of coffee with me and catch up on things a little." She also told Becky she should buy a briefcase after she saw that Becky was carrying around a grocery sack with all her papers in it.

Becky sat down on the vestibule chair and put on her tan work boots, lacing them up tight. She said, "You know, when the day comes that you work your field, and you got a problem with your land, and you can't just walk off you land and defend yourself—that's the day the system will collapse around you. My work boots and grocery sack will have to do. I'm not going to change my appearance or my demeanor just to come off like someone perceives I should—how they see me is how they get me!" She picked up the remaining papers she had on Debbie's dining room table and added them to the sack. "Come on Deb, let's go. Thanks for going in to work late." The two of them left, each getting into her own car at the same time.

It was Becky's first day in court. She showed her pictures of the gray house to the judge, and she told her story, simply and straight-forward, that they had run out of money because they couldn't sell lots in their subdivision and, as a result, they filed bankruptcy and lost their house. She did not revisit the details of the bankruptcy because the bankruptcy hearing was over, and her allegation as plaintiff would be heard in a tort action two floors up and two months later. But Becky used the opportunity to ask deliberate questions of the lenders that she could use later to trap them in their lies.

"So, when you first noticed our house had been damaged, it was the day you were there to take down the realty signs on the other lots, right?" Becky asked because she expected them to say yes. Charlie and Ruby had told Becky that they saw First Trust's employees removing the signs, the same employees Becky had introduced them to when they met to get financing. Charlie and Ruby made it their business to keep an eye on the gray house after the Blaines left.

The mortgage banker answered right on cue, "Yes, I mean"

"Objection Your Honor," First Trust's lawyer chimed in, "objection as to the relevance of the question. We're here because the Blaines tore up the house we were foreclosing on, not over whether or not some signs were removed off the property we hold title to."

But Becky didn't care what the lawyer's response was. She had gotten First Trust to admit on tape that they had removed realty signs – therefore they knowingly and fraudulently encumbered the incorrect parcel of land. The plaintiffs continued to try and beat her down with lies, and they scoffed at her, but the judge reprimanded them by saying, "That'll be enough. She seems to be batting a thousand so far."

Becky prevailed that day. Her first major victory. She had proved beyond a reasonable doubt that she and Will had nothing to do with the damage that had been done to the house after they left town. First Trust Mortgage was found to be negligent by not securing the house properly after the Blaines left. Vandals and kids drinking beer had probably been the cause, according to the police report that had been filed per Becky's request after she had received notice of the allegation. The police had taken pictures of the beer cans and cigarette holes in the carpet. Thus, it was deemed the cause on record with the court. Now there was only one remaining issued to be tried—her case of fraud against First Trust Mortgage.

On the way out of the courtroom, First Trust's lawyer spoke to Debbie, who had decided not to stay at work that day and surprised Becky by showing up in court to give her support. "I'm going to kick your friend's ass!" the lawyer said to Deb. Becky said nothing, but put it in the back of her mind, as she knew she would use his remark and many of their remarks against her and Will later. *Keep it up, you jerks. The next time I see you in court, you'll rue the day!*

Becky couldn't drive back to Wisconsin that night. She was spent. But she did call Will from Debbie's house and told him how things had gone, and asked how the kids were. Will didn't seem impressed. He took it for granted that she'd win, Becky guessed. Debbie tried to convince Becky that Will had never understood the magnitude of the problem. That night after Debbie's two sons went to bed, the two women sat together and ate popcorn and drank wine. Becky never mentioned Robert to her best friend, because she didn't think about Robert that night, and on her long ride home the next morning she was surprised she hadn't.

Chapter Nineteen

It was becoming more and more difficult for Becky and Robert to find time to be alone together, not just because of the lawsuit, but because Robert's wife seemed to be around him more and more and she was showing signs of jealousy. It seemed obvious whenever Becky was around that Ruth was sick of the way she saw her husband and Becky interact.

Ruth worked at her relationship with Robert, but it was not natural for her to do so. She arranged for them to go to a bed and breakfast, out to dinner, movies, and massage appointments for two, according to what Robert told Becky on the phone. But it was a failure for two people only pretending to be in love. Robert still wanted Becky.

Will, on the other hand, did not seem to care about his marriage to Becky, or at least that was what Becky thought, because they didn't do anything together, their communication was nil, and they each felt no respect towards each other. Becky didn't have time to spend with either of them, nor did she want to.

Robert began planning his semiannual three-week trip to Latvia, where he had told Becky he performed clinical trials. He wanted to see Becky before he left, so he paged her. She responded to his page and phoned him. "Becky," Robert said, "I feel so lost because we haven't seen each other lately, and now I'm leaving for three weeks. Is this the end, or what?"

"Bob, look," Becky said. This was the first time she had ever called him Bob. "We both have a tremendous amount of responsibilities, and those things come first."

"Will you come over here and give me a kiss, anyway?"

"Bob, I can't—with the way your wife has been creeping around you, I wouldn't put it past her to just show up there."

"She never comes to my office—you know that!"

"Well, she might now. She seems to be showing a newly found interest in you." Becky sarcastically continued, "She wants to know what you are doing and who you are doing it with all the time!

She even did rounds with you the other day, which by the way, you never told me about."

"How did you know that?"

"You know my friend Carol, who works on your floor? She saw me in the lunch line and told me."

Becky was trying to create tension to distance herself. The time that Becky had spent away from Robert, since she was no longer in school had shown her she didn't need him, nor did she want him.

Robert tried to assure Becky that Ruth's artificial pampering annoyed him, too, that he feigned acceptance of her affection, and harbored resentment whenever she showed up unexpectedly. But Becky could not take time to care about Ruth's drivel. She had enough anxiety in her life and knowing she was choosing to distance herself from Robert gave her a sense of power—power to know that alone she would be all right.

Robert became depressed, and he was confused as to how he could spend more time with Becky. Becky, on the other hand, continued to let go, even though at times she missed what a good listener he was, and how he had allowed her to pretend and dream again. The stress at home, dealing with the lawsuit, and the empty tomb of her marriage were difficult. The respite she would have if she and Robert could remain just friends who saw each other every now and then would be perfect. But for now, staying away was the best choice, and she chose to distract herself with responsibility and altruistic endeavors that made her feel good.

Becky joined a rowing club. She appreciated the sense of freedom on the water and the synchrony of the oars moving together, one stroke after another, like the steady rhythmic flow of notes coming together in a chorus. She practiced once a week and took the children with her when she did. Oddly enough, Will went along too, and she could see them all playing in the sand and water as she rowed offshore. When the club entered into a regatta, Becky had the opportunity to row in competition. So she gathered together a group of women, choosing the seven that were needed to complete the "women's eight," fun friends she had competed against in other local regattas who consistently rowed well. They took third at the Badger State Games, making Becky want to push harder. The outlet felt great. The team went on to the Chicago Sprints. During the race there, the coxswain's electronic speaker went dead, so Becky, rowing the four-seat, chimed in as a substitute in the middle where those in front and behind her could hear the orders and stay the course, and so no one would "catch a crab." The scull was propelled to victory.

Becky also wrote grants for the Wisconsin Children's Choir that Beth sang with to help sustain their fiscal responsibilities. She was nominated and elected as their Vice-President. She designed their brochures and programs and took the pictures used in the brochures. Becky enjoyed photography and how the process utilized her creativity. She had reclaimed her life and was finding pleasure in it without Robert or Will. She didn't let any dust settle under her feet, only in her house, for she found contentment in staying busy and helping other people.

That same fall, Becky worked with Hillary Clinton's Social Secretary and was able to secure an appointment for the church choir she put together to audition and eventually sing at the White House for Christmas. Becky asked her mother to join them, and it was a very special memory that the three generations enjoyed. Becky's mom sent her a copy of her hometown newspaper where they published the event on the front page with a big picture of Becky, Beth, and Grandma. As an encore performance, the Governor of Wisconsin invited them to perform at his Christmas party. Robert saw the write-up in the newspaper, and he called Becky to let her know how proud he was of her, somehow validating her, and she was surprised how good it made her feel. Will didn't seem impressed, and even though spouses were also invited to the Governor's Mansion, Will declined.

Robert had been back in the country for over a week and Becky didn't contact him. He paged her incessantly, but she did not respond. When Becky got home one afternoon, she was revisited by the same First Trust junk in the mail. They were at it again.

"The Defendants, by counsel, moves the Court pursuant to Trial Rule 12(B) (1), (2), (4), (5), and (6) of the Indiana Rules of Procedure, to dismiss the Plaintiff's complaint"—four new reasons outside of the first attack of frivolity and damage to the gray house. Becky had learned through reading that asking for a dismissal was almost always first-line defense, so at first the document didn't bother her. She continued to read the Defendant's Motion to Dismiss. "Listed as grounds for dismissal: the court lacks jurisdiction over the subject matter; the court lacks jurisdiction over the person of this Defendant; there is insufficiency of process and service of process as to this Defendant, and the Plaintiff's complaint fails to state a claim upon which relief can be granted pursuant to Trial Rule 17." *What does all this mean? Oh my God, help me.*

Although there were problems listed in the motion that would cause duress for Becky, she worked hard to stay confident that she could overcome. It was good that the Defendants pointed out she did not state a claim upon which relief could be granted. All along, the Defendants did not realize it, but every now and then they were actually helping Becky by inadvertently tipping her off to something she was missing or doing wrong. In this instance, she was required to cite the statute, and hadn't. Once First Trust Mortgage complained, she complied. It was no problem. She worked backwards many times, sometimes intentionally waiting for their response so that she knew in what direction she should go next. She often used their precise language, only in reverse order, trusting that they were more familiar with format and procedure than she was. The only difference was that when it came to citing statutes and presenting the Findings of Fact and Conclusions of Law, she had to make sure that they were cited as a direct result of *her* research and not *theirs*.

Becky went to the law library the next day and found what she was looking for by using her reverse order strategy. Robert happened to be there, too, which caught Becky off guard. She saw him reading behind a bookshelf not too far from where she stood. She only saw the top half of his face, but recognized him right away and walked over to him. "What are you doing here?" she asked.

"I needed to look up some information regarding a malpractice suit I'm testifying for," he said, and smiled at her as if tickled to see her, like he used to look at her when they would secretly meet. Becky showed busy indifference, yet asked as a friendly gesture, "How was your trip? How's Ruth?"

"Oh, the trip was rewarding," Robert said, "and Ruth is fine. Well, actually, she went to visit her mother while I was gone, and hasn't come back yet. The boys are staying at her brother's."

"Oh. Will wondered why the boys hadn't talked to Erin and Eli recently. Where does her brother live?"

"Not too far, but far enough that they can't ride the bus to school, so Ruth's brother drives them back and forth. I'm too busy to care for them alone, so they'll just stay there for now."

"Well, sorry Robert," she said. "I really don't have time to talk anymore. See you around, okay?" She turned and walked several sections over to continue her work.

She tried not to be distracted by Robert's proximity, as she looked up Trial Rule 17. She thought about how if it had been a few months earlier, she would be leaving the building with him. She continued to read so she would be able to understand what she needed to do to state a claim upon which relief could be granted. She took careful notes, eventually forgetting that Robert was there.

She left the library to call First Trust's home office in an attempt to determine how they could claim insufficiency of process and service of process. Since she had sent them Return Receipt Requested and had the signed return copy in her file. First Trust Mortgage did know she had mailed copies of documents to the defense counsel, but their counsel wrote as if they knew nothing. Becky figured good defense lawyers must use any tactic they can think of to tire and confuse the opposition. No one in the home office would give out any information, which didn't surprise Becky. She felt compelled to exhaust simple remedies first before playing detective. The lawyer who had claimed he wasn't on the case anymore wouldn't give her answers either, and Becky was running out of places to turn. Finally, she thought, *instead of trying to play their game, I'll invent one of my own.* So, instead of trying to figure out who should be sent her motions, she sent a copy to the counsel at the home office, past attorneys, and corporate heads. She also sent a letter and made reference to the court that no party had filed a formal motion to intervene, nor were there any substitutions filed. If there were misdeeds, she would use them against First Trust Mortgage later. Two months later she would figure out what they had done.

Finally, she needed to address the issue that the Court lacked jurisdiction. This claim would be trickier to prove in her favor. She knew in her heart that she was right—that she was entitled to bring suit in that Court, but she would need to locate the right statutes to substantiate her claim as a matter of law so the judge would dismiss their Motion to Dismiss. *Their motions, my motions, my motions, their motions.* Becky had motion sickness! And of course this meant that after she had all of her ducks in a row, she would need to file a formal response to their Motion to Dismiss and respond as soon as possible, because again, she did not technically know how long she had to respond. She worked as fast and hard as she could. Everything she typed and processed was sent via overnight mail with return receipt requested, even when she really did not have the money to do so. Her family scrimped and saved change for postage and gas money.

Becky questioned herself as to who might have jurisdiction if it wasn't the Superior Court. Then she remembered that her and Will's bankruptcy had taken place in another courthouse, a Federal courthouse. *Maybe the Defendants contend that this claim is still part of the bankruptcy,* Becky thought. It should not have been because they had waited until the bankruptcy was discharged and had been ruled a "no asset case" before she filed the lawsuit. But, nonetheless, she thought perhaps there was something she missed. *Maybe the bankruptcy trustee had put an end to any pending or future litigation.* If so, her lawsuit would be meaningless. She figured something like double jeopardy would preclude her from trying her case. Becky knew she had made it clear to the trustee during their bankruptcy proceedings that she had intended to look into litigation, and she remembered that the trustee had said he looked to see whether the claim was worth going after. In the end, he had declared it a no asset bankruptcy.

She called the bankruptcy court clerk to see what was on file. The clerk brought up several things. One was that Becky needed to know whether all facts about pending litigation had been brought up before the bankruptcy Judge and how she could prove that. If they had been, and if she could prove it, the jurisdiction would fall back to them. Becky was relieved to find the answer was yes because this meant she did have a case outside of the bankruptcy court. Another issue was that all facts had to have been disclosed to the bankruptcy judge, or future settlements would need to be awarded to the bankruptcy court and distributed to creditors, and the jurisdiction would therefore be in the bankruptcy court. All facts were in order and available as evidence, so Becky proceeded to create her reply brief.

Becky thought again how unfair it would be if her complaint were dismissed as frivolous. It had merit to her. Becky felt weak as she contemplated the possibility of defeat, not only for what it would mean emotionally, but also if they did, she'd probably end up having to pay First Trust's legal fees and expenses. She felt the risk was worth taking.

The clerk told her he thought they had enumerated everything, but just to make sure, he said she should obtain a copy of the bankruptcy hearing—a tape-recording of it—and have it transcribed. Becky shook her head that nothing came her way easily. Even without the cost of a lawyer, gas, transcription costs, photocopies, and postal charges were more than the Blaines could afford. Nightly, Will and Becky sat figuring and refiguring their meager budget to see if they could continue with the lawsuit. The unsettling possibility of defeat and being stuck with the Defendants' legal fees was a continual risk. They consistently weighed all the facts, and that was about the only time the two of them discussed the trial together.

The clerk further stated to Becky that the determination as to whether or not the bankruptcy Trustee would have tried the case could only be made by the trustee directly, as he was the one who stood to make a percentage of any assets forthcoming, and that Becky should read what he had written in the record. Becky followed up on her conversation with a phone call to her bankruptcy lawyer to see if he had disclosed all relevant information she was referring to at the last hearing. Then she asked him if he could fax her a copy of what was in the record. He told her he thought they had indeed enumerated everything, but just to make sure, he reiterated the need for a tape of the hearing. *More hassle,* Becky thought. *Another trip to Indy.* She could not keep even a part-time job.

"You'll probably have to have portions of the hearing that pertain to this particular evidence transcribed," the lawyer told her, but by this time Becky already knew that.

"I know, the clerk said that too," she said.

"Of course there is a charge for the services," he said.

"Of course."

The lawyer finished answering Becky's questions. She thanked him. Then she phoned the Bankruptcy Court to make her request. The secretary said that requests needed to be made in writing, and that a check should accompany the request to pay for labor and expenses. Long-distance phone calls, overnight mail charges, transcription fees, loss of wages, no time for higher education, gas money—scrimp and sacrifice in the name of justice. First Trust Mortgage was still taking from Becky and her family.

I'm going nuts. The more I do, the harder it gets—more complicated, time-consuming, and costly. No wonder so many people count their losses when they are screwed and just walk away. But she could not stop to contemplate how crazy she felt. She needed to get her response before the judge before he ruled on their Motion to Dismiss. The clerks were too slow, the receptionists were too slow, and the mail was too slow. There was no clear articulation. Records were sloppy, inconclusive, and unreliable. She had to see the documents for herself. She would drive to Indianapolis and do the work by hand, relying on no one for interpretation or collection of data. She would review the tapes herself, figure out a way to get what she needed transcribed so she could attach them to her response, type the response in the State Library, and then walk it across the street to the Superior Court.

The trip was extremely hard on Becky. She was so tired. It was hard on the family, too, although this time she traveled for only one day. She would drive back during the night on Monday so Will only had to miss one day of work. Their car needed repairs. It was using too much oil, and the tires were bare. It backfired at stop signs and stalled whenever it wanted to. She and Will were afraid that it would not make it. Again, however, they were left with no choice, so Becky headed for the highway.

Thankfully, the car made the trip, and Becky, haven driven during the daytime, was happy just to feel awake. She found a parking space, put change in the meter, and entered the huge Federal Building. She made her way to the appropriate department and, through a series of events like talking to people and being directed hither and yon, was finally able to get her hands on copies of the tapes. Holding them tightly, she asked the clerk if she could use her tape recorder to listen to the tapes. The clerk told her no. They had a specific machine that had to be used, and that a deputy would need to be present to make sure she didn't vandalize the records. While Becky waited for the clerk to make the arrangements, she walked back to her car to close her eyes for a few minutes. Sitting in her car inside a gloomy parking garage, she laid her head back and took a nap. Her few minutes lasted almost an hour, and she could hardly believe that she had slept that long. She got out of the car, somewhat disoriented, and walked back to the Federal Building. She had a lot to do before she would be done and able to get her paperwork on file with the Superior Court before it closed at four o'clock.

She identified herself to the deputy with her driver's license and began to replay the horrible set of circumstances—her lawyer's words to the judge during the bankruptcy proceedings. Listening to First Trust Mortgage's untruths made her frustrated and depressed. Reliving the past via live audio was chilling. Becky cried. Yet the words motivated her because they reiterated the desperate need for justice.

Becky listened to the entire hour-long tape and nothing, absolutely nothing, was on there about their possible future litigation. *Dog gone it. Have they given me the wrong tape? Now I have to go all the way back, talk to the clerk again, and now, for sure, I won't have time to get my response done and in before they close. Oh well, all I can do is try.* Becky was racing against the clock because she knew that once a judge made a decision on a motion, it would be difficult to overturn. She didn't want to stay in town another day either. It might cost her the opportunity for the part-time job she was interviewing for back in Madison, and staying in town would make her feel more depressed because she knew instinctively she'd want to go home to the gray house that First Trust Mortgage had taken through fraud—go home to the gray house with Will and the children waiting there. She shook her head to rid herself of sentimentality. She sought to get over this hurdle so she could prepare for the next one. In the midst of her running, Robert paged. Becky felt bothered. But for some reason she found a phone and called him collect.

"Robert, I'm in Indianapolis and pressed for time. What do you want?"

"It's been so long since I've seen you, Becky. I thought maybe we could arrange a meeting."

Becky thought for a minute, and said, "Sure, whatever. I have to go now. I'll call you when I get back." She hung up the phone and got back to work.

Becky called the bankruptcy people again. She was really getting sick and tired of talking to them repeatedly and going over the bankruptcy they never should have had to file in the first place. She was embarrassed by this, and to her, it was yet another way that the Defendants were able to harass her. *They can't imagine what it is like for me to have to humble myself and talk about this. We weren't bad people who didn't pay our debts. They were the bad ones!*

The final conclusion that afternoon was that the tapes had gotten screwed up. "Usually doesn't happen," the clerk said.

"Of course," Becky said. The list of clients' cases had been typed for the particular day that the Blaine's case was heard, and the secretary listened to the tapes in that order, but when it came to the place in the list where the next case to be heard was the Blaine's, there was a blank, an empty spot on the tape.

"I just don't understand it," the clerk said in a southern drawl. "I bet the court reporter left the pause button on by mistake—you know they pause between each case."

Becky didn't answer the clerk, but mumbled under her breath, "Sure." Why couldn't anything go her way? Becky would not be able to support her response with any findings on record with the Bankruptcy Court. She drove home empty-handed, all for nothing. She prayed for the best, after all, she had done her best and could do no more. She waited for the judge's response without the proof of jurisdiction.

After Becky had slept off the disappointing trip with six hours of sleep, she was once again back at it. She began to look for alternative ways to win the lawsuit. She realized that the only way to get the information she so desperately needed was to call the Bankruptcy Trustee directly at home to see if he would respond to her like a decent man should—off the record, yet *for* the record. She would ask him in person—why not—if he could, in some way, remember the Blaine's case. Maybe he would have a recollection of the case—perhaps personal reference notes he had kept. She called the Court and asked for the name of the trustee that had presided over their hearing. She then called Directory Assistance and asked for the name she had been given. She said a prayer and dialed the number. A man with a soft, deep voice answered. Becky asked him if he was a Trustee for the Federal Court system, and he told her that he was. She awkwardly described who she was and why she was calling, and she explained what had happened during her last trip to Indianapolis.

Much to her surprise, he remembered the case. With a little prompting, he was also able to remember the facts about their case that had intrigued him from the first day he had been exposed to it. He told Becky that he would like an opportunity to review his notes, and he promised her he would phone back the following day. He also said he would have no problem providing her with an affidavit as to the facts. Finally, Becky would get what she needed.

The next day the trustee came through, and Becky found an office store not too far from their house that he could fax his affidavit to. By the time Becky retrieved it, she the documents prepared and ready to be mailed overnight to the Superior Court. While the trustee had been doing his research and preparing his affidavit, Becky was not wasting any time. She was preparing her response, relying on what she anticipated would be received via the fax. Everything went smoothly from there on out, and she enclosed copies of the return receipt requested mail slips which she used to support her claim that the Defendants were properly served and a copy of the affidavit that gave the Superior Court jurisdiction over a "no asset case" declaration. Less than a week later, Becky received a 3 x 5 card from the Court that the judge had denied the Defendants' Motion to Dismiss. This was a major victory for Becky.

Becky felt relieved, which was why she allowed herself to see Robert that day. She knew she shouldn't, but she wanted to share her victory and hear his praise. She paged. He answered. They would take a bike ride on the trails through the woods and to the lake. Becky told Will she was going for a ride to relax and left the house. She dressed in a free-flowing skirt and a loose-fitting cotton blouse, not to catch Robert's attention, but to feel free and windblown and happy. She strapped on her helmet, got onto her off-road bike, and took off. The wind on her face felt very good. Becky had achieved another victory through patience and cunning, and that made her exuberant. She rounded the first curve while still getting herself situated in the gears, fussing with her helmet strap, bra straps, and anything else she could arrange perfectly before she felt all put together. By the time she got to the first part of the flat stretch, she knew she had seventeen minutes before she would see Robert.

Having caught up on sleep gave her a clear head and enabled her to analyze her relationship. For some reason, knowing she would see Robert made Becky peddle faster, and she didn't like that she was so excited. He was just a friend, no commitments, no expectations. She almost turned around.

It was a perfect day—sunny and not too breezy. As she approached her last hill, the most difficult one, she could feel the muscles in her legs burning. Exhausted, she wanted to slow down, but she realized that her heart was at war with her brain and wouldn't let her do it. She tried to dispel her feelings but she couldn't. Finally, she reached the top of the hill and saw Robert's green bike with him on it at the bottom. Becky flew on down the hill, finally acknowledging how very much she had missed him.

She greeted Robert with a big smile. "Hi you!" she yelled out. She wanted to reach forward and give him a big kiss—more out of not seeing a good friend in a while than out of any loving emotions. At least that's what she told herself.

Robert returned the smile and said, "I've missed you!"

"Which way should we go, Robert?"

"Why don't we go straight and catch up with the bike trail behind University Avenue?" he said.

"Yeah, that sounds like a great idea. I like it there. Want to stop at the park for a little while?"

"Sounds like a plan to me."

They headed for the park. There were swings and trees there, as well as a garden that the community took care of on a space donated for its use by the county. Volunteers planted vegetable and flower gardens and harvested the fruits. It was very pretty and bountiful. Plants were at four corners, and more than one butterfly species found them attractive. As soon as the trail ended at the park's informal entrance, there began a slightly worn path with an oak tree to the left and a park sign to the right. They parked their bikes and, without saying anything to each other, headed for the swings.

Robert was in a particularly peaceful mood, and he asked Becky if she would be interested in writing a few lines of poetry. She obliged, and he handed her a pen and paper from his backpack. He suggested a topic that they both might write about. The scene reminded Becky of a painting called "The Kiss" by Dante Gabriel Rossetti, which glorified the romance between King Rene of Anjou and Isabella of Lorraine. Becky knew that King Rene was an author of poems and romance stories and Robert was her idea of a king, a monarch like the butterflies that were all about the garden that morning. "Instead," Becky offered, "let's write about wind and water, maybe a storm or something." She wanted to stay away from romance.

"Okay," Robert said.

They got off of the swings and found a place beside the edge of the garden where the flowers met the lawn. Becky took notice of the sweet smelling flowers and grasses, and she knew Robert noticed too.

Many minutes passed and neither of them spoke. *Nothing could be more perfect,* Becky thought. A *sunny day, a garden, butterflies, and writing poetry with someone you really enjoy being with.* It seemed they were at last just friends.

When they were finished writing, Robert sheepishly said he would go first to share his poem with Becky. He was a bit shy because he felt that Becky would be more sensitive to writing poetry and that somehow she would be judging him. She listened. When he finished, he eagerly said, "Now you read yours."

Becky was pensive, for while she was writing her poem, she had gotten deep in thought. She leaned back on the oak tree not too far from where she was sitting and quietly spoke, almost in a whisper:

"The wrinkles formed when caressed by the storm
But no wind could touch the deep.
And the surface tore when the wind swept more
Though the peaceful core did sleep.

As the crests arched up to meet the sky
So to handle the forces of foe,
The sun shown through the reflectiveness
As to guide the below where to go.

When the waters tumble and the earth does rise
Giving way to unnatural chaos,
There is a calm that persists above all.
This is just the way He made us.

So the wind can come and torment the sea
For it knows not of its presence.
Yea, the truth of the sea lies deep within,
To acknowledge it is forever."

Robert leaned over and touched Becky's arm. She quietly leaned her head onto his chest, and there they sat in silence. They could feel the sun on their faces. Becky knew they didn't belong to one another. What they had created in their dreams had sustained them before, but Becky knew, like she had known all along, that what she had with Robert was only fantasy. But right then Becky felt safe in Robert's arms. Robert raised his arm and let his hand fall to touch Becky's breast.

"Let's go into the woods," he suggested softly.

"What for?" she asked, and she resisted by standing up and almost fell backwards over a tree branch that lay broken on the ground. Robert suggested again, "I want you in the woods." Now Robert looked impatient and he grabbed her arm hard and Becky just glared at him in disbelief.

"Lift up your skirt," he told her, pressing her up against the tree, his breath hot on her face.

"I think we should go now," Becky said, her voice shaking because of his puzzling demeanor that frightened her. Robert looked back at her with a blank stare. She backed away from the tree. He let go of her arm without a struggle or any attempt to hold her there. She took several more steps backward, saying, "What's wrong with you?" Then she got on her bike and rode away, numb. She couldn't cry. She just rode steadily in the direction of home, though she was so stunned she really didn't know what direction she was going, and the scowl painted on her face showed her despair.

That afternoon Robert paged Becky. She shuddered at the sound of the pager going off. *Should I return his page with a call? No—maybe.* Curiosity compelled her to phone.

"Becky, is that you?"

"Yes, it's me," said Becky.

"I'm sorry. Can we talk?"

"Go ahead. I'm listening,"

"No, I mean in person."

"No—I'm not going through that again."

"You won't have to go through anything. I promise. But I have to tell you some things in person. Important things," Robert said.

"Maybe I don't want to hear them. You scared me." Becky spoke in monotone.

"I said I was sorry. Please, I have to talk to you in person."

Becky gave in, although she questioned why she even cared at this point. She met him at the medical school. It was the first time she had been there since she dropped out. She probably would have felt more emotion as she walked through the front doors, but she was on a mission that distracted her from anything but walking up the stairs to Robert's office. He was giving inoculations to research volunteers as part of a grant project. She waited for his last patient to leave. Becky stared at him in his white lab jacket that she used to find so attractive. He stared back, then walked around her to the door and closed it. Then he turned the latch, locking it.

Becky became visibly uncomfortable and said, "Why did you close and lock the door? Open it!"

Robert did not reply. He only stood there, looking at Becky. Finally he said, "I apologize for this morning." Becky moved away from him to the end of a long table way out of his reach, and she folded her arms and sat down to use body language to ward off possible advances. She wondered with all she had going on in her family and the lawsuit why she would even bother showing up to be in the presence of someone she had convinced herself she didn't want to have anything to do with anymore.

"I just wanted to feel closer to you—we've been apart for so long," Robert said.

"What?" Becky said. "You called me all the way up here to tell me you wanted to feel closer to me? We've waited so long—what do you mean, Robert? You know it's over between us. I thought we could be friends, but obviously, we can't."

"But I want you," he said.

"No, we never were a real couple, Robert, we were a fantasy. Fantasy, like a winged Pegasus waiting to fly us off somewhere. I don't know what I was thinking when I first had coffee with you. I was lonely I guess. But what we had doesn't cure loneliness and wasn't right. And neither was your behavior this morning," Becky said. "I've never seen you like that. It scared me." She stood up to make her point.

"I know, I know, I'm sorry. Come here, please. I'd like to hug you." He opened his arms. Reluctantly, Becky neared. They began to hug. Robert leaned into Becky to suggest she sit back down on the table where his files, papers, half-full container of sharps, and freshly drawn vials of clinical trial serum were arranged in the corner. Becky leaned back into him as her way of saying no.

Robert grabbed for the bottom of her skirt, pulling it up before she could struggle away. He sat her down hard and attempted to fit his body between her legs. "Come on, Becky, I've locked the door. No one can get in here. I've got to have you. You don't want Blaine, you want me!" In horror, Becky watched herself and Robert in slow motion, a moment surreal.

Becky didn't want anyone. She just wanted to get away. Then things started to happen quickly as she shoved him back and yelled, "What do you think you're doing? Let me out of here!" She lurched toward the door. "Open the door, right now," she demanded, turning the doorknob in furious frustration. The door had been locked from the inside and she could not wiggle it open. "Open it," she insisted.

Robert walked toward her. She didn't know what to expect. They were in a locked room in the old part of the medical school with no inhabitants but lab rats in cages. No one would hear her if she screamed. What would she do if—and then he reached past her and unlocked the door. Becky shoved the door open and ran down the stairs, past the offices where less than a year earlier she had turned in her final application for medical school.

In disgust, Becky ran to her car, sat down, and slammed her car door shut. She started her car and took off, leaving a patch of black tire marks behind. She drove up and down the streets aimlessly. Her windows were open. Her mind was shut. She was numb. What had happened? Becky couldn't cry. She couldn't solve any more problems.

When Becky got home, the mail had already come. She opened the mailbox with disgust in her motions. More assertions by the defense. Shit. She walked from the mailbox to her apartment, angry. Every day she felt punished by the ridiculous communication from the half-assed lawyers who really thought they were going to beat her into submission. She opened the front door, walked through it, and slammed it. She marched upstairs and threw herself on the bed. The envelope was still in her left hand as her head sank into her pillow.

Chapter Twenty

The phone rang first thing Monday morning. It was a First Trust representative on the line. He said, "If you persist in your action against First Trust Mortgage, we will invoke the provisions of I.C. 34-1-32-1, which read, in part, as follows." Becky stood next to the phone dumbfounded and pissed, but listening. He continued, "In any civil action, the court may award attorney's fees or a part of the costs to the prevailing party, if it finds that either party continued to litigate the action or defense after the party's claim or defense clearly became frivolous, unreasonable, or groundless." Exactly what Will and Becky had been afraid of. They had discussed this before—the possibility of losing and ending up owing thousands, maybe hundreds of thousands of dollars in attorney fees—a life sentence for the innocent.

The defense had nothing but dishonesty to present before the judge. There was no exculpatory evidence. Becky suspected that what they were trying to do was to have the case thrown out because they knew they would lose. Of course, they tried to tire and confuse Becky, to shove her past the point of understanding—force her to give in, but these were idle threats. They knew she was vulnerable, so they put pressure on her and hoped she would succumb. She did not.

In the following weeks, First Trust Mortgage bombarded Becky with many legal maneuvers. One of their worst came when they launched a "Cross and Counter-Complaint on the Note and to Foreclose on the Mortgage." Much more complications, more confusion for Becky. She didn't know who was on first or who was on second. The Counter read: "First Trust Mortgage is a Connecticut Corporation duly authorized and licensed to transact business in the State of Indiana.... accrued interest thereon bear interest after maturity...that if any deficiency and the payment of any installment under the note are not made good prior to the due date of the next such installment, the entire principal sum and accrued interest shall at once become due and payable without notice at the option of the holder of the note." *Whew!* Becky was lost. She felt crazy. She kept going over and over the paperwork.

In the beginning, First Trust wouldn't correct its mistake. When they wouldn't fix it, the Blaines quit making their mortgage payment in an effort to get First Trust to pay attention to their complaints and make things right so they could continue to sell lots. That didn't do any good. First Trust wouldn't even answer their phone calls. Will and Becky eventually couldn't pay the mortgage even if they had agreed to. Will's business failed because no bank would loan him money to build houses. Their credit problems kept getting worse with their inability to pay bills since they were not selling lots. With no remedy in sight, the Blaines were forced into a bankruptcy not of their own making, lost their house, their cars, and their self-esteem. What was First Trust Mortgage doing making a Cross and Counter-Complaint? *How can they ask the Court to enter judgment in favor of them?*

It was also wrong to label Becky and Will as the defense—they were the plaintiffs! Seeing them labeled as such infuriated Becky because she felt it gave a false sense of who was suing whom. She and Will were the Plaintiffs. Period. So when she wrote her response she corrected her and Will's position so the judge would not lose sight of who had initiated the lawsuit and who had pursued the case of fraud. At least that was what Becky thought. The original petition was clear, and she wanted and needed to keep it straight when addressing the new Cross and Counter-Claim. Becky was drowning in the water that was way above her head. As much as she wanted to maintain control, she felt she was being pulled under. First Trust Mortgage asked the Court for an order directing the Sheriff of Marion County, Indiana, to immediately levy upon the goods and chattels of the Defendants, William and Rebecca Blaine, until such judgment was satisfied in full; to enter an Order that upon the expiration of the statutory period of redemption and the execution by the Sheriff of Marion County, Indiana, of the conveyance of the real estate sold hereunder…assignees in full, peaceful and quiet possession of the real estate without delay. *In other words, give them the land and go away. Sheriff's sale? When? No way!*

Becky had thought that there could be no scare tactic left that First Trust Mortgage could use to frighten her into submission, but they were getting close. Her heart raced often, and she couldn't sleep. She was dysfunctional, not only as a person, but also as a mother. She was lethargic and did not want to be involved in anything outside of her obsession to win this case and overcome the warmongers of justice.

Robert paged often. Becky refused to answer.

Through her research, Becky was aware that Thompson vs. Fourth National Bank of Montgomery gave her the right to affirm the contract and sue for damages, or she could set up damages as defense or Counter-Claim if she sued on contract. However, if they were able to foreclose on the mortgage, then affirming the contract would be moot. They were taking away her options, and she didn't like that. Not only that, all the talk about sheriff's sales and money owed for an indeterminate time in the future scared her. Sure, she waited until the bankruptcy had been dismissed as a "no asset case" declaration so that she could legally invoke the provisions set forth by the Boucher case, which essentially gave the title to the right of action against First Trust Mortgage, back to the Blaines. In this case, the bankruptcy court no longer had subject matter jurisdiction over the Blaines, and she was free to litigate the civil tort. Becky had figured out that much. She could see that what the defense was trying to do now was play a quick game of chess with her. They were trying to corner her so that no matter which way she moved, she was doomed. Checkmate, screw you!

If she did indeed apply the Boucher case appropriately, which simultaneously the trustee was agreeing with in his affidavit that was forthcoming, then the Superior Court *was* the correct forum to decide the outcome of the Blaine property, thus giving the defense an opportunity once again to foreclose. They could no longer contend that Becky was shopping for a forum.

Becky worked pulling more all-nighters at the law library and prepared her Answer to Affirmative Defense and Counter-Claim to Plaintiffs on their complaint. More pages from Robert. She ignored them. Robert showed up at the library. Becky thought it suspiciously coincidental that he was there when she was. Maybe he had gone there just hoping he would see her. He knew she saw him, but she looked down at her feet to avoid eye contact. He left. When the copy center finished collating her copies of the transcripts she needed to accompany her reply brief, she left, too.

As Becky sat in her car getting her papers in order, she couldn't help but notice the twelve or so students waiting on the corner. They were waiting to be picked up and taken to the hospital, no doubt to fulfill their rotation requirements. She knew they were medical students because they were standing in their white lab jackets by the back door to the anatomy lab, the room that housed the cadavers, the room she knew so well, and the same room where she had met Robert. She envied them as they stood waiting and behaving as if the cold weather was the least of their problems. Nothing compared to Becky's melodrama. She envied their dress clothes that showed through their open jackets every time the wind blew—the sharp looking ties on the guys. They probably got them as presents from their proud parents—the parents of their soon-to-be doctor sons. Their shirts were ironed with "I am important" care, and some had their hands in their pockets to protect the little book—a mini version of the Physician's Desk Reference and the important notes they had taken during other clinical rotations. The ones standing by the door where Becky once stood, kissing Robert goodbye one night, were the ones who had passed their tests and had earned the right to do rounds with other physicians. She scanned the happy faces to see if she could recognize any former classmates. Becky stared and swallowed hard, holding back tears. She was now waiting where she used to wait, but not for the same reason.

The Blaines and First Trust Mortgage were playing for high stakes and, since Becky was unwilling to dismiss the case with prejudice, she knew that to pull out now and quit from exhaustion would cost her a bundle. There was no way she and Will were going to give up. As from the beginning, their determination to right the wrong fed them forward.

Complications and more pleadings, plots, and conjured up lies continued to dominate until a pre-trial conference led to the preliminary hearing, which had finally been scheduled before the judge. At the meeting Becky questioned her witnesses with facts that, although irrelevant to the Adversary Proceeding, were relevant to the case that would be heard in Superior Court as to fraud. She set them up. They objected to almost everything that Becky mentioned. Some things were sustained, and some were overruled, but every bit was recorded, which was what Becky wanted. She'd use that tape later and prove that they were liars. Becky's questions were planned at the first hearing to corner First Trust Mortgage in the second one. She had devised a system to discredit the lead prosecutor, and he fell right into it. Becky caught him completely off-guard. Had he maintained honesty, integrity, and the truth, her questioning wouldn't have mattered, but because their only offense and defense dealt with lies and deceit, the prosecutor needed time to cover his tracks and figure out which way he was walking. Instead, he tripped all over his own feet, which ended up in his mouth. Mr. Shortino's arrogance oozed around the room like slime. Whenever Becky had an opportunity, she treated him like he was nothing; as he spoke, she looked right past him as if nothing he said mattered.

About one third of the way into the hearing, Becky called Mr. Shortino to the witness stand. "Your honor," Mr. Shortino complained, "I am the Counsel here—I should not be and never have been called as a witness."

The judge said, "Raise your right hand!"

Mr. Shortino looked annoyed and embarrassed.

"Do you solemnly swear to tell the truth, the whole truth, so help you God?"

"I do," said Mr. Shortino, looking at Becky with contempt.

Becky approached the witness stand, standing close to him to assert her control. "Will you state your full name for the record?"

"Daniel Shortino."

"Mr. Daniel Shortino, will you tell the court what you do for a living?"

"I am counsel with Baird, Cook, and Cook."

"And who do you represent here today?"

"I represent the interests of First Trust Mortgage and their assignee."

"So can it be presumed that since you have been retained by First Trust that you represent their best interest, Mr. Shortino?"

"Yes, I do."

"If it please the Court, Your Honor, I would like to refer to Exhibit 37." Becky walked over to the court clerk to enter her exhibit.

"Objection, Your Honor," said Mr. Shortino.

"On what grounds?" the judge asked.

"On the grounds that I am not a recalcitrant witness and my testimony is moot. This is—"

"Let her finish!" interrupted the judge.

Becky continued, "Exhibit 37, page three, paragraph two, line seven reads, 'First Trust Mortgage was always in first position, holding title to all the land. This has never changed.' This is your testimony taken from the hearing about the damage that had been done to the gray house, was it not?"

"Um, er, okay," said Mr. Shortino.

"Answer the question, Mr. Shortino."

"Yes, it is."

"Then, Your Honor, I would like to refer the Court to page 37 of this same document, there, half way down the page. Mr. Shortino, would you read this for the Court?"

He grimaced, then began to read. "At no time did we ever claim title to all of the land . . ."

"Stop, please," said Becky. "Let the record show, Your Honor, that not only has Mr. Shortino offered conflicting testimony, but that his statements do not even represent his client's own interests. I'm finished with this witness, Your Honor."

"You may step down," the judge said. Becky noticed that he was shaking his head and looking disgusted with Shortino.

Becky had succeeded in getting what she sought after—written testimony that showed First Trust Mortgage presented consistent testimony about what exactly happened with the Blaine mortgage. The witnesses' testimony conflicted with their own counsel. Legal falderal at its best. The judge ruled in Becky's favor, that the case would continue. Mr. Shortino tried to convince the judge that Becky was irresponsible and inept. The judge looked at him and said, "The next hearing is set for sixty days from today." Now Becky would be able to concentrate all her efforts on the paperwork that represented her new set of legal issues—the fraud, as she referred to it.

The Marion County Superior Judge put forth an Initial Pre-trial Order with a date by which all discoveries had to be completed on Becky's Petition for Fraud and that all other motions would be consolidated. This meant that all parties had to exchange documentary evidence no later than the close of the discovery period. Becky found out what "discovery" meant and how to do it by looking up the definition, then looked to see how litigating parties did it by going through other cases whose documents were a matter of public record. The judge further stated in his order that the case would not be set for trial until one of the parties filed a Praecipe for Trial Setting. Becky didn't know what that meant either. She looked it up at the law library also and then began to ponder who should Praecipe—the Defendants, the Plaintiffs, or did it matter?

Becky knew that details meant everything, and it haunted her that First Trust Mortgage probably laughed at board meetings where they strategized that sooner or later she'd screw up or that they would be able to throw her such a curve ball she'd miss or strike out.

The judge went on to say that such Praecipe had to be accompanied by the Movant's Proposed Findings of Fact and Conclusions of Law, and that this must be accompanied by the Movant's Brief containing a Statement of Material Facts supported by citations to admissible evidence, and must cite local rules S.D. Ind. The mound of procedural concerns were unbelievable to Becky who would go to the law library many times a week for hours at a time, collecting and gathering books and literature, stacks and stacks on long tables. At times she was surrounded by so many stacks of books you could hardly see her blonde head sticking up over them. She'd look something up in one book, and it would refer her to three others, then to another for better examples, more for case law, and related cases with current rulings, and related cases that gave more depth and breadth of certain subject matter as it related to the origin of disputes and their historic resolutions. Becky began to be intrigued by a process that taught her much. She loved to learn. She loved books, and her studies now became a blessing to her instead of a curse.

Becky thought only momentarily that maybe the judge was babysitting her when he mentioned a book he had written about courtroom procedures and what constitutes admissible evidence. So she purchased the *Indiana Trial Rule Book of Evidence*, tabulated it, highlighted it, and then memorized it. Then she reasoned as she was the Plaintiff, the one who filed the original petition, she would be the moving party to praecipe for trial. Something the Defendants probably never thought she'd do. They underestimated her.

Becky was grateful to be able to use what she felt was her advantage from the Adversary Hearing because the judge, after he published his decision, had written a formal Findings of Fact and Conclusion of Law. Now Becky had an idea of what they were talking about. She made sure that she always included in any papers she drew up the phrase "all the relief just and proper in the premises." She was afraid if she ever forgot, they would stop the case right there. She was getting paranoid about all the possibilities for failure. *I don't want to lose on a technicality*. She also made sure she always sent copies to everybody with return receipt requested envelopes, because she didn't want First Trust to try the same trick it had before and say that it hadn't been properly served. She was catching on.

Becky figured that she must be making headway for First Trust Mortgage to be fighting back so hard. In her opinion, it was a good sign. The next thing to come was a claim First Trust Mortgage made that a same claim was pending or adjudicated in another State Court. At first, Becky thought that First Trust Mortgage was back to the *Same Claim* that the bankruptcy court still had jurisdiction in the matter, but then she realized they were using the same hearing to raise another issue in defense. That by *res judicata*, this claim could not be re-litigated and, thus, should be thrown out. They gave the inference that the matter had been heard before under a different auspice and in a different court. They went on to say that it was clear that the Court ruled in favor of First Trust Mortgage and against the Blaines on the Complaint and the counter-claim. Although this was not true, it was yet another bunch of research, strain, trips, and confusion for Becky. Despite her legal obsession, she and Will continued to do things with the children. Will worked and, as usual, to friends, neighbors, those they went to church with, and even to their own children, the ill effects of what Becky herself was going through could not be detected. Will paid attention from the sidelines, but he really had no clue as to what it took for Becky to fight the lawsuit.

First Trust Mortgage sent the Blaines another letter, and in it made the statement that the Court had made a Jacket Entry in the Court's file showing Partial Summary Judgment entered with entry to follow. Becky was amazed at how diabolical First Trust Mortgage was. They used a disguise, a way to show that a fictitious hearing had taken place on November 30. Preposterous of them to sneak the last three words in: "Entry to follow." An entry was *never* made. Becky was sure of this. The entire claim was false—a deliberate lie. Becky looked it up to make sure of course, and she was right. But just in case she made a response to their claim and filed a request to have the judge's ruling overturned in the event that a hearing had indeed taken place and an entry was made that she was not aware of. She remembered only too well when the McGruders had remonstrated in court, how their microfiche had somehow mysteriously disappeared. The last note that the defense put in their claim was "to allow the Blaines to continue to shop for a forum to overturn Judge Robinson's decision would truly be an injustice." No decision had ever been made because there had never been a hearing in the first place.

Becky thought of every way she could imagine to approach all that was coming at her so fast. She decided she would attempt to get the judge to overturn, rehear, retry, reverse, or whatever, the business of a hearing she "didn't bother to attend" as the defense had claimed. *No way. I wouldn't have missed any hearing. This can't be true.* Whatever it was that was allegedly heard that day because she hadn't been given a chance to be there to defend herself needed to be readdressed if the judge would give her the opportunity. If there had somehow been a hearing that she didn't know about, it would be because she wasn't properly served. For proof, Becky got a written statement from the clerk that there had *never* been an entry made.

NO ENTRY WAS EVER MADE. No *res judicata* here! More failed attempts by the defense. Another victory for Becky. Then Becky made a request for another Status Conference, a teleconference, a brief discussion period for all parties and the judge to discuss where they were at now and how they should all proceed. She was granted her request.

In preparation for the Status Conference, Becky outlined her entire dialogue. She knew that in certain circumstances, if she got nervous, she would not make clear and concise points. She planned to ask the judge to make an on-the-spot decision to bifurcate the cases, split them into two so that through two hearing times the defense would have less of an opportunity to muddy the water and attempt to direct the judge away from the real issue at hand. Becky knew that by having the Counter and Cross-Claims heard at the same time as her case of fraud, would confuse issues. She wanted one thing taken care of at a time. She really didn't want to have a part in the claim that the other parties were making regarding the land either because she knew that First Trust Mortgage had used the land as collateral, and that other parties, namely Henry Roth, also held title to it. Should the Blaines default, and yes, it appeared to Becky in finding remedies for fraud, she probably could have gotten the land back, but there was no way that she would go after possession of the remainder of the property. Becky knew the defense counsel would not want the case bifurcated, so her rebuttal was planned, a surprise sentence or two she would slip in during the conference to plant the seed to the judge to show how the Blaines had been victimized, all because of the McGruders and First Trust.

The defense had now hired a new formidable firm out of New York to assist them in the lawsuit. "No joke suits," Becky laughed as she told her friend Debbie about them the first time they showed up in court, whining about the conference being rescheduled. They also complained that their heavy schedules kept them so busy that surely all parties would need to succumb to their schedules and asked that the case be delayed. Their whining made Becky stronger, and she convinced the judge to keep the trial date where it was so the case wouldn't drag on. The Blaines needed closure.

Becky asked the judge to approve Court Appointed Mediation. She thought he would look at the request as a noble attempt on Becky's part to resolve the conflict, as she would contend later on that she had tried to do right from the beginning. Call it a mutual mistake, be open for mediation, try to avoid further litigation. She wanted to establish credibility. She knew the mediation would fail, but she wanted to show the judge that all along she was willing to compromise and look for simple solutions in a complicated set of circumstances. She hoped he would respect her for that. He agreed, so she purchased a copy of the Rules for Alternative Dispute Resolution and set out to live by the Book of Habakkuk. She would use their evil deeds against them.

Becky sat on her bed in their tiny apartment and looked at all of the litigation papers that were piling up against their walls, leaving now only a small path around her bed in which to walk. She waited for the phone to ring that would initiate the conference call. It finally rang. Feeling important, Becky went to answer it. Her heart was beating fast. She would have the upper hand against the five corporate lawyers on the other end of the line, and the judge as listener, director, and mediator. They would all be manipulated, Becky planned. She spoon-fed what she wanted them to have and gave nothing.

When the timing was exactly right she said, "I told you guys I wouldn't settle for a million." The defense quickly chimed in, "You can't say that!" Becky knew that she couldn't let the judge be aware that there had been any settlement offers, but she was *pro se*—it would look like an honest mistake! The defendants could ask for a mistrial, but Becky gambled they would not. She had now planted the seed to the judge that the defendants had offered to settle, and for how much.

Becky counted on the judge viewing their offer as a sign of guilt. The figure Becky made up, she hoped, would set a figure in his mind as to what First Trust thought they were culpable for. The judge warned Becky. She didn't care though, because she had gotten in what she wanted to.

Should she win the case, the judge would need to make a determination of damages, and she wanted him to have a large figure already in his head from somewhere. She knew that during the Status Conference, the opposing counsel would not make an argument and start bickering that the amount she stipulated was not correct, for it would only make her allegation that a settlement agreement was offered even stronger. Becky knew she shouldn't rely too heavily on her *pro se* status as an excuse to carry her through on many issues where she was overstepping her bounds, because she knew the laws made *pro se* litigants follow the same rules of procedure as any lawyer. There was enough bend in the laws that the judge could make her sorry she ever set foot in his courtroom. Becky would learn when and where and how to use each tactic. The best defense is a pre-designed offense based on knowledge gained from mistakes. To be *pro se* was no excuse for ignorance or special favors. This time Becky's mistake would be taken as an honest one, and a minor infraction. It was well worth the risk. By the end of the call, the case had been bifurcated, and counsel was instructed to sign off on the other case with prejudice. Becky got her way. The mediation was held, and it failed.

By this time, Becky could tell the judge was finally able to see through First Trust Mortgage and that she and her case had merit. The favorable rulings indicated so. She continued to push their buttons outside of the court and counted on the defense being reactionary, exactly how Becky wanted them to be.

Becky continued to work at getting the transcripts from the Adversary Hearing where she had questioned Mr. Shortino about his role in the case, as well as the testimony of several of his witnesses. She knew that First Trust Mortgage, Mr. Shortino, and some of their witnesses had conflicting testimony, and the written proof highlighted from the transcripts would serve Becky well. Unfortunately, the tapes were in Indianapolis. She would have to make another trip down there. Time and money were scarce, as usual, so this time when she went, she decided to make it a two-day trip so she could hopefully get a lot accomplished and not have to return for a while.

Again Becky would stay with Debbie. It would be about the fifth time that Becky had stayed with her old friend, and she was grateful she had a place to stay where she felt relaxed and at home—though she still wished she could just return to the gray house and have things like they used to be. Becky had known Debbie for about nine years from the time they first met at church. When Becky first started staying with her after her and Will's move to Madison and subsequent need to return to Indy often because of the lawsuit, she felt she was an imposition. But now, staying with Debbie was commonplace, and, though Becky's trips were usually short, they enjoyed their time together.

Debbie was a great friend. She would leave her door open, and when Becky pulled in the driveway, she could simply go inside, climb up the stairs, and go to bed without waking her. In the morning there was always fresh coffee and cereal available. Debbie was a divorced mother of two children and, as she got them ready for school, packing their lunches, making sure their hair was combed and their teeth were brushed, she and Becky would chat and catch up on things that had gone on since the last visit. Debbie had been dating a guy from church, and there was a lot of scandal about that because Debbie's ex-husband, whom she had only been divorced from a little more than a year, still attended that same church. Becky would sip her coffee and listen. Then Becky would catch Deb up with the latest lawsuit falderal and give her short snippets of information about Robert, but not much. It embarrassed her to admit to her personal weakness that conflicted with her religious beliefs. Besides, Robert was now a past tense subject. So she shared happy stories with Deb and her two sons about what Erin and Eli had been up to, their hockey games, or fishing, and how grown up Beth was getting, and how she was babysitting part-time now for the family down the road from them.

Debbie's and Becky's children had been friends all the while the Blaines lived in the gray house. Erin and Eli enjoyed playing together frequently with Debbie's children, and so every now and then when Becky needed Will to be present at a lawsuit hearing, or if Will wanted the family to get together with Junior, they brought the whole family and then stayed with Debbie and the boys, and they all had a good time.

The children loved seeing each other, so the trips to Debbie's house were a blessing, really. Becky knew that Debbie was having a hard time raising the children on her own, so she made sure that she and Will brought a big bag of groceries whenever she came to town, and they took Debbie and the children out to eat, even though they couldn't really afford to. They made it a party-like atmosphere for the children, and they were always eager to see if Junior could be a part of the fun. Will missed Junior now that they lived so far apart, but he was glad that once he was out of high school they'd get to be together more often. At night, Becky rented movies for the kids, and bought all the fixings for ice cream sundaes. Debbie popped popcorn. Becky tried to keep the children occupied so that they didn't think about the house they were forced out of and missed so much, and she and Will intentionally stayed away from familiar areas in town that would spark discussion of the past. The only time they went near the gray house was on their way to church. The Blaine Valley United Methodist Church was a stone's throw from the gray house, and they always went to church when they were staying with Deb and prayed for peace, resolution, and forgiveness.

However, Becky took *this* trip alone. She slept well and got up in time to have a quick cup of coffee with her friend before she had to leave for work. Debbie was always a good inspiration for Becky because she boosted her ego with all sorts of thoughts—ways that Becky could use to "beat the crap out of those horrible men!" Debbie, being somewhat of a brazen redhead, never held her tongue when it came to her opinion of what First Trust and its band of scalawags was doing to her friend. Debbie told Becky she was surprised she'd had a phone call from "that Robert guy you told me about," and that he had asked that Becky return his call.

"How did he get your phone number?" Becky asked, and neither of them could figure that out. Becky told Debbie if Robert didn't quit calling and paging her, she was going to get a restraining order against him. She didn't answer his call.

Becky drove to the courthouse to listen to the tapes. She knew she didn't have the money to just buy them. She needed to listen and to decide on the exact testimony she could use. She would pay for only that portion to be transcribed. The clerk sat Becky in a room of long tables and recording equipment. She showed Becky how to use the equipment and then called in a guard to ensure that Becky didn't do anything to the tapes, just like she'd been through before. Becky listened to the complete eight hours of testimony, and she recorded the numbers of all of the testimony she would ask to have transcribed from the recording equipment. When she was done and before she left, Becky arranged to get the transcripts sent via next-day air to New Jersey, which for some odd reason was where the tapes would be transcribed.

When Becky returned to Madison, she phoned Robert to arrange for one last meeting where she planned to reprimand him for calling her at Debbie's place and to reiterate to him that if he bothered her again, she would get a restraining order.

When the transcribed testimony arrived, however, it was incomplete, and parts were inaccurate, at least according to Becky's recollection. *The transcribers must have been in too much of a hurry*, Becky thought, and she was extremely dismayed at what she'd have to do to fix it. She needed enough testimony to prove to the judge how the defendants lied under oath, how they had conflicting testimony, and how they connived to obstruct justice.

Becky met Robert in the medical library on the third floor of the hospital. They sat at a table in one of the private study rooms. Becky's feelings for Robert were cold and businesslike. He had what looked like two days of unshaven growth on his face and chin, and he was wearing a long black coat, despite the very warm temperature in the room.

"Have you had to work a double shift on the floor?" Becky asked him, searching for an explanation for the scraggly beard.

"No. How are you, Becky?" he said in a scratchy, hoarse voice like he hadn't slept much recently. He paused, and there was no reply. She just looked at him with a blank expression like she didn't even know him.

Robert continued, "I've paged you, and you haven't returned my calls."

Becky opened her mouth slightly as if she were going to say something.

Robert interrupted. "I saw you with Will the other day. He had his arm on your shoulder. Why was he touching you?"

Becky winced in a puzzled way. "Where did you see us?" she asked.

"At the grocery store by your house."

"What were you doing on the West Side after ten o'clock at night?" Becky asked.

"I followed you, Becky. I follow you everywhere." He paused, and his eyes pierced right through her. "I was in Indianapolis last week, too. Why did you spend so much time with that male clerk?"

"What?" Becky said in disbelief. "You were in Indianapolis?" Her face felt red and hot. She felt dizzy and sick.

"Becky, get under the table. I want you right here." Robert stood up. "I'm not leaving until I've had you! If Blaine can have you, why can't I?" And he moved toward her.

Becky felt trapped. She fell into a chair with her back against the wall. The room was small. The door was locked, and Robert was right in front of it. "Robert, what's gotten into you?" she asked. She was convinced that he was mentally unstable and she decided she would need to manipulate the conversation so she could escape. "I thought you loved me. How can you act like this?" she asked. She continued to try to reason with him before she would scream, but then she wondered if he had a knife or a gun under his coat. He might kill her before someone could help her.

"Let me leave," Becky said, moving aside and pushing away from him. "We can't see each other any more, you know that." She bravely tried to reach the doorknob.

"What's wrong, Becky? You want me, and you know it! Don't act like a prude. I know how you really are—feisty and strong. Come on." He grabbed her by the hair and stuck his fist up under her chin. "You know what I mean?"

"No—okay, Bob, let's talk—we can talk this out," Becky said.

"I wanted to marry you," he said in a quivering voice. "You want to stay with Blaine. You've always stayed with him, even when he messed up the subdivision, even when he started the fire." He unclenched his fist as Becky stood straight with her arms to her sides and face to face with him.

"What do you mean, started the fire?" Becky said. She had told Robert about the fire, but she had never told him about any suspicion that Will may have started it.

"Forget it, bitch—just leave. Have it your way!" With the palm of his hand he shoved her head to the side, throwing her off balance. Robert put his right arm behind his back and unlocked the door without taking his eyes off Becky. She said nothing. She gave him one last look and rubbed past him and out the door.

Becky trembled as she entered the elevator. She avoided the back stairs for fear Robert would follow her. She passed many people who were working in the library, all who were oblivious to what had just transpired in the room less than five feet from them. They just kept their heads down reading text. Becky could have screamed in fear, but she didn't. She thought about going to the police, but questioned herself as to what her complaint would be. There was no physical harm that had been done to her. Her head hurt from him pulling her hair and shoving her, but it would be her word against his.

She tried to get a restraining order out against him, but the court orderly told her she had to prove she was in fear of her life or that there was a successive pattern of harassment before they could do anything. The music in her head was disjointed fragments of unfinished measures, chaotic and unsettling.

Becky lived in constant fear now, almost always watching her back. She had many unanswered questions, but no time to sort through the rubble to find the answers. The pages eventually stopped coming. Becky let her guard down and tried to forget Robert for good.

Chapter Twenty-One

Becky had to make yet another trip to Indianapolis, forcing her to come up with more money for gas and court expenses. Again she went out into the garage where Will kept the change he emptied out of his pockets at the end of each workday and threw into his tool box. Becky shuffled the dirty nickels, dimes, and quarters back and forth between the rusty tools until she had counted up to forty dollars. This trip meant she would have to spend more time away from her family and her new job at an optometrist's office. She had gone back to doing what was comfortable to her to make a reliable income. No more unexpected or wildly large projects. Her part-time job was all she could manage now.

It was difficult for Becky to realize that in the ten years that she had hoped to be a practicing physician, she was doing no more than what she had done to support herself through college. It was disappointing for her to realize that she had made many steps forward, but had made more steps backward, or at least it appeared to her that way. She felt frustrated and unfulfilled. Becky looked to God for answers, but nothing was clear like she thought it ought to be. Her life right now certainly wasn't part of *her* plan. And, even now, the simplest of jobs were in jeopardy because of the time off she had to take on a moment's notice for court work. Part-time, fill-in employment was all she could commit to, not a career, and that bothered Becky. Another opportunity in her life was gone because of the time she had to spend trying to right things that had gone wrong. It seemed like everything in her life dealt with trying to right the wrongs of injustice. Perhaps this *was* God's plan for her.

Becky looked at her watch. Only fifteen minutes had passed from the last time she looked. She was in the car, again, and the road seemed to go on forever. Nothing had changed, not even the scenery. Every trip from Wisconsin to Indianapolis was the same. She was always tired. She was always stressed. Over three hours and you're almost to Bloomington, halfway there. The sun will start coming up, and you're there—seven hours, no problem. She grabbed a cup of coffee, turned up the music on the radio, and watched for the exit.

Indianapolis hadn't changed much either in the two and one-half years the Blaines had been away, but Becky had. There had been so many disappointments. But as she drove on familiar streets and through familiar places, she worked at blocking those things out. Sometimes her efforts worked, and she heard music, and she let her mind travel to far off places that would protect her from her pain. She traveled to France with its history and architecture, and Burke and Will's tree in Australia, the 19th century explorers who were adventurous like Becky but who lost their lives searching for what had become their passion. Becky could relate to them. But when it came right down to it, the Blaines could never disguise the high anxiety brought on by the continual lawsuit. If she saw an old friend, she smiled, but she didn't really notice, like when she saw Sally. Sally had gotten heavier and didn't dye her hair any more, but Becky looked right past those things and thought about the courtroom, or the judge's last words, the most recent motion she had received, or the answers to some of the discovery questions. She wanted to prove the truth, but to even try she had to block out the sentimental stuff.

Sure, a cup of coffee with an old friend might have been nice, but she didn't even consider it. She didn't have the strength to go to the church any more either; it would deepen her heartache. She missed going with Will and the children by her side in Blaines Valley United Methodist Church. The preacher was caring and wise, and the congregation was loving. But if she went there now, she would just cry and want things to be just as they used to be. Becky had been an integral part of the congregation—on the Board, part of Missions, and the Vacation Bible School—but she couldn't go there now. It would involve too many feelings and too many questions. She knew that Charlie and Ruby would be there, though; if only she could sit with them and go unnoticed by the others, she would go.

She ignored the temptation to turn down the old road to the gray house. As she drove alone down the long highway that no doubt had served to lend time to many weary travelers sorting out all their troubles, she struggled with her past.

Robert, I loved you so. You were tender, loving, attentive, caring, full of laughter, and wisdom. What happened? We shared love and music, song and dance. Kahlil Gibran once wrote, "But let each of you be alone, even as the strings of the lute are alone, though they quiver with the same music." These are words I understand.

Yes, it is true, alone with the same music. Shared visions and sunshine, laughter, and love. My soul flew when I was with you, and I am grounded in the despair of what could have been. It's so difficult to let go. Even as you have betrayed our love with advances beyond reasoning, for some reason I forgive you. It sounds sick, I know. But deep down I know you still love me, and it means something to me even though the timing was not right, and your actions were not right. Contemptuous love, let go of my heart, free me from the bondage and suffering which causes my body to ache in your absence. It is getting easier now. I can accept it, knowing that I can't change destiny. We knew it would end, each of us living separate lives—this once in a lifetime love. We were so lucky to have experienced it at all. Having felt the perfect love, even if only for a little while, is sustaining. Becky thought of the Yaqui Indian quote, "Which is the right path in life? The right path is the path of the heart." *Ah*, Becky thought, *but infatuation is a leader of fools. It is emptiness that allows room for infatuation.*

Becky drifted, as she often did, but never stayed in the past very long. There was too much time to think in the car, so she told herself, *Don't think!*

Becky drove to the courthouse and up the parking ramp. Her car could almost navigate itself; they'd been there so many times. *Walk across the street. Take the elevator to the fourth floor, and breathe hard as the adrenaline kicks in. Then wait to be abused by a closed system where I don't belong.* She wasn't a lawyer, and everywhere she went to try to proceed, she was met by opposition from those who were. They didn't want to be bothered by a non-lawyer. They didn't want to be bothered by some idiot who was unfamiliar with the system.

Her insides had become cold and calculating. Her actions now deliberate. The sweet, naïve, young girl from a small town in Northern Michigan had grown up. She had been educated through adversity, and she could now find her way through any maze. It was more than a matter of survival now. She had become like them, but *better* than them. Becky would outsmart the First Trust Mortgage lawyers. She would anticipate their every move. She was always ready.

She stopped in the restroom, emptied her bladder, and threw cold water on her face. *Time to go to work*, she thought. Lots of overtime. No pay. All the days and all the nights. Becky left the restroom, walked down the hall, and entered the room to her left. This was the office of the law clerk, the vestibule of the judge's chambers, where all cases were scheduled and trial briefs were kept. She had trained herself to always look at her file whenever she came to Indianapolis—pull it out to see if it matched *her* file, stuff she'd sent, stuff First Trust Mortgage sent that some times didn't match.

Becky anticipated that the defense was going to try something prior to going before the judge, so just to make sure nothing new was in the file, she asked the clerk if she could look at it. Becky had a keen sense for the most outrageous possibilities, and her instincts led her to seek out the evildoers' deeds. Becky had learned she could not simply accept the scheduled appointment and walk into chambers blindly. She had to be attentive and searching, aware of her surroundings. She looked for anything out of place. She noticed the slightest looks between the clerk and secretary when she asked questions. She recognized the handwriting in notes made on her file and, thus, knew who had put them there. She intuitively knew what was going on around her, what the other side was thinking, and Becky could anticipate what could be pulled off if they tried.

Sure enough, when Becky rummaged through the file, she found a document she hadn't seen before. First Trust Mortgage must have faxed it earlier, knowing they would send a copy of it to Wisconsin, but the mail system bought them time. The new information would be in front of the judge, before it was seen by Becky. She would have been unprepared. Going through the file gave her a heads up. They hadn't planned that Becky would realize or find out what they had done. But she had, and she would make sure the judge knew what they had done, too. They were trying to buy themselves a couple of days—give themselves the advantage of presenting information that Becky hadn't had time to research or come up with a rebuttal. She would use it against them.

The ritual of browsing the court files had served her well. Sometimes there were documents the defense had supplied to the court that were intentionally incomplete, or that were a wee bit different in content than the hard copy she had received in the mail, or that were not there at all. Becky kept tabs and filed away what the defense might otherwise have gotten away with. First Trust Mortgage would only think they had gotten away with something. She would show their pattern of deceit.

The clerk retrieved the second binder to Becky's file. It was one of the thickest this court had ever housed, and the clerk made a comment of annoyance when he slammed it down on the counter. Becky picked it up and walked over to a table, sitting down for the long, tedious job of looking through every lousy page in the file. She read her motions and their answers and their motions and her answers. Her back ached. Her head pounded. She couldn't believe she had to sit on the hard wooden chair half the day and go through this.

Next to her was a picture of the signing of the Declaration of Independence. All the rhetoric that ate families alive and kept lawyers in business. She wished she could just open a big window of the City-County Building and throw the whole file out. Let the papers scatter everywhere and float down in disarray to the concrete below. There. Done. Gone forever. Then she could go home and live a normal life. Plant a flower garden. Take the dog for a walk. Hang laundry out on the clothesline. *No! Read on. Read on. Read on.*

Hours passed. Becky didn't even realize that she should eat. No time. She still had to go up two floors to the library and look up statutes, ordinances, and provisions in the law. She had to pick up new tactics and find new angles. *Horns Book of Remedies* had not revealed enough information for Becky to feel adequate in her Summary Judgment. She needed more information to draft her Findings of Fact and Conclusions of Law. She could not stop nor ignore any step, for as sure as she did, First Trust Mortgage would find it and trip her up. She couldn't let this happen. If there were one just more page to read, she would read it. It had been a long time from the first day she walked into the law library at the University of Wisconsin and asked the receptionist where she might look to find the definition of fraud. Now she seemed to be proving it against an international company. Even if she lost, she would know she had done her best and in this her heart sang.

Becky felt sorry for all the people she had met along the way who couldn't afford to fight injustice. She cried for the man she met on the elevator that day. He was considerably shorter than Becky, wore a tweed cap, and very worn, hunter green wool trousers. He smelled of an old house, and looked aged by distinction, a stance of pride, and hands that showed hard work.

"What brings you here?" asked Becky, who liked to speak to older people. She truly cared about what they had to say.

"Da State of Indiana is doin' a takeover—da land my pap and his before him had worked to own after comin' from da old country." He spoke in broken English—broken by the remnants of language carried over the ocean by his forefathers. "I doubt I'll live long enough to see what happens to it."

The conversation made Becky's heart ache. Her mission was made more real, and when the elevator closed and the man got off, she knew she'd never forget him. As the days and nights went on, Becky continued to work hard. She stayed for three days, and she really missed the kids. But she felt she was making progress. She asked the clerk for her file one last time before the Status Conference where the judge would set the trial date.

She began to look over the most recent entries. The motion she had never seen before read: Albert Pomp, III, filed a *Motion to Intervene*. Becky read on, "Samuel T. Cromwell, by counsel, moves the Court, pursuant to Trial Rule 24 (A) (2), for leave to intervene in this action, and in support of this Motion, states: Cromwell is the assignee of defendant First Trust Mortgage's interest in and to the mortgage which is the subject of this action. . . . that judgment entered or finding made in this action as to the enforceability of the mortgage is *res judicata*." Becky started flipping the pages of her legal terminology dictionary. Confusion. Six hours after the original *new* motion had been filed, yet another was listed. This one was a Motion for Substitution, which talked about a substitution because the investor, Henry Roth, was now deceased. Becky felt scared. She had the all-too-familiar feeling that they were going to outsmart her on a technicality that she couldn't understand. Three new things had taken place right before the hearing—all while Becky was driving from Madison to Indianapolis, and none of which, even after reading them in the file, could she understand or comprehend.

Only minutes before Becky thought she had the upper hand or at least felt in control, but then the floodgates opened, and again she felt like she was drowning. *What am I in for when I walk into court this afternoon? I don't even know where to begin now, and it will take more time to comprehend things and establish my new position than I have. A bunch of people all staking claim to part of my property, and I've never even met half of them!*

Becky suspected that the assignees' lawyers and Dan Shortino from First Trust Mortgage were in bed together. And who was the new person claiming interest in the property anyway? Then it really hit her. The fellow that she had met in her biomolecular chemistry class—the one that had taken such an interest in her and had become a financial investor in their subdivision was dead. *How can he be dead? How did he die?* Her imagination made her wonder if he had been killed. *Where to start?*

The Status Conference had been originally set up as Becky requested so she could dispel the defendant's lie that an entry had been made. Their assertion of *res judicata* was unfounded. First of all, no entry had ever been made, fraud had not been discussed, so *res judicata* did not apply. Sure they would claim it had, but she had the tapes to prove that it hadn't. But now at the last moment she had all the new issues she hadn't expected—and at the last moment. *What to do? What to do?*

Jeffrey, the young, coy assistant to the Clerk of the Court, gave his usual annoyed look as Becky set the file back on the counter. She had tried to win him over in the past by asserting her jovial conversation, but it hadn't worked. He was a young law student who was working toward becoming a litigation attorney, and here she was litigating such a large case by herself. That annoyed him. Yet, whenever a new entry came, he would read it. He would chuckle every now and then at her persistence, but he never let on to Becky.

Prior to having the case bifurcated and long before the Blaines had even moved to Madison, Becky had hired a law firm in Indianapolis to try the case. The firm eventually withdrew because Will and Becky couldn't afford its fees. It would be too difficult a case to prove, and it would take too long. No other firm in town would take the speculative case on a contingency. So, Becky knew that there were at least two lawyers in town from the firms she and Will had met with before that were vaguely familiar with the case, *if they could remember it.* She would give them a call and see if she could pick up a couple one-liner bits of information that could help her sort through the myriad of new legal conflicts that were challenging her with no time to sort through on her own. She asked the receptionist for directions to the nearest phone and headed for the hallway two doors down from the courtroom she would soon be entering.

There was no privacy around the telephone, and that bothered Becky, who was showing visible signs of agitation—no doubt what the other side had hoped for. The hallway was lined with people waiting for their cases to start. They appeared indifferent to what Becky was saying, but she knew they were listening. She cupped her hand around her mouth and receiver as she watched the demeanor of those that waited to be called for their trial. Some huddled in the corner with a cigarette. Indiana's no-smoking laws hadn't gone into effect yet, and the smoke bothered Becky too. Others just hung around like they'd never had a good day in their lives, and Becky judged most of them as loser reprobates—downtrodden for no other reason than they chose to be. They were unshaven and wore messy clothing. One woman tried to look worthy of winning in her red high heels and matching lipstick. By the courtroom sign posted above the waiting area, Becky knew some were fighting over custody, divorce, petty theft, or urinating in the street, some such mindless, ridiculous arguing. Becky couldn't figure out how these people could even afford to be involved in a lawsuit. *Who was representing them?* Becky dialed the phone number of the law firm and the receptionist answered.

"Sure, just a moment, I'll see if he's in," she said in what Becky considered a dumb-blonde, "got-to-file-my-nails-now" kind of way. Becky shifted her weight to her other foot as she waited. Then she tapped her foot. She felt like people were gawking at her. *Mind your own business,* she thought. She was testy because of all the pressure.

"Hello," a man answered.

"Is this Mr. Jackson?" Becky asked.

"Yes, it is. May I help you?"

"I don't know if you remember me, but about five years ago…" She spoke quickly because she didn't have much time, and she kept looking at her watch. Becky went on to give him the scenario of her case and brought him up-to-date to where she was today. "Can you help me figure out what you think it is they're trying to do?" asked Becky. She knew that First Trust Mortgage was trying to muddy the water and confuse all issues, but she needed to understand the terms and merits. "I can't understand what selling off part of the property to an assignee means…" She continued to try to elaborate on her position, but he cut her off.

Mr. Jackson had listened intently to what she was saying at first, but closed their conversation with the offer to have his law clerk run over and glance through the file and that he would get back to her. Becky felt anxious as she was running out of time with only two hours left before she had to be in chambers, but she thanked him and decided she would wait for his response. As she waited, she grabbed a bite to eat from a deli across the street. She wasn't really hungry, but knew that she'd better get something in her system or the shakes that started while she was on the phone would get worse. She was conscious of her irregular and rapid heart rate, and she took one of the heart pills that the doctor in Madison had prescribed for her. She took a migraine pill, a few swigs of her diet drink, and swallowed the last tablet she had gotten from her purse—something for her sick stomach. After a few bites of food, she couldn't sit still anymore. She went for a short walk around the town square, and then walked to her car so she could sit down and try to relax without any outside clatter. She ended up falling asleep for about forty minutes, then jerked awake with fear that perhaps she had dozed too long. She looked at her watch and quickly gathered her purse, folders, books, and headed for Jackson's office.

When she got there, the receptionist told Becky that Mr. Jackson would be in meetings all day and then handed her an envelope. Becky thanked her and disappointedly turned around and headed out the door. She had hoped to speak to him, even if briefly, in person.

She felt hot all over. Her blood pressure was up. Her heart pounded. She opened the envelope with anxious anticipation as she walked. Her eyes were immediately drawn to the words DECLINE INTEREST. She had hoped that he would appreciate how far she had come and how close she was to winning, and that he would join her and split the judgment or at least throw her a morsel of understanding, but there was nothing. With her hands shaking, she read his letter: "During the course of our preparation for the issues raised by First Trust Mortgage in the Superior 1 case, it came to our attention that the Court in the Superior 2 case had previously granted a Motion for Summary Judgment in favor of First Trust Mortgage and against you on the various Counter-Claims you filed for Fraud, etc. This ruling will probably preclude you from pursuing any further relief from First Trust." *What? Where did this come from? No wonder First Trust Mortgage asserted frivolous and groundless! But there was no ruling. Why do these idiots all feel there was?* "Although you may believe you now have evidence you did not have at that time, the Court will consider the issues closed by reason of this prior Summary Judgment ruling. The fact that you did not oppose the Motion for Summary Judgment will further hamper your efforts to combat the effect of the Motion." The voice she heard through the words began to fade as Becky slowly shut herself off from their meaning. Her eyes passed over the words, and nothing further sunk in. The pains in her stomach were getting worse. *Think—think what to do—what to do?* She was empty, alone, and confused.

Time had run out for Becky. The only thing left for her to do was to show up in the courtroom and try to work through whatever was passed her way. She felt defeated, but she persevered nonetheless.

Robert paged. Becky was completely thrown off, not only because he had paged, but by the timing. As she walked through the busy streets of downtown Indianapolis, she threw the pager on the street. She punished herself for the bad decision of ever having gotten involved with Robert. She missed the children and worried about her job. *How can I find which courtroom I'm supposed to be present at in fifteen minutes? I need to get to that restraining order against Robert.* There was too much in her head. She was on overload, and the way her posture looked, rather slouchy with her head bent down toward the ground as to ignore eye contact with passersby, showed her agony.

She ran up a flight of stairs to the second floor hoping she was headed in the right direction. She found one of the defendants standing outside one of the doors and figured she had found the right place. Flustered, she entered Room 210.

"All rise."

With those two words from the bailiff, everyone stood up, and the judge walked in. "Please be seated," the judge announced. "We'll begin now." Becky lost track of what the judge was saying because she was busy looking around to the other side of the room where many unknown faces were present in the defendant's corner. It had been a long time since she had seen some of these people face-to-face, and some she had no clue who they were. "Counsel, please give your brief."

A tall person resembling Lincoln stood up and began his egregious chatter. He pointed his finger at Becky and spoke loudly, saying things that were untrue. He made Becky out to be in the same category as a criminal. The only thing Becky heard was, "And, Your Honor, she should be thrown in jail for practicing law without a license!"

Becky stared straight forward in disbelief. Of course, they were bluffing. They had no grounds to make that assertion. But he had. Becky felt hot and stared at one of the new guys she had never seen before. *He must be the one who intervened.* The new group seemed to spin wheels around the counsel she had been used to dealing with. The defense had pulled in a great replacement. Becky had no clue how to object or what to say.

"Mrs. Blaine, do you have anything you would like to say?" the judge asked.

"Well, ah, I, um..." Becky was at a total loss for words. Opposing counsel had given all the reasons to the judge why they thought they were entitled to Partial Summary Judgment and how the assignee was entitled to... "Wait a minute," Becky said. "How can you say that Albert Pomp III believes the Blaines were wrong? Mr. Pomp has only recently been added to the list of lawyers, and he doesn't know us from Adam. To make statements about our character and false accusations about our agenda is inaccurate, groundless, and wrong."

The judge interrupted Becky's testimony with a reprimand. "Excuse me, Mrs. Blaine, but it seems to me that First Trust Mortgage's counsel is correct in their assertion that you have no business defending Mr. Blaine. Your name is not on the deed. So before you go on with your long diatribe of..."

"Diatribe! These lying warmongers of justice come in here and start yelling and pointing fingers at me like *I'm* the criminal here..."

"Excuse me, order in the court!" said the judge. "There will be no more outbursts here unless you want to be thrown in jail for contempt."

Becky quit talking and sat down. *Corporate lawyers are good at making lies believable. I guess that's their job.* She wondered if perhaps they knew the judge personally outside of the courtroom because he was letting them get away with so much.

Becky's mind drifted, and it took her away from where she was to a place where the words were just noise with no meaning. And the music was deep, slow, and methodical—a back and forth bow on a bass with resonance that surged even with Becky's pulse.

All of a sudden reality jerked her back, and Becky spoke up. "Your Honor, may I make a few statements on behalf of myself and my husband?"

"No, you may not. Defense counsel has shown me that your name is not on the mortgage, and you have no business defending your husband. This is against the law, and they are right. You could be thrown in jail for practicing law without a license."

"Your Honor." Becky threw caution to the wind and said, "Your Honor, they are incorrect. I *am* on the mortgage. What they have shown the court today and entered in as evidence before today's hearing, your Honor, is our *original* mortgage. What they have failed to show you is a copy of the Quit Claim Deed that was subsequently filed."

"Do you have a copy of that with you to prove what you are saying?" asked the judge.

"No, Your Honor, I don't. But I do not lie. I can produce this for you if you allow me time, Your Honor. Additionally, the sequential series of events that opposing counsel is laying out is incorrect too. If I may, Your Honor ..."

The judge continued, "The Defendants have already said through their Motion for Summary Judgment that a ruling has been made against you on your Counter-Claims and Petition for Damages Induced by Fraud. Isn't that true?"

"No, no, Your Honor, this isn't true." Becky tried to begin to set the record straight.

Mr. Pomp interrupted like he had eminent domain over the courtroom, and in a tone of voice that made Becky almost gag. "Very, very basically, Your Honor, what this case involves is that there was an unplatted"—*unplatted,* Becky thought, *another lie; the subdivision was platted—*"subdivision by the name of Canal Estates, consisting of 12 lots, owned by Mr. Blaine, in his sole name. It was not joint tenancy with Mrs. Blaine." *Yes it was! How could they lie like this and get away with it?* Becky had to bite her tongue not to speak her thoughts, lest the judge bang down his gavel and threaten her again.

"There was a house that the Blaines built, owned by, again, Mr. Blaine, sitting on what was called Lot #1. First Trust Mortgage made a loan to the Blaines and took a mortgage to secure that loan. And the mortgage by its terms, Your Honor, covers the entire real estate. All right? We have filed suit to foreclose that mortgage; there was a default; there's no issue that there's been a default."

But wait a minute, Becky thought. *We stopped paying the loan when you guys would not correct your mistake. It is obvious now that what you were attempting to pull off was fraud. You led us into a miserable bankruptcy where we lost everything, and now you're saying that we're to blame?* Becky wished that she knew how to object, or at least on what grounds she could claim an objection. If she could only get another shot at them in court, she'd be prepared next time.

"The issue as to the Blaines," Pomp continued as Becky sat listless, "was the Blaines contended that the mortgage was only supposed to cover Lot #1, right where the house rested." He showed the court the rough plat. "And the fact that their mortgage covers the rest of the real estate. Well, anyway, that's where we find ourselves."

Becky held tight-lipped. *This isn't fair!* She showed great constraint by not saying a word.

"Just as the parties indicated they did at the hearing."

"Wait a minute," Becky interrupted without any forethought of procedure and consequence, "there *never* was a hearing." Her voice was elevated and pronounced. She proceeded to pull out the transcripts that she had gotten a few weeks before, and she asked the judge if he would please refer to them. They contained the judge's own words as they pertained to what the opposing counsel was asserting. The testimony would prove right then and there that the defense had deliberately misquoted the judge from the first hearing two years prior. Becky refreshed the judge's memory.

"Normal procedures for a hearing were not followed that day on record, Your Honor," Becky continued, "and the atmosphere was unstructured. This was a *pre-trial* conference—a place where both parties and you came together to gain understanding about the case and to decide where to go. Your Honor, you did not require that the documents be entered in as official evidence and there never was an entry made."

Becky walked a copy of the transcripts of the pre-trial conference to the judge. He laid them on the corner of his bench and acted like he wasn't paying attention to them. But Becky knew that he was reading them over, and the defense counsel knew he was, too. The judge allowed the defendants to continue on with their story. They walked themselves into a corner as the judge probably allowed them to do.

Mr. Pomp continued, "And the subdivision was never formally platted. There are no separate descriptions of these plots on record, Your Honor." *Another lie,* Becky thought. She was sitting quietly and more patiently as she had regained the feeling of control, and she listened to the story, as they would have liked it known. *No descriptions, heavens. There have been legal descriptions for these lots from the day the plat was approved by the city. The engineers have them on file!* Becky knew where to get hard copies of the evidence to prove that the First Trust Mortgage lawyers were fraudulent liars, if only the judge would agree to set a trial date.

"Okay, I've got it," said the judge.

Mr. Pomp said, "There were allegations by First Trust Mortgage that the Blaines damaged the house in question here, and the court ruled against them with a non-dischargeable debt in the amount of four-thousand dollars." They made it sound like the Blaines had been charged with damaging the gray house to discredit Becky. Counsel was disgustingly polite to the judge, and Becky was disgusted by their artificial persona. *You make me sick, you in your stupid blue suit, suspenders, and horned-rim glasses!*

"Excuse me," Becky interrupted for clarification and truth, "the court ruled *in our favor* that we were *not* malicious and willful. We owed a small amount of money because the cabinets weren't in the house—that was all—four thousand, not eighty thousand like *you* petitioned." She pointed to Pomp. "The house wasn't finished when you did your inspection, so the cabinets didn't have to be in there when we left. The only reason that we're paying for them now is because when a house is finished, the cabinets should be in; but again, the judge ruled that we were *not* willful and malicious—we only sold that stuff so we could get money to feed the family."

Mr. Pomp said, "There's no reason why we now can't go forward, Your Honor." Becky thought, *Your Honor, Your Honor, if he says that one more time I'm going to smack him. He's deliberately personalizing his conversation with the judge in hopes of making a more favorable connection—ugh!*

Mr. Shortino, the defense attorney, decided to get involved now that Mr. Pomp had established himself as the big, fast, overpowering speaker who would win the debate. "The way we got to the Summary Judgment, well, the hearing that was held before..." *No it wasn't a hearing,* Becky wanted to stomp her feet to make her point! "...First Trust Mortgage propounded a request for admissions to the Blaines, deeming among other things, requesting them to admit that the mortgage was intended to cover the entire lot, etcetera, etcetera, etcetera. Okay? When we got back responses, they were totally unresponsive and contained, among other things, the long, diatribe about how we got here." *Is this the best you can do? Unresponsive—you've got to be kidding. We have been very responsive.*

Mr. Shortino continued to take many quotes from Becky's hand-written response to previous interrogatories taken out of context, but now the judge could see right through them. The judge had finished reading the materials that Becky had placed on his desk, and finally he said, "Let me ask you a question, Mr. Shortino. Why was an entry never tendered?"

"Well, ah, I, um." The same mumbled words of despair that Mr. Pomp had chewed on were now coming out of Mr. Shortino.

"So, tell me again now, why was an entry never tendered in three years? Or two years...no, it's been over three years now. Now why was that?" the judge demanded.

Mr. Pomp said, "Other than a..."

The judge interrupted, "I am asking Mr. Shortino, not you, Mr. Pomp. He was the original counsel here."

Mr. Shortino said, "Well, I..."

"I will ask you a third and last time, Mr. Shortino," said the judge, enunciating each syllable and sounding infuriated. "Can you tell me why was an entry never tendered?" Becky could see that the judge was becoming increasingly intolerant of Mr. Shortino.

"No, I cannot."

Mr. Pomp said, "The only thing that wasn't agreed to at the hearing..."

The judge interrupted Mr. Pomp again in disgust, "But you see, nothing happened. Why in the world three years later wasn't an entry ever proffered?"

"I was waiting for a Meets and Bounds Description that I couldn't get," said Mr. Shortino. *There have been Meets and Bounds on all twelve lots from the outset, and they know this, too.* Becky flipped with her fingers through her hair and looked up with disgust, a common facial feature this day. The engineering guy, being an old friend of Will's, had called them at home about a month previously and informed him and Becky that First Trust Mortgage was snooping around trying to get their hands on documents. One of the things First Trust Mortgage had taken copies of was all of the legal descriptions for the lots. They knew darn well where to get a Meets and Bounds, and if they had cared so much over the last three years, they could have easily retrieved them long ago. Three years with no entry was a lousy excuse for why this case should be dismissed.

"Initially," Mr. Pomp said, "I was trying to put together one entry so that we could get it all cleaned up in one entry."

"Explain to me what that means?" said the judge.

"I was wanting to prepare an entry foreclosing the Blaines' interest in all of the real estate and partitioning Lot #1 off so that the lien holders could argue that out, somewhere in a trial."

"Okay," said the judge.

"It didn't look like it was going to go by Summary Judgment and on the original Motion for Summary Judgment which was heard back in ..." began Mr. Pomp.

"Well, we really didn't *hear* anything," interrupted the judge. "We had a discussion. This is *not* a hearing, come on. There was a *discussion* about who was making agreements with whom. So, did something happen between the time you were here and the time you circulated the entries?"

"No, nothing has changed," said Pomp. "I would like to add, Your Honor, in the admissions that were deemed admitted, it specifically sets out that there was no fraud involved and that's been deemed admitted by the Court, which pretty much takes care of what I would see the Counter-Claim as."

"Well, let me just tell you, procedurally, this case troubles me," said the judge. "I have read the transcript over and, even then, procedurally this case troubles me. To have represented to the Court that everything was okay, and I assume it was, I don't think anybody misrepresented me, or did they? To be three years later, and we still don't have an entry, troubles me. It troubled me at the time, and we talked about the fact that I have no idea what happened…as I've reviewed this file, I think that it seems to me procedurally that what ought to be done is to take a step back. I really don't know, and maybe Meets and Bounds descriptions are so distasteful to engineering firms that you can't get anybody to do them—I thought they were hungry. When I get them in divorce cases and other cases, I have to fight them off with a stick. But apparently you had trouble doing that."

He was giving it to them now! "The status, seems to me, in fairness and justice…" the judge continued. *What? Fairness and justice?* Becky thought, and she perked up and smiled.

"…And in terms of all the competing claims, this is a real boondoggle. What I think we ought to do, which is why we're here, and I guess I don't know any better or more artful way to describe to you as I review the file, it seems to me the appropriate thing to do is to take a half step back, or maybe it's a full step back. And again, as my file reflects, First Trust Mortgage still has some things even now that need to be taken care of—like you want to make a proper substitution." *How did the judge know they tried to slip in a substitution only hours before the hearing?*

"The case will be set to be heard in its entirety pursuant to Trial Rule 56." Becky didn't know what that meant, but she felt from the judge's tone of voice and the fact that they were taking a step back, three years according to the judge, that she stood a chance to be able to tell her story. Becky felt victorious. She had gotten a trial date. They were over the petty semantics the defense had used to have Becky's case thrown out. She could now get her story out and if she didn't screw up on a legal technicality, she could stand a chance to win.

Chapter Twenty-Two

Becky was feeling the rush of momentum building in her favor. Over the next three weeks she was busy, but nothing traumatic happened. She had not seen Robert nor heard from him, so she didn't file a restraining order. It was over between them for good. Becky focused on the job before her. There was no time to waste if she was going to try to get this thing called a Summary Judgment pursuant to Trial Rule 56 in order. The children were doing well in school, and Will was content in his job. Life went on: the boys climbing trees and building snow forts; Beth growing up to new hair and clothing styles, music and friends.

Becky went to the law library and looked up books on civil procedure and Summary Judgment. She bought a black binder and began to categorize her project. Then she entered the confines of her daughter's room and began to summarize her claims on the computer. *Where to begin—let's see.* She was used to the formatting process now. Title: MOTION FOR SUMMARY JUDGMENT, ANSWER AND AFFIRMATIVE DEFENSE OF WILLIAM D. AND REBECCA A. BLAINE TO FIRST TRUST MORTGAGE'S MOTION FOR SUMMARY JUDGEMENT AS TO COUNTERCLAIM AND ANSWER AND AFFIRMATIVE DEFENSE OF WILLIAM D. AND REBECCA A. BLAINE – MOTION FOR PARTIAL SUMMARY JUDGMENT. *Develop the opening.* "Comes now William D. and Rebecca A. Blaine, Plaintiffs herein, without counsel, and files Notice of the Answer to the Motion for Summary Judgment as to Counterclaim and Notice of the Answer to Motion for Partial Summary Judgment and moves the Court pursuant to Trial Rule 56, etcetera, etcetera.

Becky went on to write the short synopsis of her reply, and she followed it with their Brief in Support of William D. and Rebecca A. Blaine's Motion for Summary Judgment. "The Blaines, without counsel, respectfully submit this brief in support of their Summary Judgment filed concurrently herewith…followed by an introduction: The Blaines bring this matter before the Court and do hereby state the following:

1. On March 8, 1990, the Blaines and First Trust Mortgage, executed a mortgage that is attached hereto and marked as Exhibit S.
2. At all relevant times prior to and including March 8, 1990, the Blaines intended and agreed with First Trust Mortgage, to grant to First Trust Mortgage, a mortgage on only one lot of their subdivided property (Lot #1) (consisting of approximately one-third (1/3) of an acre) to secure indebtedness to Household.
3. At no time did the Blaines intend nor knowingly agree to grant First Trust Mortgage the entire subdivision property, which consists of approximately five and two-thirds (5-2/3) acres.
4. At all relevant times prior to and including March 8, 1990, Household, by and through its agents, agreed and represented to Blaines the mortgage would cover only the one-third (1/3) acre known as Lot 1.
5. First Trust Mortgage's representations as to the property mortgaged were false, were known to be false when made, were made with the intent to induce the Blaines to execute the mortgage, were material, and were fraudulently made. (Becky had retrieved the elements of fraud that she needed to prove from many resource books, and it was instinctive to her that she needed to work backwards in her motion to lay the groundwork of her complaint for the judge).
6. That the Blaines reasonably relied upon First Trust Mortgage's material misrepresentation in deciding to execute the mortgage.
7. First Trust Mortgage, knowingly, intentionally, and fraudulently inserted or caused to be inserted on the mortgage the legal description of the entire subdivision property owned by the Blaines, consisting of approximately five and two thirds (5-2/3) acres, and failed to disclose the same to the Blaines.
8. As a direct and proximate result of First Trust Mortgage's fraudulent conduct, the Blaines have sustained damages, including the loss of profits from the development of the

subdivision caused by their failure to deliver marketable title by reason of the mortgage, other damages, attorney fees, and the costs of this action.

9. The Blaines are entitled to punitive damages against Household, which damages will deter First Trust Mortgage, and others similarly situated from like conduct."

Becky went on to develop her Summary Judgment by laying out the facts—facts that ended up being twenty-three pages long, with seventy-three exhibits. The defense surely didn't expect the pansy clad, downtrodden housewife, mother of three children, to have any substantive merit, evidence, awareness, or knowledge to be a real challenge.

Becky enjoyed writing her arguments, a culmination of years of pain. She finally got to tell her story.

"THE BLAINES ARE NOT COLLATERALLY ESTOPPED BY THE BANKRUPTCY COURT'S FINDINGS OF FACT AND CONCLUSIONS OF LAW AND JUDGMENT FROM DISPUTING THAT THE MORTGAGE IS A VALID AND ENFORCEABLE MORTGAGE AGAINST LOT 1.

"THE COURT HAS SUBJECT MATTER JURISDICTION OVER PLAINTIFF'S CAUSE OF ACTION.

"In the present case, Marion County Superior Court, Civil Division, clearly has the authority to hear issues pertaining to fraud and misrepresentation. The main question is whether the Bankruptcy Court has jurisdiction over Plaintiff's claim or whether jurisdiction has reverted back to this Court.

"THE COURT CAN AND SHOULD GRANT WILLIAM D. AND REBECCA A. BLAINE SUMMARY JUDGMENT.

"Fraud may consist of misrepresentation of material fact as to subject matter of contract, the actual result of which is to substitute subject matter different from that which buyer believed he was purchasing. Bankers Fidelity Life Insurance Company v. Morgan, 123 S.E. 2d 433, 104 Ga. App. 894.

"In cases of fraud, a court of equity should not hesitate to interfere, even though the victimized parties owe their predicament largely to their own stupidity and carelessness. Klingensmith v. Klingensmith, 185 N.W. 75, 193 Iowa 350."

Becky put this in there just in case there was an issue made out of the fact that they had signed the original mortgage, and so were accepting theoretically the document the way that it was. However, it was clear that the Blaines did not know initially which legal description was used, but had trusted the mortgage company to use the correct one. Further along in the trial, Becky would show where four different companies had written the legal description separately, but for the same piece of ground. The results would be very compelling for the court because there was no way, not even when she called an expert witness to read over the legal descriptions and identify which one belonged to which lot in the subdivision, that the judge would be able to tell which description belonged to which. The point was that the Blaines were without technical expertise to realize at the time of signing, whether First Trust Mortgage had used the correct legal description or not.

"Fraud, in equity, includes all acts, omissions, and concealments which involve a breach of either legal or equitable duty, trust, or confidence. One is justified in relying on a representation made to him in all cases where the representation is a positive statement of fact, and where an investigation would be required to discover the truth. Where a person's simplicity and credulity is taken advantage of by shrewdness, over reading, and misrepresentation of those with whom he is dealing, and he is thereby unwittingly induced to do something, the effect of which he does not intend, foresee, or comprehend, and which, if permitted to culminate, would be shocking to equity and good conscience, a court of equity will with propriety impose.

"When a party professing to have some knowledge falsely represents a thing to exist, and makes representations to secure an undue advantage over a person with whom he is contracting, he is guilty of fraud, though it may not appear that he knew that his statements were false. Ordinarily, a misrepresentation must be material, that is, it must relate to a material matter in the contract; and the test is whether or not it operated to induce the deceived party to enter into contract. Fraud is material to a contract when the contract would not have been made if the fraud had not been perpetrated. Fraud and damage must concur, and neither unaccompanied by other is ground for defense. The defrauded party may affirm contract and sue for damages, set up damages as defense, or counterclaim. Where a false representation is charged to have misled a party into signing a contract, he must not only show the falsity of the representations, that he was misled by such and induced to sign the contract, but also that he has been damaged, and the extent of his damages. Misrepresentations which are made by one party to a contract, as of his own knowledge with intention that the other party, who is not informed as to the truth of falsity of the misrepresentations, rely on them, are 'fraudulent' in equity.

"CONCLUSION: For all the above reasons, William D. and Rebecca A. Blaine's Motion for Summary Judgment should be granted, and First Trust Mortgage's Motion for Summary Judgment as to Counterclaim should be denied. The Blaines have shown the theory of fraud and proven its elements. The Blaines have proved the Court has jurisdiction. First Trust Mortgage *is* guilty of fraud and is responsible for damages."

Chapter Twenty-Three

The sun was coming up now, and the beauty of a new day revived Becky. She felt blessed. She knew she was close to Indianapolis now. The route was so familiar. Over the last three years though, the road had become more bumpy from the weather, hot to cold and back again, unpredictable, rough in spots, much like her life.

She passed Falcon Creek to her left. Her mind drifted to the days when she had lived in Indianapolis and sat on the banks to watch the Olympic rowing qualifications. The day had been pleasant, laid back, and without negative clutter. There, she absorbed the rays of the sun and stared at the rowers thinking how she might like to be one of them. Becky wished she had time to row again, because the synchrony of the oars balanced her mind when her breathing became one with the drift of the water. When the coxswain rattled out an order and the stroke picked up the pace, she could feel the strong flow of freedom which brought peace and happiness to Becky.

As she passed the creek, the smooth calm water became warped with the storm of the litigation. *I am so sick of this*, she thought. *When will this nightmare be over?* She hated the lawsuit. *Come on, you ruthless . . . I can't say it.*

Becky was angry, but she didn't want to be. She felt sad, too, as she struggled, knowing she didn't like to be that kind of person. She didn't like to swear and act tough. But when she was tired and overcome with stress, it was difficult to contain her emotions. The heat of her anger and the sadness in her heart seemed to melt her restraints away. The trial made her low with despair, exhausted and so wanting for peace. She often knelt down by her bedside in prayer, and through tears, she asked God, whom she gave credit for helping her almost daily, for strength, guidance, and forgiveness.

Becky pulled off the exit, turned left under the bridge, and slowly approached her final destination. She noticed that although she felt like she had been a million places and had done a million things since the last trip down, the concrete graffiti looked about the same, the last predictable curve, and familiar panhandlers. Becky wondered if they'd ever left the spot since the last time she had rounded that same corner.

She slowly approached the parking ramp. It was about six o'clock in the morning, and the streets were quiet. It was just past sunrise. The morning was new, but she was already tired and weary. She fought with restlessness what she knew she would soon face. The day would be long and arduous. It would be many long and difficult hours spent in the courthouse before she could even begin to think about the long drive home.

The City-County Building across the street from the parking ramp was a large square and made of limestone. It looked like a typical City-County Building—probably something that might have stood out about twenty-five years before, but the City had grown so much that now it was just another large building among many. The only real distinguishing factor was the American flag that waved to its visitors. Many life-altering events happened in that building. Marriage licenses were obtained there. Divorces were started there. Child support complaints were managed there. Criminals were prosecuted and jailed. People won cases, and people lost cases. Usually, no one was a winner. Becky saw the sheriffs' cars coming and going with the changing shift. She wondered what their night had been like.

There was a common world of people out there getting up every day with the same old routine. But for Becky, she felt pulled away from any degree of normalcy or routine, and she knew that until the judge hammered out his final order, she would not let the outside in, including Will. She couldn't. She had to stay alone and strong. She would rest when the court rested.

Becky pulled into a parking spot and began to gather up her books and papers. She no more felt like being in Indianapolis this day than being the man in the moon. With her head heavy and defeat at her back, it took every effort just to make it across the street. She fumbled through the turnstile and bumped through the congregation of misdemeanors that had just been released from the county lock-up.

She was surrounded by people now. For some, the night was their day; the daylight exposed markings of being down on their luck.

"Hey lady, got a quarter, gotta call my kid." Some of them cared for nothing more than where their next drink or fix would come from, or where their next john would be found. They seemed to have no direction, just standing around smoking, looking hung over and lost. Many were unshaven; some walked with a Thorazine shuffle. Some were wearing layers of old make-up and had uncombed hair. Rotten teeth showed through half-assed smiles. All around was the stench of yesterday's cheap perfume. Becky wondered why they didn't seem to care. To them it was just another day.

Becky walked with a tired lope toward the lobby, head down, watching her feet put one foot in front of the other, and past the receptionist, until she got to the eight elevators. There were four on each side of the hallway that took people up to thirty-some floors. She took a deep breath finally accepting, without too much resistance, the job she had to do that day, and she looked up to see which elevator would be available next. She had her hands behind her back, rocking back and forth sideways to music as indistinguishable as her mood—unattached—there, but not really. A few hours earlier she had been optimistic and felt peaceful. A few moments ago, anger. A few seconds ago, lethargic. Presently, she was impatient, tired, bored, and determined. She barely knew where she was for a moment, and then she looked up at those who had joined her in the elevator. She took a blank stare because she was face-to-face with the judge that would hear her case. *What are the chances that I would drive all night, that he would leave for work that morning, and that both of us would arrive at the same elevator at the same time?* Becky's adrenaline rushed, and she quickly woke up. "Good morning, sir," Becky said in a polite way to acknowledge him.

"Good morning," the judge replied, with no apparent recollection of who Becky was.

Becky nervously began small talk. Knowing her encounter would be short-lived, she wanted to say something that would help him identify who she was. She wanted him to know how hard she was fighting for what was right in his courtroom.

"How was the traffic coming in this morning?" she asked.

The judge courteously said, "Fine, thank you. How was it for you?"

"Well," Becky started. *Now is my chance to identify myself.* "Actually, I've been driving all night, and the roads weren't too bad. But I'm really tired. In fact, I don't know if you recall, but I'm the *pro se* litigant from your courtroom. I'm here to observe the posture of your court. Well, I guess that's what you call it." Her statement sounded aloof, but nonetheless, it was out. She was tired, and that was the best she could do.

The elevator hadn't moved from the time they got in, and the judge replied, "Seems like this elevator is broken. Let's get out. I know the back way. Want to walk up the stairs with me?"

Becky felt excited, yet awkward. She wished she could say, "Hey, Your Honor, want to go have breakfast? There's a lot of stuff I want to tell you about this awful company I'm suing!" Becky knew better though than to say much more. She didn't want to jeopardize her position with the judge. She wanted to earn his respect at all costs, and she also knew that if she discussed the particulars of the case, there would be the possibility that he would take himself off of it. She didn't want to lose him. She had come to trust him to be fair. She respected and admired him too. She hoped in time, he would come to respect and admire her also.

"Well, here's the door. I guess you are going to the same place I am, right?" the judge asked. Becky mused that since the clerk and receptionist had come to know her, they were probably wondering why she and the judge had come in together, especially so early in the morning. The office wasn't officially open yet, and here was Becky! The judge had offered to let her in. He walked back into chambers. Becky headed for the front desk.

He would see her again soon. The reason Becky had driven to Indianapolis this time was to sit in on some of the other trials that Judge Fairchild was hearing. Becky had phoned the Clerk of Court ahead of time to make sure that Judge Fairchild had cases scheduled. When Becky was certain the judge wasn't within an audible distance, she asked the clerk more specifically what time his first case started and how many he had scheduled that day. She would need to wait about forty minutes.

She didn't waste time sitting around, but rather than getting her file this time, she dug through her purse for the John Grisham book she had been reading, *The Runaway Jury*. She began reading where she had left off. A friend had recommended the book to Becky's mother, knowing that Becky was involved in a trial. She, in turn, recommended the book to her daughter, who had never heard of the author until then. She had purchased the book and found that she couldn't put it down because of the mystery and courtroom intrigue that mirrored her own real life drama. She was intrigued in anticipation that the book would be brought to life. She sat down on the same hard, wooden chair that she always sat in while she waited for whatever business she was in the clerk's office for, and she began to read. Becky became completely enthralled in the book to the point that she almost forgot where she was. After what seemed like just a few minutes, the clerk interrupted her, and told her that the trial was going to get started later than originally planned and that maybe Becky had some other things she needed to do. She stood up, stretched, and thanked the clerk for alerting her about the delay. She looked at her watch as she thought about what she might consider doing while she waited the extra two hours that the clerk thought it would take.

"Well, I don't know exactly what I'll do," Becky said, as she waved to the clerk on her way out. *I could go to lunch, but it's too early.*

"I guess I'll look through my file," she said to the clerk. "Never know what I might see in there." She winked at the clerk to acknowledge that after all this time he finally seemed to be more personable to her.

"No problem," replied the clerk. He didn't even bother to ask what name he should look under to find Becky's file. Of course by now he knew who Becky was, and so did most of the others in Fairchild's court, where Rebecca Blaine had become a household name. At first, she annoyed the staff with her naiveté and the way she stumbled through their system, but now she was as much a part of the process as they were.

After a while of tense reading, Becky's head began to pound as well as her heart. She pushed herself back from the table, stood up and looked out the window at all that was going on outside of the confines of her miserable situation. *In about fifty years, none of this is going to matter to anyone anyway,* thought Becky. Yet, she knew that if everything turned out all right, there would be a positive message somewhere in all of this for her children and for other people too. But would her kids turn out to be political activists because of their exposure to the verbal grievances they had overheard their mom going crazy over? Or would they become hermits and hide somewhere in the mountains where no one could ever find them, protected from people and the nasty old world by trees and the sweet smell of freedom flowers? She didn't know. All she knew was that she, Will, and the children had done nothing wrong. They were left with no choice but to walk away from the subdivision, the historic land, and the house they built themselves. Becky was left with no choice but to defend them against the false allegation of willful and malicious intent and damaging the house. She was left no alternative but to leave medical school and file a lawsuit. It was a matter of principle to file the summons and complaint of fraud against these sneaky, lying corporate war mongers of justice.

Becky could feel herself becoming extremely anxious, and her heart danced even more. She left the hallway to find a water fountain so she could take a heart pill. On the way she passed a large window. She felt faint, so she turned around and returned to her seat.

She thought about the window again and about throwing all the papers out of it. They would scatter everywhere and be gone just like she wished the trial were. She stared. She could open the window. She felt dizzy. *Just think, out the window, onto the bare, cold concrete below. Not just the papers—me too!* Becky got up from her wooden chair again. Her head felt numb. She was mesmerized by the chant of hatred and injustice that kept running through her head. *I hate this! I hate this!*

She walked closer to the window. She thought of nothing else but ending it all. No more suffering. *What do they want? Do they want me dead? What's in it for them if they win—an international company? It won't change their world if they lose this case. Why don't they just pay me off and leave us alone? They have the historic property, the subdivision, and hundreds of thousands of dollars in improvements with sewer and roads. Isn't that enough?* She stepped closer to the window.

Becky tried to open it, but it was nailed shut. She hit her hand on the pane. "Damn it, damn it to hell!" and she cried, a nervous and out-of-place frustrated kind of cry. She raised her arm in the air as if to beckon the secretary. "Why the hell is the window locked? Can't a person get any air around this place?" Becky asked her. She bent over at the waist, folded her hands on the sill, and cradled her head in her arms. She began to sob.

Get a grip, she told herself. *You've got to hang on!* She shook her head, sniffled her nose clear, and squeezed the last bit of moisture out of her tear ducts and sat down. She felt better. *Read on. Read on. Read on!* Hours passed. Becky transcended into obsessive mode now. Facts were sinking in again. She probably just needed a good cry. The case was far from over. She could hang on.

The clerk tapped his finger on the counter and motioned to Becky. One quick glance at her watch, and she realized that it was time to make her way back into the courtroom. She could not let herself be late. There was no way she would ever allow the judge to see that her conduct was anything but respectable and precise.

Becky walked in the back doors to the courtroom entrance and tried to act inconspicuous. Perhaps there was no need, but whether it was first time excitement, or leftover hype from the book, she imagined that many eyes were on her—people wondering why she was in the courtroom. Was she a newspaper reporter or a spy for the other side, an intern or a future witness? She scouted a place to sit down. In the lecture hall at the medical school she always sat down to the right, so now she thought she would sit down to the left. It just seemed like the thing to do. She also wanted to be close enough so that the judge would see her face. She hoped he would realize how dedicated she was and be aware of the serious steps she was taking to sit before him in her own trial.

Becky prepared to use the skills she had acquired when she took a class in court reporting at night school while still in high school. She utilized her shorthand training to help her to keep up with trial notes. She recorded how the plaintiff's attorney made opening remarks, who went first to begin questioning, how they entered in evidence, and how they brought forth witnesses. The two classes she had enrolled in some twenty years earlier to help ensure she would be able to find a job when she graduated from high school and got married came in handy. She took several pages of notes, and she learned the posture of the courtroom.

At the end of the day, Becky could tell that her plan had worked. She not only had learned procedures and how to conduct herself in the courtroom, but the judge had noticed her. After several hours of intriguing testimony and heated cross-examination between experts in the field of tobacco use, they wrapped it up for the day. As Becky began gathering up her things, she thought she heard a voice call her name. She looked up and glanced around.

"Rebecca—isn't that what you said your name was?" asked the judge. It *was* her name that she heard. She looked toward the bench squarely at Judge Fairchild. The room hadn't even emptied yet, and he was speaking to her.

Becky stayed fixed, looking directly at him and said, "Me—are you speaking to me?"

"Yes, would you please approach the bench?" asked the judge. *Did I do something wrong?*

"Rebecca, I saw you this morning and then again this afternoon at the trial and was wondering who you were. It finally dawned on me that you have been in my court before and are scheduled to be back in here, right? My clerk tells me it will be in about two months. Is that correct?"

"Yes, sir, that's right," Becky replied.

"I also understand that you are *pro se* in this matter, is that correct?" he asked.

"Yes sir, that's correct," Becky said.

"Well, may I suggest to you that you get a copy of the *Indiana Trial Rule Book of Evidence*? I co-authored this book, and I think you should familiarize yourself with it," said the judge. Becky thanked him even though she had already purchased the book, turned her back, and walked out. Same fears, different day, but with an air of fairness she left the courtroom, notebooks in her arms like a student, walking proudly, head held high from her accomplishments that day.

She didn't think for one moment that the events of that day would influence the decision of the judge, but she simply felt they were events for good measure. She was on cloud nine when she drove to her friend Debbie's house, even though she was exhausted. They shared pleasantries that evening, as Becky was less tense than usual. They hugged good night and retired early.

Morning came about five hours too early for Becky, as the long trip down and the events of the day before had completely worn her out. But she could not stop. There was still one last thing she had to accomplish on this trip, which was to meet with the lawyer who had handled their bankruptcy. Becky felt he would be an invaluable resource in directing her to which books she might read, or to some articles he might know of that might help. Becky always enjoyed his company anyway, so she looked forward to seeing him and telling him where she was at with the case, since he had seemed interested in what she was trying to do the last time they had seen each other. He was tall with curly hair, and he had the cutest smile she had ever seen. He was intelligent too. Becky enjoyed being around intelligent people, especially when they made her feel bright as well.

Phil was his name, and he was organized. He ran his law business like a grocery store, maximizing on the amount of people he could run through his office in one day, and doing so methodically. It was Becky's conclusion that he was someone who would not waste time, but would work efficiently to keep the line flowing smoothly. Becky felt honored that Phil had agreed to see her.

Becky left Debbie's house shortly after 8:00 a.m., drove downtown and, after much anxious anticipation, finally found a parking spot. She took the black binder out from behind the seat, the one that she used to store her trial data in, the one that was getting thicker and thicker. She locked her car and headed for Phil's office. Once there, she was asked by his secretary to have a seat to wait. Another one of the routines that had become commonplace throughout this trial—*have a seat and wait!* She had a cup of coffee offered to her, and about fifteen minutes later was escorted to another room where Phil finally entered.

"So, what is it that I can do for you today?" he asked. Becky was thinking of several ways that she could answer his question, but thought she'd keep it to serious conversation rather than interjecting humor in his apparently busy schedule. She proceeded to fill him in on the latest—what First Trust Mortgage's people had been putting the family through and how the defense was hiding documents. She told him it should be obvious to the judge what they had done, but if only she could get her hands on the original loan application. Phil suggested a procedure known as a Motion to Compel. He explained to Becky that he was in no way giving her legal advice, but that she might read up on the motion and see if it would be appropriate for her as a remedy. Not wanting to take up any more of his time by asking him to walk her through preparing this motion, she chose instead to thank him for his time and left to run over to the law library and look up the Motion to Compel before she left town. As she jogged up the street, Becky felt official with her legal briefs neatly hole-punched into her three-ring binder. She hurried so she could beat the rush hour traffic. If the Motion to Compel would help her get her hands on the original loan application and the appraisal, their original intent of fraud would be crystal clear.

Becky began to feel a thrill through what she was doing. She *was* capable. The lawyer in her was finally accepting its position. It had been months since she mourned the absence of medical school. It had been weeks since she last thought about Robert. She was intrigued by the task before her.

As Becky continued making her way through the downtown streets of Indianapolis, she remembered the woman she had befriended that used to work in the bankruptcy court, but who had left to accept a position with the Indiana Supreme Court. Peggy (she didn't know her last name) was one of the most intelligent women Becky had ever met, and she decided since she was in the neighborhood of the Supreme Court, she would drop by and see if she was in and to say hello. The last few conversations that the two of them had were on the phone months earlier, and Becky was delighted even then when Peggy seemed interested to hear the results of the bankruptcy turned fraud case. But because the adversary hearings took place where she had been legal counsel, it would have been a conflict of interest for her to listen to Becky or to comment on the case. She had to stick to strictly business then. Peggy surprised Becky, though, one day when she left work early, picked her baby up at the day care, and drove back to the courthouse just to witness Becky in action. As time passed, the bankruptcy case was over, and Peggy had a new job, and now she and Becky enjoyed mutual friendship and respect over the telephone, talking about their children and never the trial.

Becky had come a long way from not even knowing the difference between civil tort and civil plenary, and she was proud to have survived thus far. She had made many interesting, intelligent, and successful friends along the way—successful in the sense that they were self-actualized. That was a benefit that came from the litigation, and it gave Becky a sense of importance and satisfaction. She wasn't the loser First Trust had tried to make her out to be. How quickly she had made the transition from medicine to law. But as she left her friend, she couldn't keep the high, for who was she really? Somebody's daughter—yes. Somebody's wife—yes. And for sure, mother to three children. *Doctor—I'm not one! Lawyer—I'm not one of those either!*

Chapter Twenty-Four

When Becky got home she ignored the dusty table tops and went on a long walk with Erin, Eli, and Beth. She missed them so. Even her brief absence felt way too long. She conversed about superficial things with Will, what he had done while she was away. He didn't ask what she had done, nor did she want to discuss the case. Becky needed to forget about it for a while, and she immersed herself in the children, good books and preparing large family meals. The chronic and heightened state of anxiety made Becky fatigued and weary. The short respite would do her good. She would sleep better.

Becky thought she was handling things pretty well, but she knew that the neighbors talked in their driveways, a meeting place for the cul-de-sac families, about how Becky seemed depressed. They were right. Becky was feeling beat down and a failure. She had failed medical school and the subdivision, the conservatory was gone, and her marriage was far from the way it should be.

We should live in a house, not an apartment. There should be memories all around me and in it. There should be a spot—a familiar same-old spot in the floor that creaks, and it should have creaked for years. It should be a predictable creak that the whole family would be aware of and that they would hold in common. The same sidewalk should have been shoveled every winter, and the same flowerbeds weeded through the summer. Peace, security, freedom eluded her like colored balloons let loose by a child. She felt sorry for herself and for her children. *The kids—once raised, they're raised. You can't go back and relive. You only pass through once.* She wanted to make sure they were being raised the way she would have despite the adversity that robbed them of so much. To make matters worse, she felt distant from God. But she knew if she relied more on prayer, she would experience more peace. She would pray more.

Sitting curled up on the sofa, she reminisced her longing to be a rural practitioner, the role she would have played in a small community somewhere. She wanted to cultivate her need to start the day by doing rounds in a nursing home. But those days would never be. It didn't stop her from thinking, though, and whenever she walked past the medical school on the way to the law library , she looked for her former peers and watched the, like she would school children who were out for recess.

Becky selfishly thought about how nice it would be to be dead. She was aware that she was depressed and had most of the classic symptoms, including the inability to find joy in normal day-to-day things, lethargy, and thoughts of death. But that wasn't a choice.

The constant barrage of pre-trial paperwork didn't help her situation, as it was unrelenting. She had only just returned from the trip to Indianapolis when there to greet her were more legal renderings that would beg a response. Becky had waited until now to open it, and she sighed as she tore the envelope open. This time the document was titled "Second Request for Production to William D. and Rebecca A. Blaine."

Second request? Bastards. They've never sent me a first request.

The request came in the form of an interrogatory nineteen pages typed in the form of questions that had to be answered. Difficult, multifaceted questions that required much research, vivid details describing times, dates, and sequential descriptions, any and all statements, recorded in any fashion, sworn or not sworn to the witnesses of the cause of action, and *probably a request for my first born son,* Becky thought. Becky reacted in the manner the defense had undoubtedly hoped for, and in frustration she opened the door to her bedroom and whipped them in, not caring where they went, and slammed the door. Later, after hours of paper shuffling, hours of transcribed dictation to sort through, myriads of communication documents and notes of conversations, signed contracts, title work, promissory notes, eviction letters, foreclosure notices, utility receipts, quit claim deeds, insurance binder quotes, and even thank-you letters from brokers that had been hired to pre-sell lots, she would begin to form her response. She would try to substantiate their claim that the lots had been platted and could be defined by "meets and bounds" descriptions. Becky, a complete novice in understanding the law, was thrust into the responsibility of comprehending and putting into use tools that policed a nation and helped it survive over two hundred years.

Becky sat back in the only piece of furniture in their living room—an old couch that had been placed less than six feet in front of the television because that was the only space where it would fit. She thought and thought about what to write. She prayed as she reached to the floor to retrieve a pad and paper that she always kept next to the couch and on top of a pile of books that doubled as an end table, and she began to design her response: "Defendants William D. and Rebecca A. Blaine have no way of knowing what documents First Trust Mortgage, with counsel, have or do not have. But they believe that First Trust Mortgage is in possession of or has available to them everything that the Blaines are in possession of." In her sketching, she went on to say, "We affirm under the penalties for perjury that the above is true to the best of our knowledge."

But the reply wasn't all that she had in mind this time. Indeed, she was catching on to the miserable game. She would put an end to their deliberate attempts to make her look bad, uncooperative, inattentive, and incompetent. She wrote a letter addressed to the lead counsel with a blind copy to the judge that described in it that the Blaines, having received a document entitled "Second Request for Production," had never received a document of that nature as a *first* request. Becky also wrote that she had phoned them to inquire about the matter, and that the defense had acknowledged that it had indeed been their first request, but that they just wanted to make sure they had all the documents she had. A lie, of course, as any copies of documents that Becky had could have been obtained from the Court were a matter of public record. In fact, every question posed had already been addressed over and over again in depositions and reply briefs, affidavits, and transcribed testimony. She exposed their harassment and highlighted their intent. She refused to be drawn into their abusive, time-wasting device and wrote one-sentence answers to each response after that.

It was true: Becky *was* weak and tired. She was tired of the fight, and she wrestled with fatigue. She cried a lot. All she wanted to do was sleep. Her apartment was really a mess, but she didn't want to clean it. A beautiful world was going on all around her, but she was in the middle of a dark hole. A dark hole that extended all the way into her bedroom which she kept off-limits to everyone but Will. To enter would expose all that was going on inside of her, Becky's world, her private place to be left alone. There, her secret insides were laid out next to legal documents and miscellaneous notepapers that lined all four walls in the small room. The piles were at least four feet high and were leaning—sloppy layers that had accumulated by loosely thrown correspondence and copies of correspondence mixed together with more and more layers of legal papers. There were photocopies thrown on top of rough drafts and a few binders of biochemistry notes left over from her medical school days interspersed with clothes that lay in piles in the corners. Some clothes were clean, and some were dirty. Some were new from the Christmas before that had never been used or hung up. Socks were unmatched and lying in heaps in crannies made by two sections of paper stacks coming together. When she needed a pair, she dug into the heaps. The stacks were impractically high, and the ones by the door doubled as storage bins more than anything else. There was only about an eight-inch path around her bed where she could walk, and the blinds on the windows were never open.

She found miniscule solace at night when she finally crawled into bed, a small opening in the blinds creating a sliver of light through one of the slats that was broken, and through it she could see the dim reflection of the top of the street lamp. She gazed through the crack as a ritual, for it mesmerized her to see the flicker of obscurity. There was sameness through the crack—security and peace. When it snowed, she could see through the yellow hue, the little white flakes that seemed to dance their way to the street below. She was carried back to her childhood then, where she had also found pleasure in her room as she dozed off watching the snowflakes fall through the dim rays. She was at peace, and she could hear music then.

On the nightstand next to her bed, she had many small stuffed animals lining the back part of it next to the wall. Sometimes she would pick one up and cuddle it, even sleep with it—her arms wrapped tightly. If no one was around, she would kiss the little rabbit, bear, or dog—the precious, innocent little animals that caused no pain and provided great joy and comfort, her inanimate friends.

Becky worked day and night in preparation for the hearing for the Summary Judgment. She didn't quite understand what it was going to entail, but according to the research she had done, a Summary Judgment was just that. Becky felt that if she had all of the work completed, placed sequentially in a black binder, and to the judge by the due date, she was prepared. She would have done what was expected of her. The judge would then read both plaintiff and defendants' briefs pursuant to Trial Rule 56 and, on the day of the hearing would simply read his decision based on the Summary Judgment.

Becky felt that the facts were pretty straightforward. She felt organized. The only things left for her to do were to file her Motion to Compel, to make a formal Request for Admissions, and interrogatories. She needed to go back to the law library and figure out how to do one.

She found a basic format and used it as a template for *her* format. Number one—identify the individual(s) answering these interrogatories on your behalf. Leave room for the answer. Number two—identify each individual who provided information or otherwise assisted in the preparation of your answers to these interrogatories or your response to the foregoing Request for Admissions, and state specifically, for each individual, the information or assistance which he or she provided. Number three—if you denied either of the matters in the foregoing Request for Admissions, either in whole or in part; then, as to each matter denied…five, six…eleven. Please indicate whether or not, at any time, First Trust Mortgage claimed prior first mortgage on all twelve lots in the Canal Estates Subdivision. Becky learned that she needed to make a Request for Admissions so that she could then deem them admissible. Luckily for her, she understood what she had to do.

She received First Trust Mortgage's reply. The respondents were extremely vague with their answers—intentionally, of course, but Becky got enough in her Request for Admissions that she would be able to prove the inconsistencies in their testimony. In one document, First Trust Mortgage claimed they were aware of the subdivision—in another they said they were not. Sometimes they claimed they never intended to secure the mortgage with all of the property that encompassed the subdivision. Other times they said, with certainty, that this was their intent. Becky could hardly wait to get her hands on the original loan application and the appraisal through the Motion to Compel she had submitted. Documents had been mishandled, and there had been lies, corruption, and coercion among fellow employees, and unexplainable deception. She had no way of knowing for sure what she would see—if and when she ever got to review the original documents, which had been missing or lost from the beginning. Several documents were lost. Some had been tampered with—deliberately destroyed and, in some cases, illegally recreated. Becky could prove it too. She had been all places, looking at every document for a long time. It was the only way she could stay ahead of the defendants.

Becky made her formal Request for Production of Documents to First Trust Mortgage: "Comes now plaintiffs, William D. and Rebecca A. Blaine, by counsel, pursuant to Indiana Trial Rule 34, and request Defendant, First Trust Mortgage, to produce a copy of its entire file concerning . . ." Becky knew that preparing this document was simply a matter of semantics because there was no doubt in her mind that the file would come back incomplete. So before she even got the response to her request, she prepared her Motion to Compel Discovery.

Becky was aware of discovery deadlines, and she knew if there was any way First Trust Mortgage could detain her, they would. Therefore, simultaneously, she was spending time in the law library looking for solutions to the *anticipated* problems. She would be unable to complete her discovery because of the Defendants' cover-ups.

She asked herself: *Was there an extension of time she could ask for? Would the judge give her extra time if he could?* Becky drove herself nuts trying to think about all of the "what-ifs." She knew she had to anticipate all players' possible moves at all times, and she reviewed every detail with equal importance, for one word or one small detail missed or misunderstood could change everything.

As expected, First Trust failed to provide discovery on time. They were consistently costing her time and money. Becky decided she would ask the Court to require the defendant to pay the expenses and fees incurred by the plaintiff bringing the Motion to Compel. *Pro se* fees are not usually recoverable, but Becky found Federal statutes to support her request. Her request was granted, and her fees would be reimbursed. This was a small victory.

When the time was right, Becky pointed out to the judge that the file they had requested came back incomplete. She questioned the whereabouts of a key document that she felt had been intentionally lost and kept from her. "The Defendants have failed to respond to Plaintiff's discovery requested or to request an enlargement of time to respond or object hereto. Plaintiff has incurred expenses in bringing this motion in the sum of four thousand dollars, and reimbursement of expenses is appropriate under Rule 37 (A) (4)." She had learned many months earlier that anything said as a statement of fact had to be supported by statute, and she found one. Every request, whether in the form of a question or a production of a document, had to be justified by and certified by case law. First Trust Mortgage had destroyed the original application. That was that! Becky would ask them for it in court. Not having it would make them look bad. She would also show they *misplaced* the appraisal.

Becky went after a copy of it another way. She knew that the investor who had died before the case was closed had a copy of the appraisal, so Becky struck a deal with the dead man's lawyer and retrieved a copy of the appraisal. Even better, she got a copy of the original mortgage, which she never knew he had. The appraisal revealed exactly what she had hoped it would. The legal description *was* for one lot only—Lot One of Canal Estates. The comments listed revealed: "The subject is located in a newly platted subdivision in southwestern Marion County near the small community of Blaine's Valley. The addition consists of twelve residential sites located on Blaine Lane . . . the comparables were of lots the same size as Lot One, not of other subdivisions . . . the subject is the first home constructed in the subject's platted addition." *Perfect*. Becky planned to emphasize their mishandling. First Trust Mortgage was stacking up cards against themselves. Back in their office, the lawyers were readying themselves for a counter-attack. But not legal counters. Conventional law could not survive the challenge put forth by Becky and the Court. They would have to think of something else.

Becky completed her Summary Judgment and sent it to the judge. All in all, it was two hundred and thirty six pages. She had eighty Exhibits and thirty Affidavits. Her binder was tabulated and numbered. She felt confident this would be sufficient for the judge to render a decision. She had put everything she could into it and felt that October thirteenth would be judgment day for the whole family. She would finally be able to put the insanity of the lawsuit to rest.

This would be Becky's last trip to Indianapolis. She would listen for the judge to announce her and Will's victory. The family left right after Becky and Will got home from work. The minivan was loaded to the hilt with documents, binders, clothes, kids, toys, and two dogs. They said a prayer together before they left and asked for traveling mercies and the Lord's will in whatever would take place in the courtroom.

Will and Becky knew that the kids would fall asleep shortly after they stopped for dinner, so they didn't mind the overly anxious noise when they first started out. Stopping at Cracker Barrel had become a tradition on their multitudinous trips to Indianapolis because of the home cooking that everyone liked so much and because of the play area there for the kids. Will and Becky were right—soon after dinner and back on the road, the kids got cozy in their sleeping bags. It was dusk, and they admired the orange-purple-pink sky. Becky counted her blessings and suggested her children should too.

The car was filled with the scent of coffee, the sky was beautiful, and Becky's children were safe. Her Summary Judgment was complete, and she felt at this moment that she had the world by the tail. For the first time in forever, she actually felt good, and she savored the moment.

Will tried to hold a conversation with Becky, but she chose to ponder instead. He just kept his eyes on the road, and Becky kept her eyes on him to make sure he wasn't getting tired.

At about three o'clock in the morning, they were less than a mile from the gray house they had loved so much. Becky sat up in her seat and readied herself to find strength to ask Will if he would be willing to stop at the gray house—just so she could look at it. He agreed since the children were asleep. They turned onto Wicker Road, the same road that Will, before their move, had turned onto for forty years. At first it was when he was a little boy and lived with his grandparents. Then it was when he was driving as a teenager. Next, it was when he became a parent himself. Becky wondered what Will was thinking as they approached the house that he had built with his own hands on the land that had been his forefathers' for over a hundred years. She had a lump in her throat because she knew that although the court case had taken a toll on her, the real pain was Will's, and she felt sorry for his unspoken sorrow.

Will pulled into the gravel lane that was in front of the gray house. He idled the van for several minutes. Becky looked up at the windows that she used to look out of to watch the sunset from their master bedroom. Her eyes wandered over to where Beth's room had been and then to where the twins' room had been. She could picture exactly how things were the last week in the house—watching the children sleeping peacefully with all of their special things neatly tucked in their special places—and even as things were the day they left the house. She remembered the kitchen, the last time she had done dishes, and the last night with her neighbor raking by the light of the moon. *How is it that they were parked outside?* Becky wanted to walk in, put the kids in their beds, and live in this home, but she couldn't.

"The children are supposed to be up there right now, sleeping in their cozy little beds," she told Will. "Instead, look at them. They're crammed up here in this car!" Becky began to cry. She wished Will would take the initiative to hug her. He did not. He just sat there not saying a word, but he became visibly agitated. The children woke up, and the dogs became restless because the car was no longer moving.

"Let's get out of here," said Will. The children saw where they were and could sense their parents' anxiety. They too began to cry, though they didn't say exactly why.

Will backed out of the gravel lane and back onto Wicker Road, headed toward the main road, and passed Ruby and Charlie's house on the way. No doubt Charlie and Ruby were sleeping soundly. Becky missed them so much. She would see Charlie the next day, though. She knew that for sure, because he never missed a trial date. He showed up come rain or shine. He didn't attend the status conferences, so this would make his third appearance. When he was present in the courtroom, he was Becky's constant pillar of strength and encouragement. There were times that she bucked up to deliver sentences when she didn't think she'd be able to, just so Charlie wouldn't be disappointed in her.

The next morning the whole family walked into the courtroom to listen to what the judge would say. Charlie sat in the back of the room to the right, and Debbie a few chairs over. Becky's adrenaline was pumping. She took her pills that would lower her blood pressure and sat in the chair, motionless.

The judge walked in. "All rise." There were the routine opening remarks by the bailiff and court reporter. The defendants were allowed to begin.

Wait a minute—I'm the plaintiff! I should get to go first. Why did the defendants get to start? Becky felt like a six-year-old in a game of tag, whining and carrying on when it looked like things weren't going her way. But she had reasons for her distress. If First Trust Mortgage got to go first, they could get the upper hand just by virtue of setting the stage and, sure enough, they did. They put on a show. The judge said he was totally confused, probably because of all of the random information the defense was scrambling to throw at him. It appeared their plan was to muddy the water and detract from the real issues. *These were tactics that must be taught in law school,* thought Becky. She bet that the judge couldn't even figure out what the real merits of the case were. She guessed if she got an opportunity, it would be her job to tell him.

"Rebecca Blaine," the judge said, "do you have anything you would like to add to all this?"

"Excuse me, Your Honor, *add* to this? I haven't even begun," Becky said. She felt she didn't get a fair start. She felt lost, unprepared to dig herself out of a deep, sand-filled grave. The issues had been so misconstrued and things portrayed so out of whack she didn't know where to begin. She couldn't have objected because they were only giving opening remarks. She bent over for supportive documents and picked up a copy of case law. It had a copy of Robert's handprint from the day long ago when they had been in the law library in Madison together. Becky stared at the handprint, remembering the lifelines, the tender hand of Dr. Raine that used to stroke her face with loving adoration—long strokes that outlined her face as he took in all he could of the love he felt for her.

Becky took a deep breath. "Your Honor, I thought that when a case was heard pursuant to Trial Rule 56, that both parties had to submit their motions for a Summary Judgment, pass back and forth interrogatories, present affidavits . . ."

"Ms. Blaine, you are here today to present your case," the judge interrupted in a condescending tone. "Get on with it."

"Well, Your Honor," Becky began, "everything is in my Motion for Summary Judgment. Surely you don't want me to read it. Haven't you read it?" Becky didn't mean to sound as if she were questioning the judge. Of course he had read it, or was expected to read it—that wasn't the point. Becky knew her lack of formal training had her in a bad position. She didn't know what to do. Everything she had done over the last two years had built up to what was supposed to be the pivotal turning point for her this day. She had planned everything and completed everything perfectly. Surely it wasn't going to end this way. A tear ran down Becky's face. She was overwhelmed. *They won. I screwed up on a technicality.* She hadn't prepared to put on a defense about anything. She had shut down most of the facts, which normally vacillated obsessively through her mind. Now she could barely remember the defendants' names. She couldn't remember the order of events that led to the demise of the subdivision and the painful bankruptcy. She was wiped out and could recall nothing.

Becky sat back, cried, and looked at the judge in disbelief. Her legs were outstretched, and she sat slouched. Her face was pale, and her eyes sunken in defeat. *Lord, what were the last two years and leaving medical school all about?*

Becky had listened intently to the defendants and what they were asking for. She listened to the loud spectacle. Hopeless and feeling like she couldn't lose any more ground than she already had, she looked up at the judge and asked, "Your Honor, really, haven't you read my Summary Judgment?" Becky did not mean to sound disrespectful or infer that he hadn't read it; she really wanted an explanation to her confusion. If he hadn't read it, maybe she would read parts of it to him. She didn't have to think or recall things then. Innocently, she continued. She truly thought that her job had been completed when she turned in her Summary Judgment, that the judge would read it, and that he would render a decision based on the facts and evidence presented in the document. She had showed up in court today prepared to hear a verdict.

She glanced over to the other side of the room. The defendants smirked as they realized that Becky had ticked off the judge. They were shaking their heads like they couldn't believe she could be so stupid. They felt victorious. They knew they hadn't played fair. They stayed true to form—dirty pool at all costs. Who cared? What difference did it make to them? They had no principles or scruples.

The room fell silent. It had been silent for quite a while, but Becky hadn't noticed because the voices in her head were too loud.

The judge backed off. He ruled that neither side had won and that the case would be set for bench trial. Becky was so disturbed by being caught off guard, she didn't catch what he said at first. But when she did, she was surprised, amazed, and happy—the other side hadn't won. It didn't take long, however, for her to realize what the judge's ruling meant the case wasn't over. It would go on again, who knew how long. Physically and mentally she had convinced herself to allow relief to set in, that this would be their last trip to Indianapolis for the stupid trials and tribulations surrounding the Canal Estates Subdivision. The judge's decision would come and, either way, it would be over, and the Blaines could finally move on.

She knew her heart and her nerves wouldn't allow her to survive much longer. Now she was faced with an even bigger task—a bench trial. Affidavits would need to be turned into subpoenas. The defendants could cross-examine. Becky would be forced to perform at an even higher level. More craziness. *How in the world will I ever be able to get ready for a real trial? No training. More research.* "God, I can't," she whispered. *I can't locate all of the people from the past to subpoena. I can't figure out how to lay out our evidence.* Trial Rule 56 had failed her.

Becky was quiet for the first few hours of the ride home, then she allowed herself to think, reached into the bag by her feet, and pulled out a yellow tablet and pen. She began a conversation with Will.

"Okay, Will, we can't let this get us down. We have been given an opportunity to continue. At least the judge didn't rule in their favor. It could have been worse. This is what we're going to do. Did you hear all that stuff they were telling the judge? I believe these are the only issues they are going to try to win with. They exposed their hand today, Will. This is good. They believed the judge would rule in their favor. They took a lot for granted, and they lost. Now I know what they're really thinking—what they feel. I will be able to figure out how to tear them down. Don't worry, Will," Becky said. Will kept on driving down the road.

Will smiled and said, "You know Becky, you're like a wild filly that roams the prairie and tames the west—you wouldn't ever try to break her—you'd break her spirit." His comment was about as close to a compliment that Becky had gotten from him in a long time, and it made her feel good.

While sitting together in the car for the long trip home, Becky began questioning Will on everything he could remember about the case, and she made notes so the two of them together would formulate a united front of understanding. She started to put things in order as to the series of events. She made more notes alongside the outline of documents she had created and a list of those she would need to retrieve to prove a particular point or event. She added sequentially the people she would need to subpoena—people who would be expert witnesses to prove even more points.

In about five hours, minus one potty break, she organized the details of their story backed up by exhibits and testimony that Becky hoped would win their case. The kids had been a pleasure in the car as they watched their parents work together happily side by side. By the time they got back to Madison, a trip that seemed a lot shorter than the way down, Becky already had a great start on their last hurrah.

Becky was emptying her suitcase as she listened to the answering machine when they got home. Friends and neighbors had called, anxious to hear the results of the trial. When Becky returned their calls the next day, they were all disappointed when they found out that their ordeal wasn't over. They sympathized with Becky and empathized with Will. They gave her praise and encouragement to continue, and together with the reservoir of support from Will, she felt energized. That night she got on her knees, folded her hands, and prayed, "Dear Lord, there are many lonely people in this world, empty people, and people who are afraid. All they need is to feel loved, Lord, and their lives would be so different. Lord, please give them love. Help me to give love—to be more loving—to feel full of love and to share this love. Please use me to put your loving arms around them. Heal them. Heal me." Becky got into bed next to Will, put her head next to his, put her arm around his chest, and fell asleep.

Less than a week after they got back, Becky received a Notice of Deposition in the mail. Already they were going to have to arrange another trip and be questioned by the defendants in a formal and recorded session. *What information did they think they were going to get that they hadn't gotten before?*

Becky responded with a Request for Deposition to Be Denied. She begged the Court: "To demand that William D. and Rebecca A. Blaine and family drive to Indianapolis, Indiana, is indeed a hardship. This case has been litigated for three years, and the Plaintiffs feel that no additional information will be gained from further testimony not already presented before the Court. Further, William D. and Rebecca A. Blaine stand to lose their present employment stemming from the necessity to be absent from their duties so many times for this case. Additionally, the Blaines would be away from their children the two days prior to the first day back to school, and the twins are young and need their parents. Finally, the family needs to remain in Madison as much as possible before the trial, and the financial burden of yet another trip would be devastating."

The Blaines phoned Mr. Shortino, the defense lawyer, to inquire about what additional information they could possibly need. Mr. Shortino said that the company wanted to know the breakdown of the damages Will and Becky were seeking and they needed to have a discussion regarding an offer by First Trust Mortgage at an independent arbitration meeting, which originally had fallen through at the Plaintiffs' insistence. Becky informed Mr. Shortino that as a result of pre-arbitrary preparation, that First Trust Mortgage already possessed the settlement breakdown, and that in the Blaines' opinion, there was no need for a deposition. Becky's conversation with Shortino closed in the way she had expected, and she typed the last sentence to her reply to the court: "The Plaintiffs are requesting that the Court deny First Trust Mortgage's request for the Blaines to travel to Indianapolis, Indiana, for further Discovery prior to the December 17, 1996, bench trial."

Two days after Becky sent out her Request for Deposition to Be Denied, she got the Order Requiring Attendance at Deposition that had been rubberstamped by the judge. Becky thought for sure that the judge would have denied their request knowing firsthand how much their family was suffering, and he should have known there would be no new discovery. She couldn't believe he would allow the defense to put her through more rings of fire. Becky wondered if he had sent the order before he even received Becky's Request for Denial.

Becky tried one more time with another form of written plea to the Court, a Motion to Rescind Amended Order Requiring Attendance at Deposition. This time she wrote, "Defendants' counsel stated in its Motion to Compel Attendance at Deposition that cause for the Blaines to travel to Indianapolis was due, in part, because the Blaines didn't attend one that was previously scheduled by notice more than four years ago. This statement was false. The Plaintiffs feel that defense counsel has had four years to depose us in Indianapolis, and this was sufficient time to have conducted depositions, particularly in consideration that all parties have been present in Indianapolis, Indiana, for at least four hearings involving this case where Defendants' counsel could have held depositions. The Plaintiffs are not trying to escape the depositions, but if they must take place, they request to have the depositions held in the Blaines' home county. The Blaines request at this time that the judge sign an order granting that the Blaines do not need to travel to Indianapolis to be present at a deposition, but may be deposed in Madison, Wisconsin. Further, the Plaintiffs have used up all their vacation time and several days without pay over the last year making trips to Indianapolis, Indiana, for hearings and conferences for this case and stand to lose their jobs if a request for more time off is made to their places of employment. The Blaines have been extremely compliant over the last three years to provide all counsel in this case with any and all information they were in need of to fairly and honestly litigate this case, and they feel that the defendants' prolonged harassment and constant lack of consideration or even moderate compromise, is almost more than Rebecca Blaine can physically and psychologically handle. Rebecca Blaine has been to a physician in Madison, Wisconsin, who has put her on Nortriptyline to combat the severe depression she is sustaining as a result of pre-trial preparation for the hearing that is scheduled . . . ."

The defendants responded with a Motion to Compel Attendance at Deposition, and the judge ordered it to be so.

Becky made the trip back to Indianapolis alone. The children cried when she left, and it tore Becky apart to miss Beth's Homecoming. Becky had waited all her life to see her daughter get ready for Homecoming, and Beth had been voted queen. Becky wanted to be together with Beth while she got her hair done, and she wanted to take pictures and to be a part of the excitement. She wanted to drive Beth to her date's house to meet his parents, to go to the football game on the cool autumn night with Will and the boys, to laugh, and to cry watching her daughter becoming all grown up and being crowned. Once again, Becky and her family were cheated. The only thing she got to do that was of her own volition was to cry, and that she did. For the entire eight hours of the grueling depositions, all she did was cry. She had brought her crocheting along, and she sat in the corner, surrounded by all the people who had been so mean to her—causing her family great pain and suffering, committing fraud, knowingly and willingly. Becky cried and crocheted. She didn't look up. She just cried, crocheted, and answered their questions. They had no pity on her, and they fired hours of unrelenting questioning, trying to get anything they could to use against her in court. The very people who had been so cruel to Becky and her family continued to beat her into the ground showing no mercy to her pain. She cried more and moved her crochet needle back and forth.

Yes, Becky did cry real tears not being able to attend Beth's homecoming dance, and for being exhausted and forced to take antidepressants, and forced to quit her job lest she be fired. Indeed she was troubled by her and Will's difficult financial situation, but she manipulated the overflow of tears during the deposition. She intentionally wore one of her floral church dresses, and cried for effect. She crocheted so as not to be bored. Her dress and her crocheting were props. She wanted to leave the impression of being a weak, tired, ignorant, and deflated woman. As soon as the defendants asked their last question and had left the room, she shoved her yarn and needle into her bag, went to the restroom to get out of her dress and throw on some sweats and, with strength and determination, left the building looking back like it was a house of fools.

The defendants continually worked in the weeks that followed to redesign their strategy. Becky worked to frame it. In the minds of the defense, they decided that because she cried and whimpered during the last trial, that she wasn't in control during depositions or on the phone, their day in court would be a piece of cake. They underestimated her. All along, she was writing the score for the orchestra to play, and the music she heard was jubilant.

When Becky got home and was alone in the house, she did cry her private tears, for she had missed the kids, and she had felt tortured and unreasonably pressured by a system that wouldn't leave her alone.

Later that night Will asked her how things had gone. "You cried for how long?" Becky's eyes were still puffed almost shut.

Becky slept for twelve hours straight that night. She was glad to be in her own bed. She spent most of the next day in quiet reflection. Adversity revealed Becky's character, and her steadfast faith kept a torch in her hand—a torch that would lead her home. In her mind, she held the torch high, like the Statue of Liberty, and thought *she too stands alone in the harbor.*

Becky came from a long line of strong, brave characters. Among her ancestors was William H. Seward, the Secretary of State, who was responsible for the purchase of Alaska. Another, the longest living survivor of the Boston Tea Party. Becky would try to be like them. She could do it. With tenacity she would be able to properly expose the facts, and prove the truth beyond a reasonable doubt—the preponderance of evidence.

Becky received many hang-up phone calls that started not soon after the deposition ended. She felt the defendants were taunting and harassing her to keep her full of anxiety. There never seemed to be a peaceful moment in her life now. She sat and held Erin. The phone rang. She cuddled and didn't want to get up, dreading it to be a hang-up call. She picked it up. No one was there. *Damn.* She sat back down. Her blood pressure rose. She continued to hold Erin. Later she ran up from the laundry room. Hang up. She ran in from outdoors. Hang up. She got out of the shower dripping wet. Hang up.

Chapter Twenty-Five

There were more back and forth motions from the defendants. Then *the* phone call came. It was Mr. Shortino. He was not a very bright man, and had no manners. He sounded like a bill collector, condescending and belligerent whenever he spoke. It seemed as though the corporation relied on him, but to Becky his actions were foolish. He played the "heavy"—the guy who would try to bully his opponent into submission. Becky had no respect for the incompetent, mean-spirited fool. The phone call did, however, make her shake in anger. If it would have been possible, and if she could have gotten away with it, Becky would have reached her hand through the phone and choked him. Will seemed to share her sentiments, and after seeing what the lawyer was putting his wife through, he extended his hand toward her, saying with an impatient voice, "Here Becky, give me the phone!" But Becky smiled and declined. She said she would handle it.

"Mrs. Blaine," Mr. Shortino said, "First Trust Mortgage has authorized me to offer you a settlement. You understand that you are going to lose." And there was a pause. "We just thought that rather than all of us spending any more money, we would just pull the plug now and give you say, thirty thousand dollars to end it right now. What do you say?"

"I say you're out of your mind! You really think this is about money? We aren't going to settle. This is about principle. We've already lost everything. There is nowhere to go except up from here, Mr. Shortino. We don't want your dirty money," Becky said.

"But that's precisely what I was saying. We realize you have lost everything, so why don't you take the thirty grand and get a fresh start?" the lawyer suggested.

"Fresh start," Becky said, her voice escalating in volume. "That's what the bankruptcy lawyer told us when we went into his office frustrated and downtrodden because you and your band of gypsies took everything from us. Get a fresh start, right. You make me sick. Leave me alone." She slammed down the phone and began to cry. "Will, they just won't leave us alone!" Becky buried her head in the pillow on the sofa, then picked it up and beat it against the back of the sofa.

Will said, "Why did you even talk to them? I don't like that they call you up and get you all upset."

"What do you mean why did I even talk to them, Will? I have to talk to them. It's my job. I've got to try to keep up with what they're thinking so that I might be able to figure out what they're going to do next. Every time I talk to them I learn something. Sure it gets me upset, but they reveal things about themselves every time they open their mouths, and I want to hear what they have to say. It speaks of their position, and it allows me to get into their heads."

"Well," Will said again, "I don't like it that they get you all upset." Becky acknowledged and appreciated Will caring about her, even though she really thought he cared more about losing than her feelings.

The kids walked home from school that afternoon and told their mother that a man in a green car followed them all the way home. Becky felt a chill go up the back of her neck. *Could it be that they're following us now?* She quizzed the children as to why they thought they had been followed. Had that man been waiting at the school? When did they notice they were being followed? Was he going so slowly that he kept pace behind them as they walked? What did the driver look like?

Beth explained to her mother that when she met Erin and Eli at the corner where they usually met when they didn't get a ride home, that the green car was already there. But she didn't think much about it until every turn they made onto the short streets through the neighborhood that led to their house, the green car made the turns too. She said a man was driving, but as soon as they entered the cul-de-sac, he took off. The children said he had on sunglasses, and they couldn't tell if they knew him or not.

Surely the children are mistaken. She told the kids not to worry, but that she'd be picking them up from school from now on. Becky tried to convince herself that no one was really following the children, but in the back of her mind she knew the possibility existed. Maybe it was a pizza guy looking for the right address, or a Jehovah Witness looking for his next stop. That evening, there was an anonymous caller on the phone that said, "You better watch yourself!" She felt paranoid to be home alone, and she never let the children out of her sight even if they just went outside in the back of their apartment to play.

There were more calls—harassing calls. Mr. Shortino called again. This time he said, "You know you can't make anyone aware of the settlement offer, but I've been authorized to offer you seventy thousand right now—take it or leave it. And if you don't take it, well, you'll be sorry you didn't. You and your husband are going to lose, you know. You brought all of this on yourselves. You're lucky to get this offer, and you're fools if you don't take this money!"

Becky's friend, Debbie, called and said that some guy had been calling her and asking questions about Becky—trying to dig into her past. "Who did he say he was, Deb?" Becky asked.

"He didn't say. He just said that he was a friend and wondered when you were going to be coming down and if you were going to be staying with me again."

"Well, what did you tell him? Did you tell him when?"

"I told him that if he didn't tell me who he was that the answer was none of his business. He didn't seem too pleased. Becky, he sounded like a real creep!"

Becky began to feel intense panic. She couldn't figure out who could be calling or why, if they were keeping track of every move she and her family made, or how far they'd go to further aggravate her. She was certain of one thing—she'd never accept their bribe.

A couple of days went by. Becky stopped at Chin's Wok a few blocks from where she lived to order Chinese for dinner. Becky asked for the order to go, and she poured herself a cup of tea that was offered to "while-u-wait" customers. She leaned back against the wall and watched two tall, young men walk in and place an order. They were dressed to the hilt—shiny shoes, business suits and trench coats. They began to talk to each other.

"The meeting today sure was boring, wasn't it?" one of the men said to the other.

"It was, but we have to sit through it, you know," the other one said in an even louder voice.

"Yeah, I know. With these tactics, First Trust Mortgage will really prevail in the marketplace. We didn't become international on our looks." The two laughed.

What? First Trust Mortgage? Becky felt they had been following her. They intentionally went into Chin's Wok just to make Becky realize they knew where she was. She left without taking her order. She went home and locked the door behind her. She wondered what lengths they would go to so that she would give in to their demands. *Harassment—how can I expose them?* The police could do nothing because no crime had been committed. She was helpless, and Will offered no solutions. Her migraines became worse, and she threw up often from stress-induced esophagitis. Her high blood pressure made her bedridden at unexpected and inconvenient times. Everywhere she went she looked over her shoulders.

Then one day it came to her. As if by some miracle, she thought of a new tactic. She would see if there were any local First Trust Mortgage offices. She looked in the phone book and found that there was an office not too far from home. She would go there and pretend that she was inquiring about a loan, be observant, and see what she could find out. Maybe she'd see the two guys from the restaurant. She would let them know that she was aware of what they were trying to do and that she wasn't intimidated. She left the house, cautious as she locked the door behind her, and always looked ahead by the bushes in front of the apartment complex. She glanced in the backseat of her car before she got in even though it had been locked. She drove to the First Trust Mortgage office, parked, and prepared herself. She didn't know exactly what she was going to do when she got there. When she walked in, she was nervous and felt light-headed. She saw no one that was familiar. A young woman approached the counter and asked if she could be of service to Becky.

Becky said, "Well, my husband and I are new to the area, and we wondered what we need to do to apply for a mortgage. If we find a house to buy, what would be our next step?" Becky was uncomfortable telling fibs, and she felt her face flush. She was so flustered that when she saw movement in her periphery, she could have sworn it was Robert heading toward what looked to be a conference room off the main hallway. *No, it wasn't him. No way, what would he be doing here?*

The woman gave Becky a short run-down of procedures, and then Becky realized that she would use the opportunity to gather evidence. "So, if I gave you a loan application today, would you keep that in your file for a while?" she asked.

"Oh, certainly. We keep all transaction records on file for seven years. You would be active from the day you filled out the application until about seven years after you would close on your loan," said the young woman.

"Really," said Becky. "You mean that you don't get rid of the original loan applications—you keep them?"

"Yes, it's company policy," the woman said.

"Could I get you to write that down for me? I mean, I'm not good at explaining things to my husband, and I want him to know that if we go through the trouble of filling out all the papers, past employment, past address, earnings, assets and debts, that we won't have to do it again, regardless of how long it takes us to find a house," Becky said. She knew that this was a lame excuse for wanting the company policy in writing, but the young woman seemed inexperienced enough to go along with her request. Becky hoped that she would just take care of it and not ask too many questions. It was worth the risk.

"Have you ever been a customer of ours before?" the young woman asked.

Becky almost choked her reply. "No, no we haven't."

"Okay. I just need your name and address to enter into the computer, and then I'll write this out for you." *Name and address—Oh boy, I sure don't want to give her our name! I'll give her a fake one.*

When the young woman handed Becky the signed note Becky thought, *you know, I really should have this notarized to make it something I can use in court. This woman will think that I'm nuts!*

Becky went ahead and asked the woman if there was anyone in the office that was a Notary Public. The young woman looked confused, but told Becky she would need to get a supervisor. The young woman walked away, and shortly afterward a tall, older woman in high heels strutted out from behind the door and approached Becky.

"Now, what is it exactly that you need from us?" the older woman asked.

"I just need this notarized to prove to my husband that I was really here and that what you said was really policy," Becky said.

Becky was going to offer more of an explanation, but she figured that she would only make the situation more unbelievable, and for now she had said enough. Becky figured that the lady would do it for her just to get her out of the office. The woman asked her the same questions as the younger woman had asked—about the name, address, and if she had ever been a customer. Then she went over to the computer to punch the information in again. Again, Becky felt her face get hot, like she was committing a crime and she was about to get caught.

Finally, after about forty minutes from when Becky had first entered the office, she had her notarized statement. She would use it in court. She felt a sense of empowerment over First Trust Mortgage. When Becky got home, she was excited to share with Will what she had accomplished. She got one over on the defendants again, and it invigorated her. She decided to rest from the litigator stuff and do something she hadn't done in a long time—clean the house. She started in the garage where there were bags of things, especially papers they had brought with them from Indianapolis. Until now she had been too worn out to consider going through them, even though she knew there could be legal papers in there that she could use in her preparation for trial.

Becky put on a comfy pair of sweats, some old tennis shoes, and headed for the garage. She started pulling things off the top of a dusty bookshelf that hadn't been used in three years. There was no place for it in the apartment. She wondered if she would find anything she could fit and use now, just to add something different to the apartment. *Oh, forget it; there's too much in there already.*

But she kept digging anyway. She came across a bag that had some of Beth's old dolls in it. *Wow! It seems like yesterday when she was running around the house with her little baby doll, changing her clothes, and pretending to feed her. How time has gone by! I thought when we left Indianapolis that these bags would be unpacked so she could continue to play with them. But we never had the room to unpack these bags, and now Beth is too old and wouldn't want to play with them.* Becky once again felt cheated of the youthful memories that Beth had missed because of the ruthless creeps from First Trust. She looked around at all of the things that filled their two-car garage. Most of them were from the gray house.

Becky could hardly remember what she hadn't seen in three years. *I ought to just have a truck come and haul all this stuff away. I mean if we've done without it for three years, we probably don't even need it! Oh, what's this?* Becky pulled out some of Will's graduation papers. Then she found his old track trophies that were packed loosely in a big brown box. *Where did these come from? I would have thought they would have been burned up in the fire!* She began to dig through an old suitcase filled with stuff like the jar of fifty-cent pieces that Will's Dad had given Will Junior for his tenth birthday—before the fire. How did all these things fit into the series of events that played over and over in Becky's mind? *How did all this stuff survive the fire?* In the back of her mind Becky had always questioned whether Will started the fire in the farmhouse. Had she just uncovered the proof? Again, she played the restaurant scenario of that cold December night in her mind. *Let's see. Will got up from the table to make a phone call to check on the children. He was gone for a long time. How long? Long enough to start the fire? When he got back he was visibly uneasy. Why? Why didn't I question him then? He was almost always distressed—that was nothing unusual, so why would I question him?* He had no good excuse that Becky could think of for being gone so long. He was distant and not very talkative when he came back to the table. *He did it, didn't he?*

Becky wondered again why the policeman was at the smokehouse that day when she was gardening behind the trailer they lived in. *What to do now?* She questioned Will's honesty and integrity, and she got chills to think she still slept in the same bed with a man that had perhaps set his own house on fire. But she chose not to question him on anything that she found. She would listen, watch, and wait.

Her findings that day made her less and less tolerant of Will. He was again subjected to Becky's cold shoulder.

"Becky, why are you acting so cold toward me lately? I thought we were working things out."

"I just don't think I like you, Will. I don't trust you," she said.

Who was she to talk about trust? There had been Robert. *But an affair when you need love isn't like arson, is it? Which sin is worse?*

Will wanted the two of them to go for counseling. Becky was amazed he would take the initiative to suggest such a thing. *He never took the initiative for anything emotionally based before!* She agreed to go with him, but not for her sake—for his. Becky was stubborn and didn't want to change her position. She didn't feel loved. She didn't love him or trust him. And that was that! She had no desire to work to keep the marriage together. She had had enough. *Besides,* she thought, *if a marriage takes this much work, then it's probably not worth it anyway.*

The children felt no ill effects from Becky's and Will's difficulties because Becky wasn't outright mean to Will in front of them, and they kept their conversations private. She would put up with Will sticking around just until the lawsuit was concluded, and then she figured he should probably get a place of his own. Now wasn't a good time for a formal separation. The children didn't deserve the added pressure of insecurity. They too had been through enough. That was the only thing that Becky really hated about her notion to eventually leave. She hated to break up the family unit that she had worked so hard to get. She wished she could think up another solution, but she couldn't. For now, she would hold her suspicions in a secret place next to her heart and put up with the status quo. Her marriage had been empty and void for as long as she could remember, so what was the big deal now, to stay together as co-plaintiffs and co-parent for the sake of the children?

Will began to spend a lot of time away from home when Becky was there with the kids because it hurt him too much to be around where he didn't feel wanted. Becky wondered where he'd go when he'd leave for so long. What other secrets did he have packed away in dark corners?

Chapter Twenty-Six

It was time for another trip to Indianapolis. This time, she decided to leave early in the morning instead of driving half the night. She got to Debbie's about an hour after Debbie got home from work. Debbie was expecting her and had already made a pot of coffee. The two of them sat at her kitchen table to have a good old-fashioned gossip session, as Debbie put it. Becky had a lot on her shoulders, and it was calming to talk; she just couldn't quit. It was unusual for her to expose her private and personal life events, marriage, and problems, but she did. Debbie really enjoyed that Becky was on a roll because the soap opera chat was fun for her. She listened in amazement to the allegations Becky had against First Trust, her questions about Will, the speculation of the outcome of the lawsuit, and how the children were faring, which was quite well, considering the circumstances. Becky didn't tell Debbie everything though. She didn't tell her about the extent of her suffering. She couldn't—for it was too inconceivable to put into words.

Becky was surprised by all of Debbie's stories. Becky had problems, yes, but Debbie's faith was tested by many things. They made Becky feel like she sure didn't want to trade places with her. "Becky, you know how we met at Blaine's Valley United Methodist? I don't go to church anymore. In the last five years, I lost my baby to crib death, lost my husband soon afterwards, was forced to move from my home to this apartment because I couldn't afford to pay the mortgage, and now my sister has a brain tumor."

Becky got up from the table and held her friend as she cried. She stroked her hair, and the two of them stood there for the longest time. They had been through so much since Will and Becky had moved to Wisconsin, and the two wished they could go back in time to the way things used to be.

Becky just wanted to go to bed, to pray, and to sleep off the bad news, but Debbie wanted her to stay up and talk some more. "You know why I got divorced, Becky?" she asked.

"No, not really," Becky said. "I knew you guys weren't getting along, but to tell you the truth, I never, ever expected that you two, of all people, weren't making it. I mean, he was studying theology and all. I thought if anyone made the perfect family, you two did. I used to admire the incredible closeness you displayed during Wednesday night Bible Study classes, and you two and the kids all dressed up on Sunday mornings—you seemed to have it all."

"I never told anyone how bad things were between us because I didn't want people to talk. So I just left the church and moved to the north side of town where I didn't have to see anyone I knew," Debbie said. Becky told Debbie it pained her to watch her and the children going through the divorce, but she assured her she was not judging her. "You never know what other people are going through in their lives," Becky told her. Becky wondered how they had managed to survive the pain, and she wondered, too, if maybe Debbie had somehow blamed her husband for her son's death. Debbie continued to fill in the gaps caused by a distant friendship, and the clock ticked away late into the night.

"Barry always had two sides, Becky, like Will. We'd come home from church, and he was mean to all of us, yelled, demanded chores for all of us, even me, using harsh words, and he also had a girlfriend. He continually put me down verbally. I stayed as long as I could, Becky, but I just couldn't take it anymore," Debbie said, visibly shaken. She went to the cabinet and brought out a pack of cigarettes and a crystal rock on a chain.

"I didn't know you smoked, Deb. When did you start that?" asked Becky.

"About two years ago. I do it after the kids are in bed. Cigarettes are kind of like my friend. Just me and my cigarettes—and I have my crystal, too. I read that it can help give direction—here, watch. If you don't know what to do about something, you hold it in front of your heart—hold it really still. Then if it sways to the sides you should *do* whatever you're questioning, because the crystal is confirming it. If it doesn't move, you *don't do* whatever it was you were questioning," Debbie said.

Becky watched her friend become a person she barely knew right in front of her eyes. Like so many of Becky's friends who had gone through divorce, they all said in the end that they just couldn't take it any more. What was "it"? Becky thought about the rules in the Bible and how if couples followed the basic principles, things would work out. *But solutions don't come easily, and they don't always come when we want them to.*

"After he dumped his girlfriend," Debbie continued, "he blamed the failure of that relationship on me too. It was crazy. He left the ministry, you know."

"No, you're kidding," said Becky, who by this point wasn't surprised by anything Debbie said. She thought it was surreal that there were so many odd and abrupt changes from the perfect family life they seemed to have.

"Yup. He left the ministry and got a job as a security guard at the mall," said Debbie.

"No way."

"He has two girlfriends now," Debbie said, "and as I understand it, they all three like to be together—if you know what I mean. And he never sees our sons."

"That's really sad, Debbie. You never really know a person, do you?" said Becky.

Debbie continued to tell Becky lots of things—like how she had surgery to make her breasts bigger with insurance money she had gotten after her son's death, figuring it would help with her low self-esteem. Becky couldn't understand why someone who was hurting financially would spend money on something like that, but she thought that perhaps in Debbie's mind, an outward change would help her inward self. Becky thought of her own experience she had had with Robert; who was she to judge? Debbie said she had started working out at the gym too, hoping to get in shape, maybe "catch herself a man." Becky shook her head in silent understanding at the strangeness of life.

There is a thread that would need to be measured in nanometers to judge the closeness between good and bad. People seem to be held together by such fragility. "The night is short, Debbie, but the day will be long. Let's get some rest now." Becky got up from the table. It was three o'clock in the morning. She hugged her friend and whispered a prayerful "Goodnight."

The next morning Becky left for the courthouse early to watch and listen one last time to how court trials were conducted. She was tired, but at least she didn't have to do anything this trip but listen to the trial, which she thought to be boring. *Another poor soul stymied into years of bickering, heightened anxiety, and elevated blood pressure. What will the litigants be left with after it's all over? Years of not having a life of their own, and for what? Money? Principle?* Becky hoped that it would all make sense to her one day.

Becky was still disgusted with the judicial system, and she could feel herself getting even more depressed as she listened to the two sides battle out their differences. It was a way of life for her now, too. Good moments, then bad. *Count your blessings,* she said to herself. She got up and left the courtroom in a half-dazed huff because she couldn't take one more minute of it. She headed up the stairs to the law library to look up a few things before she left for home. She had a scornful look on her face and questioned what purpose was served when people were miserable and they couldn't control their misery. *You have no choice. You have to just continue on—the continuum of misery. Or should you give up? Let injustice go until the afterlife when God judges all. No. He gives you a brain and expects you to use it. No clear answers. Keep the faith. Keep on trudging along.*

Becky made it upstairs and decided she needed a break from all of her serious thinking. *Chill out. Take it easy on yourself. Everything is going to be just fine.* Becky walked into the City-Country law library in Indianapolis up three floors from the courtroom she had been in and took a seat at the small round table in the middle of the main room. She sat in a chair and slouched back in it, legs straight out. The room itself was small, and there were only two other people there, the librarian and one other patron who left soon after Becky entered. Becky began to speak quietly to the librarian, who was facing the copy machine and had her back toward Becky. Becky sighed and decided to unwind a little with idle conversation. Becky asked her how her day had been going so far. When the librarian walked a little closer in order to hear better, Becky noticed that her right side was paralyzed, like she had had a stroke or something. *Here I am again, feeling sorry for myself when someone else has more problems than I do.*

"So, how long have you been a librarian?" Becky asked, and the woman looked puzzled that anyone would ask, but she walked even closer to Becky to answer her.

"I first started out as a volunteer checking books in and out at my high school library many years ago. That was the only experience I had before coming here, and I've been here ever since," the lady said.

"Really. Experience is the best teacher. What high school did you attend?" asked Becky.

"Oh, a high school on the south side of town," said the librarian.

"Yeah?" Becky said. "My husband went to a south side high school too, Southport High School."

"You're kidding. I went to Southport too. Small world," the lady answered. "Small world."

"Yeah, you're right about that," said Becky. There was a pause. "I enjoy libraries, always did I guess, but didn't realize how much until I've had to spend so much time in them lately. Books are not only my friend, but I can go anywhere I want to go when I read a book, you know. And you can get to know the most influential people that way too."

"That's true," the librarian said.

"So what year did you graduate?" Becky asked.

"1973," replied the woman.

"That's when my husband graduated. Did you know Will Blaine?" Becky asked.

Becky sometimes felt like she herself had gone to high school at Southport because over the years, with their barn parties and get-togethers with Will's friends, she had grown to know so many of them. Will had been the class president and all-star running back in football, and he had been really popular, so Becky thought perhaps the librarian had known him.

"Will Blaine? Of course I knew Will. Everybody knew Will. Did you know Dustin Johnson, too?" asked the woman.

"Yup, I was a really good friend of his wife, Nancy. I haven't seen them in years, but the last time I did, I heard she left beauty college, went back to school, and got her nursing degree. Everyone used to tease her that she wasn't very smart. I mean to drop out of high school, marry Dustin, and have three kids right away—but she sure showed them! She got her degree in cosmetology, became the director of the beauty school, and now she's a registered nurse at some hospital around here and doing real well, last I heard," said Becky. "I love stories like that."

"Good for her. I always like to hear when a local person does well, especially when no one expects them to. Town's getting so big now though, it's hard to keep up." The librarian paused to put a book on a shelf. "Hey, did you ever know Raine? Gosh, I can't think of his first name now," said the woman. "Oh, hi. By the way, I'm Margaret," she said, smiling and extending her right hand.

Becky shook it, and said, "Hello. I'm Will's wife, Rebecca—most people just call me Becky." And as she was talking, she was almost choking on the name that Margaret had just spoken. *Raine?* She hadn't thought about Robert in so long. Becky got goose bumps when she heard the name. She sunk quickly into an analytic state of mind, recalling Robert and the irony and coincidence of Raine's name with her own.

"No, I don't think I ever knew a Raine," said Becky, as she repeated her last name to herself, then Robert's: *Blaine, Raine, Blaine, Raine.*

"Raine, you ought to know him," repeated Margaret. "Remember—I'm sure Will's told you how the two of them used to call themselves the Brain Brothers? They took the first letters of each of their names—Blaine, Raine—Oh yeah, Robert, that's his first name, Robert!"

Becky stopped breathing for a moment.

"Yeah, 'B' for Blaine and 'R' for Raine—they added the common endings of their last names, 'aine' and started calling themselves the 'Brain Brothers.' It was really a silly high school thing to do, now as I remember it, but they were sure proud of it. If Will's never told you, you'll have to tease him about it. The two of them used to really play it up to lend validity to their namesake. They were something else—that pair. In their junior and senior year they came up with a whole bunch of schemes and doing weird things to people—playing jokes. Like the time they were hunting for rabbits, and Robert and another friend got back to the camp before Will, or so the story goes. Robert skinned the rabbits and left the blood on the snow, and when Will got closer and his buddies could hear the snowmobile getting closer, Raine told his friend to lie down. When Will pulled up, Robert held his rifle up in the air and said, 'I didn't mean to do it, honest, I didn't mean to do it.' For a few minutes Will thought Robert had accidentally shot their friend. Isn't that terrible? I mean, their tricks were something else! Robert thought up most of the schemes, but together they were always getting into mischief. I think Robert went on to become a doctor though—he was really smart, and Will's in real estate, right?" the librarian said.

"Doctor." Becky again choked down emotion. "What did you say your name was again?" Becky asked.

"Margaret—Margaret Zowolski."

Becky felt dizzy as she tried to make sense out of what she had just heard. She said, "With a name like that, how'd you end up in a state south of Wisconsin? Sounds like a 'yuper' name to me. I'm from Michigan, and it sounds like a name you'd find more around there than in southern Indiana."

"That's funny. You're right and very perceptive. My parents *are* from northern Wisconsin, and we moved here because of my Dad's work."

Becky continued to make small talk while trying to get over what she had just heard. *Could this be the same Robert Raine that I had loved? It's too coincidental. No, it's—well, maybe possible—probable—no, improbable, impossible.*

Becky tried to think back to her and Will's days together in Indianapolis to see if she would have any recollection that might suggest ever having met or heard about Robert Raine before, or that the two Robert Raines might indeed be the same person. The only thing she could think of was a night she remembered vaguely, when she and Will had gone to a beautiful lake to drift around on an inner tube by the light of the moon and get a reprieve from the Indiana heat. It was late, and the lake was dark. You couldn't see faces, and you could only hear voices of other people nearby. Becky herself was slightly intoxicated not only by the water, the moon, and the music within her, but by the wine she and Will had enjoyed that evening. She thought hard about what she could remember. There were no mosquitoes; the lake was flat and serene. She recalled the shadowy impressions of others that were by the lake, and one couple that was in a canoe nearby. They too were just floating and relaxing, and were Will's old friends. Becky recalled Will talking to his friend about how they both used to go inner tubing all the time when they were in high school, but now that both of them were married, they really didn't have much time for that sort of thing any more.

Becky couldn't remember any formal introductions, but recalled a stinging memory of Will yelling out a "goodbye" to his friend that evening when they got out of the water. "See ya, Brainy—don't make it so long next time!" Becky couldn't recall even wondering why they hadn't been introduced to each other, but she didn't really care or notice much the lack of formality on Will's part. Slowly, Becky began to recall bits and pieces of the evening. She remembered that Will had told her that night after "Brainy" had left that the real reason he believed his old friend didn't do much with his high school buddies anymore was because his wife was so controlling. She was one of those psychology majors who needed psychology management herself, Will had explained. "Why do you think most of them go into that field in the first place?" she remembered Will asking her. Will had said Brainy despised his wife. He felt trapped from getting a divorce because of their kids. They had two boys. "Two boys," Becky whispered. "My gosh, *my* Robert has two boys!"

Becky got up and thanked Margaret for her conversation. "I'll be sure to stop by and see you next time I'm in town," she said. "Sorry, I've got to run. I almost forgot that I have a meeting."

"Make sure you tell Will hello from me," Margaret responded. "He'll remember who I am."

Slowly and thoughtfully, Becky made her way out, taking the stairs instead of the elevator. She left for Southport High School.

Once there, she went to the library to look in the archives section for the yearbooks. She wanted to see if she could find Robert

Raine. On her way up the stairs she ran into an old friend she hadn't seen in a long time—another one of Will's old friends who, over the years, had gotten to know Becky.

"Anne, is that you?" asked Becky, and they both stopped on the stairs to look at each other.

"Becky, oh my gosh. What are you doing here? Long time, no see."

Becky was nervous and out of breath, looked distracted, and felt fragmented. "I know. It's been forever since I saw you last. What are you up to?" asked Becky.

"I'm a secretary over at the law school now, and I love it."

"That's great," replied Becky.

"What are you doing?" asked Anne.

"Well, I don't live in town anymore. You knew that, didn't you?"

"Yeah, I had heard that."

"It's a long story. I don't think you'd have time to hear it," Becky said.

"Tell you what though, what are you doing tonight? I'm going out after work with a friend, and I'd love it if you could meet us. You won't believe it, Becky. I'm dating this guy who is the president of the Indianapolis Bar Association." Anne, being a "talker," kept on while Becky just looked at her, preoccupied. "I met him in law school one day when he came in to one of my classes do a lecture series. He's real cool. Why don't you come along? We can catch up on what we've been up to then. I just came over here to pick up some forms for the school. I really can't talk long now either."

Becky thought for a second, then without much hesitation said, "Heck, why not? I need a break. This'll be great. Where should we meet?" They went on to exchange plans about the meeting place and time, then parted ways.

Becky sprinted up the stairs. She thought about what courtroom procedural questions she could ask Anne's friend. Becky was *always* thinking. She found the yearbooks she was looking for after searching shelves. She looked up the Class of '73, turned to the back index, and looked up Raine. *Robert Raine, pages 18, 23, and*

56. Becky couldn't turn the pages fast enough. Page 18 showed a bunch of guys in football uniforms, and their faces were covered up with helmets. *Darn.* Then she went to the front of the book where the individual pictures were, but there was no picture of Robert. There was a list of names of the kids who hadn't turned in a picture for the yearbook. *Damn it!* Robert was one of them who hadn't. There was no picture of him. Becky then turned to page 23. *Maybe this could be him. Hmm, class vice president. There's Will—president. Shoot, I just can't tell.* Then Becky turned to page 56—a page that had been put together in a collage format with just a bunch of kids doing random school things just so their picture could be in the yearbook. *Search, search. There he is. Oh my gosh! It is Robert. I can't believe this. Look at him. He's got his arm around Will, and the two of them have hiking packs on their backs, with mountains in the background. Yup, Will said he had hiked the Smoky Mountains with some friends when he was in high school and that his closest friend that went there with him was also the guy that lived with him for a short while during his first year of medical school.* Becky threw her head back in disbelief and slammed the book shut. What was she to think? She and Robert and his wife and Will had become friends in Madison and even camped together there while on vacation and neither Will nor anyone else had said anything about knowing each other before that.

Becky felt very confused and was finding it next to impossible to make her way to the bar where she had promised to meet Anne. She decided to keep the date though, get something to eat, and then leave to head back to Madison. She would call Debbie to let her know she had decided not to stay another night.

When Becky got to the bar, Anne was already there and had a table. The two of them talked and reminisced about the good times they had when their girls were little. Anne had two little girls close to the same age as Beth. "Weren't the two of them so cute dancing in their little pink tutus?" remarked Anne, as the two moms reminisced about the days when they both took their daughters to dance classes.

"I know, and now they're into prom dresses," said Becky.

"I miss those days, don't you?"

They ordered their dinner and drank their Long Island Iced Teas as they waited for the food to come. Becky wasn't used to drinking, and with her lack of sleep and no lunch that afternoon, the drink went right to her head. Before she knew it, she was laughing and telling Anne about all the junk that had been going on in her life since their move. She told Anne everything, including Robert and her most recent findings.

"What do you think it means that the two of them were friends, and I didn't know about it?" she asked.

Anne was a bit tipsy herself. She sat up straight, poised herself, and then philosophically said, "Well, I think that the two of them are doing what they used to do best in high school. They were diabolical." She laughed as she slurred her words. "They probably have a plan, Becky. You better watch out!" Becky and Anne laughed—then laughed some more.

"Yeah," Becky went on. "These two brain brokers are going to learn a few things from me when I get back."

"You poor thing," Anne said, as she tried her best to be serious in her reply. "What are you going to do?"

"I don't know for sure, but I'll think up something," said Becky.

Anne stood up. "Becky, I've got to go to the bathroom. Come with me."

"Sure, I've got to go too," said Becky.

When Anne got into a stall she motioned for Becky to come in there with her. "What are you doing, Anne?" Becky asked, slowly twisting herself into the small stall.

Anne reached into her purse and said, "Oh, I've just got some magic little happy powder here. Wanna have some?"

Becky had never been a drinker in high school, even for kicks, had never tried marijuana, and would never consider whatever this was. "What is that stuff?" Becky asked, suddenly wishing that she had never seen this part of her friend.

"It's coke, Becky. It's no big deal. Everybody does it. Try some."

"No way," Becky said, opening the stall and backing out. She immediately thought of Beth and the boys. *What would they think to have a mother who did coke? What would Anne's girls think?* Then she thought about the football player she had read about in the news recently. He had tried it once, got addicted, and died. She tried to convince Anne not to use the stuff.

"Come on, Becky, you deserve it," Anne persisted. "This stuff won't hurt you. You'll feel great. You deserve it. Think about those lousy men, and the shitty lawsuit. Come on, let yourself go and relax a little bit."

Becky re-opened the bathroom stall door to try to coax her friend out, but just in time to see her friend snorting the coke from a small mirror. *How disgusting and stupid!* Becky backed up and stared in innocent dismay. "You pay to do this?" she asked.

Anne coughed and sniffled. "I don't have to buy it. The lawyer that I've been seeing gives it to me. They all do it, Becky. Don't be so naïve. Probably every judge up there listening to your stupid case does it."

"No way, I don't believe that," said Becky.

"Well, it doesn't matter. We do," said Anne, and she laughed as she put her things back into her purse and walked out to wash her hands as if nothing had happened.

As Becky stood back and watched her old friend, she thought about all the reasons why Anne might have picked up this destructive habit. Becky's faith, common sense, and love for her family would never allowed her to do such a thing.

About twenty minutes later the two women emerged from the bathroom and found their way back to their seats. Anne's boyfriend, Russell, walked in and joined them at their table. Anne introduced him to Becky, and he bought them a round of drinks, and Becky deliberately let hers sit, watching the ice melt while the two of them chatted. Becky was excited to be at the same table with the president of the bar, and she enjoyed it when Anne bragged about the trial Becky was involved in, even though the drugs escalated her story. Russell listened and conversed only a little, his salt and pepper hair looking handsome against his dark gray suit. He flashed a cheap smile. Becky still enjoyed the fact that he took an interest in her case, even though she realized it was only a superficial caring. One real reason Becky figured was that he too had been drinking and hitting the bathroom stall. He didn't want to eat dinner with the two ladies, but rather suggested they go down the street to a dance club, which they did. When they got inside, Becky realized then that it was a gay club. Russell asked if Anne and Becky would have a dance together. "Just one little dance," he begged. Becky wished she were in her car and on her way back to Madison to be with her children.

As Becky and Anne watched Russell order another drink, Anne said, "Isn't he great? I have so much fun when I go out with him."

"Yeah, he is fun," Becky said, rolling her eyes.

"This whole evening is just what you needed," Anne told Becky.

"Thanks," Becky said with a half-baked smile.

Russell staggered over to Becky and Anne and said, "Let's drink up. I want to call for a limousine." Becky was glad to think she would finally be driven back to her car.

When the limo pulled up, Anne said in childish wonder, "Can you believe how cool this is?" Becky was not at all impressed.

Once they were inside the limo and heading for home, the driver drove for about fifteen minutes and then pulled up into the circular drive of the most luxurious hotel in Indianapolis. Becky couldn't figure out why. Russell assured the ladies that they just needed to relax a little before they went home. *Give the drugs time to wear off,* Becky thought. She was annoyed, but she didn't have any choice unless she wanted to leave by herself. Since it was already two o'clock in the morning and Russell instructed the limo driver to wait for them, Becky followed him and Anne into the hotel, where they took the elevator to the eleventh floor. Russell assured Becky that she'd relax with them and go home. Will would tell her later he couldn't believe how naïve she was. Once inside, Anne took more drugs. Becky wondered what she should do. She had been uncomfortable the entire evening, and could not stand the outrageous behavior any longer. She imagined what she had read before in the news about the awful things that people do when they're stoned.

Russell could freak out, or Anne could. I could end up dead. Becky made her way to the door and her stoned-cold friends didn't even notice that she was gone.

Becky was lucky. She hailed a cab—a luxury that she couldn't afford, and made it back to her car. It was now after four o'clock in the morning when she got behind the wheel of her own car. On her way out of town she kept thinking about the evening. Becky thought how she needed to be more in control of her life. She learned big lessons that night. As she drove out of town and away from the city lights of Indianapolis and into the abyss of the long, dark road, she took one last look in her rear view mirror at what and who she was leaving behind.

Becky was excruciatingly tired, so right before the sun began to rise, she pulled off at a wayside to sleep for a while. As she dozed off, she thought about how all she ever wanted was a good husband, a small house, five children, church on Sundays, and a clothesline in the back yard. Peace and contentment that seemed miles away.

She was fighting an international company to prove fraud; Debbie's sister was dying of a brain tumor; Debbie's husband had left the ministry to become a gigolo; Debbie had found inner satisfaction through a boob job; Anne was doing drugs; she had had an affair; and Will had set his own house on fire. *Where is God in all of this?* She wondered what could be next, and she imagined as she drove through the darkness that the spies from First Trust Mortgage could kill her. Then she got a hot rush up the back of her neck and remembered what she had found out in the library that day. She felt afraid and alone. Becky wondered if the entire world was crazy, and she said it out loud before she dozed off.

About forty minutes later, as the dawn lifted the shade to expose a new day, Becky started driving again. She passed the reservoir and watched as a bird lifted off the misty water and rose into the air. She could feel the energy build with each crescendo and flap to the very beat of her heart. Like the bird that inspired her imagination, her mind and the music brought her to places few have traveled, and it was beautiful there. She felt the vastness of the knowledge there too, and she gestured after it. She saw a global purpose for her oneness, and she sensed a togetherness and peace just then that made her personal experiences with roguery somehow matter.There was a field that Becky could see not much further ahead, where the mist was still and a small green knoll protruded out, beckoning her to come and sit. She did. She parked the car on the side of the road and made her way to the knoll, barefooted, so as to feel the cool dew between her toes and on the soles of her feet, and it felt good. There was not a problem in the world between the dew and her feet.

Chapter Twenty-Seven

Becky was confused still, as usual, and tried to think of all possible conclusions to her personal mystery. She surmised many possibilities, none of which made true sense. She and Will had had difficult times in their relationship, and so had the Raines. But how could any of the knowledge she had gained in Indianapolis, the time she had spent with Robert, and Will's laissez-faire attitude amount to any logical conclusion? Yet she had discovered something about herself that she hadn't noticed before. She was a sinner headed in the right direction. She sought after and experienced forgiveness as she tried to be a better person. "Wisdom combined with goodness is justice." Becky was a good person and nothing anyone would say or do from here on out would change what she knew in her heart. She would deal with circumstances, pleasant or adverse, as they came to her.

"Good morning, Becky," said Will.

"Good morning," Becky said. She began to clear the table. "Kids, if you guys are done with breakfast, you need to brush your teeth."

"Pack your book bags," commanded a stern Will. He was rarely easy going like he was in the days when Becky first met him. Nowadays, it seemed to Becky that every time he opened his mouth, it was as if he were barking out orders. Maybe she put the edge on him because just when it seemed they were getting along well, she had to become distant again.

Becky tried to help the children feel light-hearted—maybe so she'd feel more light-hearted herself, and she pointed out to them a bird that she saw on the ground outside their dining room window. "He's the male, you know," she said, pointing to the bright yellow finch that was not too far away. "See how much prettier he is than the female? He's over there on the ground next to the berry bush." Her efforts to spend time with the children, a pastime that was her favorite, made a difference to them. The children eagerly ran to the window to catch a glimpse of the bird, then loaded up their backpacks and headed down the stairs to leave for school.

"I love you. Have a wonderful day," sang Becky.

"We love you too, Mom. See you after school," both boys echoed at the same time.

Becky hadn't seen Beth yet that morning, but she could hear the shower being turned off, so she knew it wouldn't be long before Beth would appear for her breakfast. Moments later, a wet-headed Beth leaped to the table with great energy as she shook her hair to fluff it up to dry and sat down to eat. She didn't talk much in the morning, so Becky let her go without conversation and simply kissed her cheek when she was done eating. She told her to have a good day as she ran out the front door. Becky missed her little girl, who seemed to be growing up too quickly.

The news was on TV, and Becky sat on the sofa for a brief moment to reflect on the morning and plan her day. She didn't know where to begin. She sat staring straight forward at the television. It was presenting a program on paraplegics performing ballet from their wheelchairs. She watched the beauty flow out of their performance. *This is what really matters, isn't it? We all care for one another. We all feel the rhythm and experience the beauty. It's there if we choose to feel it, see it, and touch it.*

Together, the quad and the non-quad held hands and danced in the wind of their movement. Whirl to the right, sway into the sound. Drift and carry others with them. Again, the dichotomy of life. God's beauty is always present even in the midst of pain and evil. *One must look for it, take it, share it, and pass it on.*

Becky had to go to work: not on the lawsuit, but the paying job. It was a seemingly small fraction of her life since she was down to only two days a week at the eye clinic. That's all the time she could spare, but it was enough income to subsidize their legal expenses, gasoline, paper, photocopies, and postage. After work, Will took the kids out to a fast-food restaurant, and Becky drove to the law library. She looked in the Indiana Digests at cases relating to Competence of Witnesses. She wanted to subpoena the defense lawyer for his role in the fraud. It was not common procedure to sue a defense lawyer, but she felt so compelled. She wasn't concerned that he would quash her subpoena with his communication, but she was concerned about his acts that were *not* protected by the privilege to quash a subpoena. She looked in the statutes and found that Title 34 had an appendix with rules of conduct for attorneys . . . "except for disclosures that are impliedly authorized in order to carry out the responsibilities." Becky read over everything she could locate on the topic, and then decided she would prepare a formal Subpoena for Mr. Dan Shortino, attorney for the defense.

Of course, in short order, she received his Memorandum in Support of his Motion to Quash the Subpoena and Testificandum, where he offered the Court, "As with all assignments from clients, the matter was offered and accepted on a professional basis to provide legal advice and assistance to the client. It has long been public policy to provide privileged communications to parties with special relationships. Included herein is the attorney-client privilege that has been codified in I.C. 34-1-14-5 (2). The attorney-client privilege applies to all communications to the attorney. Further, the communications are strictly confidential"—*not when you're obstructing justice by withholding evidence,* Becky thought—"The privilege exists to facilitate the full development of facts essential to provide proper representation, to encourage people to seek early legal assistance, and to give full and frank disclosure to the attorney"—*privileges,* thought Becky, *he thinks he's privilege*— "It is the ethical obligation of the attorney to hold inviolate all communications with his client in the strictest of confidence. Here, there is no question that all of the information counsel may have, has been provided to him in his capacity as attorney and for the purpose of providing legal assistance. For these reasons, the subpoena issued to Dan Shortino should be quashed."

Becky responded within twenty-four hours because she had anticipated his response. Her Response to Motion to Quash Subpoena stated in support, "That on September 18, 1996, William D. and Rebecca A. Blaine, Counter-Claimants herein (Blaines), had served upon the office of counsel for First Trust Mortgage, a subpoena and Testificandum, summoning Dan Shortino to appear at trial to testify for the Blaines. A true and accurate copy of said Subpoena is attached hereto and incorporated herein as Exhibit A on October 17, 1996. That the Blaines' subpoena was served summoning Dan Shortino as a means to ensure that he would appear at the hearing so as to be called to testify as to the truth or falsity of conflicting testimony he has given throughout the six years of this litigation." Becky had a feeling that First Trust Mortgage, having made a Motion for Substitution, would see to it that Dan Shortino didn't even show up at the trial. "That it is imperative for the Blaines to ascertain knowledge of a fact in truth in order to establish solid, lawful grounds with which to prove their case. That the Blaines in no way wish to obtain knowledge from Dan Shortino that in any way conflicts with the statutes outlining attorney-client confidentiality. That the testimony given by Dan Shortino on behalf of his client during adversary proceedings and status conference is relevant and admissible. That to not allow the Blaines to question Dan Shortino at trial would prejudice the opportunity to establish and prove that there is no genuine issue as to the facts. Wherefore, the Blaines respectfully pray the Court for an order to deny quashing the Subpoena and Testificandum issued to Dan Shortino and for all other relief just and proper."

Becky supplemented her motion with a memorandum in support of her Response to Motion to Quash Subpoena and Testificandum and further stated that "Dan Shortino has represented First Trust Mortgage in the above matter and has given conflicting testimony during many hearings and through interrogatory questions raised by the Blaines, and the Blaines are simply trying to get at the truth. That Dan Shortino is an actor in this litigation, and the Blaines are not concerned about his communication with his client, but rather his *acts*, which are *not* protected by the provisions, set forth in I.C. 34-1-14-5 (2). That the Blaines are not asking that the lawyer reveal any information as to his communications with his client. That Dan Shortino cites in his Memorandum in Support of Motion to Quash Subpoena and Testificandum D.R. 1.6 of the Rules of Professional Conduct saying, (a) a lawyer shall not reveal information relating to representation of a client unless the client consents after consultation. However, Dan Shortino did not finish what the Rules of Professional Conduct conclude, which is as follows: (a) a lawyer shall not reveal information relating to representation of a client unless the client consents after consultation *except* for disclosures that are impliedly authorized in order to carry out the representation and *except* as stated in paragraph (b) (2) . . .

to respond to allegations in any proceeding concerning the lawyer's representation of the client." The document continued, "The lawyer is part of a judicial system charged with upholding the law. One of the lawyer's functions is to advise clients so that they avoid any violation of the law in the proper exercise of their rights. The rule of attorney-client confidentiality applies in situations *other* than those where evidence is sought from the lawyer through compulsion of law. Here, there is no question that information from Dan Shortino is imperative in establishing for the Court that there is no genuine issue as to the facts, and there is no question that the Blaines are *not* interested in attempting to disrupt the attorney-client privilege as they apply to the confidentiality of such communications. For these reasons, the subpoena issued to Dan Shortino should not be quashed."

Becky prevailed. She had overcome all the major obstacles put in her path by her opponents. But could she win at trial? Her confidence rose to the challenge. Her latest win fueled the motivational engine within her. She was getting healthier and stronger with each new chunk of adversity that fell into her lap. Now she wanted to talk to Robert—to face him. She was ready. She paged him.

Robert responded back within minutes, almost as if he was waiting for her call. He appeared cordial over the telephone, even apologetic. Becky wasn't fooled by his antics. She knew things now that neither Robert nor Will were aware of—that she had knowledge of their past friendship. She would fight the fronts of two battlefields—one in the courtroom and one at home.

Three hours later, Robert and Becky were face-to-face, like in the old days, yet now presenting with diametrically opposed forces. Robert had suggested meeting in the lab, but Becky didn't want to be where he could force isolation, and she didn't want to be in a medical environment because of the negative feedback from all of her memories there—after all that she had been through, she had to stay strong. Instead, they met on neutral ground where there would be a lot of people—at a park bench next to the lake by the campus. The air was sultry with barely a gentle breeze. Becky got out of her car and watched Robert watch her. He was already out of his car, and leaning against it. He commented on how beautiful she looked when her hair was slightly curly from the humidity and wispy on the sides. He looked down at her dress and watched how it moved with the sway of her stride as she walked toward him, but he said nothing about it. Becky stood looking at the cattails, arms folded before her and looking past Robert, whose hair was cut shorter than she had ever seen it. He was almost completely shaven and had a goatee that barely covered his chin, but that reached up to his lower lip.

"I've missed you," Robert said, in a soft, husky, sullen voice. "I'm really sorry about. . . . You know—I wasn't myself." He paused and shuffled his feet a little in the dirt below them. Becky had heard this line before. He had his hands in the pockets of some very tight jeans, unlike any she had seen him wear before. He seemed distracted, as she looked about, first at one thing over by the trees, then another, sort of looking down the street. "I just couldn't get over knowing that you were leaving me."

Of course, Becky knew there was much more that he wasn't saying, but she felt strong and unafraid. "Oh, so that's your excuse?" She paused and then went on. "I really thought you were different from all the other men, you know? But you aren't. From the beginning, I asked you not to hurt me. If it didn't work out, I said please, just don't hurt me! The way you acted—you scared me."

Robert started to move closer to her, and she let her arms fall to her side to warn him he better not step closer. "I didn't mean to frighten you. I just didn't know how to handle my frustration," he said.

Becky restrained herself, knowing that a confrontation would serve no purpose. She wasn't meeting with Robert to get back together or to discuss misgivings. She was meeting to solve the puzzle of Robert's relationship with Will and how it played into her life. She didn't expose her frustration, but rather played along with Robert and, looking at him softly, she waited for him to speak again.

Robert began a long monologue; as he spoke, Becky just watched his lips form the words. She didn't hear him speak because her mind drifted, and she heard music. Robert wasn't with her in song this time. She was alone with her music and it allowed her pain to drift away. Long ago when their relationship was new, the beauty they saw in each other drew them together. Not physical beauty, but beauty found in the appreciation of things that most people do not notice. They felt connected through those things spiritually. But who were they kidding? Where is honor and integrity when you love someone outside of your marriage? Robert and Rebecca together seemed refreshing, energetic, resourceful, creative, and fun loving, but so shallow to ever think that those things were real when they were created under the guise of self-righteousness. Still, Becky wished it to be true. At the time it seemed so perfect. If only he was who he had pretended to be. *But who was I?* Perhaps she had only fooled herself with the lust for another man's affection. It felt so good to be loved.

Becky empathized with Robert's frustration, though she dared not show it. She had been there before herself, downtrodden because of a failed romance, an unfulfilled professional career, and the lack of a partner with the sameness of soul. She could see this now, things she couldn't before that were shrouded by loneliness. But she had never really been alone; she had the love and companionship of God. Yet her human frailties allowed her to miss the dreams she had about being with Robert and the commonality they shared over important things—medicine, love for the elderly, the nursing home they wanted to design, the poetry they loved to write, and the books they wanted to read, write, and illustrate. For a while, they even heard the same music. *But he ruined it.* And she paused. *No, he hadn't.* There was a purpose to her travails, and she would find balance and meaning through the ying-yang of life on her own—the good challenged by the evil such that goodness would prevail.

Becky jerked herself back into the one-sided conversation. Robert had pulled a piece of paper out of his pocket and began reading a poem to her that he had written, "Forever seems too short for you and me, for we have consumed the hours that were seconds. However seems too vague for us to breathe, for we have promised the sustaining air." Becky loved him so—the man she thought him to be.

"Bob, I found out that you didn't make tenure," she said.

He looked stunned. "How did you know?" he asked.

"There is a lot that I know," Becky said, as she took charge of the conversation and where it was heading by changing the subject and putting him on the defensive. She trusted that the *other* Robert would show his ugly teeth, and she would work with that. "How is your family taking the news?" Becky had learned through talking with people in the valley that Robert's father was a prominent physician; in fact, all the members of his family were successful professionals. Robert was proud of their successes too, and Becky knew he must have felt like a failure—like a black sheep.

"You know Robert, I loved you with all my heart once and, although I am reluctant to admit it, I still fantasize about the 'us' that used to be. It was so beautiful. But that wasn't you, Robert. At one time I fooled myself into thinking it so, but I was wrong. Even now, I can say that love must be sick because there is a part of me that peers through time and sees us together when we're eighty—my foolish love, the person I thought you to be. Is this potent and forgiving love I'm talking about—an understanding love? My intellect tells me a different story than my heart."

Robert just listened.

There was a pause, and Becky had a tear in her eye. She looked at his beautiful face. To her he had been a king—a monarch. "Why didn't you tell me you knew Will before you knew me?"

Robert stared at her like a marble statue—eyes carved with no pupils, the windows to the soul not there.

"Robert, do you have anything else you would like to tell me before I leave?" She would get no answers. She handed him a white feather and whispered, "Forever after, Robert." He took the feather with lifeless hand. "Please remember that, and know what it means then." Becky recited something Emily Dickinson had once written after she was smitten with an unrequited love affair. "Hope is the thing with feathers that perches in the soul—and sings the tune without words and never stops at all." To Becky, the gift was a symbol of purity and hope, freedom—free to float through the air—aimless until it might land quietly onto the ground. Becky was grounded in her faith now, and she would sing the tune without the words and never stop at all.

He looked at her in disdain. She blew him a kiss and the sign language for "I love you" but only for a moment. Then she thrust her hand downward as if to throw the sign into the sand—leaving it to be washed away and carried to distant shores by the evening tide.

Robert silently walked to his car and drove away. Becky took her shoes off and walked closer to the water's edge. She still had no answers, because she knew they were not to be found in Robert. But she had her own kind of closure, at least for now. Her mind wandered to distant hills.

Up o'er the horizon where the pine trees speak of freedom,
We dream our wild airy dreams and trust that they will follow.

The waters wind around each bend, unknown what may come,
Yet we wait around and search about for what's left of our tomorrow.

The road that leads us upward now, will meet
The path that leads us down.

And we rise and fall through passages
With what's left inside us all.

The limestone walls will crumble down.
The baby pine will grow.
The bluffs will cause us wonderment
Wherever we may go.

Signs of a lifetime sit and wait
To be passed and left behind us.
But we'll meet again—along the road
All the things that we have trusted.

Becky put her toes into the water—back and forth, teasing the ripples at the shoreline. She felt dizzy and backed away. Then she lay down. She pushed her arms outstretched as if she were making angels in the snow. The imprints stayed in the sand. The sounds of the water came together with her music, and it rose and fell with each gentle tide, a crescendo and decrescendo until the last echo of eventide slowed her pulse, and a healing breeze fell above her to hush the last noise of the mist that settled as night approached. She thought about all the things she liked, church steeples when they dot the landscape, the people inside worshipping and trying to do better. She thought about barns and the hard-working farmers that were rapidly diminishing and being replaced by modern inventions. Becky thought how the work ethic formed in the fields was also being replaced. She thought about how the farmers helped define America, their large hands with work lines deeply engrained—in their faces too, work lines cut in by the wind, the rain, and the worry for a good harvest.

Becky felt herself relaxing as she continued to follow her wandering mind. She pictured the mailman who years ago rode the rough paths between mailboxes and the important job he had as the major communicator for the people. She pictured a woman leaving her kitchen and running out the squeaky front door with her apron strings flying as she went to meet the him, she standing on one side of the picket fence, he on the other. She knew the exact time her rider would show up, and she anticipated his arrival. She hoped for a letter and relied on the cheery hello she received along with a little gossip from town. The mailman was a precious part of the American family back then. He could laugh with them and cry with them because he knew all about the letters they got. A letter from a husband in some far-off place, trying to find work when it was scarce, or a son who had gone off to college or to war. He knew things about the core of their existence, and he shared those moments with them. Becky thought how she liked to share sacred moments and how being a physician would have given her that, the intimate details of human existence—fear, joy, love, and the source of their derivation. *As a minister, you are there too,* Becky thought, *in the commons of all humans. We are all the same. We cry the same; we laugh the same; we fear the same; and we love the same. None has a barrier for which any of us are protected.* The simplicity of that time—so different from now in the world of fiber optic connections and worldwide websites. Peacefully, she escaped her complicated life.

I hug a quiet snowfall when everything seems muted. The sky is deep. I feel the cold calm on my face and the crispness of subzero when the snow creaks below my feet. Ice crystals glitter then too, and my nostrils stick together.

I like old women when they wear cotton dresses and sweet perfume. I like walking down a gravel road and seeing a grove of mature trees; it's a sign of a place where a house once stood. I stop and stare at that place and picture the children laughing all about, swinging on their tire swing and running through the fields. Where are they now? Memories to some—maybe nothing to most.

A railroad track on a warm summer day. It smells of creosote and dust. I see buttercups, bumblebees, and wild strawberries.

The top rock of a cluster of boulders as I get closer to them—walking through the tall grasses. God. I look over the field, and the sky is dark with rain clouds, but the sun adds yellow to the green and golden wheat. The colors are vivid and distinct. Everything is still.

I like to see co-ops and granaries. Days gone by. Large packages of feed. The local merchant who has been there forever.

I think about the deli I once visited downtown. How one man, Sam, always ate there for lunch, and Flo, the waitress, knew exactly how he liked his coffee.

I like hardware stores. They have work boots, workin' men supplies, and hardware stuff for middle-class Americans who can get their home fix-it and maintenance needs there.

Becky daydreamed right into a night dream and lost sense of where she was.

Hold on tight to what makes us special—symbols of American family and tradition—faith.

Her thoughts carried her to a kitchen in the forties. There was a man and his wife enjoying their noontime meal. *She looks at him as he wipes the corner of his mouth. He is content now after eating the dinner that she prepared for him. They call the noon meal dinner—it couldn't be considered lunch.* She could see the woman preparing the meal for him. *She makes sure to fix it just the way he likes it because, after all, no one knows how he likes it but her. She owns this special knowledge. This brings a pleased smile to her lips, and her heart is content.*

It's Sunday morning. The husband and wife walk into the chapel together as the organ music harmoniously begins. His hand reaches for hers. Her pocketbook is draped over her other arm. She has finished greeting friends. He watches her and smiles. He adores her that much. Her handkerchief is tucked into her belt. They sit down in the same spot in the pew as they do every Sunday. He sits in his suit in a way that I can see the strength in appearance that he gives—proud, sound, and content. She grabs his arm with secure admiration.

Becky thought of her children. *Ah, the sweet little faces that the pillows caress at bedtime. Those special little fingers—even when they're sleeping I can put my finger in their palms, and they close tightly around mine. Even when they're fourteen, like Beth, they look like they coo while they sleep. I can't stand it. I have to hug and kiss them—these tender sleeping bundles of joy. Father leans against the doorframe. The dim lights pass through the crack in the door, and he looks on. He watches her. This is a man's pride and a mother's dream!*

Becky lay still in the sand. She closed her eyes and let the setting sun cover her. Her mind was still wandering, and she heard sweet music that her heart spoke, and her heart listened for the answers to come as in I Kings. The heart can be personified. Becky knew from her Bible that the heart feels pride, yet is humbled—it can love, and it can hate, and it searches (Jeremiah 10) and meditates (Psalms 4), is hardened (Proverbs), yet makes merry (Judges), and fears (Deuteronomy). And it rejoices: "therefore my heart is glad," and it cries, and it is comforted. Could her heart rejoice just then?—she asked her Lord. *Can my heart feel comfort now?* And Becky fell asleep, and she rested.

About a week later, Robert began calling Becky again. He couldn't stay away from her. Seeing her had rekindled the flame of obsession and hearing her voice lit a fire he couldn't control and had never been able to control from the first time he had laid eyes on her by the light of the moon on the lake in Indiana five years before. Becky called the sheriff's department and, because he kept calling her house and hanging up, they told her to purchase Caller ID so she could avoid his calls and keep track of how often they came. When he caught on, he started calling from a telephone booth so she wouldn't be able to recognize the number—almost every telephone booth within a five-mile radius of Becky's house, the police told her after tailing him for several days. She was advised to obtain a restraining order. She did, but still didn't feel safe. She wanted to tell Will, but she didn't trust him either.

Chapter Twenty-Eight

Alone in the wilderness of her thoughts, Becky was anything but misguided. She lay on her bed, legs dangling off the side, looking straight up at the ceiling, humming, and thinking about Will. She searched to make sense out of what was left of her marriage. *Wild Will—indeed, that's what he was—a wild, grizzly mountain man like the one in the picture above our fireplace mantle.* The man in the picture was born to shoot a cougar from the rifle off his hip, to trap wild animals for food, to wear their skins for warmth, and to weather the mountain storms as if the need to survive the wilderness was a gift from God. Will was like that man in the picture. *He was crazy too.* She wondered what it would be like to have a normal life. *Is there anyone who is normal? Are most people victims of something unpredictable and uncontrollable?* She moved to her living room couch and just sat there staring at the walls. She felt woozy, and her vision was getting wavy on the right side. She blinked her eyes, thinking it might be tears. But then half of her visual field went black—a hemianopsia. She tried to get up and walk, but her arm was tingly, and she had paresthesias all the way into her fingertips. She thought she was having a stroke. She stumbled over to the telephone with great difficulty and tried to call 911. Her brain was not working right because she couldn't remember how to do it. She grabbed the telephone book and opened it to the emergency numbers. Even though she could see the number, she couldn't make her brain tell her fingers what to do. She fell to the floor, unable to dial for help and unable to speak. *My God,* she prayed, *please forgive me for my sins. Am I going to die?*

The next thing she knew she was waking up in a hospital room. Will had come home and found her on the floor. He called for an ambulance. The doctors gave her every test in the book to try to figure out what was going on. Their final diagnosis included several possibilities. More tests would be required, and a longer hospital stay. The doctors figured either she had had a complicated migraine, which sometimes can present itself like it did, a stroke, a brain tumor, or an aneurysm. Will told the doctors that Becky was under an incredible amount of stress—more than he himself even admitted to, and the doctors chose to medicate her for the night so she could rest.

The next morning, Becky woke up feeling odd and displaced. She felt drugged, but she knew where she was. She felt like she was being lifted from her body and was heading for a white light in the upper right corner of her room. She was happy to be heading toward the light. She felt peaceful, and never once thought of the sadness of leaving her children because sadness was an earthly conception, not a divine one. Then she heard a voice that told her to go back. She didn't want to go back there and, as she lay on her white sheets, she started to cry. The minister from her church walked in to visit and was surprised to see Becky crying.

"Peggy and Aileen told me you were doing much better, but I guess not. What's wrong?" he asked.

Becky told him why she was crying and what had happened. He did not seem surprised, and he told her that she wasn't the first person to have experienced something like that. Becky remembered thinking, *I will never fear death, for thou art with me.* But she didn't tell the pastor about Robert, Will, the extent of her confusion, the upcoming trial, the stress, or the depression. He just bid her "good day" and left.

Becky went home that afternoon shortly after being told that she probably had experienced what the doctors called a complicated migraine, precipitated by stress and fatigue. They told her to take it easy and to call them immediately if she noticed her vision beginning to get wavy again.

Becky's faith had been strengthened by her experience in the hospital. She did not fear death. She had experienced what she felt was her soul leaving on a journey to heaven. She felt that through divine intervention she was able to feel that no matter where she was headed, she was going to like it there, and those she left on earth would be protected enough by their faith also. Becky understood life better; the importance of coming into what God had called her to be.

Her schedule didn't permit her to think about her experience much. As soon as she got home, there was more mail about the trial and much to be dealt with.

The Counter-Claim Defendants filed a verified Request for a Pre-trial Conference. They sent the order with their motion so that the judge might just sign off, as he sometimes did. Standard procedure. *Request for Pre-trial Conference on a complicated matter—sure. Rubber stamp. Not this time!* The judge had gained respect for Becky, and he took her seriously. He reviewed the paperwork and denied their Motion.

Becky learned that the judge assigned the defendants only three and a half hours to present their case. She was given equal time. She questioned how she would manage to prevent opposing counsel from eating up part of her time. She anticipated they would deliberately use up her time by gibbering a long cross-examination.

"Can we use timers?" Becky questioned the Clerk of a Wisconsin court. "Can I go first without them being able to cross-examine?" *Give them an opportunity to call my first witness on their time,* she thought to herself.

"We can't give you legal advice," said the clerk. Becky didn't know the answers, and she couldn't find them either. As a last resort she called the law clerk in the court where her case was to be heard. The clerk told her he would send her some basic guidelines. Becky told him she was grateful.

What will happen if the judge isn't fair? If he doesn't closely scrutinize the guidelines, he could easily give them more time by allowing them to ramble. It had happened before. How can I protect myself? When it was her turn he could cut her off by overruling objections. *What if the judge is the one who keeps track of the time in his head?* She wouldn't stand a chance if opposing counsel got on a roll again like they had succeeded in doing in the past. *Clearly, this is not just under the law. What can I do to protect myself?* she questioned again.

Becky had run across many statutes she felt were insufficient to protect due process. Maybe someday she would have her chance to facilitate change, if she could achieve a level of respect and knowledge. She knew she possessed the perseverance. She wanted to change laws and help people.

As the trial date got closer, the pressure to meet deadlines exploded. Becky had to chase all over town to different photocopy centers to receive faxes as responses from depositions. A fax machine would have really come in handy, especially when she had requested that the responses from witnesses be returned as soon as possible. She was trying a case several hundred miles away and was at a disadvantage, especially when past records and notes from the file were in a town so far away. It was crucial for Becky to get deposition responses as fast as she could, but she and Will could barely afford groceries. There was no way they could justify buying an extravagant fax machine. With each passing day Becky's preparation for the trial was becoming more difficult. Will watched from a distance as his wife worked frantically on the case. One afternoon, feeling sorry for what he saw her going through, he surprised her with a fax machine. Becky was so grateful she cried. Will knew it would help make her life easier, and she appreciated his sensitivity. That night at supper the kids had to eat around the fax machine because the dining room table was the only place in the apartment where it would fit. No more driving halfway across town to pick up faxes that came over the wires of a copy shop. Will thought she deserved a little bit of convenience, and his empathy toward her did not go unnoticed. Oh how she wished she could let her guard down and love him, trust him, rely on him, and enjoy him. But her guarded walls were up and supported by unanswered questions she couldn't explain or get answers to, at least now. For those reasons, she couldn't get close.

Becky had to make another trip to Indianapolis to see what witnesses she could find to add to the Tendor of Witnesses that she was compiling. Will and the kids went with her. The main reason for the trip was to talk to the people she would subpoena—to remind them of who she was because for some of them, it had been years since she'd seen them. She wanted to bring them up-to-date on what had happened since she had last had contact with them. She gave them the court date, made sure they wouldn't be a hostile witness, and told them in what order she'd call them to the witness stand. Becky planned to go through a dry run of her line of questioning so she could assess their response and suggest the best way for them to give their testimony. She couldn't take any chances—no surprises. She knew which witnesses she wanted an expanded testimony from and which ones she only wanted a one-line answer from. She was deliberate and precise in the story she wanted the judge to hear and how she would support the truth with evidence.

Her first stop was to drop Will and the kids off at the park. They went there to relax and play while Becky worked. She splashed water on her face from the park fountain to freshen up before she left for her first appointment.

While Becky was talking to the real estate broker who had originally listed the lots of their subdivision, she knew that Will was giving underdogs to Eli, Erin, and Beth on the swing set. When Becky was finished, she went back to the park. It was the same one that they used to play in before the fire—before the fraud. She missed Indianapolis and the memories before the pain. Becky played with the children on the same equipment there—the rocking horse, the old rides, the swing set, and the monkey bars. They knew the park so well and enjoyed it, then they were forced to move. Forced to move from all their comforts of home. Becky thought how easy it would be to go to the gray house in Blaine's Valley not far down the road. How strange it was that they couldn't just get in the car and drive home. First Trust Mortgage and their goons could never have fathomed, nor did they care, how adversely they affected so many peoples' lives with their egregious acts of deceit and fraud.

After Becky's short break to be with the family and to laugh for a bit, she gathered them up and dropped them off at a fast-food restaurant while she drove to the bank that had originally given them the money for their construction loan. She contacted the loan officer that had initiated their loan with First Trust Mortgage. He was now the president of his own company, and she thought maybe now that he was no longer employed by First Trust Mortgage and in need of protecting his job, he would come forward with the truth. She was right. She subpoenaed the real estate broker, and she subpoenaed the banker too. Then she drove all the way to the north side of town and met with the engineer who had designed the subdivision. He had insisted that his counsel be present. They informed her that the opposing counsel had been there the week before and had wanted to dig through their files. The engineers told First Trust Mortgage that they would need a court order. They got one. According to what the engineers told her that day, it was interesting to Becky to see how First Trust Mortgage twisted the facts of the events that had transpired in order to contrive a story to support their favor. Becky prepared how she would expose their tricks and lies to the judge. She decided to subpoena all of the engineers.

Before she left town, she contacted the appraisal company and spoke to the gentleman who had appraised their property and who could testify to the truth or falsity of the documents that First Trust Mortgage had hidden in their possession for so long. The appraisal would show the intent of what the Blaine loan had been for: one lot, not the entire subdivision. That would be the best piece of evidence yet, the next best thing to the first page of the original loan document that First Trust Mortgage stated they had lost. Becky had filed a Motion to Compel to get it, but First Trust Mortgage kept to their story. It was unthinkably deceitful. Becky figured the judge would lose respect because their cover-up was so obvious. She counted on it because she would then corner and expose them. It wasn't easy for Becky to determine how she was going to authenticate the information she needed in the appraisal, because she didn't know whether to subpoena the original appraiser or the president of the company, who had ordered and approved the appraiser's work. She knew the possibility existed that the defendants would object to either person she chose to testify; she would subpoena them both. The owner was not very happy and balked at having to appear in court. He did not want to be a part of her problem. She realized by the end of her conversation with him that if she did subpoena him, he would probably be a hostile witness. She tried to think of ways that she could get the appraiser to authenticate the appraisal document in a way that the defense wouldn't object. Then she wouldn't have to call the owner to the stand at all.

The appraiser himself was a nice guy and, after a short conversation, easily remembered the property and the job. Becky discussed what he would be testifying about. He was concerned that he really needed to work that day because he needed the money. Becky knew better than to offer to pay his day's wages, because then the other side might make an allegation that she paid him for his testimony. That wouldn't work. She was just going to have to continue to feel sorry for him and subpoena him anyway. Part of life. She would send him a check and a thank-you note after the trial.

Once Becky was done for the day, she and the family went to Debbie's house. It had been a hard day's work, to say the least of the emotional energy spent, as the Blaines drove by many familiar landmarks that were imbedded in their memories—both happy and sad things they had done over the last ten years together when they lived in Indianapolis. They drove by the funeral parlor where Will's Dad's service had been held less than two weeks after the fire. They recalled that the whole family had been together then—even Will's three sisters from many parts of the United States, who buried their father and watched their brother and his family suffer in other ways. They drove by the grocery store that Becky and Will had shopped at for the many years they had lived on the farm. Becky could remember it like she had gone there yesterday—planning Sunday dinner and running to the store to get the fresh meat, rolls, and vegetables. The last time she was there, Beth was small enough to ride in the cart. Becky also chuckled to Will about how she always used to make sure when she went to the store that she had her make-up on, and she wore her best jewelry because she didn't want to be caught without it in Indianapolis. Madison was so different. Becky hardly ever wore jewelry or make-up there. People were different—jewelry and make-up didn't matter as much. Maybe it didn't in Indianapolis either. Becky just thought it did. "Hoosiers seem to be vastly different creatures than Cheese Heads," Becky said to Will, and they laughed together.

They were grateful to be able to stay at Debbie's place, not only for the company and accommodations of home, but because a hotel room was out of the question on their budget. They could barely afford the postage for a return-receipt letter to the other lawyers. Their income was down to mostly just Will's salary, and expenses were mounting.

They were about a block from Debbie's place when Will took an unexpected right turn and told Becky he had decided they would get a hotel after all. "We deserve a break, Becky. Time alone, a bed instead of the couch and floor, and the kids can swim in the pool. Besides, all day I've been thinking, and I want to talk to you tonight, alone and in private after the kids are asleep." Becky was reluctant to go along with the idea. There were so many unanswered questions and unresolved issues, resentment, and suspicion, and she didn't know if she had it in her that night to discuss all of it. But if Will was taking the initiative, she hated to turn him down.

As they drove, Becky sat stoically. She stared out the window at familiar landscape, and the music in her mind was loud, but she sat quietly. Now that Will had brought up talking, she started to think about all the questions she had put aside until after the trial when she felt she could deal with them better. Now they were in her face. She would ask Will if he set the fire. She would ask Will about Robert. They would confront issues, and she would wait on his answer.

When they got to the hotel, Becky called Debbie to let her know they wouldn't be staying with her, and she thanked her and told her she'd call her the next day before they would leave to return to Madison. Becky was afraid to confront the truth, but she knew she had to hear it. She had rehearsed her response to different scenarios, yet she dreaded whatever she thought he might say.

The wear and tear on the family of the lawsuit alone had all but destroyed them many times over the last five years, too. Their lives had not been their own, and the tragedy itself was overwhelming. Humans are capable of withstanding the most violent and heinous acts that mankind puts on its own, and it was difficult for Becky to fathom that one small group of people could do so much damage and devastation not just to two adults, but also to three small children. She couldn't understand why the opposing counsel hadn't used common sense to end the problem before it had snowballed beyond a point of no return. Becky was committed to face each issue head-on and with strength and dignity until the truth was known. Will—Robert—the fire—the fraud!

That evening, after the children were tucked in and asleep for the night, Becky and Will sat down on the sofa at either end. "I know it was your idea to come here to talk, Will, but can I start?"

"Sure, Becky," Will said. "I don't care who goes first. It'll all come out the same."

Becky stared at Will, then said, "Your high school days with Robert, Will. Why didn't you tell me about your relationship when you first found out he was my professor and friend?"

Will stared at Becky. He said, "Becky, I was in shock when I first realized that it was him—oh, Becky." Will shook his head. "I should have told you sooner. Remember a few years ago when the sheriff came to our trailer, and I talked with him outside that evening but never shared our conversation with you? Well, he was an old Valley Boy, and he came to tell me about my old friend, Robert, who had lived with me in the old farmhouse after my divorce, during the rough times he was having during his marital separation, and while finishing his residency in medical school. He lived with me until he got a place of his own and his divorce was final."

Will continued, "He went nuts after that, lost his house and his residency appointment, never really cared about losing his wife, but losing face with his family. His dad especially. You met 'em, though—remember that night when we went inner tubing on the lake?"

Becky said, "The night by the light of the moon?"

"Yeah, that guy—that was Raine," Will said.

Becky sat idle and listened.

Will continued, "Well, anyway, according to my old buddy Sheriff Watson, I guess he *really* went crazy. His wife reported him missing, and Watson thought that maybe he came to our place looking for a place to stay. Again, I didn't tell you because I didn't want to frighten you. Watson was real concerned about what Robert might be capable of, because he'd heard Robert was into drug running and was considered armed and dangerous. His ex-wife had reported that he was delusional, and sometimes didn't even know her. We moved and I didn't hear any more about him until I met your 'friend' for the first time. I didn't recognize him at first because he had gained so much weight, and he was balding where he once had long hair." Will sighed.

"I almost fell over when I realized it was Raine. He acted like he didn't know me and, well, I knew for sure then that he was crazy then. One day, he called me from the opposite end of the soccer field and told me if I interfered with his relationship with you, he'd kill me. Right away, Becky, I phoned the police and hired a private investigator to follow you to keep an eye out for your welfare. I let the police tell me what to do. The cops have been trailing him between Indy and Wisconsin for over a year. The whole time we were camping I knew, but I couldn't say anything to you. I could only observe and report. Becky, he's involved in some pretty serious stuff. The woman you know as his wife is his third. She's been trying to have him committed, and according to what the cops tell me, he has what you call two personalities. Seems like he can outsmart everyone. Being a doctor made him believable, I guess."

Will continued his story. "I was so happy when you got the restraining order on him. You got it easier than you otherwise would have because of the detective I had hired, and the involvement with police. They are aware of Raine's two personalities, and familiar with his threats, his stalking, and his other problems. And you know what else? When Robert lost tenure with the hospital and needed money, from what the detective tells me, he started dealing drugs again and left town. He hasn't been around in a long time, but I continued to have you followed—the kids too, until Robert is behind bars."

"So it was a detective who was following the kids," Becky said.

"That's right, and they're still working on the case. I can't interfere with how the detectives want to handle it. I wish we had been getting along better, Becky; it would have made things a lot easier. I just tried to keep my distance until the dust settled a little."

Becky confessed that Robert had done some bizarre things and had scared her, but she handled them on her own because she had to handle what she had started. She confessed to Will her intimacy with Robert, and she was sickened now by the thought that she had fallen in love with him in the first place. "I wanted affection, and to be with someone who didn't argue all the time and who seemed happy," she said. "You rarely seem happy, Will. Most of all, I wanted to be someone's something special."

"I understand, Becky, I really do," said Will. "I know I haven't been the best for you, but I love you and I want things to get better between us."

He didn't press her with lots of questions—it was just the way he was. They both sat and stared at each other as if wondering what to do next. Then Becky said, "I saw two personalities too, Will, and it was scary."

"Well, that's not all, Becky," Will interrupted. "Wait'll you hear this. An informant told the detective that Raine has been to First Trust Mortgage, trying to strike a deal with them about testifying against us. I think *he's* the assignee we've been hearing about—you know—the new party who recently entered in as the new owner of our property. I just know it's him. I can't tell for sure what he's up to Becky, but it has to be no good."

Becky tipped her head back against the couch and closed her eyes to take in with disbelief all she was hearing, then in fear of what she might see in Will as she began to question him about who *he* was. "Okay, Will," she said, sighing, "what about the fire?"

"What about the fire, Becky?"

Becky put her head down, just looking at her knees, and spoke softly. "Will, I found things in the garage—things I don't think we should have—things that should have been destroyed in the fire." Her voice rose. "I was going through boxes looking for old court documents, and I found—"

"Oh, Becky, dear sweet Becky," Will interrupted. "You think I started the fire?"

"Well, where were you for so long that night—you know—when you left the table at the restaurant? And how come that stuff didn't get destroyed in the fire?" she asked.

Will shook his head, saying, "I left the dinner table that evening to use the restroom. On the way back I met an old girlfriend standing by the arcade games. We talked for a minute—well, maybe it was longer, but I didn't want to mention it. Becky, our relationship was so unstable at times. I didn't want to bring her up because my cousin knew I used to date her, and he would have made a big deal about it, and you would have gotten mad."

"Yeah, but that doesn't explain all the stuff I found. What about that?" Becky asked.

"We were remodeling the house, Becky, remember? I intentionally took some of our belongings out of the house so that they wouldn't get ruined. Remember, we were knocking out walls, sanding, doing lots of construction. If I hadn't boxed 'em up and moved 'em down to the root cellar and the barn, they could have got broke and dirty for sure. We were just lucky, that's all. Lucky some of our things got spared."

Becky sat and listened to her husband's story without moving a muscle. She and Will continued to talk, and they had moments of truth. He told her how he felt changed after she had gone to the prayer service and prayed for their marriage, and she told him about her white light experience and how she too felt changed and had wished for a long time that things would work out between the two of them, but that she just didn't know how to get there from where they were. Becky appreciated that Will had tried to protect her, and he told her he didn't blame her for her weakness for Robert because he admitted he knew he hadn't been there for her emotionally in ways she needed right from the beginning, but that he'd now grown especially closer to her. And he wanted her.

They embraced. They asked each other for forgiveness. They kissed. They joined forces. They had an ally in each other. They started to plan together, to laugh together, and to love together, just like they had so long before.

Once upon a sprouting bloom
There came the chance for change.
And all around, the sunswept room,
There lies the open range.

So on she grew, no thought for risk
To open up and grow.
To push 'ere out the leaflet starts
To wander to and fro.

And off they went, those dancing leaves
That moved with graceful all.
To wind around in limitless
Less n'er a place to fall.

Love bears all things, believes all things, hopes all things, and endures all things. I Corinthians, 13:7.

Chapter Twenty-Nine

It was now two weeks before the bench trial, the case of William D. and Rebecca A. Blaine versus First Trust Mortgage and Assignee. Becky had dropped her case against the title company that had missed the encumbrance. They were lucky. But again, comparing her circumstances to war, she had enough fronts, and she chose the significant battles. The title company had assured her during her investigation that First Trust Mortgage had not recorded the deed, so their argument as to why they hadn't filed the deed before the title search was completed in the first place should have been deemed a culpable offense, but Becky had to make difficult decisions and move on. So much had gone wrong for the Blaines and the project. Now Becky was scrambling to get last things in order as she ran out of time: completing every document and priming every witness. Only last-minute details could be fit into her already demanding schedule, and no stone could be left unturned.

Becky phoned the Attorney General's Office and did research with them regarding First Trust Mortgage's background. She looked for prior complaints and lawsuits, and she found what she was hoping for—another opportunity to suggest a pattern of deceit. The Blaines were not the first clients of record to have filed complaints. This was a good find for Becky. She paid attention to court issues of predatory lending practices.

She was also getting the family arrangements in order. She wanted Will's sisters to be present at the trial so the family could experience first hand a little of what Will and Becky had gone through over the last several years. It would help them understand why Will and Becky lost the family farmland and had to move away. She also wanted them to see the trial because she knew it would serve the family well to see how they struggled. It was an opportunity to bring them closer together—to be a part of their pain. She would be responsible and astute, and she wanted them to be proud of the woman Will had married. She wanted them to know how much she, Will, and the children had suffered, and she wanted them there for moral support because she really enjoyed their company. Becky wanted her mother to attend, also. She felt her mother had made a sincere attempt to bring comfort and support after she finally understood that First Trust Mortgage had committed fraud against her daughter and family. She cheered her on with prayers and strengthening words of encouragement. She had always been astounded by what ultimately ended up happening to the development, the fraud, and the move. She too wanted answers. She wanted to face the "creeps"—as she referred to them—eye to eye for herself. She wanted them to be punished for their wrongdoing. Becky did everything in her power, both physically and financially, to see to it that she and Will both had someone from their respective families to be there for and with them. Charlie and Debbie would be there, too, for neither had ever missed an appearance.

Becky went shopping to get a new outfit for court; she had a specific look in mind. Something smart. Something serious. She looked around in several stores until she found the outfit that demanded the respect she sought. She meant business, and she wanted to look the part. Still, she needed an outfit that she would be comfortable enough to move around in—a non-restrictive outfit so she would feel free and unencumbered. She chose a brown, tan, and black tweed skirt that fell just above her knees; a tan, thinly knit top; a black, wool suit jacket; black nylons; and black shoes. She scratched off another item on her list of things to do for the trial.

Becky spent considerable time writing her opening statements, and Will seemed attentive and helpful, spending quality time with the children, which Becky enjoyed. He gave her a kiss on top of her head while she was typing. Becky gave him a smile back. They were flirtatious.

Once she got her opening statement finished and felt good about it, she got out the photo negatives of the gray house from pictures she had taken and chose the best one she could find to enlarge for display during her opening remarks. It was one that made the house look the best so that when she showed the devastation it would have more of an impact. She wanted the judge to realize that their home wasn't just a little shack that had been foreclosed on, but a large and beautiful home constructed with utmost care by Will and Becky, down to every last detail of an ornate Victorian home. In her closing argument, she planned to tell about the research she and Will had done to accomplish vintage accuracy. She would also use the enlarged photo made from a negative of a picture she had taken on the last trip to Indianapolis, so that she could show the Court what the house looked like once the defense took possession of it. The house looked terrible. The windows and doors were boarded up, and some of the siding was hanging down from strong winds that had passed through over the years. Becky borrowed an easel from her church to display the pictures, and then crossed that task off her list.

Becky was sure of her work, and minced no words when she said that the only way they were going to lose the case was if she lost on a technicality. She felt that she understood all of the procedures. She had read many books and felt prepared. She couldn't sleep. At four o'clock in the morning she found herself scribbling notes with whatever she could find—using eyeliner pencils, crayons, unsharpened pencils she found in places where there was no sharpener, so she'd bite the wood off the pencils to get to the lead. She had notes on tissue paper and notepads all over the apartment. She had papers sticking out of the pocket in her purse, and red notes written all over the days of the week on the calendar. About once a week she'd gather the notes and sit down to compile one long list. From the list she created an outline on large graph paper so that it would be easy to add or delete something. Then she propped up the eleven-by-seventeen-inch sheet of graph paper and typed everything into the computer. She generated page upon page of proposed testimony and enumerated questions she intended to ask the witnesses—a procedure that was extremely important to her because she knew that she needed to tell her story and prove her points in a very concise and orderly manner. Then she mailed a copy of some of her questions to a few of the witnesses she had chosen to read and study, depending on what she was expecting out of them.

Her presentation needed to be chronological and easy for anyone, particularly the judge, to follow. She had to prove each step sequentially. In her mind, she pretended that the judge knew nothing about the case, and she was starting from scratch in attempting to show him exactly what the defendants had done. Every word she uttered needed to be supported. She had to anticipate every objection and when, where, and how they would object. She needed to know what evidence or statute she could use so the judge would overrule the defendants' objection. So when Becky put her three-ring binder together, she did so in story form with all of the supporting documents, whether it was a paper or a personal statement tabulated and highlighted nearby. She put an initial in capital letters followed by a colon for each question she would ask a witness. She went over those questions with her witnesses right after she subpoenaed them, and would review with them intermittently until the trial. She would do it again the day before the trial. She kept useful records of their replies, then she streamlined her questions to make them more pointed, more specific, and easy for even a novice to understand. She put the witnesses in the order that her story was being told. Becky made notes when she had to prove something at Point A so she could sequentially move on to Point B, and so forth, until she was at the end. Along the way, she wrote in red ink in the margin where she anticipated an objection and how she would go about showing why it should be overruled. She had her exhibits in sequential order, and she was ready to fill them in on the recorder's list and get them labeled the day of the trial and before it began. She had learned to do this from watching as an observer at the other trials.

Becky reviewed her opening statements. She made follow-up phone calls to her witnesses and informed them about what time she thought she'd need them, in order of her presentation, and she went over her line of questioning again. She ended conversations cordially and with grateful thanks and appreciation. She made sure that just in case she ran out of time, the most important and least important witnesses were prioritized. Then she began to develop her case by typing exactly what she needed to say to each witness to qualify them—who they were, what their field of expertise was, how long they'd been at their job, and what their association had been with the Blaines. Her questions were precise—no long speeches—just short and to the point. She instructed her witnesses to give brief answers. She only had half of three and one-half hours to get her six-year saga out to the judge.

Becky was undecided almost to the trial date whether or not to accept a settlement offer, or to counter offer for more, because

Will cast a shadow of doubt about their ability to win. He didn't want them to walk away with nothing, and maybe owe their legal fees if they lost. But for Becky, the case wasn't about money—it was about principle. She had to admit to herself and finally to Will that she agreed, money could certainly help compensate for what they'd been through, and her family did deserve to get something back, but not by way of a bribe. No. Becky and Will had a few discussions in the kitchen, away from where the children could hear, about what to do. Money—no money. Lots of money—a little money. In Becky's mind, Will just didn't understand. Becky finally said, "The only way we're going to make a difference for anyone else is to have our day in court. If the judge rules in our favor and we've proved fraud, it's a scarlet letter to them. How many other successful companies out there have committed fraud?" Becky never could understand why a successful company would need to be dishonest. She couldn't understand why there was no compassion for one man from another. When he saw his brother hurting and in pain, where was decency?

Becky had read many cases in preparation for the trial, and she was all too familiar with the notorious actions of large companies. One in particular came to mind. A misguided and deceptive insurance company paid way below indemnity on an accident claim just because they knew that they could—that their staff attorneys could keep up the rhetoric long enough that the family would settle. *Standard practice for large corporations who feed like wild animals off the fat of their kills. It's called making a living—making the numbers work—just doing their job. Where is the brave, honest soul who would stand up and say, "No, this is wrong."?*

She gave in to Will and sent a substantial settlement offer of what she felt they were entitled to. Becky knew they would reject it, but she went through the motions to appease Will and, also out of curiosity, to see what First Trust Mortgage would come up with. Becky prepared an outline of their losses to include loss of credibility, loss of historic homestead, loss of lifestyle, loss of feeling of well-being, mental cruelty, loss of family heirlooms, sustaining bankruptcy, leaving a professional career program, loss of business, moving expenses, loss of appreciation of house, loss of the conservatory, building contracts, all of which came to two million, seven hundred nine thousand, three hundred and twenty dollars.

Under the law, Becky knew she had choices. She could have rescinded the contract and asked for the house and property back which would have resulted in the Blaines having to leave Madison and move back to Indianapolis and assume all subdivision debt. That also would have meant they could have continued on with the historic subdivision. Becky didn't want to do that because she and Will had already established themselves in Madison, and they didn't want to uproot the kids again. They didn't want to go back in time. They had gone through too much. Sure there was family history, and there were memories in Indiana, but they had already adjusted to the losses they had experienced there—the hype and momentum of the subdivision was gone. They no longer wanted any part of it. The other option was exactly what they were doing. They wanted to go to trial, win, be compensated for their losses, and try to set a precedent so the company couldn't hurt anyone else.

Becky's mom drove to the apartment two days before they were set to leave. The show had started. Becky told Will that it was like being in labor. "It won't stop now 'til it's over, and the experience will heighten and become more intense the closer we get," she said.

Will's sister, Diana, flew into the Madison airport. Everybody was getting anxious, excited, and nervous. Diana asked Becky to try to explain the story to her because her family had never really understood. Becky did her best to explain the more pertinent facts to Will's sister and to her mother. They sat and listened intently. Will chimed in periodically with tales of First Trust Mortgage's behavior—their tricks and schemes.

Becky did not reveal that she had come close so many times to a nervous breakdown. She had had thoughts of death—either her own or First Trust Mortgage's lawyers. There is a thin line that separates good and evil, and sometimes there is a silent and secretive crossover where human nature experiences moments of weakness and unrestraint—some more than others.

The defense attorneys called Becky again. This time, they tried to smooth her over with a layer of pure silk, but she saw the moth holes. They asked her to sign off on a Stipulation of Admissible Exhibits, telling her that what they were trying to do was save them both time in court so the case wouldn't be continued. Becky knew better than to believe their bull. If it was First Trust Mortgage's idea, it had to be no good. *Why were they asking for this?* Becky thought about what they were saying and realized that what they really wanted to do was to get their exhibits signed off on so they wouldn't have to enter each one and put themselves at risk for objections. That would be too easy. They still thought Becky was a pushover. They had to at least try. If she had signed off, it would have left them more time on the clock to litigate their point of view. *No way.* They took a chance, but it was a foolish one. They had exposed themselves. This was a perfect opportunity to seize control again, so she replied, "Sure." They sent her a list and, just like she had anticipated, she was able to see more closely what they were thinking, what they were planning, and the order of their attack. She was able to see what evidence they were going to try to use to prove their points. If she missed anything when she analyzed their strategy, she now had two days over the weekend to figure out a rebuttal, an objection, or a witness that could dispel their theory. But she had already sent in her witness list. Could she add another one or two at the last minute? More research for Becky.

She put herself in defense mode so she could figure out how to beat them at their own game. She had to think like them. Based on the evidence, she wrote down more of her objections and continued categorizing and re-categorizing her information methodically. She developed cross-questions based on the order of their exhibits—the ones she knew for sure and the ones she anticipated. Trusting her own intuition and knowledge of events that occurred, she felt even more ready and complete than before. She was glad that she had given the defense the impression that she was a dumb blonde who was weak and naïve.

Becky discussed with First Trust Mortgage's counsel as to where they should meet in Indianapolis to sign off on the Stipulation of Admissible Exhibits, and what time they should do it. Becky acted eager. She allowed them to believe that she was falling for their acts of sincerity. After they hung up the phone Becky laughed to herself. She knew she had no intention of meeting them on the morning of the trial. They would be left hanging alone at a motel many miles away from the courthouse waiting for Becky, who would never show. Or, maybe they had planned on doing that to her. At any rate, she wouldn't be there.

Becky pulled herself away from the family on several occasions so that she could rehearse her lines. She could not be too prepared. The trial binder she had put together and tabulated read just like a book. She also had a second binder that she called the "Just-in-Case File." It listed several things she thought the defense *might* bring up and, if they did, she wanted to be able to quickly refer to her notes on what she could say about the issue and the statute that would support her assertion. For instance, if the defense brought up her Motion to Set Aside Summary Judgment, she could raise issue that it was moot because there was never anything entered—"see Transcript of Evidence from November 11th hearing." She felt confident she could address each and every issue they could raise—even the little things that the defense had sneaked into the file so they could grab it out later. There were little one-liners that would be intentionally ignored until the day of the trial, and Becky was aware of them. She also knew they would try to make the small one-liners into major headlines. She knew that if they had not brought it up previously in their moving papers, they couldn't enter new stuff in during the trial—another small detail she had picked up in her court travails.

Becky's third binder was titled "Copy of Plaintiff's Summary Judgment Motion," and her fourth, the "Copy of Plaintiff's Trial Exhibits." Because the four volumes were in order, she told Will that if something happened to her on the day of the trial, all he had to do was read each page out loud like he was reading a book, and he could try the case. She taught him her system. She had written her opening statements, called each witness, and typed her outline of questioning. In the margins in blue ink, next to each issue, she had the statutes that supported everything she was trying to do, and red ink of the anticipated objections and her response. She also referenced the title page in the Indiana Trial Rule Book of Evidence to correspond and tabulated that book so she could quickly flip to the appropriate page and tell the judge why their objection should be overruled. Her depression had subsided. She felt in control of her life once again. She felt close to Will, as they were approaching together what at one time looked to be a nightmare that would never end. A season of trauma that went on and on. They were not unscathed, but they had survived, together—through perseverance and faith.

The minivan was packed to the hilt. Becky even made sure that the kids had stuff to play with in the swimming pool at the motel. They took Claire, their cocker spaniel, with them and the kids' favorite pillows. Grandma and Aunt Diana were there. To an onlooker, it would appear that they were all just going on a marvelous family trip. But also crammed into the back were four black binders filled with the story of six years of hell. Becky's new outfit for the trial was also in the back in a small suitcase right next to the binders. There was a peculiar feeling in the van. Each person had his or her own set of thoughts that were racing through his or her mind as they headed down the road for the last trip to Indianapolis. Becky wanted to win for so many reasons. She wanted to make Will and his family proud. She wanted to make her mother and father proud. She wanted to prove to herself and family that they were right all along, and that they had done nothing wrong to deserve all that they had been through and, more importantly, that Becky would not cease on her unrelenting quest to find justice. Many family members and friends had speculated that Will and Becky surely must have done something wrong to lose everything. They were wrong.

The trip was a happy one. They sang songs together and played games. They stopped for breakfast and enjoyed the late autumn air. They pulled onto the exit ramp that would take them to the Indianapolis airport where they would meet Will's other sister and continue on to their final destination. Step A to step B, and on to step C. The momentum was escalating, as was the excitement and anticipation. Becky's planning was methodical down to the last detail, and they arrived at the airport within minutes after Aunt Carol's plane arrived. Becky's orchestration was perfectly timed and melodically tuned. The van kept getting more and more full, but that was all right. The plan was to be together, to commune on their way there and to celebrate in quiet understanding how far Becky and Will had come.

The fact that everything was falling into place was a sign in Becky's mind that all would go well from here on out. Aunt Carol seemed overwhelmed to see her favorite niece and nephews. She said she could hardly believe that only two hours before she was home in sunny Florida. This was the first time that she had been on a direct flight, and she was tickled not to be jetlagged. She quickly got caught up with the emotions inside the van and was part of the gang of travelers on a mission of discovery and truth. There was a common undercurrent of excitement because the family was together, despite the unspoken apprehension. They stopped at Aunt Carol's favorite restaurant for lunch, and Becky's mom picked up the tab. Then they proceeded into town.

The first thing that Becky wanted to do was to take everybody to the gray house. She wanted her relatives to see what the house looked like since they were last there. The last thing they remembered was a beautiful house that Will had built, Becky had decorated, and that had been filled with lots of beautiful memories. They were greeted by their own shock. Tears welled up in Diana, Carol, and Becky's mother's eyes. Will put the van in part, got out before anyone else did, put his hands in the back pockets of his jeans and walked toward the house like he was just coming home from work. Diana openly wept as Carol searched for her camera, to preserve the awkward scene. Weeds had grown up and tangled around the porch posts and across the front steps as if to disallow trespassers. Becky helped the children out of their seats. Erin and Eli took Claire on her leash towards the field where years earlier they had left a toy truck and on this trip they found. Beth waited near the gravel lane for her mother. The house looked like part of a movie set for a haunted tale. Abandoned, for sure. Shingles were hanging here and there where wind had blown them off, but no caretaker was around for repair. Windows were boarded up. Slowly, each walked through the tall grass like cotton pickers in the South, or berry pickers in the North, interspersed in the patch of green and somewhat stooped over. Beth walked around to the side holding her mother's hand. They noticed that the door of the porch was wide open. Cautiously, they walked inside. In disbelief their eyes scanned the vandals' damage. The mantle above the fireplace had been torn clean off the wall, and lay on the beer-stained carpet. Hand-painted tiles from the kitchen were smashed, and bits and pieces crumbled under Becky and Beth's feet as they tried to walk around the mess to get to the stairs. They kicked beer cans aside and began their ascent to Beth's old bedroom. Beth wiped a few tears from her cheeks. Becky looked down the hall into her twins' room. She too began to cry. Will was still outside, but Carol, Diana, and Becky's mother had made their way upstairs and they formed a group hug in the hallway where Becky used to walk her crying baby twins in the night, by the landing where she used to sit and study for her college exams after the children had fallen asleep. A bird flew past them to its perch in Becky's old closet, and startled, they broke the huddle.

Without saying it, they all knew when they had seen enough. They walked out to the van and got in, exhausted from what they had seen. This, the beginning of a trip back in time. Their next stop according to Becky's itinerary would be the firehouse. There on the walls were a series of five photos that had been taken by the fire chief, an old friend of Will's family, of the original Blaine homestead. When they got to the firehouse, Becky identified herself to the captain and asked if she could take her family to see the pictures. Will led his family single-file to the gallery of works that began when the firemen first arrived, and they progressed to the last picture, of a solitary structure, the chimney, the only thing that evidenced where a house once stood. Anchored by smoldering embers and the ghostly smoke that rose up far into the sky, a story now in pictures.

This time it was Aunt Diana who became overcome and left the building crying. She had wanted to see the pictures, but could not have prepared herself for the trauma that she felt. She would tell the rest that it was not only for what her brother and family had been through, but all that went through her mind as she viewed the emptiness, the farmhouse forever gone. The farmhouse she had grown up in. Seeing it put her right there with Will and Becky the night of the fire. It made her tremble inside. Once out of the firehouse she sat down on the curb with her hands covering her face and her head bowed into her lap. Will followed after her and put his arms around her and told her that he was sorry, sorry for her tears. The story that had been unfolding in the van became more lifelike with each segment of their trip, just as Becky had planned. Page by page, Becky allowed them to enter her book—the story that she, Will, and the children had lived.

After they left the fire station, the van was much more quiet and much less festive. But there was work to be done to finish the story. They arrived at the hotel and one by one, each person took a bag out of the van until it was unloaded. One by one they filed into their rooms.

It wasn't too long though before Eli and Erin started bugging their grandma and aunts to take them to the swimming pool, and they did. Once again there was laughter and giggling. The reunion was very special. Becky sat on a pool-side chair, but she was quiet. She was entertained by the people she loved the most, though she wouldn't remember much else.

She didn't remember ordering pizza for dinner, or whether the kids ate. She couldn't have told anyone what the weather was doing outside, even though the pool house was paneled with windows, or what was on the news, even though there was a television set tuned to the news less than five feet away from her. Becky didn't pay attention to what anyone was wearing, and she never even noticed that the music in the billiard room nearby was entirely too loud and drove everybody nuts. Her world was quiet and she heard no music, only dead silence.

The evening passed quickly into night. They were all tired and went to bed easily, even the children. The morning light soon filtered through the half-drawn drapes, and no one moved or spoke. Becky was in one bed with Beth, and Will was in the other bed with the twins. They watched as the shadows moved with the passing of time. Both Becky and Will had been awake for a long while.

When they all began to stir, each did everything Becky had instructed them to do. The children got dressed without complaint.

Becky had their outfits laid out so there would be less hassle. Becky walked over to the window sill and ran her fingers over her black binders, placed side by side like books on a library shelf. Then she took her clothes into the bathroom to change. She pulled up her nylons and put on her slip. She put on her blouse and tweed skirt. She left her jacket off until the very last so she wouldn't get overheated. She looked at the heart pill she had laid out, but decided to wait until later to take it so its effect would peak during opening statements, if everything went as planned. She made sure that her extra pills were in her purse. She fussed with her hair in an obsessive-compulsive sort of way. *Should I pull it back—no, leave it down.* Then she looked in the mirror. *Should I put it behind one ear—yeah, no, pull it back with a ribbon.* Nope, the ribbon would bother her neck. *Take it out. Damn it. Put it up in a clip—looks neat, and it's out of the way.* She was used to wearing it that way—it would be fine. She checked to make sure that all of the binders were loaded into the van. She went back into the bathroom, closed the door behind her, and rehearsed her opening statements and closing arguments one time only. She said a prayer. She put on her black jacket and told the family, "Come on, let's go."

Will's sisters and Becky's Mom stepped into the hallway walking out at the same time. They too ready to go, and were there when Becky told them to be. No one spoke. They all left Becky alone with her thoughts. They carried their somber feelings with them.

Once in the van, each found a place to sit with no discussion of who would sit where, no hassle, no controversy. They were mindful of the importance of Becky's state-of-mind, even the children, odd for them not to struggle for a particular place to sit. Becky broke through the silence, and said, "I forgot my glasses—we need to turn around." Each person instinctively looked around to see if maybe she had dropped them somewhere in the van. She found them in the pocket of her jacket.

After about a mile Becky reminded the passengers that First Trust representatives were probably at the meeting place where she was supposed to be to sign off on exhibits. She wondered if they had gone there or had just made the whole thing up.

Becky didn't want to get to the courthouse early because she didn't want to give the defense an opportunity to say something aggravating that might throw off her meditative state. It wouldn't take much. Yet she fought her instincts to arrive early to get acclimated. But she thought, *I've been here enough; I'm acclimated.*

Both sides were now present, lined in rank as of readying for Pickett's charge—one line leaning on the walls on one side of the hallway, the other on the opposite. The clerk stepped out to Becky, pulled her aside, and told her that one of her witnesses had called and was not going to make it to the trial. He was in the hospital.

"Why?" asked Becky.

"I don't know Becky," said the clerk, who had come to know her over the years.

"He's subpoenaed, so I could ask to reschedule, but there's no way I'm going to do that. I *have* to do this trial today," Becky said. She threw her head back and closed her eyes, and she didn't care what the defense thought she was upset about. Will walked up to her and asked her what was wrong.

"Nothing," Becky said, as she opened up one of her binders and rapidly took her pen to write in the necessary changes. She wanted this witness, but she would have to do without him, circumvent his testimony, get it from another witness. She tried not to let the situation throw her off. *Was anyone else not going to show?* She would follow up on what had happened to her witness after the trial. She ran her fingers through her hair in a nervous gesture. *I wanted him. The judge knew him personally. He would have been a very impressive witness.*

Five minutes before nine o'clock, Becky entered the courtroom to set up. This would be the fifth time in the past two years that she entered through the same doors either to be present at a hearing to study the posture of the court or to attend one of their status or pre-trial conferences. She always sat on the same side of the room because she was a creature of habit. Today would be no different, for the sameness brought her comfort, in the same way traditions offer comfort to children—a sense of security. So she walked in the direction of her seat, the long wooden table by the door. It was her comfort zone. When she got to the table, however, she was surprised to find the defense had deliberately set up camp on *her* side of the room. She stared at the table that was heaped with stacks of documents that represented the Blaines' years of suffering and struggle—stared it down as if by telepathy their briefcases and paperwork would move.

Now what am I going to do, God? I have to sit on the same side of the room or I won't feel in control. They can't get to me before I even begin today. What will I do? She stepped back and quickly scanned the room looking for answers, the eight wooden chairs around the table by the judge, the place where the recorder sat, the jury section. Could be a distraction. *No, this won't do.* Like a commando, a member of a small force trained to raid enemy territory, Becky set herself in motion. She had weighed her options; she had to prove their stuff. She waited for the defense team to get out of eye-shot. Then she quickly moved all of their briefcases and stacks of papers to the table on the other side of the room. She knew they would be furious, but what were they going to do—whine to the judge? *Judge, she moved our papers! No, they can't do anything about it,* thought Becky.

She could feel her adrenaline surge as she organized her binders all over the table. She threw her coat on the back of the chair and sat down with a pencil in her hand like she'd been there for hours. Becky's support team had watched her actions from the sidelines and was quietly laughing to themselves, but had stayed out of her way.

Becky had asked that Will sit in the back of the room so that his body language would not distract her. The defense team entered through the doors right behind where Becky was now sitting. They were momentarily puzzled by what they saw. Dan Shortino approached Becky red-faced and began to reprimand her sternly. "I could ask for a mistrial, you know. You're not allowed to touch our things!"

Becky looked indignant but said, "I'm sorry, Mr. Shortino, I won't do it again."

He was infuriated as he realized once again for the umpteenth time that she had foiled him again. This set the stage for what lay ahead. She had gotten the jump-start on him twice that morning.

Becky watched as he rearranged his dossier, then pulled back his chair. He sat agitated and uneasy.

Becky, on the other hand, felt put together. She was as prepared as she could be. She had worked hard. All of her evidence was in place. She didn't feel arrogant or overly self-confident. She was realistic and knew the challenge ahead of her would not be easy. The defense was disproportionately armed with years of experience, law degrees, and a counsel of eight to confer with. She looked around and saw Debbie and Charlie sitting in their same old spots—they were her fans, and she knew the exact direction she needed to turn and how far she needed to twist her neck in order to see them. She winked at Charlie, and he gave her the thumbs up. Debbie was less inconspicuous and said in a brazen voice, "Get ‘em, Becky!" No one in the room could miss her voice, and the two defense counsels stopped working their pens and looked up to find the source of their distraction.

Becky got up for a minute and walked over to the court reporter. She asked that her exhibits be stamped and numbered, a technicality that she had observed during one of her visits to another trial. Becky and Will's family watched her as she walked with a confident posture; she looked like she knew what she was doing.

The rest of Becky's entourage entered, and the witnesses sat down in order of their appearance. Becky's mother found a seat for herself where she could communicate to Becky with facial gestures, and where she could see her daughter well. Becky saw her mother wave to her and mouth "good luck." Will's sisters sat together and whispered to each other and pointed now and then.

There were several quiet, busy things going on all over the room. It wouldn't be long now before the trial got underway. Charlie walked over to Will and asked, "You okay, bud?"

Will turned to face his friend of many years, the friend of his parents, the friend of his grandparents, and the only living connection to that part of his past and said, "You know, Charlie, I feel like a horse that's been ridden real hard and put away wet!"

Charlie replied with a handshake and a grin, "'Know whatcha mean, Will, know whatcha mean," and he patted Will on the back as if to say "it'll be all right." Will got a tear in his eye for what Charlie meant to him, coupled with the emotion of the day and the culmination of the many years of suffering and losses because of the fraud. He had never acknowledged recovery since the fire that had come so close together with his twins' birth and his own father's death. Will gazed longingly at Becky as she sat meditating now, trying not to allow her mind to deviate far from center.

The rest of the defense counsel had entered for what would be the last time. They had walked in and out, back and forth, several times—like a civil war re-enactment, all the blue and gray suits moving to and fro. Becky watched as their three witnesses took their seats. *Is that all they have?* Becky had eleven.

The judge walked in through the back doors, and the bailiff announced, "All rise." Then the judge took his seat. Becky asked if she could approach the bench, and the judge consented. "Your Honor, as I am the moving party, may I go first?" Becky had tried for weeks to try to understand the order of which side went first. She had never gotten a clear answer from anyone. She couldn't remember if the judge simply decided, or if like the preacipe, someone needed to ask if they wanted something. Becky was afraid that the defendants would give reasons why they should go first. She wasn't asking for special favors, but if anyone got to go first by simply asking, she wanted it to be her.

The judge announced in a very loud and impatient manner, "There will be no special favors here, Ms. Blaine. However, you may go first as you are the plaintiff in this matter." She felt her face get hot. She didn't want to start off on the bad side of the judge. She felt embarrassed. She could hear snickers from the side of the defense. She wished with all her heart that she could have explained why she asked about going first. She didn't want the other side to gain internal mental strength that she had already been reprimanded by the judge. *Oh well,* she thought, *there's nothing I can do about it now. Proceed.* Walking away from the bench she wondered if this was an indication of how the judge was going to treat her. She took a deep breath, and said to herself, *Whew—this ain't gonna be easy!*

"I would like to make a foundation statement," said Becky.

"You may proceed," replied the judge.

"Your Honor, I, Rebecca A. Blaine, am here today without counsel and stand *pro se* as Plaintiff to speak on behalf of myself and my husband, William D. Blaine, in the matter of our Motion for Summary Judgment as to the Counter-Claim and Petition for Damages Induced by Fraud against First Trust Mortgage.

"One is left to wonder after six years of litigation, whether large corporations that build their empires from the fruits of others' labors would understand the true nature of human struggle or the naked honesty found in simplistic truth.

"When my husband graduated from high school, he didn't use his scholarships for college—he stayed on the family farm to take care of his father and grandparents. When his grandparents died, he bought the family farm from the estate from his father and two uncles. The family farm represented the Blaines—the Blaines were the founding family of Blaine's Valley, the Blaine's Valley United Methodist Church, and the Blaine's Valley Grade School.

"After my husband's father died, when our twins were only six months old, the farmhouse burned down. Our five thousand square foot, one hundred and twenty-three-year-old farmhouse was reduced to ashes. After the fire, and after the mortgage was paid off, we were left with only eight thousand dollars to rebuild. We bought a trailer, put it on the land, and lived in it for two years while we saved to rebuild.

"It became apparent that we should sell off part of our land to help offset the cost of rebuilding. But when we approached the City, they would not approve any more septic systems on the property. So, to offset the cost of City sewers, we spoke with Coston Engineering about the possibility of selling three or six parcels. We ultimately re-zoned the property from farm to residential and contracted with Coston to plat a twelve-lot subdivision that came to be called Canal Estates. We chose that name because we had the last remaining untouched section of the old Central Canal on the property. The subdivision was to be an epitaph of sorts to the Blaines who founded the valley with a Lockerbie aire, cobblestone walkways and gas lamppost lighting. The plat was approved by the City of Indianapolis and, in a ceremony held on our property, the Canal Society members, a State Senator, the Blaine Valley Grade

School Principal, historians, university professors, and the Blaines dedicated our property an historic landmark. The planning for this was done as the City of Indianapolis was simultaneously renovating, preserving, and beautifying the Canal System downtown. The timing was perfect for the success of Canal Estates." Becky believed that giving a smidgen of evidence or at least a suggestion for the success of their project would perhaps support a higher judgment should they win, and at least establish worth and substantiate the value of their historic subdivision should a verdict warrant such figures necessary."

Becky continued, "Through the cold, harsh winter, Will and I, along with our four children, my brothers, and a couple of friends, built with our own hands the first house in Canal Estates, the *spec* house that was situated on Lot 1. Our construction loan had been secured with Banker's Trust Mortgage Company, but because of a merger and a change in house rules, they were no longer giving out permanent financing, which led us to seek the end mortgage with First Trust.

"This is where our problems really began and is the reason we're all here today." Becky continued to tell their story. She kept her details to the point. She referred to the picture of the gray house that she had enlarged up on the easel, and she pointed to it when she said, "We had to leave our home because of First Trust Mortgage. Will and I had to leave our thriving businesses, all prospects of my attending medical school, and the historic ground that was being transformed into Canal Estates." She went on to give a brief summary of the series of events that led them to file their Petition for Damages Induced by Fraud against First Trust Mortgage.

"The defense has tried to tire, confuse, and defeat us with multitudinous motions. The court lacked jurisdiction; the case was a frivolous action; the Blaines were shopping for a forum; that they were not properly served, and on and on. They were telling me that I could go to jail for practicing law without a license and were asking the court to make us pay for their legal fees of yet many more thousands of dollars.

"This is not an imaginary trial they refer to—a piece of fiction they have enjoyed. No! Susan Kane, Professor of Law and Political Science at USC writes, 'There is a usual pattern in don't-blame-me cases—Blame the victim!' I say the defense need not behave so acrimoniously; the reticent truth will prevail. We will finally hear the true merits of this case."

Becky stood proudly as she read her opening remarks from one of her black binders she held in her left hand like a choir folder. "The defense will raise issue of contention that their original intent was to secure a mortgage with one house on 5.65 acres of land. Our witnesses will not only prove these intentions to be false, they will prove that the Defendants' own testimonies are inconsistent. The truth is that First Trust Mortgage confirmed with us when they gave us a mortgage that they were securing it with one house on approximately 1/3 acre lot, Lot 1, Canal Estates.

"The plaintiffs, William D. and Rebecca A. Blaine, will prove today, Your Honor, beyond a reasonable doubt," she said, and a rhythmic cadence of war drums forged through her mind in crescendo as it pounded with her heart, "that the mortgage given to William D. and Rebecca A. Blaine by First Trust Mortgage was procured by fraud and misrepresentation, and that the Blaines are entitled to Summary Judgment against First Trust Mortgage for their egregious, fraudulent misconduct. The defendants have no exculpatory evidence. Their facts are purely lies of their own invention. Will and I, alone, as part of the American public, acting through our court system, stand up to these lying, deceiving, corporate war mongers of justice and say, enough is enough!"

Chapter Thirty

"Marked for identification purposes as Trial Exhibit 1, is a copy of *The Indianapolis News* dated February 1923," Becky began. "I move to have Trial Exhibit 1 entered into evidence."

"Objection." Already with the first exhibit, the defense objected because the newspaper was a copy and not an original. *I was right—they planned on objecting to everything,* Becky thought. *Using up time so the case will be continued,* or at least make it so that she wouldn't have time to introduce all of her exhibits. *I have witnesses to swear in, to qualify, and to give testimony to support each exhibit.* She was afraid she would run out of time, but she was prepared to move quickly and with expediency. She looked into the margin of her notes—red ink—"objection," then quickly flipped to her referenced spot in the *Indiana Trial Rule Book of Evidence*—blue ink—and then she responded, "Chapter 902 under self-authorization—"

"Now we're cooking," said the judge.

Becky moved on. "Marked for identification purposes as Trial Exhibit 2, is a copy of a survey of the Archibald Blaine Farm, the first of the Blaine family to settle the area. I move to have Trial Exhibit 2 entered into evidence." She brought a copy up to the judge and, according to protocol, brought a copy of it over to the defense table. "This represents the first legal description of what came to be known as Canal Estates. The relevance here, Your Honor, extends the understanding of the extent of emotional devastation experienced by William D. and Rebecca A. Blaine and family, who did not simply lose their home and a subdivision because of the fraud committed by First Trust Mortgage—they lost the land that once belonged to Will's great-grandfather. Canal Estates was designed to be an historical landmark for the City of Indianapolis and the State of Indiana, as well as an epitaph to the Blaines." She paused. "Your Honor, I am ready to call my first witness. Mr. Berry, would you please take the stand?"

Mr. Berry walked over and sat down. Becky approached him. "Please state your name for the record."

"My name is Lonny Berry."

"Please tell the Court where you are employed, how many years you have worked there, and in what capacity," said Becky. Mr. Berry answered her questions, and Becky continued, "Are you trained and authorized to prepare 'Meets and Bounds Descriptions'?"

"Yes."

"In one or two sentences, briefly describe the business relationship you had with the Blaines," Becky asked. She knew instinctively that she needed to remind the witness to be brief because of the time limitation. She also knew that the defense was going to cross-examine with a controversial question that would take some time to defend. That was predictable. Becky also knew that First Trust Mortgage would allege that Becky and Will knew from the very beginning what they were signing and that they knew all of the land was being mortgaged. Becky was prepared for that, too, and to head them off, she entered into evidence four different forms on which the legal description for their property had been described. One described the property in one paragraph, another in two paragraphs, yet another in a different format, and the fourth was over a page long. She showed each of them separately to the witness.

"Can you identify for the court which of these four legal descriptions that you have before you describes Lot 1 in Canal Estates?" Mr. Berry read each one in detail. The defense team huddled and whispered. The witness replied that he could not. The opposing counsel objected, and Becky quickly turned to her evidence book, Rule 1005, Public Records.

"You mean to tell me that an individual trained as yourself to understand and decipher legal descriptions cannot simply look at these degrees, longitudes, and latitudes, and ascertain what specific property they describe? Are you saying that you cannot tell me which legal description describes Canal Estates or Lot One?" Becky paused for effect. "Would it surprise you then to learn that all four legal descriptions, one written in two paragraphs, one in three paragraphs, and so forth, describe the exact same piece of ground?"

"Well, ah, legal descriptions can be written many ways," said Becky's expert witness.

Becky continued, "So, can you say with certainty that it would be impossible for an untrained person, such as myself, to be able to decipher legal descriptions upon brief survey of these degrees, longitudes, and latitudes?"

"Yes, it would."

Becky closed, "Let the record show that there is much diversity with which legal descriptions are written and that even trained eyes cannot simply glance at a legal description and ascertain what it specifically describes. The Blaines could not have even remotely realized that the document they were signing contained an inaccurate legal description. They relied on the honesty and integrity of First Trust Mortgage to give them a loan for what they asked for—a loan for one *spec* house, Lot 1, in the Canal Estates. The mortgage they led us to believe we were getting does not and never did exist. The mortgage that does exist is inaccurate and represents only the beginning of a long trail of deceit designed by the Defendants to commit fraud."

Becky's next step was designed to show the Court that she had tried to obtain a copy of the original front page of the loan document that would have shown the intent of what the Blaines had asked to be mortgaged, but she was unable to obtain one even with a Motion to Compel, though she did get one from the Roth family, and she entered that into evidence.

The judge asked the defense, "Is what Mrs. Blaine is saying true—you do not have a copy of their original loan application?"

The lead counsel for the defense shook his head no, and replied, "No, Your Honor, we do not." The judge took his pen and made some notes while he too shook his head.

Becky, of course, knew exactly how First Trust Mortgage would reply. Their own actions would be used against them.

"Didn't you tell me that you had lost our loan application?" Becky questioned. "Doesn't the record show that our Motion to Compel produced nothing?"

Becky continued to question Mr. Berry. "Can you tell me sir, at the time the Blaines closed their mortgage loan with First Trust Mortgage on March 8, 1990, could they, in accordance with the laws and ordinances and provisions set forth by the City of Indianapolis, have legally sold properties by 'Meets and Bounds' legal descriptions in Canal Estates?"

Mr. Berry answered, "Yes, they could."

"Can you give an opinion on whether it is normal, routine, and customary for a real estate developer to sell lots and obtain mortgages on lots by 'Meets and Bounds' descriptions after a plat is approved, but before it is recorded?"

"Yes, it is customary," answered Mr. Berry.

Becky was feeling comfortable in her role and continued with her first witness, "Marked for identification purposes as Trial Exhibit 15, I hold a Disclosure Statement of Mr. and Mrs. Robins, who owned Lot 3 in the Canal Estates. I move to have Trial Exhibit 15 entered into evidence. I call the Court's attention to the reference to the lot number at the top of the page. Let the record show that First Trust Mortgage was well aware of the Canal Estates subdivision one month before, and I emphasize *before,* the Blaines closed on what they believed to be a mortgage on Lot 1 of the Canal Estates.

"Marked for identification purposes as Trial Exhibit 16, I hold a legal description labeled Lot 3. I move to have Trial Exhibit 16 entered into evidence." Becky turned to her witness. "Mr. Berry, did you prepare the description of Lot 3, which was used to execute the Robinses' loan?"

"Yes, I did," Mr. Berry replied.

"Your Honor," defense lawyer Shortino interrupted, "we have evidence, Your Honor, that will show that Mrs. Blaine contacted this witness three days ago and tried to get him to write a legal description for Lot 1."

"Excuse me, Mr. Shortino," Becky replied in a disgusted tone of voice, "what are you eluding to? What is your inference here? Are you trying to suggest that I tampered with a witness—that I asked him to create evidence?"

"Objection, Your Honor," interjected Shortino.

"On what grounds?" Becky said.

The judge said, "Let her finish."

"I asked the witness if I *needed* to have one prepared, *could* he do it? Part of the testimony in your motion suggests that you could not file an entry because you couldn't get anyone to do a 'Meets and Bounds' description. I had to ask him this question so I could establish with the Court that yes, indeed, at any time you could have obtained a 'Meets and Bounds' Description for the property in question. You are insinuating, Mr. Shortino, and falsely so—trying to create an image to the Court that I was dishonest, trying to get the witness to do something dishonest. You are distorting the facts, Mr. Shortino, and this is an outrage! Again, I was asking him if he *could* prepare a legal description if he were asked to do so. I was not asking him to write one and slip it into the file! There's a difference!" This was the first time that Becky appeared out of control. Her anger almost led her to jump over the table and rush him.

"I have no further questions of this witness, Your Honor."

Becky called her second witness, Mr. Wyndel, who was the mortgage company's Branch Manager. She would be able to show the Court through his testimony over the last three hearings that his dealings were deceitful and that his direct testimony to the Court was inconsistent and conflicting. When she had finished, she had discredited him to a point of embarrassment—at least most people would have been embarrassed. Becky figured someone with his lack of principle was probably not affected. She wasn't sure, but she thought perhaps what he had done could be considered perjury, another issue.

She had the witness step down, and Becky continued. She called the counsel for the defense as her third witness. "Mr. Shortino, will you approach the bench to be sworn in?"

Mr. Shortino challenged the request. "I'm one of the lawyers here." Becky had done it to him again.

The judge said, "Raise your right hand." Mr. Shortino walked to the witness stand.

"Starting at the beginning, Your Honor," Becky said, "Mr. Shortino, counsel for First Trust Mortgage, when giving a general background of the foreclosure action against the Blaines, has been inconsistent in his testimony. Please refer to the transcripts you have before you that I entered into evidence, Exhibit 11, pages 37 and 38, and note please where he refers to the property as '12 lots,' not land consisting of 5.65 acres. Then, I would like to draw the Court's attention to page 63. Here, Mr. Shortino states, 'I don't believe First Trust Mortgage is claiming prior first mortgage on all twelve lots'! Please let the record show that on November 30, First Trust Mortgage did not believe they were claiming prior first mortgage on all twelve lots, but on March 1, they stated they had *always* maintained they held a first mortgage on the real estate described in the mortgage. What we have here, Your Honor, is a conflict in sworn testimony by the defendants and their own counsel as to the truth of the intentions of First Trust Mortgage at the time they went into contract with William D. and Rebecca A. Blaine and with respect to said property."

Becky turned around and faced Mr. Shortino directly, eye-to-eye. "Lies make people suspicious of devious behavior, Mr. Shortino, and the real problem with people who don't tell the truth is that you never really know when they are. Isn't that right, Mr. Shortino?"

Becky paused for a moment, then went on to drill the lawyer some more. Finally, one of the other counsel objected on the grounds that business decisions that are made between attorney and client are confidential and privileged. Becky had anticipated this objection, and said, "According to Article V, Rule 501, of the Indiana Rules of Evidence, except as provided by constitution or statute as enacted or interpreted by the courts of this State or by these or other rules promulgated by the Indiana Supreme Court, or by principles of common law in light of reason and experience, no person has a privilege to refuse to disclose any matter."

Then Becky said, "My next question is why First Trust Mortgage would allow portioning of the property. If they hold firm to their original contention, at least part of the time, they do indeed hold title to all twelve lots, always meant to, and intended to from the beginning. Why then are they willing to give away part of their assets now through the Assignee? Isn't part of the pie less than the whole? What I'm trying to establish here, Your Honor," said Becky, approaching the bench, "is that once First Trust Counsel learned that I was preparing to expose their perjury, they worked with the other counsel to find a willing party they could drag into this action and pay off to become an Assignee. Once they sold their interest to the

Assignee and entered them in, they figured the water would be so muddy, the conflict so confusing, that Will and I would give up."

Becky went on: "The defense has told the Court through their pleadings that they wanted a partial Summary Judgment so that they could minimize their losses. Wouldn't it have been better, with no loss to anyone? If First Trust Mortgage had partitioned off the property when *we* asked them to originally, five years ago, we wouldn't be here today. If please be the Court, we ask that the assignee be brought forward for questioning."

The judge responded, "Point taken. Let's proceed. Counsel, you may step down."

Becky was articulate and had gotten her point across. It seemed she had earned the judge's respect. Mr. Shortino elected not to cross-examine himself.

Becky looked forward to her next witness, Aaron Olsen, because in the last two trials, the bankruptcy and the one about the damage that had been done to the house, he had been a hostile witness—a young First Trust Mortgage employee afraid of losing his job. He had lied in court then, and this time Becky would corner him like in a chess game. She knew he would be an easy witness, and it would be entertaining to Becky to watch him squirm in his lies. After he was sworn in, Becky had him identify the original affidavit that he had signed in preparation for the case when it was heard pursuant to Trial Rule 56. Becky had intentionally taken the original affidavit, added two words that would change the meaning and highlight the truth, and sent it to Aaron to sign. She made it look identical to the first one he signed with the minute exceptions and moved a comma, which anyone knows can change the complete meaning of a sentence. She sent it via facsimile and told Aaron she needed to get it signed and returned right away. Aaron must have glanced at it, signed it, and faxed it back right away, not noticing the changes. Becky had tricked him into signing an affidavit that told the truth. He couldn't rescind it. He had signed it. Becky remembered the day well because she was elated when the signed fax finally came back to her on their new fax machine. When Becky questioned him on the witness stand, he was stuck. He had to reaffirm the truth.

Becky entered his affidavit into evidence and proceeded, "Mr. Olsen, you swore under oath and the penalties for perjury that the document you have signed and now hold before you, represents the truth and nothing but the truth as you know it to be so, is that correct, Mr. Olsen?"

The vague responses he had given in court on the last two occasions wouldn't fly that day. He couldn't protect his personal interests. Becky had too much. She hammered him. "Mr. Olsen, regarding the truthfulness of your statements, they are indeed true and based upon your personal knowledge. Do you agree with that?" Aaron was silent and stared straight ahead. He looked at his old boss, a guy with whom he had developed a friendship. He looked at him as if to say "Sorry." His friend, the liar from First Trust Mortgage, must have been thinking, *traitor*.

"So it can go on record that the affidavit entered into evidence as Trial Exhibit 19 reflects true and accurate information based on your personal knowledge?" Again, the witness paused for what seemed like an eternity, and it was obvious to everybody that he didn't want to answer the question. Becky prodded, "Come on, Aaron, just tell the truth." Mr. Olsen told the truth. Defense counsel announced, "No cross, Your Honor." Becky asked Aaron to step down.

The next witness was one of the best that Becky had; his presence was her opportunity to produce and validate the most compelling hard copy of evidence—the next best thing to the original missing front page of the loan document—an 8-½" x 11" piece of paper that would prove intent as to what land would be held as collateral for the Blaine mortgage. He was Rex Sorenson, who was hired by First Trust Mortgage to come out to Becky and Will's property and make the appraisal that would assess and describe the property that the mortgage would cover. In addition to the original loan application, it too would show the Blaine's intentions as to what would be included in the mortgage, and it would make it clear to the Court that the Blaines, with First Trust Mortgage, only agreed to secure the mortgage with one house on one lot, and that holding and encumbering all twelve lots was not the Blaines' original intent. Additional land was encumbered by fraud.

Becky pre-empted her line of questioning with dialogue to fill the Court in with a brief history—one that would set the stage to further incriminate the defense as to what kind of dishonest characters they really were. "Yes, after four years of asking, the Blaines finally got what they feel to be yet another strong piece of evidence supporting the intentions of First Trust Mortgage. The Blaines had to submit a Motion to Compel to retrieve it, and it still did not come from First Trust Mortgage, because they admitted on record they had lost it. But we got a copy anyway, from a different source entirely—the appraiser had a copy of it. We could ask the defense why it took so long to retrieve the document."

Becky looked directly at the appraiser. She was so happy to have found him, his documents, his expertise, and his memory. After he was sworn in, Becky asked, "Mr. Sorenson, please state for the record your full name."

"Rex Sorenson."

"Mr. Sorenson, please tell the Court what you do for a living, what certifications you have, and how long you have been in that business."

Mr. Sorenson answered the questions. Then Becky asked, "Did you perform the appraisal on the Blaine property for First Trust Mortgage while you were employed by Blake Appraisal Company?"

"Yes."

"Is this your signature on the appraisal?" Becky asked.

"Yes."

"Does your signature attest to the fact that you appraised what you were asked to appraise?" Becky asked.

"Yes."

He answered every question the way Becky knew he would. Becky's pretrial preparation had made her comfortable and she expected no surprises.

"Please refer to the first page of the document you now hold in your hand and read out loud the legal description on the appraisal," Becky said.

He read, "As the Court may recall from the testimony of Mr. Wyndel, Manager of First Trust Mortgage, Mr. Wyndel said under oath that he was *not* aware of the subdivision called Canal Estates."

"Please read again for the court, Mr. Sorenson, what land you were asked by First Trust Mortgage to appraise."

"Lot One in the Canal Estates Subdivision," he answered.

"It appears to me then, Mr. Sorenson, that if First Trust Mortgage asked you to appraise Lot One in the Canal Estates Subdivision, that they probably knew Canal Estates Subdivision existed, right?"

Charlie laughed out loud.

"Yes," Mr. Sorenson answered.

Becky knew that she not only had just proven beyond a reasonable doubt that the mortgage manager had lied under oath, but she had really just proven her case. She felt a wave of excitement that she was at this turning point. For effect, and as punishment, she repeated her last question and had the appraiser repeat his answer. The defense team was obviously shaken, and the judge noticed that, too.

"Under 'Comments,' Mr. Sorenson, you write that the subject is located in a newly platted subdivision and that the subdivision consists of twelve residential sites, located in the Canal Estates Subdivision, right?" Becky asked.

"Right," Mr. Sorenson replied.

"Turning to the next page, please look at comparable #1 with a site view of .45 acres, comparable #2 with a site view of .25 acres, and comparable #3 as .35 acres." The defense team and judge looked too. "I again note that the subject's property is listed at .33 acres. And again, on the next page you write, 'The subject is the first home constructed in the subject's platted addition.' Is this correct, Mr. Sorenson?"

"Yes, it is," he answered.

"Could you help me, Mr. Sorenson?" Becky could smell victory. "On your photographic addendum, moving down the street scene, can you identify where the lots are located?"

"Yes, I can," he replied. And he held up the paperwork to point, but no one was looking.

"*You* were aware of the Canal Estates Subdivision, weren't you, Mr. Sorenson? First Trust Mortgage asked you to appraise what you appraised, right, Mr. Sorenson?"

"Yes," he said.

"So, based upon your professional opinion, through the nature of your job at the time, is it correct to assume that the reason First Trust Mortgage accepted your appraisal and did not ask it to be re-done was because it reflected what they had asked you to appraise?"

"Yes, that is correct," Mr. Sorenson said.

"You never did appraise all twelve lots, did you, Mr. Sorenson? Because you didn't need to—isn't that right?"

"No, I only appraised Lot 1," Mr. Sorenson replied.

"Thank you, Mr. Sorenson. I have no further questions of this witness."

Opposing counsel, "We have no questions for this witness, Your Honor."

Becky called forward the trustee. When he got up on the stand, she realized from conversations with the President of the Bar Association that he was the witness who knew the judge. Becky noticed that he and the judge smiled at each other when he first approached the bench. Of course, they didn't know what Becky knew. It was a special time in the trial for Becky. It allowed her to have a little personal fun amidst the consternation.

Becky called her last witness. It was her last because she had run out of time, but that was okay. This one would help establish damages. She knew that she needed to show damages as a condition of establishing fraud. But the judge then called for a lunch recess, informing all parties that he had decided to scratch off the rest of his day from his calendar so that he could hear the remaining parts of the trial. "This thing needs to get settled," he said.

The defense left for the lunch recess knowing that they were behind. Becky and her clan went across the street to a deli. She was more jovial than she had been that morning, for sure. Some of the pressure was off. She didn't eat much, and she returned to the courtroom before the others. When she got there, the room was empty. She started to reorganize the binders and tablets on her table. As she was doing so, she got the feeling someone was watching her. Slightly startled, she turned around to find Will, who leaned around and gently kissed her cheek, then softly said, "You're really doing a great job, Becky. I'm proud of you." Then he left the room to give her some quiet time.

When all had reconvened, the defense appeared eager to make a statement. "Your Honor," the defense counsel began, "When the Plaintiff rested, she did not give her Findings of Fact and Conclusions of Law. We move that the case be dismissed."

There it was—Becky was going to lose on a technicality. At the end of her presentation, when her time was up, she hadn't informed the Court what the law could do for her. She hadn't forgotten that she needed to do it—she was deliberately saving it until her closing arguments. She didn't know that she needed to establish her legal position at the end of presenting her witnesses. She didn't know the legal procedure.

Mr. Shortino didn't come up with this tactic—surely it had to be one of those highfalutin lawyers from New York. Shortino is too dumb to have thought this one up on his own. Becky knew better than to try to explain to the judge that she didn't understand how the system worked—that she was a non-lawyer and wasn't familiar with all of the rules because, first of all, he was well aware of that, and secondly, non-lawyers were held to the same standards as lawyers in a court of law. *I gave it my best shot.* She put her hand up to her forehead and looked down at her papers.

Becky began to show outward signs of distress: her hand was shaking, she was breathing hard, and she started to cry. She felt like she was going to faint. Out in the stands her family and friends were trying to give her body language that she shouldn't give up. Her mother shook her head and mouthed the words "Stop it!" She was trying to be stern with Becky so she would hold her composure. Finally, Becky realized she needed to take another blood pressure pill. She motioned to Will, and he brought her a glass of water.

The judge told the defense counsel that he would take the matter under advisement, and he instructed them to move forward. Becky was still in the race—at least for now.

They called their first witness who showed the court absolutely nothing. Becky felt embarrassed for them. She waited to see what else they'd put on. She had been anxious for a long time to see what tactics they'd come up with to try to win. She was starting to feel better and focused on staying prepared.

The second and third witnesses didn't prove anything either. *They don't have any evidence to prove their position.*

But then the defense started making an issue of the bankruptcy. They made Will and Becky out to be horribly irresponsible people who didn't pay their bills and were the cause of their own demise and who were now blaming First Trust Mortgage for their problems. Becky got choked up again. She looked at her mother and whispered audibly, "That's it, I can't do this—we're not bad people—we're not irresponsible." The defense continued to make a strong argument that the entire problem was Will and Rebecca's fault and that no one would be in court today had it not been for the Blaines' bad decisions.

Becky was weak, tired, and so emotionally stressed, she didn't realize right away that they were making allegations but had presented no proof. Her blood pressure medicine began to do its job. She felt more calm and that her thinking was more clear. Slowly she began to regain her composure. The difference in her abilities then was like night and day. She was astute and was able to perform with sharp distinction. She said to the judge, "Your Honor, we are not here today to attempt to establish whether the Blaines had good or bad credit, or whether they made a good or bad decision to preserve the historic property and develop a subdivision. This has been dealt with already in the bankruptcy court. These issues are moot and have been designed as a diversionary tactic by the defense, as they have no exculpatory evidence. Their own witnesses are recalcitrant. The reason we are here today is to prove that the Defendants committed fraud. They should be trying to prove that they did not commit fraud, and it doesn't appear that they can do that."

The judge seemed happy to see she was finally in control again. The sliding scales were once again moving in her favor. Her reasons were good enough. The judge said, "Yes, this is not a bankruptcy hearing. Please proceed in the appropriate direction, counsel."

The defense's next witness was Will. Becky was hoping they wouldn't call him because she was afraid of how he might present facts or say things he didn't mean to because he was nervous. He meant well, but sometimes things just didn't come out the way he intended, same as in their marriage. Much to her delight, however, he surprised her and did quite well. When it came time for her to cross-examine him, she felt awkward. *How can I ask questions of my own husband?* She put herself in a business mindset, called him Mr. Blaine, and went on to use the opportunity as her last ditch effort to get some things on the table that she had been unable to do before recess because of lack of time. There were objections, but most were overruled.

The defense called their last witness.

"Your Honor, this will be our last witness. We present Mr. Samuel T. Cromwell, Assignee." The door opened. Mr. Samuel T. Cromwell was called from outside the courtroom where he had been waiting. "We apologize for the slight delay in calling him in," said the defense. Becky looked down at her notes to review her closing arguments. She didn't pay attention when she heard the sound of shoes as the defense lawyer and Mr. Cromwell entered. She acted bored to send the message to the defendants that nothing they could possibly do at this point would save them. She looked up to establish eye contact with the witness. She felt a chill go up her spine. *Oh my gosh—it's Robert!* Becky was aghast with disbelief. She whipped around to look at Will, who was wearing an expression of concern. Neither Becky nor Will had heard from or seen Robert in months. The last thing they had known about Robert was that the police were still working to charge him with possession. The Blaines were completely caught off guard by his presence in the court. None of their family had any idea who Robert was. Will and Becky just sat, watched, and waited to see what it all meant.

The detectives in the case later revealed to the Blaines that Robert, aware of Becky and Will's problem with First Trust Mortgage, had gone to First Trust and offered to testify that he had known Will in Indianapolis, and that Will had set his own house on fire and staging the whole series of events, to recover insurance company compensation and plotting to sue First Trust Mortgage for fraud to get settlement money from the banking firm, too. In exchange for his testimony, First Trust Mortgage would make Robert assignee. It was on paper only, but in the end, if First Trust Mortgage won the trial, Robert would be given Will's house and Lot 1 in the meantime. At least that's what the undercover detectives had told him. Robert sold pharmacy narcotics on the street for money and was counting on being able to move back to Indianapolis and live in Becky and Will's house. The police department had other ideas.

Becky drifted back to the conversations she had had with Will about him and Robert in high school. Will had said that both friends had always been competitive with each other in everything from sports to girlfriends. They were fierce, young competitors, but still friends. Will could never have imagined that Robert would have ended up like this.

The detective that had been waiting out in the hallway walked into the courtroom. His Honor was aware of the situation because the detective had been working with him before the trial. They had pre-planned to wait until Robert had introduced himself on record as Samuel T. Cromwell, the name he had used when he went to First Trust Mortgage to strike a deal. They would have him on several charges down to the rap of false identification to the Court and all the mitigating factors surrounding his arrest because of the pharmacy scandal.

After Becky had obtained a restraining order, and through Will's private investigator who followed Robert, the police detectives had what they needed to convict Robert for the illegal sale of Class 4 narcotics. The investigators also found out from old police records that Robert Raine had almost lost his medical license before because of a prior arrest for spousal abuse before he had left Indianapolis, but the charges hadn't stuck. That would help explain his abusive, erratic behavior with Becky before. The cops had taken their time to set up the sting, but now they had him.

Coolly, the judge said, "Mr. Cromwell, you have been called by the defense as their next witness. Will you take the stand, please?" Robert walked past the long wooden table where Becky sat, and went up to take a seat.

The bailiff asked him, "Do you swear to tell the truth, the whole truth, and nothing but the truth so help you God?"

"I do," said Robert.

"Counsel, you may proceed," said the judge.

Mr. Shortino, who had been told ahead of time about his witness, approached the stand. "Please, sir, state your name for the record."

"Samuel T. Cromwell."

"Excuse me, sir, could you again state your full name to the Court?" Mr. Shortino had been given a script by the Marion County detectives and was instructed on how to proceed.

"Samuel T. Cromwell," Robert said.

"Did you at any time in the last ten years reside in Indianapolis, Indiana?"

"Yes.""Isn't it true, sir," Mr. Shortino said, "that your real name—the name that is registered with the Social Security Department—is Robert Raine?"

"Robert T. Raine."

Gasps and whispers filled the courtroom. Will sat and stared at Robert. Becky glanced towards Will, then refocused her attentions on Robert.

"Can you tell the Court what you do, and where you are employed?" he asked.

"I'm the assignee in this case," Robert said.

"Excuse me, Robert—I mean, Samuel—I thought you were a physician working at the University of Wisconsin."

"I am a doctor, but I didn't make tenure so I quit," Robert said.

"I've heard enough," said the judge. "Bailiff, Officer Frank."

Robert didn't look at Becky; rather, he seemed to look past or through her. Officer Frank asked Robert to step down and they handcuffed him. As they walked toward the large wooden doors at the back of the courtroom, past the judge, Will, Becky, Charlie, and Debbie, Officer Frank began reading him his rights, but Robert interrupted, turned and looked at the judge and said, "I started the fire because I wanted her to need me." Then his ice cold eyes pierced through Becky as he turned to her and said, "I only followed you to Madison because I love you. You're mine, you know—not his!" He pointed at Will.

The trial was nearly over. Becky slapped her trial folder down on the table, sat back, and stared straight forward with her hands folded in front of her. She paused before giving her closing arguments. This was the moment she'd been waiting for after months of preparation and years of hardship.

The judge told opposing counsel that their time was up. The defendants tried to gently argue with him, asking for more time.

The judge sternly said, "We've finished."

The defendants politely asked the judge to consider this and that.

"Counsel, the trial is over," the judge repeated sternly. "Gentlemen, I've heard enough. I think the plaintiffs have given me some good evidence. We're finished here!"

Although Becky felt positive about the outcome, she was still unsure. It was difficult for her to believe that it was so close to being all over. She could feel relief, but the feeling was unnatural.

The judge said, "Becky, you may give your closing statement." Becky took down the beautiful picture of the gray house from the easel, and replaced it with the picture that showed the house the way it looked after First Trust Mortgage took it over—a shambles.

The room was quiet.

Becky began, "Like a death, the Blaine family, affected by the tragedy of First Trust Mortgage's fraud, has passed from life as they knew it, protected and nurtured by the land of their forefathers, and into a world untouched by the history that connected them. From Ben Logan's book, *The Land Remembers,* that I gave to my husband three years ago to help ease the pain of his loss, 'Once you have lived on the land, been partner with its moods, secrets, and seasons, you cannot leave. The living land remembers, touching you in unguarded moments, saying, I am here. You are a part of me.'

"Yesterday we went to our land for the last time we could call it ours. We went to dig up some of Grandma's peonies so we could plant a lasting piece of our heritage in Madison—the place we now reside because First Trust Mortgage's fraud took our home away from us. How they could live with themselves for what they've done we cannot even begin to comprehend. Anyway, realizing we needed a container to put the flowers in, Will, without thinking, knew exactly where to go on the property to fetch an old metal bucket. He told me the story then of how one stormy night, a long time ago when he was just a young man, he had gone to feed the livestock, had forgotten to bring the bucket back to the barn, and the water froze in it. 'That's why it was lopsided,' he said, 'and wouldn't stand up straight.' The land and everything connected to it was a part of him, and a part of him died when he lost it. Like a thief that robs you in the night, First Trust Mortgage stole our heritage, depleted our savings and our dignity, stripped us of our legacy, disabled us from holding jobs that utilized our fullest potential, and took us away from our professions. They threw us into a compromised way of life—six years of ugly litigation, devastating bankruptcy, and dirty lies. I left medical school to tread on the unfamiliar ground of the law library. Life was not our own. First Trust Mortgage destroyed us both financially and emotionally. They took our dreams!

"For the last six years, we have defended something that rightfully belongs to us. We did nothing wrong to deserve this, yet have had everything taken from us. For six years we have driven to Indianapolis—for the first two years in a car that barely ran because our credit had been ruined, and no one would give us a loan for a better car. Often we would drive through the night after work so we could get to the courtroom in the morning—all the while praying the car wouldn't break down. We literally used piggybank money for gas. Once, when we pulled into Indianapolis about 3:00 a.m., we drove down the lane to our boarded-up house. We sat in the driveway and cried. Our children were asleep in the back of our car, rather than in the safety of the bedrooms that we could see in the distance. Like death, how do we explain this loss to our children? Sometimes we had to appear in court during Christmas vacation, Easter, Mother's Day, our children's birthdays, and homecoming. The defense had no concern for our lives or livelihood. We would drive to the courthouse, exhausted from the trip, change clothes in the restroom, and go to court, then turn around and drive several hours home. It has not been easy for us to try to recover from such a devastating set of circumstances. And our children, too, have fallen victim of an adult crime."

Becky continued, "Daily, we have been haunted by the dreams that turned into our own personal nightmare. Every part of our world has been disrupted. The little things most people take for granted. Our apartment is so small we have no wall space to hang up our children's school pictures, yet we pay the same amount for our apartment as our mortgage to First Trust for our beautiful home in our historic subdivision. Grandma's tablecloth hasn't been on our table in six years because we don't have enough room to open up our table and, instead of the children being raised watching their mother tend a garden, they spend their time playing on the concrete outside of our apartment, except for an occasional trip to the country where they can once again catch a glimpse of the life they once enjoyed daily. They miss the valley, its hollows and cornfields, and picking blackberries with their Dad. They still ask why. Our old traditions have now become memories. They have been seared in the youth of a grown man's problem."

There were tears that could not be hidden among those in attendance, even from Will, who, until this very moment had not acknowledged how much this loss had affected him. Becky continued, and her final remarks recounted the Findings of Fact and Conclusions of Law. "First Trust Mortgage owed the Blaines a duty of good faith and fair dealing which was breached. Fraud is material to a contract when the contract would not have been made if the fraud had not been perpetrated, and fraud and damage must concur; neither unaccompanied by the other is ground for defense.

Misrepresentations that are made by one party to a contract, as of his own knowledge with intention that the other party, who is not informed as to the truth or falsity of the misrepresentations, relies on them, are fraudulent.

"The Blaines pray that the Court awards the Blaines Summary Judgment against First Trust Mortgage for its egregious misconduct and for breach of their contract, for compensatory damages, punitive damages, damages reasonable and just under the circumstances, for losses incurred as a result of First Trust Mortgage's fraudulent conduct, bankruptcy, court costs, and any and all relief just and proper in the premises.

"The Blaines have shown the theory of fraud and proven its elements. They have proven First Trust Mortgage's intentions. The Blaines have proven there is no genuine issue as to the facts, and the Blaines have proven that First Trust Mortgage is guilty of fraud and is responsible for damages."

Becky sat down stoically and again stared straight forward with her hands folded. It was over.

Several minutes of silence passed as opposing counsel gathered up their paperwork and briefcases. Their pride would be left in the courtroom.

Will slowly passed through the friends and family who were congratulating him with quiet pats on the back as he made his way towards Becky. She was sitting alone at the long wooden table, still surrounded by all of the books that represented the culmination of years of sacrifice and work. He placed his hand gently on her back, leaned forward and whispered in her ear, "I love you."

In cases like the Blaines', the judge does not award victory until sometimes thirty days later, and in writing. He has to be very specific because of the repercussions of appeal. The final outcome for the Blaines was presented in a four-page document after three weeks. The defense appealed the case and lost. With the money the Blaines received from their settlement, they built another house just like the gray house; the children helped. They bought new cars and gave the rest to charity.

Later on that evening Becky called Grandfather to fill him in on what had transpired.

He told her, "You see, Becky, you didn't beat the lawyers at their game—they simply couldn't beat you at yours!"

Becky said, "The game, Grandfather—how you play it—is who you are." Becky had listened to her own voice, the song within her, and it keeps her still.

"There is hope in every tomorrow."

Danny Glenn

Printed in the United States
24673LVS00006B/10-12